CLAIMED BY THE FLAME OF FAERY

Monsters of Faery Book Three

Mallory Dunlin

VARISTAN YLLAXIRA
DUKE OF NYX SHAERAS
THE FLAME OF FAERY

Whoever coined the phrase "write what you love"—
Thank you.
You probably didn't mean "give that man protagonist eyes, horns for steering,
an oral fixation, sharp teeth, dragon wings, a wicked prehensile tail, *and* a pair
of pocket cocks", but as one of my friends is prone to saying, "more is more."
And I love it.

CONTENTS

CHAPTER ONE

IN THE BACK

The risers for the mortal pit fighters were marked *Humans Only*. It was a necessary precaution. We sharpened our weapons while we waited for our turn in the ring, and the last thing we needed was an iron-scalded fae from the fine patina of steel. The warehouse would get cleaned thoroughly before the morning, of course, blood and sweat and iron filings washed down the warehouse drains, but for the night it was safer to enforce our distance.

I'd sharpened thousands of spears, and I almost didn't need to look at the blade as I ran the whetstone along it, keeping my stone at the precise angle for a durable edge with the ease of practice. Using a stone takes longer than a file, or even a leather strop with grit, but it eats up less steel and left a smoother edge, and it wasn't as if I didn't have time. The fights would go until at least three in the morning, and I couldn't complete my tasks until the bets had been paid out and the silver counted.

A fighter took a heavy seat next to me, shaking the cheap wooden bench. I held my whetstone away from my spear until he settled, then returned to my steady sharpening.

"Five coppers on the guard getting first blood," he said, jerking his chin towards the two opponents circling each other in the chalk circle on the floor. There was more blood than the last time I'd looked up; someone must have taken a bad hit last fight.

"You know I don't bet on these things, Sam," I said with a snort. "Besides, it's a bad bet to take. That fae he's up against is on his third fight tonight, and he's already hurt, besides. If a city guard can't manage to get first blood, it's because he does something stupid."

My companion laughed, shaking his head. "You're a lot of fun. What's the stick up your ass?"

I paused in my sharpening to watch the human fighter as he feinted to the left of the wildling fae he'd been paired against. The fae got his blade up in time to catch the real strike, breathing hard. I didn't like the match-up; Estarren was only wildling by way of the shimmering scales along his forearms and shins and his pike-sharp teeth, and while he knew enough not to get gutted, putting him against a city guard for his third fight was cruel. Fae didn't have the same endurance humans did, and Estarren wasn't a fighter by trade.

The fae jerked away from a stab, trying to close with the human guard and getting driven back. He stepped back across the chalk line—and staggered forward as a feral-looking fae shoved him into the ring again. There was rarely any escape from a fight, no matter what the rules said.

My lips thinned with distaste. Desperate people took desperate risks, but I didn't have to like it. I turned away from the sight, looking back down at my spear-blade as I returned to sharpening.

"I have plenty of fun," I said in my driest tone of voice. "It's just that none of it happens to be wasting my coppers on stupid bets." The crowd roared; someone must have drawn blood. "There, you see—"

My words died as I looked up, catching sight of the guard reeling backwards with one hand over his neck, bleeding profusely. Estarren breath bubbled out between his teeth, his opponent's blade through his hand and blood dripping off of his face in a red mask.

"Holy shit." Sam sounded shaken, his voice wavering as he stared at the scene.

I didn't blame him. I was shaken, too, and it wasn't my first time seeing a fae go fully feral in a fight.

The guard tumbled to the floor, his skin ashen. Blood painted his side with crimson ruin.

One of the two fae healers for the night finally fought through the crowd to his side, slapping her hand over the gruesome wound on his neck in time to stop the bleeding before he died.

My eyes slid back over to Estarren as he pulled the sword out of his hand. It dropped to the floor, the clatter lost to the bloodthirsty cries of the watchers. He spat a red, wet glob onto the floor, the chunk of flesh he'd bitten from the man's throat splatting onto the filthy warehouse floor, and wiped his face with the back of his uninjured arm. Blood dripped down his impaled hand, red splatters falling from his fingers.

The crowd didn't cease their clamor, the horror of it nothing but a sick thrill to them.

"Fucking hell," I muttered, following Estarren with my eyes as he stalked out of the ring, the people parting in front of him like minnows fleeing a pike. "What the fuck did he have riding on this to bite a man's throat out? It's hard enough being considered an aberration without people thinking you're gonna eat them."

"It had better have been damn important," Sam said, biting off the words. "That's the goriest thing I've seen in months."

I looked back down at my pale fingers against the bright metal of the steel, and closed them around the whetstone until my knuckles went bloodless. "You weren't here when they brought in the dekker, were you?"

He flinched. "Fuck. Can't even imagine. Those things are salad shooters on legs."

I shrugged one shoulder, forcing my hands to relax. I didn't know what Sam was comparing dekkers to, but I didn't catch a lot of the references the more recent imports to Faery used. My whole life had been spent under the boots of the fae.

"Eighteen people against one monster," I said, returning to the slow, steady *scraaape, scraaape* of my stone across steel. "People too deep in gambling debt to ever pay it back, mostly. Their one chance to get out from under it. Eighteen went in, and two made it out alive. I watched the crowd kick a man back into the ring who had his guts hanging out and his arm attached by a string."

Scraaape. Scraaape.

Sam didn't say anything, staring tight-lipped at the ring as three new opponents stepped in. The glob of flesh was gone; the healer must have put it back where it belonged.

"I was eleven. My mom went down in the first sixty seconds, and didn't get back up," I said finally. "So, yeah, I don't bet on these things, and I wish no one else would, either. It's brutal and ugly, and I don't like it."

He glanced sidelong at me. "And you're sharpening spears."

"Yep." I didn't look up from my work.

"You *fight* in the ring."

"Yep," I said again, not even tensing. I'd gotten used to my fate a long, long time ago.

"You're one ice-cold bitch, Bells," Sam said, shaking his head.

I snorted, one corner of my mouth flipping up. "I'm a pragmatic," I informed him, holding up the spear to catch the light, checking that the edge was smooth and sharp. With a sharp tug, I plucked a dark strand of hair from my scalp and ran it down the edge, pleased when it cut. "Look, I like my freedom too much to sell it for the sake of a comfy berth in some fae's mansion. This place is a shithole, but it's one of the only places where the people on the bottom can extract a little money from the fae on top."

"Brothels," he said with a smirk.

I snorted again. "What, *you* looking to take a fae cock? I'd much rather be the one sticking my spear in someone than taking it, risks of having someone bite chunks out of me notwithstanding."

"Seems like a shared career risk." Sam waggled his brows at me, clearly more comfortable with sex talk than gore, despite being a fighter himself. "There's gotta be fae who get bitey about it, even if you're the one dishing."

His playful expression made me laugh; I shook my head as I picked up the next spear. "Gotta find ways to keep it interesting over the centuries, I guess. Can't say I'm all that eager for first-hand knowledge, though—"

"Bells!"

I glanced up from my work at the sound of the pit boss' voice, raising my brows. He jerked his chin at me, so I pocketed my whetstone and hopped down the risers to see what he wanted.

"You bring your kit?" he asked, pitching his voice low to be audible beneath the yells of the spectators.

"Yeah, always do," I said, my brows pulling together. "But we've got two healers on deck tonight. Is it that backed up?"

Omari's broad lips thinned. "It's Estarren. Both the healers are refusing to go near him, and he's refusing to bribe them."

I winced. "Gods, he must really need the coin."

"Someone dumped a baby wildling at the edge of the Tangle last week," he said, his eyes going hard. "A little girl. She's in a bad way. We found a family for her, and with what Estarren won tonight and what the rest of us could pitch in, he's got enough to pay a healer to fix what's wrong with her without doing anything... unnecessary."

The way he said that made my upper lip tense, anger flaring. There was nothing wrong with wildling fae. They just looked different from other fae, or had different abilities. There was no reason to try to "correct" their bodies.

I knew life had never been great for the so-called aberrant fae – I'd spoken to enough of them to hear the stories – but things had only gone downhill for them in Raven Court since the Annihilation War with Stag Court. People looked at them and remembered the Beast who'd destroyed the city of Phazikai and eaten their crown prince, or their traitor prince who'd stolen land from Raven Court to make his own, or the Furies he'd created as war-weapons and lured away to his Windswept Court. There was a lot of bad blood there.

Even so, I could barely imagine a world in which something like this could happen. The fae had children so rarely when they lived in cities, the wild magic that let new life be created spread far too thin. Children were cherished. Had things truly fallen so far?

"I'll see what I can do, boss," I said at last. "Even clean and bandaged is better than nothing."

Omani nodded. "It's appreciated, Bells. Will you still be up for doing the drop tonight?"

"Yeah, should be fine." I rubbed at my face. "Gonna be a long night, but it'll be nice to help out with vermin control."

He smirked; the term was a popular one for the informal coalition of humans, wildling fae, and even some court fae who took it upon themselves to rid the world of their worst predators. It couldn't be formal, of course; no "kill my master and I'll kill yours" bargains were possible when one's life was magically tied to loyal service. Anyone who did vermin control went in knowing that their actions would have no direct bearing on who got selected for eradication, and so they could act in accordance with their oaths.

The mortal world had grown far less open about its slavery, and people had gotten used to the idea of being free men. But the fae didn't seem to care – or even to notice – that their bondservants were less and less satisfied with their bargains. We were making them feel our displeasure, though, as those who preyed on humanity and sated their appetites with blood began to vanish, their eternities cut short. Who better to dispose of a body, after all, than the oft-ignored mortals who kept the fae cities running?

It was beginning to be very dangerous to be a predator of men in Raven Court.

Tonight it would be the bastard who'd funded the expansion of the Lylvenore fighting ring over the past four years. They'd been reaping a pretty profit from their investments, bought with the blood and suffering of people they never had to look in the eye. We'd make them pay it back in blood of their own.

"To the back with you, then," he said, tilting his head towards the stacks of crates. "I'll have someone rack the weapons."

I sketched him a bow before hopping back up in the stands to grab my duffel bag of supplies. Slinging it over my shoulder, I headed towards the back area where the injured fighters went, giving Sam a pat on the shoulder as I left.

There's not a great deal one can do for a stab wound through the hand—not when the blade is steel, the hand is fae, and the world Faery, at least. The only times fae tended to get injured by iron was during war or in the fighting rings, so fae medical technology left something to be desired when it came to surgical repairs. Not that it would have been easy to get Estarren medical care, regardless, but as the case was, there simply wasn't any to get.

He hadn't managed to slice through any major blood vessels, but that was about the best that could be said for his stab wound. Both the middle bones of his palm were fractured, and the blade had cut one of his nerves, because he could barely bend his middle finger and couldn't feel anything on the thumb side of his ring finger. I did what I could, cleaning the wound, splinting his hand, and binding everything closed so that it would have the best chance of healing properly, but it still left me feeling helpless and bitter.

"Was it worth it?" I asked him quietly as I wrapped his hand.

Estarren huffed a soft laugh, one corner of his mouth kicking up. "Illianthe will have the chance to grow up loved," he said, his voice as quiet as mine. "She will have the chance to grow up at all, and to do so with the body she was born into, and not one shaped by the desires of society and the hand of one who ought only to heal."

He glanced down at his bandaged hand as I tied the wrapping, looking tired. "I was born with a tail, and fins running down my spine. I feel them as phantoms, even though they were stolen from me long before I had the capacity to remember. But my body remembers, and surely hers would, too." With a sigh, Estarren tilted his head back, letting me put his arm in a sling. "What's a weak hand in someone who already suffers, compared to the life she could lead?"

I put my hand on his knee, meeting his pale eyes. "You did a brave thing," I said in a serious tone, then flashed him a smile. "Stupid as fuck, but brave."

He made a sharp bark of amusement, shifting his ears in the way fae did when in high spirits. "I'll count that as worthy praise, Isabela." Estarren flashed me a smile of his own, one made rather frightening by the blood still coloring his sharp teeth. "Your assistance is appreciated, my mortal companion."

"Go home," I said. "Kiss your paramour. Take little Illianthe to the healers, and pay them to do what's right." Anger turned my expression hard, a feeling of righteous wrath burning beneath my sternum. "Let's make the sun rise on a better world."

CHAPTER TWO

DRAGONSLAYING

Three in the morning came and went. One of the matchups ran long, a barehanded fight between two heavyweight humans; by the time the bets had been paid out and the spoils divided, it was easily past four, and I'd managed to sharpen all the spears.

The delayed timeline didn't mean much to me, though. I'd expected to be up all night, anyway, and the drop wasn't supposed to be picked up until first light. In the early autumn this far north, the sun didn't rise until around seven in the morning, and first light was an hour before that. There was plenty of time to get in place before our quarry would arrive.

I made my way through the sleeping city of Lylvenore by the pale light of the crescent moon, unafraid of attack. For all its ills, one of the benefits of having humans life-bonded to their fae masters was the lack of crime directed towards those beneath the protection of those same masters. In Lylvenore, almost all the bondservants belonged ultimately to the Vicereine of Lylvenore, and harming each other in a criminal fashion was off-limits.

A fae could have offered me danger, of course, and since I wasn't life-bonded to anyone, so could any of the humans in the city. But those humans with criminal inclinations wouldn't know that, and fae so often tended to treat humans as below their notice, even when they strode through the city with a dark pack slung over one shoulder and a spear gleaming in the moonlight. What harm could one human woman do, after all?

I hit the Tangle as the moon started setting, making my way through the dark maze of thorny brambles by using the butt of my spear as a blind-man's cane. The Tangle served as Lylvenore's defense instead of walls, a forbidding labyrinth of bloodthirsty hedges and glorious profusions of roses, but like many within its embrace, I knew most of the pathways by heart.

I'd played in this hedge-maze with the other children of Lylvenore, the one human child in the half-dozen of us. Even in the moonless dark before dawn, I could navigate it, measuring the lengths of my steps and taking turns by instinct.

When I stepped out of the Tangle at the edge of the woods, I tilted my head back and breathed deeply, inhaling the cool mist of the night air at the edge of the wilderness. I didn't often come out this far, staying within the city, but I loved the taste of the wild wind. The knowledge that I stood beyond the dangerous embrace of Lylvenore, facing a world far more frightening than its familiar streets, made my skin prickle with adrenaline desire, reckless anticipation quickening my breath.

I wanted that world—longed for it. But my father was bound to the city, and I wouldn't abandon him for a little wanderlust. I lingered, letting the wind flirt with my hair, then sighed and turned, making my way over to the bare outcrop of stone designated as our drop site for the investor.

Ussan Sairal, I thought, even the name feeling like an oilslick. A fae lord, and surely not the final link in the chain of coin, but high enough up that I felt no guilt as I set the pack down, hooking the shoulder strap around a spur of stone so that he would need to stoop to untangle it.

It had taken four years to do it, but we knew who we'd be facing; every drop was carefully compared with all the people present in Lylvenore, an enormous task that ensured no one acted against someone under the protection of the vicereine. Lord Sairal was the needle in the haystack; the one man who was always in Lylvenore when a cloaked figure came to carry away the bloody profit of the pits.

Well, the duke is, too, I thought with some amusement as I ducked back into the Tangle. Omari had mentioned it the night before, and I remembered the laughter as people pointed out that there was no way the half-dragon duke would be able to hide those wings and horns under a cloak, and that our sole mage had verified the man hadn't been glamored. *Good thing he's so gods-damn distinctive—*

Some sixth sense made me turn in time to see a dark shape drop from the sky.

I recognized him instantly. Varistan Yllaxira, the Duke of Nyx Shaeras, landed in a crouch, the wind of his passage tearing the mist into streamers and kicking up dust. Even from my poor vantage point, I recognized the angle of his wings, the set of his spine. He was ready to fight.

He knew. He *knew*—

Four people broke out of the woods and the Tangle in the same heartbeat the duke landed, moving with the silent viciousness of sighthounds while I stood frozen, my spear dangling from numb fingers.

Three long paces to the stone. One leap up to the knob of bare stone where I'd tangled a pack, the dragon-winged duke lying in wait.

Spears lanced for him, the whisper-sharp edges catching the faintest gleam of dawn as first light eased the black of night.

The fae twisted, faster than thought, putting himself in the gaps between the deadly blades. One sliced across his shoulder, the steel going dark with his blood; two others clashed with a spray of sparks.

His tail lashed out, wrapping around a man's ankle and tearing his feet out from under him.

A gleaming length of steel slid past his neck. He snarled, his clawed hand wrapping around the haft. Wing whistled over his wings as he pivoted, tearing the spear from my father's hands.

The duke's arm whipped out, and the heavy bag of coin struck a man in the chest, sending him stumbling backwards. He tripped, falling down the rocky outcropping, and went still with a sudden shock as his skull struck stone.

I covered my mouth with one hand, horror making my skin cold. I started backing up, wanting to vanish into the Tangle as the Duke of Nyx Shaeras made corpses of my friends.

His stolen spear through a woman's chest as she scrabbled backwards. Blood dripping out of the mouth of a broken body on the rocks. His deadly stride as he came down the rough stone with the same confidence as a King descending from his throne.

My father, empty-handed, backing away from his enemy.

With casual ease, the fae duke exhaled a thin stream of fire against the butt of the spear. The dense wood caught flame and kept burning, licking its way up the haft as he held it angled at the level of his knees. The orange light cast him in relief, emphasizing the sharpness of his face and the inhuman shape of his body.

"You bastard," my father whispered, still backing up, trying to get to the Tangle. He knew better than to turn his back and flee.

"True," the duke said, anger sharpening the word. His tail snapped behind him like a whip as he advanced. "I must say, I'm impressed by the attempt. I wouldn't have imagined Lylvenoran humans would be able to attack a guest of the vicereine."

"I thought you a Fury." The words were clipped. Antagonistic. I could almost feel the tension in my father's voice—knew the comparison to the monsters of Windswept Court was as much to the magic binding him as the man in front of him.

A snarl twisted the duke's face, his ears angling forward and lifted high in the fae tell of focused intent. His long tail snaked behind him, the fleshy blades of the spade end flaring out. "A Fury?" he asked in a silken voice, taking one dangerous step forward. His black wings mantled over him, shrouding the world from view. "Is that what you think me now?"

My father tripped over a spur of stone, landing hard as the fae advanced on him.

The spear I held shook, my hands gripping the shaft so hard my knuckles ached. I could leave—could vanish into the Tangle, flee back to the safety of the streets of Lylvenore, go back to my life. None of this had to fall on me. Father wouldn't want it to. He'd protected me, preserved my freedom, bought it with blood—

He stared up at the fae, his mouth opening and closing like a fish ripped from the water by a hook.

"Is that what you think now, mortal?" the duke asked again, his voice going harsh.

Silence.

With slow menace, the Duke of Nyx Shaeras drove the point of the spear into the earth, inch by inch. The haft burned, the orange light illuminating his otherworldly beauty. He stepped forward, face falling into shadow, and drew his sword.

The ringing sound of drawn steel broke my will. My father's death wasn't a price I could pay for staying free. There were far worse things than being even a monster's slave.

I flung my spear down and stepped out of the Tangle, leaving the safety of thorns behind. "Wait!"

The duke's eyes snapped to me, his chin coming up and eyes narrowing as he met my gaze. "Ah. An observer." His mouth curved up into a dangerous smile. "Have you come to witness an execution, little mortal?"

"I want a bargain, your grace," I said, keeping my voice from shaking by sheer willpower. "Blood on your sword is such cheap repayment for an attempt on your life. Claim my life-debt instead of his, and have a woman's lifetime instead of an execution."

"Bells, don't—" my father started.

The duke's tail snapped out, wrapping around his throat in a strangling hold. My father's voice died in a choking gasp, his hands clawing at the black length closing around his neck.

I couldn't look, my hands trembling.

"A woman cannot serve two masters," the duke said with what sounded like disgust. "I cannot claim one of the vicereine's bondservants for my own. But you're right," he continued nastily. He sheathed his sword in one clean movement. "Blood on my sword is too cheap a repayment. I suppose strangulation will have to do."

"I'm not a bondservant!" I said, desperation wrenching the words from me. "I'm a free woman!"

The duke's eyes snapped to my face again, his ears pinning back. "And you want to be my slave? Are you a fool?" He looked back at my father as his struggles grew weaker. "Is he your lover? I'm certain you can find another."

"He's my *father!*" I cried out. "Please! Take me, instead!"

The duke went very still, in the way only fae can. Then, with care, he folded his wings down and released his grasp on my father's throat.

I turned and ran to my father's side, helping him up as he coughed and fought for air. "Dad, Dad, are you okay? Daddy, please say something," I all but sobbed out, pushing his hair away from his face and falling back on the names I hadn't used for him since childhood.

"Oh, Bells," he rasped out, reaching up to wrap his calloused hand around my wrist. "What have you done?"

"Saved your life," the fae snapped. His tail wrapped around my wrist, the scales slick and blades smooth as suede, and yanked me away from my father.

Pain sang up my arm, my elbow bending too far and my shoulder wrenched backwards. I bit off a scream as I landed badly on my hip, striking a rock and biting down on the side of my tongue. I scrambled at the ground as the duke hauled me to him, trying to take the tension off my arm, and ended up huddled at his clawed feet, cradling my arm while tears ran down my face.

"Bells!" my father cried, his voice full of hoarse agony as he reached out for me.

"Stay down, you stupid man," he said, spitting the words. "I accept your daughter's bargain." The duke went rigid, the harshness of his breath the only thing I could hear. Then, with a snarl, he exhaled a gout of flame and snapped his attention down to me.

Clawed fingers tangled in my hair, closing down. I didn't wait for him to drag me to my feet, staggering up as he pulled me up by my hair, needing to stand on my tip-toes to keep the weight off my scalp as he made me look into his eyes. In the moonlight, they were unreadable pools of darkness, until he exhaled a curl of flame between us. The heat licked at me, and for a moment I looked into the blood-red eyes of a furious monster.

"What are you going to do with me?" I asked, my voice wavering as the darkness fell between us again.

His fingers loosened in my hair, then released, and he ran the back of his claws against my cheek in a sickening caress. "If you're my bondservant, I can do whatever I want with you. You're mine, *Bells*," he said, leaning into my nickname with a sneering tone. "I require a body-servant. Someone to care for me. Dress me. *Bathe* me." He crooned the words with a dangerous expression tensing his face. "You'll do."

Goosebumps prickled down my arms at those words. Care for him? I was a fighter—a killer. I couldn't— I wasn't—

Flame curled between us again, those red eyes boring into me. I panted, starting to shake, but the duke released me and stepped back.

My body felt cold all along the front, where I'd been inches from his chest with his dragon's heat radiating against me. I shuddered, wrapping my arms around myself.

"Be in my chambers within an hour, Bells," the duke said in his silken voice. "My first command for you." His eyes swept down my body before he turned and walked up the stones to pick up the satchel of coin, breathing harder than he had been a moment before, so much so that his wings lifted with every breath. "An hour," he said again, his voice going hard. "Say your goodbyes to your father—and don't be late."

Before I could say anything, he crouched and launched himself skyward.

The power of his wingbeats tossed dirt and sparks into the air, making me throw an arm in front of my eyes to protect them. I stared after his silhouette as he flew towards the lights of the vicereine's palace, struggling to pick out his wingbeats against the stars. I kept staring, even after I'd lost him, until my father coughed behind me, taking a ragged breath.

"Oh, Bells," he said again as I turned to look at him. His eyes gleamed in the moonlight with tears unshed. "My little girl. You shouldn't have done that."

He was still kneeling in the grass.

I swallowed, looking down at the embers, and wrapped my arms around myself again. "What were you thinking?" I asked, trying to force back the choking sorrow as the weight of my future descended on me. "He knew you were there."

My father pushed himself to his feet and pulled his spear out of the ground, looking exhausted. My eyes followed his movement automatically, going to his throat as he rubbed it. "I know," he said, his voice quiet. "But Penelope moved, and I wasn't going to let her just... die..." His voice choked off as he looked at the bodies on the stone, mouth tight and trembling. "God forgive us," he whispered, the words a slender defense in the cold dawn air. "How will I ever tell their families?"

"They knew the risks," I said quietly, swallowing away the tears that threatened. "We all know the risks. They spent their lives trying to do the right thing. That's what you tell them."

Pain played across his face, and my father started scraping embers off his spear with his boot, not looking at me.

I didn't know what to say, or what to do. I wasn't like the rest of them. I'd grown up with this, a human born in Faery despite all odds, and death had been my constant companion.

At last, I sighed and walked over, holding out my arms.

He didn't look at me, his jaw tensing.

"Dad," I said, keeping my voice soft, willing him to understand. "I'm spending mine for the same reason, and I have to go. Please give me a hug before I have to go give that asshole a bath."

With a sharp sound, half-laugh and half-sob, my father stepped forward and wrapped his arms around me, pressing his cheek to my hair. "Thank you," he said, the words hushed. "I'm so sorry, Bells, but... thank you."

Tears pricked at my eyes, my throat going tight. I inhaled, trying to fix the scent of his favorite soap in my mind, remembering teasing him about loving leather so much he had to bathe with it when he couldn't wear it. "I love you," I said, forcing the words out. "You'd have done the same thing for me."

"I love you, too, ladybug," he said, his own voice rough. He planted a kiss on my hair, then stepped back, his face lined with sorrow. "May the road stay straight for you, and the wind carry you every secret you desire."

The words of one of the formal farewells of the fae almost broke me, a tear tracking down my cheek. "May you find your home and hearth before you grow weary," I said in reply, my throat tight.

His face trembled and I turned away, unwilling to watch my father weep. But once I'd looked away, I couldn't bear to stay. I started moving without commanding my feet, going faster with each step, returning to the embrace of the roses as my heart broke.

CHAPTER THREE

A DEAL WITH THE DEVIL

W hen I arrived at the guest suite given to the duke with my few posses-
sions bundled into a carpetbag, it was still within my allotted hour, and
he was already drunk.

Duke Yllaxira had downed a full bottle of wine and was well into a second.
The first bottle lay on its side on the table, resting up against a carved-crystal
wine glass. He wasn't even using the glass anymore; the man was slugging
straight out of the bottle like a soldier on his first leave in months.

He looked over at me when I came in, taking a drag off his bottle before
turning away. Despite his unusual shape, he was no stranger to my eye than
any other fae—less strange, even, because I didn't expect him to be human at
some deep, animalistic level. Sprawled across the couch, clad in black, he was
simply a man, sulking and well on his way to being completely wasted.

Still, though, he was impossible to mistake for any other man. One enormous
black wing stuck up along the back of the couch, with the other hanging off
it; they curled up at the bottom like a relaxed bat's, but the talons and scales
couldn't be anything but a dragon's. Two long fingers and a thumb rested at the
wrists of his wings, black-skinned and tipped with claws. His long tail draped
off of the couch and across the coffee table, the thick blades of his spade
relaxed. His legs belonged to a dragon in their shape, and those powerful,
taloned feet could surely gut a man.

Every inch of his warm brown skin looked smooth and almost burnished, a
natural bronze color with inhuman perfection, lacking a single mole or freckle.
That elegant face was all fae, save for the two black horns arching over his head,
wrought like a piece of artwork. His arms had more bulk and his shoulders

were broader than most fae, though, giving him the look of a fighter instead of a dancer—*Because he flies*, I thought as I examined him.

The ruby eyes and tangled blood-red curls against his black coloration and clothing made him look like a villain out of a picture book. If someone had asked me to come up with an evil half-dragon, I might very well have made someone who looked exactly like him.

Well. Perhaps rather less on-the-nose than him. As a picture-book villain, he'd really only do for children, rather than any sort of illustrated book I'd be interested in reading.

"Done admiring me?" he asked in a snide tone, holding up his wine bottle to see how much was left. "You'll have plenty of time to get familiar with my body when we return to Nyx Shaeras."

"I'm waiting for you to tell me where I can put my things, your grace," I said, keeping my tone conciliatory. "Will your grace be wanting me in the servant's room, or warming your bed?"

The duke choked on his wine, coughing hard enough that he spattered his shirt with wine and sent a lick of flame up. Drops ran down his wing and the scent of boiled wine filled the room.

He pinned me with a hot glare.

I smiled.

"I'm fae," he said, his eyes hard. "You may think little of me if you so choose, but I don't force women to my bed." His talons scraped across the glass, leaving scratches on the dark bottle. "The human disregard for choice is despicable. I would choose death before demanding that of anyone."

I held onto my smile, keeping my expression clear despite the bitterness that twisted in my gut. "The nights get cold in Lylvenore, your grace," I said, putting on the most servile voice I could muster. "Some of the residents who dislike having cold feet have bondservants sleep next to them to keep them warm. But I take it that won't be a problem for you?"

A muscle in his cheek jumped. Without speaking, he put the wine bottle to his mouth and took another long pull, keeping his baleful gaze on me.

I didn't move, meeting his garnet eyes with anger stiffening my spine. I couldn't hate him for defending himself against assassins, but I certainly could for the reasons that had put him on our list in the first place. Service didn't necessitate gentleness or affection.

The duke narrowed his eyes as he set down the bottle of wine, flicking his gaze down along my body with a possessive assessment that made me want to snarl at him. "You were with them, were you not?" he asked, as if it was of no concern. "I watched you set the drop." At my flinch, an arrogant smile curved across his beautiful face. "I recognize your stride, Bells."

His voice caressed my nickname like a lover, dropping into a lower register as his expression sharpened towards hunger. I was no stranger to the attention of men, but the duke smiled at me like he wanted to toy with me, his gaze direct and with the sort of bold confidence that I usually liked in a man.

It made me want to stab him.

"I see no reason to deny it, your grace," I said, fighting to keep my voice pleasant. "There aren't many opportunities for unbonded humans in Lylvenore. I was employed by the same organization your investments support."

His cheek twitched again, an edge of anger tightening his face. It vanished a moment later, wiped away by his sharp-edged smirk. "I'll admit that being murdered wasn't the outcome I expected when I began my involvement with our mutual acquaintance. I admire the boldness, but it was foolish. I'm not an easy man to kill." The duke pushed himself up with languid intensity, his eyes half-lidded. "Come here."

My jaw clenched at having a fae command me, but I did as he said, walking across the room to stand in front of him where he lounged on the couch.

The duke's expression went hard. "Kneel."

Rage sparked in my veins, heating my blood. But I hadn't forgotten the image of the duke outlined in firelight, his tail wrapped around my father's neck. I knew what I'd traded for his life.

I kept my anger behind my teeth, and I knelt.

He leaned forward, resting his weight on one hand. "Let me be very clear with you," he said, the words flat. "This is not the ending to my evening I desired. I didn't want to kill anyone, and I didn't want *you.*" The duke's mouth flattened. "Yet now that I have you, I have no intention of letting you slip out of my grasp. You're *mine*, and I'm far more possessive wearing dragonscale than I ever was before."

"I understand," I said, hanging onto my level tone.

"I doubt you do." The duke wrapped a hank of my hair around his clawed fingers, tugging me towards him. "You're not bound by power. You can act against me, and I'm unlikely to forget it. I won't be surprised to discover it if you seek to destroy everything I care for, or if you try to flee." He licked his lips, breathing hard. "But no matter what you do, Bells, the fact remains that you're mine. Life is bound to be much easier for the both of us if you choose to accept it instead of fighting for your freedom."

His red gaze bored into me, as if he could drill through my skull and divine my thoughts. I didn't look away, meeting the challenge in his eyes with all the steel I carried inside me. The world seemed to narrow around us, my focus falling onto the duke with the same intensity as when I met someone in the fighting ring.

"I sold my service, your grace," I replied steadily, my own breath coming harder than necessary, as if we were about to meet each other steel-to-steel. "I know what's owed."

"Ah, but will you give it?" He tugged on my hair before releasing me, sprawling back against the couch with the looseness of drink giving him boneless grace.

I didn't move, my heart beating hard enough that I could hear my pulse.

"My arm requires tending," he said, gesturing to the bloody scarf tied around his upper arm, where I'd seen a spear slice him open. "If I go to the palace healers, they'll surely want to know who cut me with iron, and such an inquiry is likely to lead back to my actions tonight, as well as to your father and those who sent him." He tilted his head back, giving me a slow smile, as smug as a cat. "I think neither of us want such a thing, but you far more than I. You may undress me and give me a reason not to endanger those you hold dear, if you so desire."

The heat in his gaze and touch of a smirk on his full mouth would have made me think he wanted sexual favors if he hadn't just been so adamant that the very idea disgusted. *He's a flirt*, I decided, examining him. *He just wants to unsettle me.*

"Very well," I said, setting my carpetbag down on the coffee table. I turned, unzipping the bag and pulling out my medical kit, trying to ignore the weight of his gaze as I moved. I'd done this hundreds of times, undoing the leather ties and rolling my kit out on tables, but my fingers felt unsteady and my heart pattered like a child running down the stairs.

I had to pause, pressing my hands on the table to steady them, taking careful breaths. I wouldn't let him get to me. This was going to be the rest of my life. I needed to be able to handle this.

With a deep breath, I turned back to the duke, unsurprised to find him watching me, his head tilted back and eyes half-lidded.

"Part of my duties included tending to the injured when the fae healers couldn't or wouldn't, your grace," I said, meeting his eyes. "I can take care of that slice for you. There's no need to bring the palace healers into things."

His mouth curled up into a lazy smile. "You have your permission already. What are you waiting for?"

I didn't answer him, giving him a nod instead. There wasn't anything for it but to follow through. It didn't matter that needing to touch the man who'd nearly killed my father made my skin prickle with adrenaline, nor that his possessive gaze set me off-balance. This was my life now, and if he truly intended for me to be his body-servant, I would be doing a great deal more for him than cleaning his wounds.

Thus chastised, I got up off my knees and bent over him, resting my weight on one knee next to him. He shifted as I started puzzling out the clasps at his collar, resting his solid thigh against my leg and skimming his gaze down along my throat to rest on my cleavage. The warmth of his body radiated into me, the sort of heat that turns a man into a furnace in the cold of night.

"I would prefer it if you didn't look at me like that, your grace," I said, keeping my words level as I undid the clasps. The cloth between his wings fell, pooling on the couch and revealing gleaming black scales armoring the top of his spine.

He hummed, raking his gaze back up to my face. His tail leaned against my leg, the casual physical contact sharpening my breath. "And how would you like me to look at you, Bells?"

My hands went to the buttons down his front, undoing them one by one. He breathed deeply, pressing his strong chest against my fingertips. Every button undone bared more of his tawny brown skin, a warmer shade than my own cool-toned pale olive. Like many fae, he was hairless, offering no distraction from the planes of his muscles or the perfection of his skin.

"Like I'm sexless," I said, trying not to look at him as if *he* was worth looking at. I had to untuck his shirt while he watched me, reaching my hands around his back. His warm skin left my fingers feeling oddly cold when I took them away, as if I ought to be running them along his sides. The sensation made my jaw tighten, disliking my innate reaction to his physical sex appeal.

The duke ran the backs of his fingers down along my arm, the look on his face one of curiosity instead of seduction. "Am I not allowed to admire what's mine? It's not as if I'm harming you," he said with nonchalance, his garnet eyes flicking up to mine. "I don't often have beautiful women undressing me, and I'm loathe to pretend I don't appreciate the sight."

I gritted my teeth, untying the scarf around his arm. The blood made the cloth stick to his skin, and the duke flinched as I worked it free.

"I find it difficult to believe that the Flame of Faery doesn't often have beautiful women in his presence." The words came out clipped, but I kept my hands gentle as I finished taking off his shirt. "You're infamous."

The movement had started the wound bleeding again, the flesh inflamed and oozing. The deep slice cut through his deltoid, but it was the sort of clean cut that should heal well. I examined it for a moment, then turned to wet a gauze pad with iodine to clean the area.

"The pureblooded fae rarely look at me with anything kinder than pity," he said in a dangerous tone of voice, not looking at me. "That name may once have been used with admiration, but since the war I have far more often heard it used as a mockery of what I've become." The fingers of his wings flexed, curling into dangerous arcs. "I seem to generally be regarded as an unfuckable monster by the women I desire. So, yes, I'm not often in a position to admire anyone."

He flinched as I started flushing the wound with saline, less gently than I could have. I had to pause to get control of myself, leashing my temper.

"There are far more people in the world than pureblooded fae, your grace," I said in my most conciliatory voice, keeping my eyes trained on his injury.

I hated that term for fae with two fae parents; the fae offspring of humans were no less fae than the others, and though they were far less likely to be magically gifted, they were also far less likely to come out of the womb with the sort of physical differences that made it difficult to fit into society. I didn't know of a single wildling born with a human parent.

He snorted, leaning forward to grab his wine bottle as I threaded the curved silver needle to stitch him up. "You say that as if I have an interest in having any other breed of partner." The duke tossed back the rest of his wine, flopping against the back of the couch. "Admiration notwithstanding, I've never had that sort of paramour. Not sky-called, not mortal-blooded, and certainly not *human.*"

The duke said the word like we were disgusting, not even worth fucking, and I noted that he didn't even bother to mention aberrations. I wasn't surprised; his reputation preceded him. The Duke of Nyx Shaeras wore dragon scales, but he hadn't been born with them. He despised the interactions fae had with humanity, and walked in the worst circles of the aristocracy. If he'd had his way, there'd be no humans in Faery at all.

I took a certain savage glee in thrusting the needle through his skin, stitching him closed without the relief of painkillers. He deserved to feel every ounce of pain, and more. He'd earned enough silver from ours.

"Far be it from me to offer you guidance on your love life." I closed his wound bit by bit, my neat stitches in a stark line across his smooth brown skin. "I certainly want no part in it."

He laughed, a harsh sound. "I suspect you're soon to become acquainted with a great many parts of my life that you'd prefer not to, Bells. I'm not a particularly subtle man, and my greed is such that I'm unlikely to allow you to stray far from my side."

I smoothed the bandage over his arm, resolutely ignoring the strength of his body as he leaned towards me, his breath smelling of wine and heated metal.

"Bells," he said again with aloof amusement, his voice caressing the word. "I can see you wanting to look. Tell me again how you desire me to think you sexless."

I refrained from squeezing his wound only by force of will.

Instead, I kept my expression carefully bland, putting away my supplies. "I don't need to look. I'm sure I'll be far more acquainted with your... parts... than I ever desired. Besides," I said, nastiness rising in my tone despite my efforts, "I was raised not to stare, even at aberrations."

His jaw clenched, expression hardening as his eyes narrowed and brows lowered. The duke took my hand and shoved my palm against his chest, flattening my fingers against his skin.

His hand was warm and strong, and the feel of a handsome man's chest against my palm was enough to spark tension between my legs. I met his angry gaze, breathing hard, refusing to be intimidated.

"I am not an *aberration*." The duke's voice was tight with emotion, his crimson gaze ferocious. "I'm fae. I've *always* been fae." A shudder ran down his body, and his hand pressed harder against mine, as if he could convince me with the feel of his skin. "I've worn these scales for eighty-one years, but I've seen three thousand and six. The heart beneath your hand beats the same as it always has."

I stared at him, not sure how to respond.

His eyes flicked between mine, some of the tension leaving his shoulders. "I'm still who I've always been. I'm still Varistan," he said quietly, as if willing me to believe it. "Even dragonfire doesn't change that."

CHAPTER FOUR

DECISIONS

I sat in silence, my heart pounding. I didn't know what to do. He was talking to me like I was someone else—as if we had a past together, one stretching back thousands of years.

I wet my lips and watched his eyes drop to my mouth, grief softening his face.

"I just wish you were..." His mouth twitched towards a smile, one without any joy in it at all. He lifted his hand off mine and brushed the backs of his fingers down along my cheek, resting them against my lips.

"What do you wish I was, Varistan?" I asked, my heart pounding as my lips moved against his warm fingers. His name felt good on my tongue, the sort of name for whispering late at night.

"Not what. Who." A rictus of a smile crossed his face before he dropped his hand, looking away. "You look a little like her. Gods." Duke Yllaxira dropped his head back with a groan, sprawling against the couch. "I am very drunk."

Against my best intentions, my lips twitched. "You seem to be holding yourself together well for two bottles of wine, your grace."

He groaned again, sagging a little deeper into the couch. "I'm not usually this... maudlin." He traced a circle on the back of my hand with one finger, the sharp tip of his claw dragging against my skin. "Or this... hrm."

"Forward?" I suggested drily.

The duke barked out a laugh, rolling his head to look at me. "Oh, no, Bells," he assured me, his voice dropping lower. He licked his lower lip, revealing a forked tongue. "I have often been quite forward. I may not have opportunities for such very frequently these days, but I've been accused of being a flirt many times." He ran his fingers along the back of my hand and up onto my wrist. "Though perhaps you're the one being forward at the moment."

My hand was still on his bare chest. I removed it with as much decorum as I could muster, my cheeks heating. "What, then?" I asked, trying not to look like I'd been caught with my hand in the cookie jar.

He smiled at me, the sort of heart-stopping expression only beautiful, sleepy men can seem to manage. "Forthright." When I didn't say anything, he sighed, tilting his head back. "I already regret the drunkenness, particularly since I'm almost certainly going to vomit up two bottles of wine before we even make it out of the city, but I suppose it can't be easily undone." His tail flipped up before smacking against the table. "Our itinerary has us departing in only a few hours. Given the bloodshed, I require new clothing. Pick something attractive."

I closed my eyes and nodded, the news that I wouldn't have the chance to say goodbye to anyone hitting me hard. *At least he let you say goodbye to Father*, I thought fleetingly, breathing with care. It was an odd moment of kindness—but then, the duke had only released him when he'd discovered our relationship. I knew he'd lost his, long ago. Maybe he remembered how to feel pity.

"Of course, your grace," I said as nicely as I could, locking away my sorrows as I got up to go dig through his things. My father was alive, and the duke didn't seem inclined to drop the hammer-blow of the vicereine's justice on my people. This was merely part of the price I had to pay: humoring the duke until he got bored of me.

I'd never handled anything as expensive as Duke Yllaxira's clothing, but even without experience I could tell that he wasn't as wealthy as he appeared at first glance. The seams had the sort of wear I was familiar with from keeping clothing until it fell apart, showing years of age, and I found several careful mends in less-obtrusive places. The trim on one of his fine shirts had small holes in the weave where threads had been picked out. It had been taken from a garment too worn to show in public, and added to an unornamented shirt in order to make it more fashionable.

I glanced through the bedroom door to where he still sprawled across the couch, most of his body hidden from sight. I knew how much profit he'd made off of the fights, and that surely couldn't be his only investment. Had someone been skimming? Was that why he'd come himself, instead of sending Sairal?

It doesn't matter, I told myself, and almost immediately thought better of it. As Duke Yllaxira's body-servant, I'd have close access to him, and to many of the things he owned. Vermin control was about doing the best we could to limit the damage, but I knew there was more than that to the human resistance. I had unprecedented access to the High Court in the shape of the King's half-dragon nephew. I could still make a better world for people like Estarren, as long as I was willing to swallow my pride for access to the information the duke possessed.

I chewed on my lip as I stared at the back of the couch, considering, then looked down at the clothing in the chest. Duke Yllaxira was a handsome man, and clearly vain. He flirted; he admired. He'd asked for something attractive, no doubt expecting me to ignore the directive, and it was obvious he didn't like the parts of him that were draconic, no matter how well he used them in battle.

So. Something that showed off the breadth of his shoulders and the tapered strength of his core, and de-emphasized the way that narrow waist gave way to draconic hips. No rings; his scaled fingers needed to fade into the background. But he had the sort of beautiful face people painted in chapels, with striking eyes and the classic sharp-tipped ears so common among the fae. Earrings, then, and cosmetics to line his eyes and darken his long lashes.

Re-invigorated, I returned to my task. I only hesitated once, coming across a set of rings clearly sized for the fingers of his wings, and decided at the last moment to add them to the ensemble. The duke owned them and had brought them with him on his visit to Lylvenore; surely that meant he had some amount of fondness for his wings.

When I finally emerged from his bedroom, Duke Yllaxira had passed out on the couch with no grace whatsoever. One of his wings was sticking up at an angle that had to be uncomfortable, with the other one folded underneath him, and he was sleeping on his arm in a way that suggested it wasn't getting any blood. He hadn't even managed to close his eyes entirely, a thin slice of white showing from between the mahogany arcs of his lashes.

Gnawing on my lip as I decided how to deal with him being unconscious, I crouched next to him and brushed his long hair out of his face. The deep red curls would have looked fake on a human, but it was obviously his natural color. Even the fine hairs where his hairline met his sharp-tipped ears were the same warm shade, a little darker than the rest. His ear shifted in his sleep, the motion so much more animalistic than any natural human movement.

The danger and exhilaration of being so close to a sleeping fae – a sleeping *duke* – made my breath shallow, goosebumps standing up on my arms. I could do anything to him, and he could do nothing to stop me. Varistan Yllaxira was utterly at my mercy, drunk and unconscious on the couch with a woman who had been eager to kill him looking down into his face.

He looked so familiar, in an ineffable way I couldn't quite place. It felt like I knew him, down to every line of his body—but, then, he was the Duke of Nyx Shaeras, and the Flame of Faery. I'd seen him before in Lylvenore, watching processions and duels with the fascination of a child. Hell, I'd seen more than a few illustrations of him. The duke was part of the royal family; his face was a familiar one to everyone in Raven Court, human or otherwise.

With a sigh, I traced my fingers down along his throat. "Your grace," I said in a low murmur, stroking his neck. I knew better than to wake up a fighter by anything other than the gentlest fractions. "You need to get dressed." I hesitated, then added, "Wake up, Varistan."

His eyelashes fluttered, the duke responding to his name.

"Varistan," I murmured again, running my fingers along his smooth cheek, trying to ignore the intimacy of the scene. "Wake up."

His warm hand wrapped around mine, a contented smile touching the corners of his mouth. "Let me sleep, dearest," he said, barely vocalizing the words. The duke drew my hand to his mouth, running his lips along my fingers before planting a heavy kiss on them. "It doesn't matter if... we're late..."

Duke Yllaxira's voice trailed off as I stared at him, my eyes wide and heart pounding. He— He had to be dreaming. Not awake enough to realize what he was doing. He was dreaming about someone he loved, someone else—

He laughed, a low sound of pleasure, and resettled his head. "So demanding," he said in a fond tone. "I can't... I can-can-can—" His brows pulled together, frustration and confusion flickering across his face. "I—can't. I... I... dearest?"

"Wake up, your grace," I said, my voice weaker than I'd intended.

His face creased again, head moving in a sharp jerk as his ears pinned back and throat worked. "Don't— Don't—"

"Varis!" I said sharply, desperation overtaking me as he clutched at my hand, breathing hard. Whatever dream he was having was turning into a nightmare, and I didn't want to be responsible.

The duke's eyes flew open, unseeing as he panted, but wakefulness followed the motion. Comprehension overtook panic, his body relaxing and grip easing. "Oh. Bells. It's you." He blinked, releasing my hand. "I... fell asleep?"

"You did, your grace," I said, my heart still pounding. "You were... dreaming."

One corner of his mouth twitched backwards. "Remembering," he said, his voice grim. He shook his head once before grimacing, looking nauseous. "I think I'm going to vomit."

I had no interest in cleaning up two bottles of wine vomited up by a dragon, and I'd tended enough children to know the sound of someone who really was on the edge of hurling. I leapt up, dashed to the washstand, and snatched the bowl for hand-washing, getting it in front of him just in time for him to grab it out of my hand and puke his guts out.

CHAPTER FIVE

PREPARATION

Instinct had me pulling the duke's hair back as he retched. It stank, the wine so hot from being in the stomach of a dragon that it steamed. I swallowed back my own nausea, not looking at the duke as his body heaved.

He looked up at me with misery in his crimson eyes, then heaved again, puking into the bowl of steaming wine. "Gods," he moaned, sounding truly wretched. "This is worse than I imagined."

I heard him gag again, followed by spitting, but he didn't vomit. I waited another minute, then said, "Um. Are you... done? Your grace?"

He nodded, his whole body slouched forward, and set the disgusting bowl on the table. "Fuck. This is deeply unpleasant." Duke Yllaxira put his hands over his face and sprawled back on the couch, looking about as unhappy as a person could. "What time is it?"

"About ten after nine." I swallowed, trying to keep my nausea at bay, then picked up the bowl of disgusting wine-puke. "Give me one moment," I said, my voice strained, walking with speed towards the bathroom.

I got it to the ensuite and dumped it down the toilet, gagging and almost puking, myself. Having not eaten anything since two in the morning saved me; there was nothing to come up. The duke didn't say anything as I washed out the bowl and returned it to its home, so I poured him a tall glass of water and took it to him, setting it and a hand-towel down on the table, along with a trio of pills.

He gave me a wary look, not touching them.

"Anti-nausea," I said, tapping the smaller of the three, "and mild painkillers. There's always a med kit in the bathroom. You'll feel better for them, your grace."

Duke Yllaxira eyed me, but he wiped his face off on the towel I'd provided, then tossed back the pills and drained the glass of water. He set it down on the towel, glancing over at the clothing I'd laid across the chair. "Why are you being... kind?" he asked, sounding puzzled. "I expected a certain level of, hm, antagonism."

I shrugged, getting up so I didn't have to meet his eyes. "I know what I bought, and what I sold," I said, my chest going tight. "You can still bring a great deal of pain down on the people I care about, but I'm hoping that as long as I improve your life, you won't be inclined to do so." *And I'm hoping that if I play nice, you won't notice me listening at the door.*

He watched me, his ears shifting as if assessing the room, then sighed, looking away. "It's not my intention to harm the people you love."

My mouth twitched back, wanting to snarl at him. His money paid for them to be hurt, week after week, and returned to him as bloodstained silver. But I kept the rage contained. I couldn't do anything for them if the duke turned me into a scullery maid. "Intentions change," was all I said, my voice quiet. "Can you stand, your grace? I have fresh clothing for you."

The duke did manage to waver his way up to his feet, though he had to balance with his wings half-spread and keep a hand on my shoulder. I took one look at his ashen face and had him sit back down, unwilling to risk getting puked on, even if all he had left in his stomach was bile. I could dress him from a seated position.

Before I started putting clothes back on him, I made sure to wash all the blood and iodine off. He mostly had it on his injured arm, but he'd gotten a shallow cut on his left wing in the fight, and blood spattered on his other arm. I cleaned him with care, trying to be gentle instead of taking out my ire on his skin.

Duke Yllaxira submitted to it in silence, observing me with tired eyes as I dried off his arm. I was used to that; many of the fighters had watched my face while I'd cleaned and stitched them. Maybe it was simply easier than watching me do the stitching, or maybe it gave them comfort to see someone looking at what frightened them with only quiet calm. Either way, having the duke's eyes on me while I worked wasn't uncomfortable, and by the time I finished, I'd almost forgotten his observation.

When I started dressing him in the overshirt he turned his face to look into my eyes from inches away. "Why this one?" he asked quietly, searching my face.

"You wanted to look attractive, your grace." I tried to ignore the way his warm breath scudded across my skin and the curiosity softening his expression, with resounding failures on both fronts.

One of the corners of his mouth lifted. "So why this one?" he asked again, with a lilt to the words.

I started closing the clasps along the side of his chest, feigning nonchalance. "You're well-built," I said, as if discussing a particularly fine horse. "The military style emphasizes your shoulders and core, and the gold braid is a good compliment to your coloration. It's the sort of thing to make people drag their eyes down your body and linger at your collarbone. Which," I finished as I closed the last of the set of clasps, "I'm certain you knew when you commissioned it."

The duke smirked at me, leaning back against the couch. "Like it?"

Reminding myself that I wanted him to keep me close, I examined him, pursing my lips. "It's doing its job," I allowed before crouching down next to him.

Duke Yllaxira stiffened, looking away as I undid the buttons at the base of his tail. When I went to undo the buttons at the front, he stopped me, grabbing me by the wrist. "Almost everything below my navel is... draconic," he said, his voice tense. "I would appreciate a lack of startled commentary or staring."

I blinked up at him in owlish surprise, but the duke didn't look down at me. His jaw clenched, a moody expression tightening his face.

"Of course, your grace," I said after a moment. "You're hardly the first fae with atypical anatomy I've encountered, after all. I'm one of the people on deck for the full moon fights, and under the light of the full moon many of the moon-called are a great deal stranger than you."

His jaw tightened, but he let go of my wrist. "I'm not sky-called."

"No, you're not." I got his pants unbuttoned and glanced back up at him. "You're a chimera."

"Amalgam," the duke corrected, his voice tense.

He lifted his hips for me, not watching as I pulled off his pants and under-things.

It was fairly obvious why Duke Yllaxira thought I might stare, or have comments. He had no external genitalia whatsoever, merely a black-skinned, scale-edged slit running from where the top of a penis typically sat on a man to where a woman's clit would be. He had asymmetrical scaling instead of pubic hair, too, with a smattering of black scales on the edges. The scaling on his hips wasn't quite symmetrical, either, going up past his hipbones on the right and barely covering them on the left.

I neither commented nor stared, moving as if dressing a mannequin instead of a fae man. The duke apparently enjoyed the soft knit cottons of the mortal world   an indulgence that was usually frowned upon in Raven Court – and all of the underthings he'd brought had been modified boxer-briefs. I put a dark gray pair on him, feeding his long tail through the hole in the garment without lingering.

By the time I got his pants on, the duke was watching me with a tense expression, his red eyes looking almost worried. "Nothing to say at all?"

"You asked for no commentary, your grace," I said with a half-shrug, picking up my jewelry selections for him. I started threading the gold through the piercings in his ears, the surely custom-made chains arcing below the gleam of garnets. "Would you like my opinions?"

His throat worked as he swallowed. "I'd rather hear them now than months from now."

I shrugged again. "You fly," I said, sliding a gold barbell through the piercing on the bridge of his nose. The gold studs would draw attention to his eyes, but would be a bit much for every day; it was a nice location for an enchanted piercing. "I can only imagine it would be deeply uncomfortable when in flight to have a more typical arrangement, and the first time you nearly lost a testicle from torsion you'd probably never take to the skies again."

Duke Yllaxira looked like he had a new regret, his skin going sallow.

I smirked at him, leaning forward to line his eyes with black. "As a person with internal anatomy myself, I regard it as sensible, your grace." I paused, considering my next words. "And, for what it's worth, you neither look like a chimera nor an amalgam. As you said, you're still Varistan, even where you wear scales."

"I didn't say that latter part," he said softly, not flinching as I darkened his lashes.

"It's true, nevertheless." I capped the tint and sat back, examining him, then held out the three rings. "These are for your wings, yes?"

He gave me a slight nod, dropping his wings forward so that I could reach his wrists. I put the pair of matching rings on the left, one on his index finger and one on his thumb, and the third on the second finger of his right wing.

When I leaned back, he resettled his wings, looking pensive. "Are you pleased with your selections?"

I frowned, my brows pulling together. "I think that's what I ought to be asking you, your grace. My opinion of your appearance doesn't matter."

The duke breathed a soft laugh, more of a sharp exhale than a sound of humor. "I think I need my hair combed," he said instead of answering, raking one hand through his tangled mane. "Did you see any grooming supplies?"

In silence, I put away his cosmetics and pulled out a wide-toothed comb. He grunted assent and swung his long legs up onto the couch, talons flexing as he leaned back and draped his curling hair over the arm.

His long hair was badly tangled, maybe from flying, and his nap on the couch hadn't done it any favors. I did my best, combing from the bottom up, but I'd never been very patient with my own hair and didn't have a lot of experience with delicate detangling, let alone curls. Eventually I gave up, disinclined to tease apart every knot by hand as if he had a baby-soft scalp. After three millennia of life, surely Duke Yllaxira had some experience with having his hair yanked on.

I took the comb, narrowed my eyes at his half-brushed sweep of hair, and dragged it against the tangles without mercy.

The duke *moaned*, his back arching and hips lifting, tail wrapping around the leg of the coffee table. Wet heat thudded between my legs at the sound of his pleasure, my pulse throbbing. Both of us froze, me with the comb halfway through his hair, and him with his head back and mouth open in an expression of raw sexual enjoyment.

The Duke of Nyx Shaeras did indeed have experience getting his hair yanked.

And he liked it.

A *lot*.

I'd never considered being in a position like this. I had no idea what to do. I went with my instincts, and for some stupid reason, that meant trying to tug the comb the rest of the way through his hair.

He let out another panting sound of pleasure, nearly dragging the coffee table up onto the couch with his tail as his thighs tensed.

"Oh. Um." I eased the pressure on his hair, slowly pulling the comb out. I couldn't take my eyes off of his face as I did, my whole body focused on his open mouth.

"Don't... do that," he said, sounding strangled.

"Uh-huh," I replied, my voice far too high-pitched to sound at all unaffected.

He settled back down into his seat, not looking anywhere in my general direction. With slow deliberation, he let go of the table, lying his tail along the couch.

The spade of his tail was fully flared, revealing a secondary spade and a series of nubs running up the top and bottom of his tail-tip. I decided not to think about what that meant about dragons. I decided not to think about what that meant about *him*.

Using the same exaggerated care, I returned to trying to comb out his hair without yanking at the tangles. My damn pulse wouldn't settle down, my fingers tingling where they touched him and my heartbeat pounding against my skin. It didn't help that he kept making little sounds of pleasure in the back of his throat whenever the comb got caught, clearly stuck on the edge of arousal after I'd flung him there.

Still wide-eyed and with nipples that refused to lie flat, I managed to finish brushing his hair, my fingers moving automatically into braiding it. He didn't protest, so I tied it off in a club at the base of his neck with a leather thong.

"All done," I said, rather like someone reading words off of a cue card.

The duke reached back, touching the braid as if checking that I'd done it correctly, then dropped his head back onto the arm of the couch to look at me. "I would prefer if you didn't tell others about... that," he said with an edge of tension. "I dislike being the focus of cruel gossip."

My brow furrowed. "I wouldn't mock you. There's nothing wrong with being submissive."

He flicked his ear in a dismissive gesture. "It's not about being submissive. Being entirely disregarded as a potential sexual partner is unpleasant enough without having my desires in the forefront of people's minds." Duke Yllaxira caught my eyes and smirked, reaching up to twine a strand of my hair around his forefinger. "Though I think you appreciated the display."

At my tight expression, he merely laughed, melting down against the couch and closing his eyes.

I looked down at him, clutching the comb so hard I thought I might snap it. Gods. How in the world was I going to keep from stabbing his smug, arrogant self long enough to take his whole empire down?

A sharp knock sounded on the door, rescuing me from my contemplations. The duke heaved a sigh, swinging his legs down and getting to his feet. He wobbled, catching himself on the arm of the couch for a moment before finding his sea legs.

"Well," he said, sounding glum. "Let's go."

CHAPTER SIX

CARRIED AWAY

People stared as I followed the duke through the vicereine's palace. I hadn't been exaggerating when I'd called him infamous; his hot temper and dragonfire were only the barest edge of the things I knew about the Flame of Faery. I'd never heard of him keeping company with a human before; if my friends didn't already know my fate, they'd hear soon enough. Gossip ran like wildfire, and my rumpled, hard-eyed self next to the self-possessed (if drunk) duke would be the sort of thing people would be talking about for days.

Lord Sairal had a hickey on his neck and a courtesan on his arm when we met him in the courtyard. Apparently he'd been having a lovely time last night instead of getting impaled like he should have been. A lucky break for him, and a terrible one for me.

The duke flicked his eyes down along his lord with a supercilious expression. "Enjoy your evening?"

The lord glanced over at me and lifted his lip into a sneer. "Enjoy yours, your grace?"

Duke Yllaxira's tail lashed, smacking me in the calf. "Not particularly, no," he said, his lazy tone belied by his tense body. "Your dereliction of duty has caused me some annoyance. Find your own way home."

"Your grace—" Lord Sairal started. He shut up at the duke's low growl.

"Take it up with Xilvaris," he advised, turning and opening the door. "After you, Bells." Duke Yllaxira gestured for me to go ahead of him with a mocking smile.

The back of my neck prickled as I obeyed, sweat dampening my palms. I didn't like having him behind me, but I liked being the center of attention even less. The last thing I needed was scrutiny.

He stepped up into the carriage behind me, practically shoving me the rest of the way in, and slammed the door behind us. The duke dropped into his seat with all the dignity of a sack of potatoes, and rapped his knuckles on the glass.

The carriage lurched into motion, giving me an immediate surge of nausea. I swallowed, hard, trying not to look like I'd left my stomach behind, and dropped into the seat facing him so I wouldn't fall into his lap.

The duke raised one brow.

"I've never ridden in a carriage before, your grace," I said through gritted teeth as the hateful vehicle swayed underneath us. "Is it always this unpleasant?"

"This is mild," he said, smirking at me with his eyelashes lowered across his crimson gaze. "We're still within the heart of Lylvenore. When we reach the dirt roads of the country, I suspect you'll think longingly of these moments."

My mouth twitched down with unhappiness. Maybe he'd hold my hair back when I inevitably became the next one to vomit.

Duke Yllaxira snorted a soft laugh through his nose and scooted to one side of the bench, stretching his long legs out in front of him. "Come here, Bells," he said, sounding amused. "It's much less distressing facing forward, and if you vomit, I almost certainly will follow after." When I didn't move, he made a sound of annoyance, tail wrapping around my ankle in a possessive grasp. "Don't make me tell you again."

I clenched my fists again, but my unhappy stomach was enough of a goad. It wasn't as if I had to stay sitting next to him. If it didn't work, I could go back to my own seat.

Grabbing onto the railing on the wall for balance, I got up and transferred sides, staggering as the carriage hit a bump and only keeping myself from falling into the duke's lap by planting my hand on his chest. He gave me a heated look, dragging his eyes down along my arm, and didn't let go of my ankle.

With flaming cheeks, I sat next to him. Instinct warred with pride: I wanted to shove myself into the far corner to stay as far away from the duke, but I couldn't bear to let him know that he intimidated me. He was stronger, faster, and larger than me—not to mention wealthy and politically connected. In a fight between the Duke of Nyx Shaeras and Isabela Keris, the duke would always come out on top.

So I sat dead in the center of my allotted half, lacing my hands together in my lap and staring resolutely out the window. To my surprise, it did help; I'd halfway expected "much less" to mean "almost not at all."

For his part, save for the tail coiled around my ankle, the duke didn't try to get into my space. He simply lounged next to me, his body heat warming my left side, slouching along the comfortable bench. Even I couldn't manage to sit ramrod straight for hours, though, and as the carriage left the Tangle behind, I settled back against the seat, watching the landscape as it grew wilder.

He watched me for a while, then made a disgruntled noise. "Is it your intention to sit there silently for the next eleven hours?"

I shrugged one shoulder, not answering. I didn't want to talk to him.

The duke growled, the sound far more draconic than fae. He resettled himself next to me, taking up more space than before but taking his tail off of my ankle. It left my skin feeling cold; Duke Yllaxira radiated heat like a wood stove, and the air outside was growing colder as we traveled up into the mountains.

He managed to hold the silence for perhaps another five minutes before saying, sharp with irritation, "It's considered polite to converse with the people trapped in a conveyance with you, and I dislike being ignored."

I took a deep breath, stopping myself from saying something sharp in return. Even if I hadn't wanted to convince the duke that I was worth keeping close, I was trespassing very close to the borders of open defiance. If I flagrantly broke the rules of life-debt, I wasn't sure that Duke Yllaxira would be held to the bargain, and my father's life was worth far more to me than pretending politeness when I wanted to knife someone.

So I turned away from the window, meeting his eyes. "I'm not ignoring you, your grace," I said, as politely as I could. "Be assured that I'm very aware of your presence and moods. But I'm also very nauseous from the motion, and the only thing that seems to work is focusing on staring out the window."

It was even true. Well, mostly true. I much preferred ignoring him to conversing with him.

Some of the tension left his shoulders, though, and his expression softened away from anger. "You act more fae than human," he said, tilting his head to the side.

I couldn't cover up my surge of outrage at that, my nostrils flaring and whole body tensing.

The duke *laughed*, a rich sound that seemed to warm the very air. "Oh, you don't like that, do you?" he asked, with the same patronizing tone of an adult talking to a small child who'd done something amusing. "A housecat who thinks herself a tigress. We're in Faery, in case you've forgotten. This is my birthright, not yours."

My fingernails dug into my palms as I clenched my fists, but I forced myself to smile. "Actually, Faery is my birthright, too," I said, managing to keep my voice pleasant. "I was born in Faery, same as you."

His brows snapped together, expression darkening. "I don't appreciate being lied to, human girl." The duke practically growled the words, his voice dropping into a lower register. "Your kind birth fae on faery soil. No human can be conceived in the presence of wild magic."

"Birth and conception might seem to happen in the same instant for someone who's lived three thousand and six years, but there's still nine months between the two of them," I said, my smile turning into a self-satisfied smirk at his narrowed eyes.

"A mother can't bargain for her unborn child," he said, sounding more hesitant than before. "As I understand it, those who seek out the dying cannot claim the life-debt of an unborn child, and so they don't choose pregnant women to save. Why bring home a servant who will only create a hungry mouth?"

I lifted my lip for a moment at that; it was such a mercenary way of viewing the world. It wasn't that I thought that fae healers should burn themselves out trying to save every injured human in the world—but the cold-heartedness of leaving pregnant women to die because of the inconvenience was alien to me. I relaxed away from it, though; what was the point? It wasn't as if I approved of taking advantage of desperate people either way.

"She wasn't pregnant." When he raised his brows, I flashed him a grin. It was always fun to see people's reactions to finding out that I was a Faery native, and that was proving to be true even when the person in question was the Duke of Nyx Shaeras. "Humans become pregnant in stages, your grace. It takes several days from the time of conception for the fertilized egg to implant and the woman's body to accept it. Until then, they're two separate creatures, and her body doesn't know what she's carrying."

"And your mother was carrying a conceived child without yet being pregnant when she was healed?" he asked, sounding skeptical. "You have a father in Faery. What of him?"

"He's my father in every way that matters." At his narrowed eyes, I shook my head. "He's the only father I've ever known, but they didn't even meet until after I was born. Can you think of a better explanation for a human bondservant giving birth to a human child nine months after coming to Faery, without ever having had sex since then?"

The duke made a face, draping his arm along the top of the seat. "I cannot, but I'm also not certain I ought to trust your retelling of the events."

I huffed a laugh and turned my eyes back out the window. It had developed fog in the corners, and I could feel the cold air emanating off of the glass pane. I'd known that the coast was much colder in the autumn than the interior, but to have proof of that before we were even an hour out of Lylvenore was a bit unsettling. I wasn't dressed for cold weather.

"I'm not lying, though there's no need for you to trust me." I lifted one shoulder in a shrug, watching the trees go by with a sense of pensive melancholy. "I'm sure you could get the birth records. However it happened, I'm fae by birth and human by nature. This is my world, too, your grace."

"Hm." I felt him wrap a tendril of my hair around one of his fingers in a possessive gesture. "That seems like a strange position to hold in the world."

I reached up and tugged my hair out of his grasp, draping it over my other shoulder to remove the temptation. "It is."

I could feel his eyes on me for a long moment before he took his hand away, the air colder without the halo of warmth from his body. "Do you dislike me touching you, Bells?" He lifted his brows when I glanced at him sidelong, but he didn't look upset, merely curious.

"You nearly strangled my father in front of me," I said, returning my gaze to the landscape outside the window. "You seem temperamental, you're certainly still drunk, and I don't know you at all. What do you think?"

The duke didn't say anything, the silence stretching past discomfort and into dead time as the minutes passed. At last, he sighed gustily and resettled himself, shifting further away from me.

"I have a tendency to be very physical," he said, sounding moody. "It took little more than a year for the new limbs I acquired in Pelaimos to become a part of my conversations, despite my dislike of them. I'm often casual with touch, and, yes, that's a behavior that tends to become more pronounced when I'm not sober."

I heard him move again, and turned to find him regarding me with what looked like unhappiness.

"I don't want you to feel... aggressed," Duke Yllaxira said, searching my face. "I enjoy touch a great deal, and I suspect that establishing my possession of you now will make it far easier for me in the future, but neither of those seem worthy of that cost."

I wrapped one arm around my chest, feeling far more uncomfortable with thoughtful regard from the duke than with him treating me like a doll. I didn't know how to react to that, and I didn't like not knowing where I stood. "You're fae," I said, sounding unhappy about it. "I know you won't do more than manhandle me. But I'm not used to that sort of thing."

One corner of his mouth tugged back in what looked like an expression of ruefulness before he turned to look out his own window. His tail coiled around his own ankles as he said, "If you name your physical boundaries for me, I will attempt not to cross them."

I frowned, looking at his tail. He sounded almost shamefaced, an emotion so far removed from the aggressive, flirtatious man I'd seen thus far that I wasn't quite sure what to do with it.

Faery culture – the culture I'd grown up in – enshrined physical autonomy, especially sexual autonomy. Rapists were executed, and the punishments for sexual assault were similarly severe. It simply wasn't tolerated, not from fae and not from humans. Even in situations with dramatic power differentials, fae didn't take that sort of advantage of those beneath them.

Such as, say, a fae duke and his human bondservant.

There were rules, and the fae respected them. Duke Yllaxira's physicality was setting him in opposition to the rules of consent for even platonic touch, and being drunk wasn't doing him any favors. But he'd respected my silent rejection of his touch, and he clearly didn't want to do worse than he already had.

"As long as it's platonic and doesn't cause me harm, you may touch me as you like," I said.

He shot me a disbelieving look, his brows pulled together. "But you dislike it."

"I'm your body-servant," I said, with a self-conscious laugh. "I'm going to be touching you a great deal, whether or not you initiate it. And since I've consented, maybe it won't feel quite so strange."

He made a soft sound of amusement, but he did relax somewhat, no longer tucking his body away from me. "I suppose you did suggest that sleeping next to me could be part of your duties, without so much as a question as to my nocturnal habits."

The dry humor in his voice made my lips twitch. "Are you a terrible bedmate, then?"

"I'm honestly not sure," he said, one corner of his mouth flipping up into a half-smile. "I have a distressing tendency to talk in my sleep, and as I'd rather not get held to promises made while semi-conscious at best, I habitually sleep alone. I don't believe I've slept next to another person for at least a millennium." His tail brushed against my ankle, and for a moment the duke looked almost afraid, as if I might change my mind after all.

I tucked my feet closer to him, leaning into the contact. The cool air drifting down from the window would have been enough of a lure, even if keeping the duke happy hadn't been useful to me. "Not afraid I'll steal your promises?"

He barked out a sharp laugh, the blades of his tail flaring out against my calf. "You're mine. You can't," he said with a smirk. "If you'd like to share my bed, that won't work as an excuse."

I snorted at that, unable to help it. His expression sharpened as he settled himself against the far corner, turning so his broad chest faced me. Without my command, my eyes skimmed down along the gold braid on the front of his overshirt, dropping down to his trim waist before I caught myself and returned my gaze to his.

The duke smirked, lifting his chin as he took a deep breath that made the fabric across his shoulders pull. He exhaled a curl of smokeless flame as I watched, the flicker of orange light casting his sharp features in relief. "You can look if you like," he said, pairing the drawled words with a lazy smile. "I enjoy being admired."

"Even by a human?" I asked, lifting my chin in answering challenge.

His smile stretched, lips parting to reveal a line of white. "What's not to like about the envy of those who want what they can't have?"

That killed any enjoyment of the moment for me, and I turned back to the window. "I have far more of you than I want," I muttered, my spine stiff.

Duke Yllaxira's tail tightened around my ankle for a moment, but he didn't respond to the volley, though I knew he had to have heard it. He merely moved back into his seat, stretching out in the pose of someone perfectly at ease, and let the silence descend around us again.

Chapter Seven

WARMTH

The roads grew steadily rougher and the air steadily colder as we traveled towards the castle of Nyx Shaeras. We were neighbors: Lylvenore sat in the eastern foothills of the Western Range, with the broad sweep of the fertile plains of Raven Court laid out beneath it; Nyx Shaeras stood on the far side of the mountains, along the coast.

As we traveled up into the mountains, the temperature cooled and the oaks and lowland trees gave way to soaring spruces. Light coatings of early-autumn snow rested on the northern slopes, protected from the sun by the shadows of the mountains, and the air beneath the old-growth forest was dark and cold enough that when we paused around one in the afternoon to eat, I started shivering as soon as I set foot outside of the dragon-warmed carriage.

I hadn't dressed for the mountains or the coast, not knowing my future, and I'd been too focused on the duke once I'd been in his grasp that I hadn't thought to add more layers. I regretted it as I got back into the carriage, my hands and feet icy and my light sweater not nearly enough to warm me. But my things were tied to the roof of the carriage, and given that we only were given fifteen minutes to bolt our food, I suspected the itinerary was too tight and the wilderness too dangerous for us to linger.

So I shivered, hunching in on myself and tucking my cold fingers up against my underarms to keep them from going numb. At least I couldn't see my breath, I thought miserably, staring through the fogged window and thinking longingly of having the duke's tail around my ankle.

"You know," Duke Yllaxira said in a conversational tone, more than an hour into the second leg of our journey, "I often admire fortitude of character, but your pig-headedness is elevating stubbornness to an art."

I shot him a sharp look, trying not to shiver.

He smiled at me, luxuriating in the expression. "You're sitting in a carriage with someone who is casual with physical contact, who radiates heat in a fashion not dissimilar to a banked fire, and who has already expressed his desire to be physically possessive with you. And *you*," he said, with great relish, "have decided to wedge yourself into the far corner, right up against the cold wall, quite as if being warm will kill you."

I hadn't considered huddling with the duke for warmth, but now that he'd been explicit about the opportunity, it was impossible not to think about it. I hated being cold.

"You planned this," I accused, glaring at him.

He gave me a rakish grin. "I didn't, but it would have been very clever if I had. You're quite at my mercy, Isabela."

I glowered, making a point of putting my shoulders towards him as I wedged myself further into the corner.

"Suit yourself," he said, sounding amused.

The lure of being warm proved to be too much for me before long. It would be embarrassing, wildly so, but my fingers and toes were turning into icicles. Maybe I could stick them on him and make it as miserable as possible.

I started grouchily scooting closer, but when I made to cross onto his side of the bench, Duke Yllaxira held up on hand with a smirk.

"Ask nicely," he purred, with a self-satisfied smile that made me want to punch him in his stupid, arrogant face.

This is useful. He has draconic instincts, right? I told myself, taking a deep breath to calm myself. *If he feels like he owns you, he'll keep you near. Just play along.*

"Of your mercy, would you allow me to warm myself at your fire, your grace?" I asked, forcing myself to relax as I met his eyes. "I'm not dressed for the weather, and would appreciate the opportunity to warm my chilled skin against yours."

The duke blinked at me, looking a bit taken aback. "That's a great deal nicer than I expected."

One corner of my mouth lifted, appreciating the look of consternation on his face. "I may not be a practiced servant, but I grew up fae. I know how to make a formal request."

"So I see," he said, looking contemplative. "You may warm yourself against me, if you so desire."

The openness of that agreement startled me; without any timeframe attached to it, he'd left himself open to having my cold fingers on him any time I wasn't dressed for the weather and wanted to use him to get warm. I didn't protest, though. Not that I was liable to sneak up behind him and shock him with cold skin against his warm neck, but it didn't behoove me to remind him to watch his words around me. An Earth-born bondservant might not catch such laxness, but I certainly would.

"You have my appreciation, your grace," I said, biting my lip. The prospect of actually crawling into his lap was a lot more intimidating than the initial thought, but with permission asked and granted, it wasn't as if I wouldn't follow through.

I waited until the carriage jounced over the rest of a particularly rough patch of the road, then slid next to him, draped my thighs across his, and stuck my hands up under his shirt. Duke Yllaxira made an undignified sound as my chilled fingers hit the warm skin of his stomach and back, his abs going tense.

I tried not to snicker at that, appreciating the small bit of revenge as his heat sank into me. "You said I could," I said, my sharp amusement slipping out in my voice. "I'm only warming my chilled skin against yours."

"I didn't expect that to include your hands under my shirt. That's more intimacy than I was prepared for," he replied, breathing harder than before. His tail wrapped around my calves, binding them to his, and he tangled his clawed fingers in my hair. "But it's alright," the duke murmured as if talking to himself, his body relaxing as my fingers warmed. "You belong to me. Your hands are mine. Your touch is mine. It's better if you're warm."

"Trying to convince yourself, your grace?" I shifted my hands to a new spot, having sucked all the heat out of his skin.

His fingers tightened in my hair at the touch, and his wing dropped down over my shoulder like a cloak, the fingers of it gripping me. "Settling myself," he said, sounding embarrassed about it. "I may not be cursed with the mind of a beast living alongside my own the way my cousin Ayre is, but I'm afflicted with a great deal of the purely biological instincts. I'm..."

Duke Yllaxira tensed, then sighed out a breath shaking his head. "You might as well be forewarned. I struggle to keep body-servants because, along with being monstrous in appearance, I'm very touch-sensitive. If you hurt me, even accidentally, I'm liable to lash out, and if you touch me in... pleasurable ways, my physical reactions tend to be immediate and strong."

My cheeks heated, remembering him moaning with excruciating detail. "Combing your hair," I said, sounding somewhat strangled at the recollection.

"Pulling on it," he said, sounding tense as his own fingers closed on my hair. "Which, unless you want me sinking my teeth into your neck to lay my claim on you where everyone can see, I suggest you refrain from doing, ever again."

Despite the fact that he was the Duke of Nyx Shaeras, that particular mental image made my pulse throb between my legs and put a very different color on having my hands under his shirt. I'd always liked a challenge when it came to partners, and the duke was far, far more dangerous than I. Yet despite the fact that the world would be a great deal better off without him in it, it was difficult to ignore the raw sexual charisma he oozed while using him as a heat source.

What had I ever done to displease the gods quite this thoroughly?

"I'm human, though," I said, carefully not moving my hands.

He snorted, his warm breath stirring my hair. "I'm selective in my paramours, but I'm neither ascetic nor blind, and hunger is so often a powerful motivator. My appreciation for the physical goes far beyond casual touch, and as I've said, it's been a long time since I've had occasion to enjoy such things." The duke's wing-thumb caressed my collarbone as he spoke, a casual gesture. "Few regard me with the ease you do, and you're a beautiful woman, human though you may be."

"You're far less strange—"

"—than others you've been close to. Yes, you've said," he said, cutting me off. "Nevertheless. My experience of your comfort remains the same even if you would be comfortable were I far more monstrous than I am." Duke Yllaxira tipped my chin up with one finger to make me look into his eyes, observing me through lowered lashes. "I'm not sure if your gaze is a gift or a curse."

"Why would that be a curse?" I asked, adding a beat behind, "Your grace."

He pursed his lips, regarding me for a heartbeat of silence. "I don't think I want to tell you."

I stared at him in momentary surprise before I realized I'd been treating him as if he was a companion instead of my master. My jaw clenched as I realized it, color rising on my cheeks. Gods, I was such an idiot sometimes. Too used to being in the company of equals, and too at-ease with those who didn't look like typical fae.

Varistan Yllaxira wasn't an aberration, and he wasn't sky-called. His wings and scales weren't the markers of safety they felt like to me. This was the man who'd spent the last four years investing in blood sports, battening onto the pain and suffering of people like Estarren like a raven on a battlefield. He'd killed three of my friends and nearly killed my father. Treating him like he might become a friend was stupidity of the highest order.

I slid my hands out from under his shirt, tucking his undershirt back in and smoothing the wrinkles of the overshirt out while he watched me. Then I shifted positions, still resting against him with his fingers in my hair and his wing across my shoulder, but no longer with such familiarity on my own part.

"Warm enough?" he asked after a moment.

I nodded, looking out his window as my stomach complained about the motion of the carriage.

"Good," he said softly. His fingers ran through my hair with gentle idleness, the backs of his sharp talons brushing against my skin.

It made me shiver, pleasant tingles running down my spine, relaxing despite myself. The fae couldn't lie with their words, but they certainly could with their actions—yet I didn't think there was any particular lie in the way he touched me. He was just... touching me.

It felt far better than it had any right to. More natural; more comfortable. But I was cold, and he was warm, so I didn't say no.

Chapter Eight

NYX SHAERAS

I fell asleep on the duke.

Motion sickness and a sleepless, adrenaline-filled night lulled me into it, falling unconscious between one blink and the next. I came awake in slow dribs and drabs, totally at ease, as if I slept in my own bed. I put the pieces together as I woke, making sense of the world as my awareness trickled back in.

The warmth surrounding my right thigh was because I'd dropped it between Varistan's legs with his thighs embracing mine, my leg resting against his groin with my shin supported by his tail. That same tail had slid around my other ankle, the tip of it coiling up my calf beneath the fabric of my pants, holding me in a loose grasp. His arm rested against my lower back, heavy with relaxation, his warm fingertips touching the skin of my side where my shirt had ridden up.

The heady scents of musk and cedar warmed me as I breathed, cut with the tang of sun-heated copper. When I tilted my head, my nose and mouth ran against soft skin, sending a tingling wake through my body. The low vibration of an almost silent sound of pleasure played against my ribs.

I was on Varistan's chest, I realized, my face resting in the crook of his neck. He'd draped himself at an angle across the bench so he could lounge with more decadence, managing to take up almost the entirety of the carriage, and he'd shifted me so that I lay on top of him.

It was a comfortable place to lie. The slow rise and fall of his chest underneath me seemed to counteract the movement of the carriage, and my heartbeat had settled into the same rhythm as his. Heat radiated up into me, enough that I felt relaxed and warm despite the occasional drift of cool air across my face.

Varistan – *Duke Yllaxira*, I reminded myself, not liking the casual ease of his company – must not have minded having me cuddled up to him, because he made no move to shift me as I woke. If anything, his hold on me tightened, the spade of his tail widening a fraction and his thumb slipping up under the hem of my shirt.

"You don't need to move if you're comfortable," he said, his voice soft and with a hint of roughness.

I blinked at that, my lashes sweeping against his throat. That didn't sound like enjoyment, or even remotely like his flirtatious voice. It sounded like... grief.

"What's wrong?" I asked, pushing myself up enough that I could look up at his face.

His jaw worked as he looked away. "When I was a child, I wanted to be nearly always carried, even when sleeping. Nothing comforted me like being held. As a man, I have generally been happiest when my life is full of physical companionship—and I don't mean sexual." The duke sighed, setting his hand over mine where it rested on his heartbeat. "Imagine, if you would, what it might be like for a man like that to have someone resting on him for the first time in eighty-one years, even if she would rather put a blade through him than belong to him."

"I think I'd rather put a blade through almost anyone than belong to them," I said in a sleepy voice, trying to ignore the pity nipping at me.

Varistan laughed, a single breath of sound. "And yet."

"And yet," I sighed. "There's things worse than belonging to someone."

He stilled in the way fae do, his breathing slowing and the casual adjustments people always make slipping towards motionlessness. "Do you hate me for it?"

The question surprised me, as did the way his heartbeat kicked up. "You were attacked in cold blood," I said, feeling him tense underneath me. "My father tried to murder you, and if he'd been able, he would have driven that spear through your heart without a single moment of remorse. So, no." I shrugged, then patted him on the chest. "A life for a life. He knew what he was doing, as did I. I appreciate your mercy, as hideous as the memory is."

The duke relaxed away from stillness as the ground beneath the carriage-wheels changed, turning to look out the window with his ears shifting to catch the sounds. "I suppose you ought to sit up after all, Isabela," he said after a moment, with a touch of humor to the words. "This is one of the better views of Nyx Shaeras, and it would be a shame for you to miss it."

I obeyed, curiosity driving me, pushing myself up and resettling my body so that I could look out the window without putting my knee on his groin. Not that I thought that would be as unpleasant for him as it would be for most men, of course, but it seemed rude.

Still draped across Duke Yllaxira's lap, with his arm around me and his tail twining up my calf, I caught the first sight of the duchy that would be my new home.

Nyx Shaeras was... breathtaking. The castle itself was built on a massive formation that was well on its way to being an island, the basalt walls stark black against the sunset sky. A narrow isthmus connected it to the mainland and two massive curtain walls cut it off from access by land, each with a pair of towers flanking the gates. Out to sea, a small island bore a lighthouse, the vivid light cutting across the sea with brilliant warning. The pastureland near the cliffs of the shore gave way to tangled salt-scrub, and then to the soaring, magnificent heights of the saltwood forest. I could see seabirds circling over the harbor, and the masts of anchored ships in a deep harbor rolled with the swell of the sea.

Varistan brushed my hair back, his claws hesitating along the curve of my ear before he drew them away. "Welcome home."

I looked over at him as the carriage veered back into the forest, the black castle vanishing from sight. "It's beautiful."

The duke smiled, though he still looked out the window, his ruby gaze distant. "It has seen better days, but it does remain beautiful," he said, with a wistful tone to the words. "I hope to be here to see it returned to the grandeur it once possessed."

I didn't respond for a while, as the slope of the carriage shifted and the sky grew darker. He didn't look away from the window, either, his arm around my waist and his tail around my leg. I wasn't used to that sort of casual physical contact, but Varistan seemed completely at ease, holding me as if he didn't even notice he was doing it. But the sort of man he'd described himself as would surely be that way. No doubt it would be stranger for him to hold himself separate from me than to have me on his lap—especially given his draconic possessiveness.

"Were you here when it was at its grandest?" I asked at last, as the coast came back into view.

The castle against the darkening sky faded away at the edges, a looming shadow, like a great seabird perched on its nest. It didn't have any spires; the central tower was broad and flat-topped, and aside from it, the buildings crouched below the level of the basalt walls. I supposed that made sense. The weather along the ocean surely included the sorts of storms that had never dared lash Lylvenore. Sticking a delicate spire into the open air was asking for trouble.

He sighed and traced his fingers down my arm, looking away from the view. "Nyx Shaeras has been a port for a little less than four thousand years, and it's been in my care for sixteen hundred. In my lifetime its greatest prosperity was in the centuries before the war."

I regarded him with curiosity, tilting my head. "I thought duke was a familial position. Shouldn't it have been yours from birth? Since you're the nephew of the Raven King?"

Varistan breathed a laugh, chucking me under the chin with two fingers. "How quickly the years fade into history for humanity." He turned away before

I could gather my anger into a glare, drumming his fingers on my side. "My mother is the elder sister of the Raven King, and the Court was born with him. As such, while she was his heir until my late cousin's birth, no positions within Raven Court could be inherited by her. It didn't exist." He shrugged one shoulder, shifting his position.

His tail slid out of my pant leg, leaving my leg feeling cold. Despite my discomfort with being touched by him, I missed the contact. The carriage hadn't gotten any warmer while I'd slept.

"...Will you tell me how you got it, then?" I asked, curious enough to venture the question.

The duke glanced sidelong at me, as if to verify my interest. One corner of his mouth tilted up into a smile at whatever he saw before he returned his gaze to his home.

"You're right in saying that 'duke' is a familial title. My mother is technically a princess, though she rarely uses the title. By birth, I'm granted the title of Lord Yllaxira, and given my bloodline, I can be granted a dukedom." He smiled, a soft expression, watching Nyx Shaeras approach until the carriage turned onto the spit of land and the duchy swang out of sight. "My uncle believed me mature enough for such a holding. He granted me the castle of Nyx Shaeras, and a great deal of the coast and inland forest, as my protectorate."

"Huh." I leaned back against his chest, considering that. Sixteen hundred years was certainly long enough to feel like forever to humans—but for someone as ancient as the Raven King, it wasn't that long at all. "Is it the same for Duchess Xirangyl?" I asked, naming the daughter of the late Elion Xirangyl—the former crown prince of Raven Court, killed in the same war that had seen Varistan changed into a half-dragon.

He huffed with obvious amusement and brushed some of my hair behind my ear with the thumb of his wing. "It is, though she's held her duchy for more than ten thousand years now. Port Kairos is rather grander than Nyx Shaeras, though I prefer my home to hers."

The carriage rolled through the shadow of the first curtain wall, the tunnel a solid twenty feet of stone. Even in the darkness, I could see the difference in the landscape as it became part of the protected land. The pale shapes of sheep dotted the pasture, and small outbuildings made soft shadows against the growing night.

"I have a hard time imagining that much time," I admitted quietly, trying to pick out shapes in the darkness. "It's not the sort of thing humans get to experience."

"Not often," he said, sounding moody. His wing-fingers trailed through my hair, a desultory touch. "Only when their lives are bound to those of the fae by the gods."

I snorted a laugh at that, trying not to be bothered by the way his fingers tightened in my hair. "Soulmates," I said, with an edge of derision. "Hard to imagine any human wanting to walk lockstep with the fae into eternity."

He made a purring sound, something sharpened by disdain. "Don't you like my kind, Bells?"

My back went stiff at the contemptuous way he said my nickname, but I forced myself to relax as he tensed beneath me. Carefully, I let out my breath, slouching against his powerful chest. Duke Yllaxira was my master and my prey; better not to make an enemy out of him before I'd even set foot in his castle.

"I struggle to imagine having much in common with you, your grace," I said in my politest voice. "You're ancient and ageless. When you look at the world, you're not thinking about tomorrow, or even next year. You're thinking millennia into the future, and you expect that world to belong to you." I sighed, thinking about the agonizing patience it took to wait even a decade when you knew you'd mark a hundred years if you were lucky. "I don't have that sort of luxury, and I can't imagine forgetting about everyone I know and love to claim it."

"Hm." The duke's fingers loosened in my hair, and he relaxed back down against the seat. "I suppose I cannot hold such a thing against you. I, too, struggle to imagine having much in common with a creature like you." He leaned forward, putting his mouth near my ear, his warm breath stirring my hair and drifting across my cheek. "But for me, I cannot imagine choosing to forgo an understanding of the great sweep of time for a fixation on the present. I think I would have chosen death in truth upon waking in this body had I not been capable of seeing the millennia set before me."

The stern determination undergirding those words startled me—but maybe it shouldn't have. Duke Yllaxira had been widely regarded as a gorgeous, desirable male, the sort of man who was pursued regardless of whether or not he had a paramour, and he'd woken up into his worst nightmare. I didn't know all the details of what had made him into what he was, but what I knew was enough. He'd gone to battle a man, and woken in the wreckage of Pelaimos as a monster.

That he held the sort of position few others who didn't fit the strict physical requirements of fae high society did no doubt mattered little to him. He'd had everything, a man viewed as the pinnacle of what fae could be, and he'd become the very thing he loathed.

"There's no doubt a lot to be said for the great sweep of time," I said, my own moodiness showing in my voice. "Yet when one doesn't have access to it, your grace, it's difficult to appreciate what things might be like when you've been long forgotten."

He hummed, leaning back as we passed through the second gate, the walls thicker than before. "Though it's not your fault you live as fleeting animals, I find it difficult to even pity your kind. You have minds to think; you could serve the future if you so chose."

I clenched my jaw. Snapping at Duke Yllaxira for his condescending tone wouldn't get me anywhere. There were far more powerful ways to show someone like him that the here-and-now mattered just as much as the distant future.

"The future is a far less enticing reward when you won't ever get to see it, your grace," I said, when I could say it without snarling at him. "Perhaps you could find it in you to recall that your affection for the millennia ahead comes paired with the expectation that you'll see them."

"I suppose," the duke said, sounding dubious. "Even in wartime, though, when the future may be cut away with a blade at any moment, fae seem to have a far greater memory for what may result from their actions than humans. Your kind so often trades the future for the most fleeting pleasures." He shook his head, sounding almost sympathetic, in a patronizing sort of fashion. "You're lucky never to have had to live in your native world. Humanity seems to be racing towards its end like a runaway horse for a cliff, the bit between its teeth."

"Faery is my native world," I reminded him, holding onto my pleasant tone. "Even if I'm the only human who's ever lived for whom that's true, it *is* true."

He made a derisive sound, waving one hand in the air, as if to dismiss my statement. "Semantics, Bells. Your kind hails from the mortal world. That you're a lucky transplant doesn't change where you're truly from."

Breathe, Bells, I told myself, digging my fingernails into my thighs. *You want him to like you enough to keep you close.*

"Who am I to argue with a duke?" I asked prettily, smiling when he shot me a disbelieving look.

Varistan might have pulled together a retort – I could almost see it forming – but the carriage came to a lurching stop, taking my stomach with it. Before he could say or do anything, I transferred myself back to the opposing bench, raking my hair back with my fingers and resettling my clothing.

Whatever I was going to face in Nyx Shaeras, I wanted to face on my own two feet, no matter how tactile the duke was. I couldn't bear for my first impression to be some sort of bawdy-girl, perched on Duke Yllaxira's lap as if I belonged there.

He watched me without speaking, waiting until I laced my fingers in my lap before throwing open the door.

Cold air rushed in, reminding me of how very underdressed I was, but I didn't let the cold drive me back into his aura of warmth. I all but leapt out of the carriage, getting my feet under me and turning to offer the duke my hand as he stepped down. He regarded me with what looked like curiosity, his ears perked forward, and accepted my hand.

I halfway expected him to stroll into Nyx Shaeras holding my hand, but Varistan treated me with the same neutrality that people treat chairs and hitching-posts. He touched me only while in motion, stepping past me with his shoulders squared and wings trailing behind him like a cloak. A little stunned – he'd had me sleeping on his chest, for fuck's sake – I fell into place behind him, walking at his left shoulder.

"So you noticed I'm left-handed," he said in a low voice as we went up the stairs to the double doors into the castle, sounding amused.

I hadn't made any intentional choice to stand at his dominant side, but it wasn't shocking that I'd noticed that subconsciously; it wasn't as if I wasn't used to identifying how people moved and where their strengths were.

"I'm very observant," I replied, trying to sound neither smug nor surprised.

The duke didn't reply, striding through Nyx Shaeras with the utter confidence of someone who knew that every stone beneath his feet belonged to him. Despite its grandeur, I could see some of the same signs of age that I'd noticed in his clothing—wear in the carpet runners of the hallways, vases holding faded ornamental twigs instead of the hothouse flowers that were in vogue, and even a cracked slate tile.

It didn't match my expectations, and that sparked my curiosity. As tempting as it was, I knew I couldn't lay all the ills of the world at Varistan's clawed feet, and the evidence of the decay of his wealth stood as proof to that. But if the Duke of Nyx Shaeras wasn't the one growing wealthy off the blood of humans, who was?

With his back towards me, I dared a smile. Whether it was Duke Yllaxira or one of the other aristocratic parasites, he'd put me in the position to find out. I wasn't going to waste the opportunity. We humans had spent long enough with fae boots on our necks.

I'll burn the world down if I have to, I promised the blackness of his wings. I'd been steeped in blood and pain, and I'd long since ceased to be afraid of it. If I had to leave the beautiful Flame of Faery broken to leave a better future behind for those who came after me, I would do it without hesitation.

My soul was already tarnished from the brutality of the world. I'd fought and killed, and I was willing to do it again. The Duke of Nyx Shaeras could either get out of my way, or be yet another casualty of war.

Chapter Nine

HEART-STOPPING

The duke handed me off to his steward without even a backwards glance, leaving me behind like a stray bit of flotsam he'd acquired. It was a true enough designation, I supposed, but it still rankled to be so summarily dismissed—especially after being flirted with, manhandled, and cuddled. It worried me, too; had all of his interaction with me merely been boredom? That didn't bode well for my plans of spying on him.

I wasn't entirely shoved to the side, though. The steward, a stern-faced fae man, took one look at me and brought me to the baths for the servants, telling me that I ought to be clean before moving into the quarters for the duke's personal servant. That statement came with an assessing look, but he didn't make any further comments once I'd taken a quick scrub, merely guiding me to the dining hall and leaving me with a wooden token he told me could be traded for a luxury like alcohol.

I pocketed it instead of spending it, of course. Such things would be far more valuable as a way to make friends than for drowning my sorrows.

Like many fae castles, Nyx Shaeras had been built to allow the servants to move through the castle without ever impinging on the important people living there, and there was an entire shadow-castle for the servants. I'd expected the place to be as segregated as the risers at the fights, but nearly half of the servants were fae, and they mingled with the humans as if they didn't notice the differences between us.

I wondered how Varistan acquired his so-maligned human servants. Typical fae snob. He disliked humanity enough to talk shit about us, but not enough to forgo the free labor bondservants provided.

A fae woman dropped down into the seat next to me and, without warning, put her cold fingers on my neck. Varistan's aplomb in the carriage put mine to shame: I shrieked and stabbed her in the chest with my fork.

She stopped my heart.

It *literally* stopped, with a wrenching sensation that left me choking for air as sweat broke out over my entire body. A second later it started again with a thudding beat that hurt worse than the stopping.

"Fuck!" she yelped, yanking her hand away as I started coughing, my chest feeling like I'd just taken a hit from a warhammer. "They told me you were his body-servant, not a thrice-damned *bodyguard!*"

Gods and monsters, the woman was a fucking *combat-trained healer*.

I dragged in air, my heart thudding hard against my sternum and my hands white-knuckled on the edge of the table. "Gods-damn," I croaked out, forcing my stiff fingers to relinquish their hold. "You pack a punch, lady." I pressed one hand against my chest, breathing slowly to try to calm my body. "I don't take well to getting touched by surprise."

"It wasn't my intention to aggress you," she said, all but vibrating with worry next to me. "Perhaps I ought to have warned you, but I'm unused to sharp reactions from brief contact."

"I take no offense from you," I said, my breathing evening out as my heart got over its brief halt. "Gods. Where'd you learn that little trick?"

I glanced over at her; luckily, my fork had been in the process of delivering a piece of mutton to my mouth, so the only damage I'd managed to do was making a big grease-spot on her shirt. The same couldn't be said for my physical well-being, but that was the trouble with fighting mages. They could kill you in the most inventive ways.

The healer flashed me a weak smile. "I can wield power through organic materials at a longer range than most healers. I enlisted during the war. Fought with a wooden stave and leather gloves."

She was a handsome woman—not pretty, but with the sort of elegant features of a high-class draft horse, broad and strong. Her nose curved smoothly, catching the eye and drawing it to her ink-dark eyes. Heavy brows arched over those eyes, and her full mouth was the kind men like to boast of kissing. She had good reach, long-bodied in a way that would have been lanky had the gods not blessed her with thick thighs and the sort of curviness that will get you through famines and give lovers a soft bed to rest upon.

In short, she was the type of woman I'd always appreciated the most, and had she been something other than fae and a healer, I'd have been tempted. But the last thing I needed was a lover, whether one with gleaming jet-black scales or one with supple brown skin.

Maybe I should get laid more often, I thought, amused at the direction of my thoughts. I'd broken up with my last partner because he'd gotten a bug up his ass about me fighting in the ring, and that had been months ago. I wasn't usually one for one-night stands, but...

"Remind me not to piss you off," I said, starting to grin. "You must have done a helluva lot of damage."

She shrugged, though one corner of her mouth lifted. "I made my presence known."

That made me laugh outright. I held out my hand, shaking my head with amusement. "Isabela Keris. Making sure I'm not bringing any parasites into Nyx Shaeras?"

"Lianka Vasetorys," she said in reply, grabbing me by the forearm in the fae style of greeting before smiling, keeping hold of me. "Standard procedure with new humans. We try to keep the number of colds circulating down."

I made a slight sound of derision, though I didn't lose my smile. "No more likely to catch a cold than your folk."

"Less likely to have immediate access to a healer, though," Lianka replied, a more compassionate take on why humans dealt with disease more often than fae than I usually heard. Her eyes went a little unfocused as she magically examined me, and a moment later she released me. "You're very healthy," she said, murmuring the words. "Better base structure than most humans."

It wasn't news to me. Though some fae Courts preferred human bondservants from more prosperous regions, most held to the thought that humans from harder lives and worse deaths would make for more loyal servants. It was probably true, but it meant that a lot of humans in Faery came with the physical damage of living hard lives and healing the old-fashioned way.

"I grew up here," I said, tilting my head and examining her as she released my arm. "You don't look surprised."

Lianka shook her head, smiling. "You feel like someone who grew up in Faery. Humans these days have all sorts of chemicals in them you don't find in fae water and food."

"Hm." I bent down and picked up my fork, examining the mutton for suspicious bits before shrugging and popping it into my mouth.

The fae made a pained face. "Must you?"

"With such an excellent healer on deck, how could I not?"

She rolled her eyes, dropping one elbow onto the table and resting her face on her hand as I ate. "Might I ask how His Grace acquired you? To my knowledge, he hasn't had a human attendant since his early youth."

Well, I supposed the easiest ways to keep from being the gossip topic of the next century would be to satisfy the gossip-mongers.

"My father gave grave offense to Duke Yllaxira, and in recompense I offered my life-debt." The words came more easily than I thought they would; it helped that *"grave offense"* was an accepted fae shorthand for *"did something terrible I don't want to talk about"*. "Luck had me present and unattached, and he accepted the bargain."

She made a thoughtful noise, examining me with sharp intelligence in her dark eyes. "I suppose you didn't expect to become his bodyguard, did you?"

"You were right the first time, actually," I said, wrinkling my nose. "I think His Grace can defend himself quite well, but he expressed a desire for someone to tend to his physical needs. I'd make a better bodyguard than body-servant, but here we are."

A smirk. "He's an excellent duke and a good master, but he goes through body-servants like an ugly man through whores," she said, grinning like a shark at my raised brows. "Scares them off," Lianka clarified, looking no less pleased with herself. "If it's not the flame and him breaking things when he gets overwrought, nor his tendency to get possessive with those close to him, it's generally his touch-sensitivity. Folk seem to find that unbearable."

"Awfully familiar terms to use for your duke," I pointed out, a bit unnerved both at her friendliness to the strange human her duke had dragged home, and by her apparent ease around him.

"Your duke, too." The healer plucked a sprig of parsley off my plate and ate it, apparently as casual about others' physical boundaries as Varistan himself. "Nyx Shaeras isn't an enormous place, and His Grace isn't a remote lord. He isn't my bosom friend, but neither is he a distant stranger. And you ought to know what you'll be facing."

I decided not to tell her how very well acquainted I was with His Grace's lack of remoteness. Nobody other than me and Varistan needed to know about me sleeping for hours on his chest, nor about the strength of his reactions to feeling good.

"He warned me about the touch-sensitivity," I said, focusing on my food so I could say it without my voice changing tone. "No doubt he'll get bored of me before long, but until then, I don't scare easy."

"Well, good," she said after a moment. "He could use a friend with thoughts betwixt her ears, and you seem like a clever girl. Maybe the duke will be a bit less restive with a body-servant who can't abandon him in the night."

The way she said that twinged my attention. Surely there were people for whom the status of being body-servant to a duke would be worth it—even fae-born. Why would they vanish?

Fae-born, comfortable with wildlings, used to dangerous men, and willing to deal with accidental flame and sex-faces?

Maybe not.

It still struck me as odd that people would leave such a position without notice, but maybe it shouldn't. For all that he was royal-blooded, the Duke of Nyx Shaeras was more infamous than he was lauded. His hot temper and prejudices had been seen in a very different light before he'd been made into a monster, and beautiful men were always treated with more forgiveness than ugly ones.

Not that I thought he was ugly, but for the fae-born? In this Court, where even hiring sky-called could get you called a beast-lover? Surely that would be among the kinder terms leveled at Varistan behind his back.

"I'm his bondservant, not his friend," I replied slowly, considering my position with more care. I chased the last few scraps of my dinner around with my fork, not really hungry enough to scoop them up and eat them. "Yet perhaps that will be enough to ease his vigilance."

"Perhaps," she said, agreeably enough. "It would make it an easier task for you, as well. Though I'd suggest not stabbing His Grace with the cutlery."

My lips twitched with good humor. "I doubt his hands are ever cold enough to stop hearts."

"Hah!" Lianka waggled one finger at me, apparently quite happy to banter with a human. "He's more likely caused hearts to quicken rather than stop. Our duke was once considered all but peerless in his beauty. Shame about the scales."

"Better than being dead or maimed," I said, my good mood evaporating. "There's no more wrong with having scales than there is with being fae."

The healer picked her head up off her hand, regarding me with curiosity. "I doubt he'll like hearing you talk like that."

"Then he can make me a scullery-maid," I said, more waspishly than I'd intended. I took a slow breath and exhaled it out in a sigh, letting go of some of my anger as I did. "Not that I intend to anger him," I added in a quieter voice. "But many of my friends in Lylvenore were wildling. I have as much of a tendency to jump to their defense as I do my own."

There was no point in being irritated with Lianka. Nyx Shaeras was a different place than Lylvenore, and despite the friendliness between the servants, people tended to follow their leaders. The Raven King hadn't roused himself to destroy the lives of the wildling fae, but general thought was that he simply hadn't gotten around to it yet. Varistan, royal and arrogant, held the same disdain for the wildlings as he did for humans. It shouldn't surprise me to hear such talk from my new companions.

"I take no offense from you," she said with a smile, her shoulders relaxing. "I don't particularly find scales attractive, so he's not nearly as desirable to me as he once was. That doesn't mean there's anything inherently wrong with them." Her smile grew and she flashed me a wink as she added, "If you're a connoisseur, perhaps you might ask His Grace to lend you his sword."

I knew it had to feel good to be on the other side of such an exchange, keeping the balance between us. Sometimes I envied the fae for their ability to feel the ties that bound people together. Lying was a lovely skill to have, but it was a lot harder to tell where you stood if you didn't have a sense dedicated to it.

Even knowing her kindness might simply be due to me not taking her to task for hurting me, I enjoyed the light-heartedness of the comment and the ease of her smile. She was acting a lot more like some of the mortal-born court fae I'd known in Lylvenore than someone who regarded humans as an underclass. It didn't entirely take her out of the realm of suspicion, but I didn't see a good reason to take out my unease on her.

So I smiled back, resting my chin on my hand. "As much as I enjoy swords in general, when it comes to His Grace, I'd prefer never to encounter any sword in his possession." I smirked at her, flicking out my tongue. "Besides, can fae dick really compare to human? The fleetingness of mortality makes men so much more dedicated to ecstasy."

That earned me a laugh and a brilliant smile. "It's been a long time since I've tried riding a human. Maybe I should pick up a new hobby."

"Tell them I sent you. I'd appreciate a little bit of swordplay," I said, catching sight of the steward as he came to take me away. I gave him a deep nod to let him know I'd seen him, then stood and picked up my dishes. "It's been a pleasure to make your acquaintance, Lianka. Perhaps I'll see you again?"

She stood with me, taking my dishes out of my hands. "If you like sparring, come to the training ground on the rising days," she said, using the term for the first and third days of the five-day feast week. Most humans never got used to the complicated fae calendar; I'd grown up with it. "We've two healers at Nyx Shaeras, but I'm the battle-trained one, so I take the fights."

"Live weaponry?" I asked, interest perked.

"Not often, but surely you know how fights are," Lianka said with a shrug. "Weapons aren't the only way to hurt someone."

"Very true," I said, sketching her a bow. "I'll come if I can."

"It would be a pleasure," she replied, smiling at me as I turned away to face the far less pleasant consequences of the day.

Chapter Ten

DUTIES

The steward gave me an explanation of the castle as we passed through it, while I did my damndest to stuff all the information into my sleep-deprived mind. Nyx Shaeras was an interesting shape, built with three bulwarks to defend against the storms off the sea and a more traditional U-shape attached to it towards the mainland. It meant there was a great deal more indoor space than I expected, with the remarkable luxury of indoor greenhouses lit by rare violet lambence, the only part of the castle that showed none of the effects of time.

Whatever else Varistan was, he couldn't be an idiot. He'd diverted his money away from visible luxuries to what was clearly a core part of Nyx Shaeras, something that many wealthy people couldn't bear to do, lest they lose face. It gave me a little bit of reluctant respect for him. Despite his obvious vanity, the half-dragon duke had chosen to protect his assets instead of his reputation. Whether that was due to a dragon's greed or a man's intellect remained to be seen, but it did color my developing opinion of him.

I had to begrudgingly raise my opinion of Varistan again when the steward showed me to my room. The man didn't confine his personal servant to a mean little closet, nor would I be trapped in the room with the only access through his bedroom. As the duke's body-servant, I was required to live in the servant's room adjoining Varistan's bedroom, but he wasn't making that my prison.

It was both more and less private than anywhere I'd lived before—the first time I'd had a room (or even a bed) to myself, and yet constantly accessible by a stranger. I had a private entrance via the servant's hall, and I'd never possessed the sort of luxury represented within. Though I wanted to swear to hate it forever, I suspected that within a fortnight I'd never want to sleep on a straw mattress again.

Of course, the impact of being given the sort of room a city fae would have been pleased with was somewhat spoiled by the fact that Varistan was lounging in it. He looked up as we entered, smirking at me while sprawled across my bed.

"Ah, Bells," he purred, unaffected by my frown. "You've arrived. How do you like your new domain?"

"It's lovely, your grace, though I appear to have been shown to your bedroom instead of mine." I didn't think telling him that his healer had stopped my heart would go over well, but I couldn't resist a jab at his hospitality. I didn't want him to think me particularly grateful to be in Nyx Shaeras, good food and a comfortable-looking mattress notwithstanding.

"They're all my bedrooms," Varistan said, his smirk growing into a wicked smile. "I suppose one could even say that you'll be sharing my bed tonight."

I sniffed at that, walking over and pointedly starting to unpack my things. "Semantics," I said, earning a soft laugh from the duke.

He sprawled down across the bed, as hedonistic as a cat, his tail flicking. "So many faery things are." Varistan watched me unpack my clothing for a few more heartbeats, then said in a warning tone, "Don't ignore me, Bells."

Despite the fact that saying such a thing made me want to give him the silent treatment for weeks, I made myself smile and turn towards him. "Is there something you'd like, your grace?"

He regarded me with half-lidded eyes, one hand resting lazily on his chest as he ran the fingers of the other along his wing. "Your attention." The duke gave me a sharp-toothed smile. "And also a bath."

Ah.

I set aside the rest of my things, resigning myself to seeing Varistan naked again. "One of those things is certainly within my duties, and I suppose the other follows along." I put my hands on my waist. "I presume you have a private bath?"

"I do," he said, still with that sultry gaze, "though you may use it, as well, if you so choose. I think I'd prefer that to you using the general facilities." At my lifted brows, he flashed me another smile, pushing himself up. "Draconic possessiveness, if you'll recall," Varistan said, keeping a light tone despite the dark expression that flickered across his face. "Having you bathe in my private suite and wash with the scents I choose... appeals."

"I'm neither a pet nor a concubine," I said stiffly, struggling not to bare my teeth at him. "Life-debt entitles you to my service, not my body."

His wings flared, but the duke sauntered towards the adjoining door as if he didn't care about my unhappiness, his tail swaying behind him. "Untrue, Bells," he said, lilting the words. "Surely a woman who claims to be fae by birth knows better. To be in life-debt entails owing your entire existence to another." Varistan cast a brilliant smile over his shoulder at me. "It isn't outside of my purview to require that my bondservant bathe in this or that room, or wear the scent of my choosing. But I'll remind you that I'm *offering*, not demanding."

He shrugged with his wings as I followed him into his sumptuous bedroom. Four-poster bed, easily as wide as it was long. Six wardrobes. What looked like a trio of full-length mirrors, shrouded by cloth. A chaise lounge *and* a reading nook.

Dear gods. Hedonistic didn't even begin to cover it.

Varistan looked back at me with one perfect brow lifted. "Is there a problem?"

I'd stopped dead in the middle of his bedroom like a deer caught in a poacher's light. I scraped together what little dignity I had left and gave him a polite smile. "I'm unused to seeing such luxury, your grace. I'll be fine."

"Hm." He looked around the room as if reassessing. "I do like beautiful things," the duke said, one corner of his mouth lifting into a soft expression. His eyes flickered back to me for a moment, skimming down my body before turning to the room again. "Perhaps I should take more time to appreciate them. It's so easy to grow used to what one sees each day."

I stared at him for long enough that he returned his garnet eyes to mine, his pointed ears lifting.

"I won't get any cleaner standing here, Bells," he said, mouth curling up into a smile. "I appreciate the focus, but given our mutual lack of sleep, perhaps we can progress a bit further than the bedroom...?"

The innocent humor in his voice was far worse than any lascivious comment could have been. I flushed so hard I knew I had to be turning crimson, my cheeks and throat heating. "Coming," I said, sounding choked, and scurried across the room towards where he lounged against the doorframe.

The duke smirked at me, his eyes heated as I ducked past him. "Usually I prefer a bit more enthusiasm when women tell me they're coming, but given that charming blush, I suppose it will do," he said, his tail brushing against my calf. "I wouldn't have expected someone as ferocious as you to blush so prettily." His claws combed through my hair as I passed by, the barest hint of contact. Tingles ran down my spine, making goose-prickles rise on my arms, and Varistan made a soft sound of amusement as he stepped into the bathroom behind me.

Gods damn, but he knew exactly what to say to make me want to draw blood—and how to say it. I usually wouldn't take offense to being called "ferocious", but when said in that tone of light amusement, it made me feel like someone's housepet who'd caught a cricket.

Kitty has claws, I thought viciously, though I kept my expression mild.

"How do you like your baths, your grace?" I asked in my most servile tones. "Scorching, I assume?"

"Cold, actually," Varistan said, his wings rustling as I knelt by the enormous granite bath. "I produce enough body heat these days that the contrast is pleasant." When I glanced over my shoulder at him, he favored me with a rakish grin. "Your cold fingers were only a trial in their unexpectedness. When we get lucky enough for freezing weather, I even like having ice baths."

I blinked at him, surprised at that, then shrugged and opened the tap for cold water. "I hope you don't expect me to take cold baths."

He laughed and crouched next to me, wrapping one tendril of my hair around his clawed finger. "Don't worry, Bells," he said in a croon. "My possessiveness doesn't quite extend to mandating you use the same bathwater as me. Besides, once I'm done with it, it's not quite so cold."

I considered ignoring his nearness to examining the enormous rack of bathing supplies, but given his reaction to having me sleeping on him, I suspected that having me return any amount of casual physical familiarity would be the sort of irresistible lure I needed to have him keep me close. It would be fun, too—edging up to the breathtaking danger he represented, both as fae nobility and as a war-dragon, and pretending I was more than prey.

So I turned towards him, looking up into his face with a thoughtful expression. As the water thundered into the tub next to us, I reached up and tucked a curling tendril of hair that had escaped his braid behind his ear. Distaste and fascination wound through me from the feel of his sharp-tipped ear beneath my fingers, the sort of intimate touch I'd never expected to share with someone fae.

For all my railing against the stark divisions between the court fae, humans, and wildling fae, I'd fallen in with humanity as strongly as Varistan had fallen in with his own kind. I'd never run my fingertips along a fae's pointed ear before, and I doubted he'd ever caressed the rounded ear of a human before mine, either.

"It doesn't seem like anything about you is cold," I said, refusing to quail beneath his gaze even as his pupils dilated and breathing quickened. He was touch-sensitive; that sort of gentle touch might have as much of an affect on him as anything else. "Every story I've heard of you paints you as passionate."

He took my hand away from his face, giving me an odd look, almost akin to fear. "I told you. I'm not a subtle man."

The wariness in his voice made me smile, suppressing the victorious smirk that wanted to settle onto my lips. I filed away the knowledge that he didn't know how to handle being approached, and turned to his collection of oils and unguents.

"Lack of subtlety and passion are two very different things, your grace," I said as I walked my fingers along the glass bottles, recognizing most of the apothecary marks with ease. A few I didn't know; I unstopped one and wafted it beneath my nose. I didn't recognize the scent, either, a heady, almost musky fragrance, but without the animal darkness of musk. It was brighter and sharper—a resin, perhaps.

"Keskyr," Varistan said, taking the vial from me. He poured a little into the water before capping it and setting it back amongst its mates. "One of the perfumes we harvest wild from the saltwood forest."

"It's lovely." I looked back up at him as he stood. "Do you export it?"

"We used to," he replied, sounding moody. The duke stood and shook out his wings, glancing down at where I still crouched. "You may undress me while the bath fills." He said it like he was doing me a favor; I narrowly resisted rolling my eyes, standing instead.

Without saying anything – I didn't trust my tongue – I started undoing the clothing I'd put him in that morning, starting with freeing his hair and removing his jewelry. The outfit was still as attractive as I'd found it when choosing it for him, and I found myself fighting the urge to linger. The fucking Flame of Faery, under my hands. A gods-damn gorgeous fae royal, his broad shoulders and powerful body looking like someone had sculpted them for the sake of admiration.

He was awful, but he certainly was pretty.

He didn't flinch this time when I undid his pants, his stance relaxed and breathing easy. His lacquered scales caught the light, gleaming with a hint of iridescence, and when he picked up his feet for me I noticed a healed brand on the outside of his ankle.

I touched it before I could think not to, running my fingers across the scale-free skin of the scar. I recognized the version of the Raven Court seal used for the Army, the triskelion ravens simplified into linear shapes within a circle.

"They brand war-dragons," Varistan said, his voice flat. "Healers can't heal scars. It is what it is."

"I like it," I said, surprised at myself.

He stepped away from my touch, talons flexing and tail swiping through the air. "Don't lie to me."

"I'm not lying." I turned off the water before getting back up, folding his clothing and setting it on the counter. "Not a lot of fae have permanent adornments. I doubt you'll like me saying it's a mortal trait, but..." I shrugged one shoulder, trying not to bare my teeth at his wary expression. "I enjoy the boldness of modifying your body in a way that can't be undone. I know you didn't choose it, but I have enough fondness for the trait that I appreciate the aesthetic, nonetheless."

His eyes scanned my face, but though he narrowed them at me, he didn't accuse me of anything else. Varistan simply stepped past me and got into the tub, sprawling out on his back in the cold water with every evidence of comfort. He kept his bandaged arm slung over the edge of the tub, his fingers tracing idle circles on the stone.

I stood there, feeling stupider and more useless by the minute, until he sighed and tilted his head back in the water.

"Do you know anything about how I came to be what I am?" he asked, in the sort of light tone people use when talking about painful topics they've shoved far away from their hearts.

"Um." I tried to find a casual pose, failed, and hopped up onto the counter like an embarrassed cat. "It was during the siege of Pelaimos, your cousin did it, and afterwards he made the Furies for the war. Other than that, not really."

Varistan made a sharp sound, one that tried to be laughter and came out laden with bitterness. "I've been told the damage a trebuchet stone does when it strikes a man is worse than putting him through a meat grinder," he said in a dark tone. "They scraped what was left of my legs and hips off the ground. There wasn't much but ashes and char of the other parts of me that met the fires that raged through the city that night."

I stared at him, appalled. He'd survived *that*?

"I've been told you could see my blackened spine when they took the burning beam off of me," he continued in a conversational tone. "That the stone held my guts and blood in, and the burning wood cauterized the damage it did quite thoroughly." He exhaled sharply, his jaw tensing. "Whatever the reasons, I was still barely alive when I was found. The Raven King let my cousin out of confinement just for me." The bitterness wound through his words, as cutting as garrotte-wire. "They killed a war-dragon, and Ayre used its corpse to make me into *this*."

The duke swept a hand down over his body, his face twisting with disgust. "I'm branded like an animal because my legs *are* an animal's. I have a tail because I needed a new *spine*, and wings because there was little left of the muscle of my back. Only my soul is fully fae, I fear." He shook his head, a tight movement, tension tightening the skin around his closed eyes. "So I don't particularly like being complimented for the brand of ownership stamped into my skin."

I wrapped my arms around my chest, feeling uncomfortably guilty. I didn't like it; feeling sympathy for Duke Yllaxira would make it a great deal more difficult for me to sacrifice him for the sake of progress.

"You said I could look," I said, even the words sounding guilty, like a child trying to find an excuse for what she knew was poor behavior. "I didn't intend to cause you pain."

He made a low sound, settling deeper into the water. "I did, and you may," he said in an even tone. "I invited you to look at me with admiration, and that invitation stands. I didn't imagine you would direct an admiring gaze to my ankles, but I suppose I cannot fault you for taking me at my word." The duke sighed, swishing his fingers through the water. "Come wash my hair, and you may retire after."

I didn't love the way he assumed that his invitation would garner admiration, but he hadn't exactly been wrong. Peacocks knew they were beautiful and flaunted it, and Varistan had been a beauty among beauties. Being admired must have become second nature to him.

Biting back a snarky retort to his command, I went over to the side of the tub and knelt. Varistan handed me a glass bottle of cleansing conditioner before I could choose one, with the apothecary labels for styrax and cedar-smoke on it. The rich scent bloomed around me as I lathered his hair, the cold water keeping the cleanser from forming suds.

Varistan leaned back into the contact, lashes fluttering and lips parting. It looked like a wholly innate response, one paired with a slight tilt of his hips and pointing of his feet, his draconic toes spreading; a moment later he caught himself and relaxed, letting out a heavy breath.

"I can rinse it myself," the duke said, his voice rough as I scrubbed my fingertips across his scalp. "You needn't stay."

"You're surely capable of washing yourself, your grace, but the whole point of having a body-servant is so you don't have to deal with even that bit of manual labor," I said, a bit nonplussed. "Otherwise why bother having me help you bathe at all?"

He huffed a laugh, opening his eyes to look up at me with a wry smile. Varistan held up one hand and curled his fingers, his sharp obsidian claws gleaming in the lambence-light of the lamps. "I have a distressing tendency to rend clothing and slice my scalp when dressing and bathing, Bells," he said in a lilting voice, with an undercurrent of distaste. "I do greatly enjoy being bathed, but I'm tired, you dislike me, and no doubt you'd dislike the cold water, as well. Being scrubbed because it's a chore isn't an upgrade from doing it myself, save for my hair."

My cheeks warmed, even though everything he'd said was true. "You could always cut them?"

Varistan snorted and closed his eyes again, leaning into my hands. "I tried that some time ago. I prefer being dangerous to blunted, even if I'm less likely to injure myself. It makes me appear to others as if I'm discontented with my body."

"...You *are* discontented with your body."

He rumbled a laugh. "Ah, but I don't *appear* to be, do I?" he countered. "I flaunt my wings and tail; I use them as if it's only natural. I burnish my scales, and I adorn my horns and the fingers of my wings. I cannot change my body, and so I must not act as if I'm ashamed of it." Varistan sounded grim, the way soldiers do when talking about the realities of war. "I am the Flame of Faery. I didn't gain what I have by making myself small, but by stepping boldly into the world. So." He flashed me a smile. "Sharp claws, and a body-servant washing my hair."

"Well," I said, giving his scalp one more scrub. "Your hair is washed."

"And I sleep in the nude, so you may consider your tasks for the day complete," Varistan said, yawning and covering his mouth with one hand. "Stay and wash me if it pleases you, but..." His voice trailed off, a smirk on his full mouth as he looked up at me through lowered lashes, knowing full well I wanted no such thing.

"It's been a long day, your grace," I said, a little stiffly. "I'll take my leave."

Varistan lifted one hand and wiggled his fingers at me in farewell.

I didn't have any good way to make an exit. There's really nothing at all dignified about being on your knees in a bathroom, nor rinsing your hands off in a man's cold bathwater. Even with my spine straight and stride certain I felt like a fool, fleeing the naked half-dragon sprawled in his tub while the warm sound of his self-satisfied chuckle chased me out the door.

CHAPTER ELEVEN

RESTLESS SLEEP

S leep had always come easily to me, and even in a strange new place and on the sort of bed I'd never slept on before, I fell into a dreamless sleep almost before my head hit my pillow. My body had no concept of what to do on such a different schedule than it was used to, though, and I woke up repeatedly through the night, each time shooting upright with a sense of horrible dislocation.

When I finally woke into predawn light, I gave up trying to sleep and hauled myself out of bed to get dressed. The duke's steward had provided me with a set of simple clothing to supplement my few personal belongings. Though I would have preferred my own clothing, I dressed in what had been supplied, telling myself it was part of winning over Duke Yllaxira. He wanted to be possessive; well, I would dress in his clothing and sleep within immediate reach of him. Dragons were greedy creatures by nature, and though he was a man, he confessed to draconic instinct.

I took a moment to settle myself, standing in front of the door to the duke's bedroom. This was just another arrow in my quiver—a necessary part of the war. I was one in a long tradition of female spies, sent to coo at their male targets and claim from them the secrets they guarded.

You can do this.

Since I didn't have any knowledge of the duke's schedule, I wasn't sure if and when I should rouse him. If he was already awake, though, I didn't want to abandon my duties. So, with care, I opened the adjoining door and poked my nose in to see what there was to see.

With the heavy curtains drawn, the pale dawn light did little to illuminate the room, and even with my good night-vision I had to wait for my eyes to adjust to the darkness. The simple act of waiting told me enough; the duke was sound asleep, his breathing slow and even. Curiosity held me in place, though.

In many ways, the duke was an enigma to me. Seeing him vulnerable carried an appeal I couldn't resist.

Slowly, Varistan's shape resolved. He slept on his side, a body pillow tucked up along his front with his arm and wing holding it close. The tangled sheets suggested a restless sleeper—or perhaps a restless tail, since it was wrapped around both his leg and another pillow.

The same sort of fascination that makes people pick up serpents drew me out into the room, padding closer to his bed. He was unfairly beautiful in repose, the arrogance gone from his lovely face and his body lax. Those broad shoulders were no less tempting bare than clad, and the black scales on his back looked like lacquered armor, as much art as protection. The fae blood-red of his curling hair looked almost black in the darkness, his pointed ears and dragon's horns growing through the tangled strands like the young shoots of plants.

His lips moved as if speaking, chin lifting. I froze, not wanting him to wake and find me creepily staring at him. But all that happened was that a gentle smile touched his mouth for a moment before he relaxed back into sleep with a sigh, his face going soft again.

He talks in his sleep, I remembered, thinking back to him unconscious on the couch in Lylvenore. The reminder of my lost home wrenched in my chest, but I forced the pain away by studying the man who had claimed me, making myself focus on the here-and-now.

The pattern of scales on his back weren't symmetrical, just like his hips. They angled up higher on his left shoulder, and further out onto his ribs on the right. His whole spine was scaled, smooth plates of armor protecting the bone, but the same wasn't true of his back. The uneven scaling thinned where it turned to smooth brown skin, a smattering of small scales along the edges. Perhaps it should have looked patchwork – like a stitched-together monster – but every scale seemed to lie exactly where it belonged. I couldn't imagine Varistan looking any other way.

His cousin must have been an artist with flesh, as horrifying as the thought was. He had done his best to preserve what body Varistan had left—maybe even working with a healer to fix what could be saved. Healers could only heal what was *there*. They could grow back muscle if there was muscle to grow from, but Varistan had been burned to the bone. They could repair bone and sinew, but they couldn't create it out of bloody scraps.

Without thinking, I brushed Varistan's hair away from the back of his neck to follow the line of scales running up his spine.

Varistan made a soft sound, leaning his head back towards my touch. "Don't tease, dearest," he murmured, his voice warm and his body still heavy with sleep. "Too early for yearning."

I froze again, my heart pounding. Instinct made me want to flee—but Varistan had to be dreaming about the same woman he'd been dreaming about yesterday morning, the nameless person I looked a little like. He wasn't calling me "dearest." He didn't even know I was here, half-roused and filling in the gaps with his memories.

"Sleep, then," I said, pitching my voice low. "I'll wake you once the maids begin to sing."

He smiled, his ear shifting. "As you like," he said in a happy sigh. Varistan wiggled a little closer to the pillow he embraced. "Don't go," he murmured as I took my hand away, his breathing slowing even as his face tensed with unhappiness. "Please... don't go. Not again."

"Don't worry," I replied, setting my fingers against the slow throb of his pulse, shocked at hearing a fae plead, let alone one like him. "I'm here."

Varistan didn't reply, but he relaxed, utterly, his entire body going lax with sleep. His heartbeat slowed under my fingertips as he slipped back into deep sleep, looking completely at peace.

Ambition and compassion warred inside of me. It would be so easy to shift him, murmuring words into his dreams and manipulating him like a vizier whispering into the ear of a King. I could do it right now—could comb my finger through his curling hair and step into the role of his paramour, this man who slept alone to protect himself and whose twilight dreaming was so dangerously real.

I wanted to do it; wanted to take every advantage of the fae duke who had killed my friends and used his gold to spill the blood of people I loved. But I couldn't separate myself from the reality of the touch-starved man sleeping with a pillow in his arms, dreaming of a woman who-knew-how-many centuries gone. I couldn't use his heartbreak against him, not with my own heartbreak so raw.

So I waited until I was certain he wouldn't wake when I left, and I took my fingers away from his neck and walked away, a tightness in my throat I didn't want to identify. Several hours and a warm breakfast later, I stepped back into the duke's room, composed again. He was still sleeping, but in the light way of someone merely drowsing, and when I opened the curtains I heard him shifting.

Varistan was watching me with sleep-muzzy eyes when I turned, the sunlight falling across his tawny skin and teasing warmth from the black of his wings. He looked beautiful in the morning light, with the ivory sheets tangled across his legs and his maroon curls rumpled, like one of those boudoir paintings of achingly lovely women.

But then his expression sharpened, a smirk settling onto his mouth, and he was the Duke of Nyx Shaeras again, arrogant and demanding. "Someone told you I enjoy late mornings, hmm?"

"Yes, your grace," I said with a pretty smile. He had, after all, even if he'd been asleep, and those quiet words had been seconded by a set of notes I'd found in my room, clearly written by at least three former body-servants, if the handwriting was anything to go on.

It contained a very interesting list of physical triggers, to which I'd pessimistically added "yanking his hair" for my eventual replacement. I'd memorized them all while waiting for it to be time to wake him, which had the unfortunate effect of making me deadly curious as to what *direction* they triggered the duke. "Don't use wool-felted soap", for example—did he hate it? Love it? If I dared to stay and bathe him, would this elicit a snarl or a moan?

I busied my hands with pulling out the outfits I'd hung up the night before, keeping my back to Varistan so he couldn't see me blushing as I considered him. My cheeks were such a curse, giving away my emotions even when I tried to stay calm. I didn't want him to call me pretty for it again.

"Will one of these suit your pleasure today?" I asked when I thought I could keep my face quiet, turning back towards him.

The duke had arranged himself in a lounge, his ebony wings a backdrop against which the warm brown of his skin looked smooth and inviting. He'd probably studied his appearance in mirrors, I thought with annoyance, determining the best way to display himself for admiration. He'd certainly mastered the task.

I kept my eyes on his face and a bland expression on mine as Varistan turned his attention to the clothing. His eyes skimmed across all three, his ears shifting slightly and the tip of his tail flicking like a cat's.

"You chose these last night?" he asked, turning back to me with a faint line between his brows.

"Yes, your grace." I tried on a smile, willing myself not to look like a hungry jackal. "I thought you'd appreciate having unwrinkled shirts."

"I... do, yes." Varistan sounded troubled, tapping his thumb against his thigh. "The storm-blue and silver will do. Did you examine my jewelry-boxes, as well?"

"Only a brief skim," I said, putting the other two outfits back into the closet before carrying his chosen clothing over to him and laying it across the chair. "I thought that perhaps you'd have opinions, your grace, and I wasn't sure how much jewelry you wear on a typical day."

He pushed himself up, disentangling himself from the sheets and swinging his legs over the edge of the bed. "Cuffs on my horns and ears most days. Earrings and rings for my wings often." Varistan gave me a slow smile, with heat in his eyes. "The bridge piercing was intended for special occasions, but if you like it, I may wear it more frequently."

Gods, he was very naked. That trim waist and those splayed thighs were far too much of a lure for my eyes. Eventually he'd catch me looking, and I knew he was going to gloat about it.

"You have unusual eyes, even among the fae," I said, keeping my gaze above his collarbone as best as I could. "I assumed you liked flaunting them."

"I do," he said, his smile broadening. Varistan leaned forward, lifting his chin so he could look down at me through lowered lashes. "They're not the only thing I like flaunting, but if that's what you notice, perhaps I should work harder to emphasize them."

I held up a pair of his boxer-briefs, trying to appear stern instead of as if I was wavering in my desire not to stare at his bare skin. "You need not dress for my approval, your grace," I said, my control breaking and my eyes glancing down along his body as he got off the bed, moving with the same liquid grace as a panther. "I'm a bondservant. My appreciation is hardly important."

The duke stepped into his underthings, an unfortunate task that left my eyes level with his groin, if I had dared to take them off the ground. He slid his tail through the hole in the garment without even looking – the warning *"don't touch his tail-blade"* from the notes I'd found flashed through my mind – and he caressed my neck with it as I stood.

"I think I ought to be able to decide whose appreciation is important to me," he purred, tilting my face up to his with the tip of his tail. "Most people here are surely used to me by now, and they no longer watch me like you do. I'm enjoying that precious struggle you're having with your eyes, and am quite willing to make the battle more difficult for you."

I pursed my lips, trying to decide how to handle him. "I was raised by humans, your grace, even though it was in Faery. It's fairly common to teach human children not to ogle when people are unclothed, and it meshes well with the faery practice of not giving attention to those engaged in intimacy. It's a difficult habit to break, even when invited to do so." I took a step back, looking into his eyes as I did. Then, with great deliberation, I drew my gaze down along his body, lingering as I went.

Varistan was built like the swordsman I knew he was, with strong arms, a well-muscled chest, and powerful core. Like most fae men, he had very little body hair, so there was no disguising the bulk of his pectoral muscles or the lines of his abs, and I already knew he flaunted his powerful build in the clothing he wore. Fighting and flight had given him strength in the obliques of his sides, too, his flawless brown skin smooth across the ripples of his muscles.

I liked that power, and the danger it represented. Most fae, even fighters, were lissome creatures, but though Varistan was considered a beauty among the fae, he was also more powerfully built than many. How much of that was the legacy of his fae birth and how much draconic, I didn't know, but he had strength to rival any wild beast.

Bulky thighs with the strength in them to launch a full-grown man into the sky, protected with gleaming black scales. The sort of calves men wear tight pants to show off. A dragon's feet, the talons gleaming like polished jet, his ankle lifted and the brand matte against the gloss of his scales.

Keeping my eyes half-lidded, I dragged my gaze back up along his body, pausing on his splayed legs and his broad chest. When I reached his face again, Varistan wore a nervous expression, his face impassive but his ears shifting in the way of an animal listening for danger.

I gave him a shark's smile. "I'll look, your grace. I'll even admire. The war with my eyes has more to do with politeness than any maiden's demureness."

He narrowed his eyes, crossing his arms across his chest. The movement drew my eye to the bandage on his upper arm—still clean, but certainly needing to be changed.

Before he could say anything, I reached out and touched the wrapping, my medic's training coming to the fore. "I should change this. I'm afraid in all the excitement, I forgot about the necessity." I made myself smile again, something rather less fierce than before. "I don't often see my patients the day after fights."

"No need," the duke said, lifting one wing in a shrug. "While my healers will likely be distressed at my injury, I need not hold an inquisition to determine how I was injured, nor search for the culprit. We can go down once I'm dressed."

"'We', your grace?" I asked, moving to grab the rest of his clothing.

Varistan favored me with his own sharp smile. "The medical care for my injury ought to be continuous, don't you think?" He held his wings and arms out for me as I puzzled out his shirt, his tail flirting with my ankles. "It seems better for the first healer to pass care directly to the second."

"If that's what you'd like, I'm pleased to comply," I said absently, working my way down the row of buttons beneath his wing.

The membrane of his wing was as soft as suede, a texture that made me want to run my hands along it. It would probably be fun to play with, too, as if Varistan would ever consent to such a thing. Pliable, stretchy, and flexible, a person could get a great deal of tactile enjoyment and amusement from touching him. He was surely far too interested in his dignity to submit to such a thing, but it was a delightful mental picture, nonetheless.

Once I had him dressed, I picked out a few pieces of jewelry for him: a set of simple horn-cuffs made of beaten silver, ear-cuffs in the shape of oak leaves, teardrop-shaped labradorite earrings, and in a fit of pique, a simple barbell for his bridge piercing.

Varistan smirked as I slid the piercing in, giving me a smoldering look with his lashes lowered across his crimson gaze. "Is it a special occasion?"

I screwed the ball onto the other end of the barbell. "It's my first day in Nyx Shaeras."

He laughed, a disbelieving sound. "And you think I ought to celebrate such a thing?" Varistan raked his claws through his hair, shaking his head. "You're a far worse hangover to me than anything alcohol has ever done."

That made my spine straighten, indignance sparking in my chest. "You don't even know me yet! I might be an excellent acquisition!"

"I'm certain someone would think that about you," he said in a condescending tone, as if he was speaking to a toddler. "I, however, would have preferred never to encounter you."

I could feel my cheeks heating alongside a growing desire to shove the duke down a flight of stairs. "How have I done badly?" I demanded, planting my hands on my hips. "I've done everything you've asked. I'm even trying to anticipate what you might need! It's only been one day!" At his raised brows, I blushed harder. "Um. Your grace."

"You're belligerent," he said, lifting his chin to look down his nose at me. "Aggressive. I might even go so far as to call you 'hostile'. As far as I can tell, your interest in me is primarily due to wanting me dead, and any amount of compliance is due to not wanting your father to suffer that same fate." The duke shook his head again, tail swishing behind him as he strode towards the door. "I didn't want you, and I remain of that opinion, regardless of the enjoyment I get from playing with you."

"Why make me your body-servant, then?" I asked, trying not to sound accusatory as I trotted after him. "Why not stick me in with the pot-scrubbers?"

The duke flicked his wings with a *snap!*, an aggressive motion that sent a jolt of adrenaline through me. "You're *mine*," he snarled, his tail snaking through the air next to me. "Be grateful that's as much closeness as I demand. You're fucking *lucky* that I have eighty-one years of experience with a dragon's greed, for if I'd laid claim to you even a few decades ago, you might have ended up chained to my gods-damned *bed*."

Flame lit the hallway, flickering in his breath. Sweat broke out across my body at the anger in his voice, my skin prickling with tension and my pulse picking up. I wasn't afraid, precisely, nor was it the animalistic response to danger that I'd anticipated. I felt like I was about to step into the ring with a deadly enemy, my focus narrowing and all the anticipation of battle brightening my vision and tensing my body.

"I have very few things that are utterly mine, Isabela," Varistan continued in a more level tone of voice. "Even Nyx Shaeras belongs first to the Raven King, and only thereafter to me. But *you* are mine, body and soul." Another flicker of flame lit the hallway as he stalked down the stairs. "I cannot hope to convey the depths of possessiveness I feel over things that belong to me. It doesn't matter that I don't want you, nor any amount of dislike I feel for you. You're mine, and by the gods, I will strive to keep you."

CHAPTER TWELVE

A HEALER'S TOUCH

I didn't have any answer for the duke, but it didn't seem like he required one. Privately, I felt a good deal of relief at his outburst. I was painfully bad at acting like a bondservant, but apparently that didn't matter at all. If "chained to the bed" was in the realm of possibility, I no longer had to worry about being able to get access to the private parts of his life. I probably had to worry about the opposite problem – being so coveted that I wouldn't be allowed to interact with anyone else – but given his behavior thus far, I didn't think he wanted that to happen.

I'd do my job, of course, since that was the price of my father's life, but I could stop throwing myself at the impossible task of being as demure and obeisant as a model servant. I was doing a terrible job of acting like I was pleased to be Varistan's dog, but apparently it didn't matter, after all. All I'd have to do would be to follow Varistan around; I suspected that if I expressed interest in being near him, he might not even be *able* to send me away.

So I walked at his left shoulder, feeling a great deal more relaxed about my future and adding to my mental map of Nyx Shaeras instead of fretting about how to get Varistan to like me. He didn't *have* to like me. The simple fact of our bargain meant that he couldn't bring himself to do anything but keep me near. It was enough to make a woman want to skip her way down the hall in glee.

To my surprise, Varistan took us not to a healer's ward, but to a large indoor arena. It reminded me somewhat of the training grounds for the Lylvenoran guards, with several different activities occurring in different parts of the room. On one end, a grizzled-looking human woman worked with a class of mixed-age humans on sword forms; on the other, next to a mirrored wall, a smattering of fae practiced solo forms with various weapons. The center of the room was dedicated to sparring, with dueling circles marked out on the floor with white paint.

I dutifully followed after the duke as he skirted the activity and made his way over to the sidelines, where Lianka sat with her legs propped up, reading a book. Now it made sense—it was the third day of the feast week, and since Lianka was the battle-trained healer, she was probably the one who knew how to deal with iron wounds.

I didn't think I'd be embarrassed by her opinion of my work. As angry as I'd been with the duke, I'd still taken care of him as best I could.

Lianka looked up as we approached, swinging her legs down and marking her place in the book with a ribbon. "Your Grace! I didn't expect you. Were you planning on joining the sparring today?"

He smiled at her, a warm expression, one without any sexuality or aggression. "I think not, for today," he said, draping himself onto the bench next to her. "Bells can explain."

The healer switched her gaze to me, raising her eyebrows as I blushed.

"His Grace received an iron wound while in Lylvenore," I said, trying to maintain my aplomb with Varistan looking at me like a cat enjoying the unhappiness of a cornered mouse. "I have some training as a medic and tended him to the best of my ability, but given that there's a healer of superior skill present in Nyx Shaeras, I turn his care over to you."

"Grave offense indeed," she said, pursing her lips as she turned back towards Varistan. "Where?"

"Upper right arm. Clean cut through the deltoid, deep enough for stitches but not for internal ligatures."

She made a sound of consideration, picking up her healer's kit and beginning to lay it out on the folding table next to her. "Well, let's see it. If you could remove your shirt, your grace...?"

Varistan looked at me, his lips curling into a smug smile and his garnet eyes half-lidded. "Bells."

I didn't need him to give me an explicit command—after all, my official purpose here was to take care of the things he couldn't do with ease, given the sharpness of his claws. Without commentary, I undid all the buttons I'd done not even half an hour earlier, and helped the duke out of his shirt.

He was no less beautiful for the intervening time, nor the vista of his shirtless body any less tempting. Lianka didn't seem to notice, though, going straight to the bandage on his arm. For his part, Varistan kept his eyes on me, still wearing that self-satisfied smirk. His tail wrapped loosely around my ankle, a warm embrace that felt more comfortably familiar than it had any right to.

"Clean stitchwork," Lianka said, sounding pleased. "Decent job cleansing the wound, too, though there's some minute traces of iron and oil remaining."

"I didn't want to cause His Grace further damage," I said, wrinkling my nose. "There's often a trade-off between thorough cleansing and ease of healing when doing such things by hand."

"I meant no offense," she replied in an absent tone of voice, framing his wound with her fingers. "You did very well for an amateur. If His Grace would be willing to share your services and you're interested in the task, I could use an assistant like you in the afternoons when I'm here at the training grounds."

That perked me up, despite feeling a bit flattened at being so easily pegged as an amateur. I supposed it was inevitable; fae healers received a great deal of training, and since she'd been on the battlefield in the Annihilation War eighty years ago, she'd almost certainly been a practicing healer for a century or more.

"I would love to serve you in such a way, your grace," I said, looking at Varistan hopefully. Given his possessiveness, I took care to frame it as something I was doing for *him*, rather than any other sort of pursuit. I wanted to get involved with the fighters here for my own purposes, and if Varistan supported that pursuit, it would be much easier to do.

His tail tightened on my ankle, though that might have been from discomfort as Lianka forced the last traces of iron and spear-oil out of his wound. "You may, though I shall expect you in my chambers at the fifth hour of the afternoon to prepare me for the evening meal."

I crossed my wrists over my chest and gave the duke a deep bow, wanting to show him my appreciation. He didn't like me, and the feeling was mutual, but he was giving me some liberty despite his draconic instincts, and I knew that had to be unpleasant for him.

"May I remain, then?" I asked, sounding eager even to my own ears.

Varistan snorted a laugh. "You truly are your father's daughter, aren't you?" he asked, with an edge of derision. "Stay if it pleases you. I'll see if I can appreciate a day without your presence."

Lianka gave me a sidelong look at that, curiosity wrought across her handsome features. When I didn't offer an immediate explanation of the duke's antagonism, she merely started re-wrapping his wound, which was no longer inflamed and in no danger of infection.

I stood by, doing my best impression of a statue until she finished. Without waiting for Varistan to give me the command, I started re-dressing him, treating him more like a mannequin than a man. He put up with being manhandled, apparently as eager to be parted from me as I was from him. When I finished, though, he caught my hand before I could take it away, pressing my palm down against his strong chest. His heartbeat thudded against my hand.

"You'll be there at five?" he asked, tension around his eyes and ears pulled back.

My heart rate picked up alongside his, my pulse felt in my throat. "I'll be there, your grace. I won't forget."

The intensity of his expression didn't bode well for his ability to leave me behind, but after a moment Varistan jerked his chin down in a nod, breathing a little too hard. "Do *not* be late," he warned, his voice tight. The duke stood, still holding my hand to his chest. "I doubt it will go well for either of us if you are."

"I won't be late," I promised, meeting his vivid eyes with my plain hazel ones. "I give you my word."

Even though I was human, the words made Varistan relax. It worked on a lot of fae, even those used to interacting with humans. The binding force of their own promises made it so much harder to remember that humans could lie, and the Duke of Nyx Shaeras was well-known for avoiding humanity with assiduous care. As long as I kept my promises, I doubted it would even occur to him that they might be lies.

A useful trait to have in an enemy.

"Very well," he said, the tension in his shoulders dissipating. He stepped back, letting my hand fall away, and glanced down towards Lianka. "If she chooses to enter the ring, don't allow her to leave the arena injured."

She put her hand over her heart and inclined her head to the duke. "As you say, your grace."

That was apparently enough, because Varistan turned and stalked away, releasing his tail's grasp on my ankle only when he had to do so or yank me off my feet. He didn't bother avoiding the fighters this time, striding through the dueling rings without looking, clearly expecting people to get out of his way.

They did, of course, pausing their combat while their duke crossed through, and returning to battle once he'd safely passed, but it remained a breathtaking display of arrogance. It was easy to miss someone outside of the fight impinging on your space, especially in an arena, where your ground was all but guaranteed to be free of interlopers. Maybe he was looking to pick a fight—or maybe putting himself in the way of danger was some sort of fucked-up coping mechanism.

Stupid either way, I decided, dropping down onto the bench Varistan had vacated. At least the duke wouldn't be my problem for a solid six hours. That was a blessing.

"You seem to have struck his fancy," Lianka said in an idle tone as she tidied up.

I wasn't fooled. The woman clearly loved gossip, and Varistan and I were the obvious topic of interest.

"Trust me, it's not as interesting as you're imagining," I said, dropping my head back with a groan. It made me nervous to be under the command of a fae, but she seemed easygoing. As long as she was behaving in a friendly fashion, I would try to do the same. "Draconic instincts, all the way down. He didn't seem to have any trouble leaving me with his steward yesterday, but apparently you're a different story."

She laughed, stretching her legs out in front of her and flipping her book back open. "Well, a steward is a great deal like an extension of self for a noble," she pointed out. "The expectation is typically that a steward knows his master well enough to anticipate him, and act accordingly. Besides, His Grace and Sintuviel have been together since long before His Grace was granted Nyx Shaeras. I've only been here for forty-odd years, and the training grounds are rather more dangerous than the dining hall."

I grinned, amused at the idea of forty years being "only". In comparison to sixteen hundred, it was, but I wasn't used to seeing the years like that. "I'll admit, I was growing a bit concerned that I was going to spend all my days following the duke around like a duckling. I appreciate the rescue."

"Well, I truly would appreciate the afternoon assistance," she said with a smile, her eyes twinkling with good humor. "But I also recalled your vigor of yestereve, and am familiar with His Grace's possessiveness. I thought it prudent to give you an excuse to spend time here, and one that has more merit than 'I like hitting people with swords.'"

"Spears, actually," I said with a laugh. "They're an excellent weapon for a human facing down a fae or monster, and not too shabby when paired up against someone with better reach than me."

"There's a few who favor the spear here." Her attention turned towards the sparring ring at a shout of pain, but when the fight continued she relaxed again, keeping one eye on the duel. "Do you have much experience with fae combatants? The duke keeps enough human swords and spears to meet the Crown's mandate, but they're generally trained for Army fights, not duels."

I raised one brow in curiosity. Cities like Lylvenore, under the control of a viceroy or vicereine, had to maintain guards for policing and defending the city, and were also required to supply and train portions of the Raven Army, but Nyx Shaeras wasn't a city. I didn't know how it fit into the complicated web of the peacetime Armies.

"He's landed nobility," Lianka said, in the tone of one stating the obvious. "Ducal estates are required to maintain a quarter of the Army levies for their land in peacetime."

"Seems excessive," I said, watching three fae doing a triad duel. It was a good fight, and beautiful to watch, even though such things rarely occurred outside formal duels.

She only shrugged, focusing on her book.

I watched the fighters until the duel concluded, with one kill and one disablement. One of the fae clapped another on the shoulder; she rolled her eyes and stalked off, clearly with a chip on her shoulder from getting hamstrung.

"Why the humans, if that's the case?" I asked at last, unused to sitting there without anything to do. I wasn't particularly hungry for conversation with a court fae, but I didn't have anyone else to talk to, and I was getting nervous sitting there in silence. At least it wasn't unusual for combat healers to have human assistants, since the humans could handle iron without risk. It wouldn't look that strange to the human soldiers for me to be friendly with this particular fae, so I wouldn't be hurting my chances of connecting with allies by sitting here.

Lianka licked the tip of one finger and turned the page in her book. "I think the First Army levies for Nyx Shaeras are entirely fae, but for the War Army, mostly humans." She made an apologetic face, glancing over at me with her ears leaning back with discomfort. "Fewer years to be cut short on the battlefield. It's costly to keep getting more, but less so than the payment many fae require for the danger of open battle instead of monster-hunting."

It wasn't news to me. In Lylvenore, at least two-thirds of the guards were human; we were disposable. I could understand the logic behind it, even if I hated the execution of the idea. If all went well, a fae might live to see the death of the sun. A man counted a hundred if he was lucky. Measured by years, a single fae might live as long as a nation of humans. Who would want to risk that?

Humans gambled with their lives all the time on Earth. I knew that. Many of the human guards and soldiers of Lylvenore were pleased with the bargains they'd made, and the lives they had. It was the ones who were bound to bargains they hadn't understood that filled me with anger.

"Well," I said, when the silence had grown too uncomfortable for me again, "I've plenty of experience facing fae in the ring, though mostly wildling. If the fae here would be interested in sparring with a human, I'd be happy to play."

She made a sound of consideration. "If you're good enough, I suspect most will be willing to join you in the ring. Not all, though."

"Eh." I started to smile, leaning forward to watch the combatants with more focus. "I'm not too shabby. Maybe they'll change their minds when they see me fight." In my experience, the bigots were only too happy to get in the ring with a human, expecting to mop the floor with them. I enjoyed being able to go toe-to-toe with fae and giving a good showing.

"Join me, then," a nearby fae said, pulling off his helmet to let a cascade of sweaty blond hair tumble down. "I hadn't planned on sparring today, but I'd be interested in blooding His Grace's new pet." Despite the dismissive diminutive, it didn't strike me as sneering, necessarily—but I downgraded that opinion when he glanced down along my body with a haughty expression, one ear flicking in a contemptuous gesture.

I looked him over, taking in his stance and body. He was one of the ones who'd been practicing solo forms, wielding a longsword, and though I hadn't been paying attention to him I had some instincts about him from seeing him move in my periphery. He struck me as a classic fae soldier: brash, confident, and with the swordsmanship to back it up. He'd probably fought humans before, and plenty of them.

Oh, this would be fun.

"It would be my pleasure," I said, and meant every word.

CHAPTER THIRTEEN

SPEARS

I gave my specifications to the glamor artist as I limbered up, rejecting two spears before settling on one that was within both the skillset of the artist and my comfort with polearms. As I didn't have any armor, he supplied me with a glamored set of light infantry armor, which suited me well. The quilted linen, gauntlets, and helmet wouldn't stop a strong swing from breaking my bones, but I didn't have the training for full plate, and in a fight against a fae opponent, mobility was key.

My opponent was already in the ring when I stepped out into the arena, excitement sparking in my veins. Despite everything that came along with it, I loved this—the anticipation and the physicality of it; the wild-animal desire to kill or be killed.

The glamor artist, serving as the arbiter, called out the rules for a simple exhibition duel: no exiting the ring, no maiming, and the duel to end at death-blow or yield. Though I rarely fought under such rules, they were familiar to me. Without access to good healers, it behooved you not to maim your opponents. After all, you were likely to face them again, and there would be no one to protect you when you fell if you spent your battles crippling people who could have been your comrades-in-arms.

He stepped back, holding up one hand. My opponent settled into a fighting stance with lazy disdain, looking at me the way wolves examine lambs.

You'll learn, I thought, skin prickling with adrenaline.

A *crack* split the air, and the battle began.

We started circling, making small adjustments of our postures and weapons as we sized each other up. I held my spear level, the tip pointed at his heart, the world falling away as all of my focus settled on the fae across the ring.

He moved first, rushing forward with the sudden burst of speed of an attacking lynx. The clatter rang across the room as his blade struck the haft of my spear in a fast series of hits, *tak-tak-tak!*, striking towards me with his sword outstretched.

I side-stepped to take the force of the hit, stabbing forwards. The jab forced him to step back, sword lifting. I used my forward hand as a fulcrum to slice my spear downwards against his longsword, wood against steel.

A sharp stab forwards, making inches of progress; a sweeping step to the right as his sword clashed against the length.

We broke apart, a snarl on his face as he looked at me through narrowed eyes. He swung his sword in a lazy circle, limbering his wrist. "Aw, someone taught you how to hold that spear," he said in a mocking sing-song. "Know better than to get close to a real fighter?"

I didn't answer, my eyes hard and calm. He was a stranger; I didn't know enough to aim a barb that would get under his skin, so why waste my breath? Silence could be every bit as unnerving as words.

He feinted, jerking forward without committing, the sort of bluff wild beasts used to frighten smaller predators.

I'd faced monsters from the wilds of Faery who would have eaten alive as people paid for the pleasure of feeling the blood spray. He didn't scare me. I held my spear level, the tip pointed at his heart.

Some people say fae are superior to humans in every way. They're faster, stronger, and move with liquid grace, leaving mortals in the dust. What human could ever hope to match up to a faery opponent? They're simply better.

It's not true.

The fae came at me again, blade flashing in the air. He drove me backwards, my foot almost hitting the ring before I crouched and drove my spear forward. He jerked out of the way, my blade slicing across his armor with a screech before I yanked it backwards. The fae swung his sword in an aggressive gesture, his eyes lighting with feral anger.

I dug my toes against the rough stone, surging forward as I drew my spear back, using the momentary advantage to get away from the edge. Blood pounded in my ears, my breathing light and easy.

Steel on wood, *clack-tak!*. Disengage; retreat.

Circling slowly, holding him at bay. There was no reason to search for a killing blow. I had all the time in the world.

He did not.

Fae are like wildcats. They move like lightning, vicious speed combining with precision and strength to make a deadly enemy. A fae wins his battle quickly, striking down the enemy in seconds. Even war-trained fae, capable of being on a battlefield for hours if not days, can't spend those long hours fighting without reprieve. Fae war-tactics always rotate the fighters, giving them chances to breathe. The price of speed is endurance.

But humans are *wolves.*

I took an offensive, striking forward with short forward jabs, forcing my opponent to halt my progress with powerful swings, his sword extended. He redirected the tip of my spear, making me strike the air next to his throat and to his side instead of his heart, his heart, his heart.

He snarled, batting my spear to the side with a brutal swing to try to trap it beneath his arm.

I thrust it down, leaving myself open for a terrifying moment as I whipped the long haft of the spear around. The butt struck him in the shoulder with a sharp *clang!* as metal struck metal, the blow hard enough that he was forced to step to the side.

The sword slammed against the haft of my spear as I held it like a stave, negating the advantage of the spear's reach. His eyes gleamed, the wild ferality of a fae in battle turning him into a predator, and his strength so much more mine.

Eyes calm, I twisted, the sword whistling past my shoulder as I whipped the tip of the spear around and up, gouging a screeching line along the armor of his thigh.

A strike. Another. He came for me with stymied anger, the humiliation of being held at bay by a mortal too much for a man like him to bear. I blocked, stepping back, letting him drive me as I recovered my position, breathing hard.

But not as hard as him.

Eons ago, before there were swords or spears, humans were hunters. We didn't hunt like the leopards or the lynx, lying in wait before attacking with a burst of vicious energy. We didn't hunt like the serpents, tracking down our prey with slow deliberation and striking once.

We hunted like the wolves we made our companions. We chose our prey, and we ran it to death.

We're slower than fae. We're weaker. That's true. But we can run for hours. For *days.*

To defeat a fae, you must *outlast* him.

He got a hit in on me, leaving a heavy bruise on my thigh and a trickle of blood soaking into my pants. I left pale marks on his armor and a prick on his shoulder that blossomed into red. His expression grew grimmer as the fight wore on, sweat marking both of us. Salt stung my eyes and trickled down my spine.

The fae stopped attacking with such vigor, choosing his attacks with more care, so I started harrying him. I gave up some of the distance of the spear, moving my hands forward to give myself more precision and power.

"Tired already?" I taunted, watching his spine go stiff with outrage.

Testing him, I moved forward, stabbing at him with sharp jabs, forcing him to block or move out of the way. He reacted slower than before, using the minimum force necessary to keep my spear-tip from striking him. I struck harder, disguising my drive in another flurry of blows, but the fae slammed his sword into the spear with vicious power, going on the offensive.

Tak-tak-tak-clang!, steel against wood against steel. I leapt backwards, disengaging, the smallest smile touching my lips for the first time as we resumed circling.

He held his sword in front of him, the blade angled to defend him from the death I carried.

I held my spear level, the tip pointed at his heart.

Without warning, the fae committed everything he had left. Snarling, he surged forward, every sharp movement of his body taking chips out of my spear as his blade clawed against the wood. I had to fall backwards, side-stepping onto my injured leg over and over to keep from being driven out of the ring.

My leg gave out under me. I could see death coming for me as he whipped his sword to the side and drove the tip straight at me, leaping through the air with the same focus as a falcon stooping on prey. In the same heartbeat, I jerked my spear up and back, bracing the butt on the ground and the haft on my thigh, turning myself into the human equivalent of a spike trap.

You can't always evade death, but you sure as fuck can make it hurt to claim you.

Agony seared into me as his blade struck me like a lance, piercing me through the shoulder and down into my ribcage. The force of his bodyweight striking the tip of my spear slammed into me in the same instance, pain blazing across my thigh and wood cracking as his scream joined mine.

A second later, the pain vanished as the glamor-artist dismissed the weapons, and I got flattened as an armored, swordless fae hit me like a sack of bricks.

I started laughing, all the endorphins of battle hitting me at once, and kissed my opponent on the cheek when he groaned. My pulse throbbed through my skull, an edge of wooziness from having struck my head on the stone ground, even with the helmet. He couldn't be feeling much better.

The fae spat out a curse and thrust himself off of me, staggering backwards. "Mayfly bitch," he ground out, a wheeze edging his breath. "You won't win every time."

A hand appeared in my field of vision. I took it without looking away from my opponent, giving him a feral smile. "I'll go again, if you like. Best two out of three? I'm just getting warmed up."

Anger twisted his face, but a quick glance at the faces around us made it obvious that he had no allies, and he turned and stalked off, smacking away the fae who'd helped me up when she moved to give him some support.

She rolled her eyes as he plodded away, turning to me and holding out her hand to me again. "Well fought. Isabela, is it?"

I took her hand in the fae form of the greeting, grasping her wrist in a handclasp. "I suppose rumor flies fast in Nyx Shaeras. Yes, I'm Isabela. My friends call me Bells."

She released me, the slightest smile touching her broad mouth. "Stellaris," she said, introducing herself. "How in the wilds did a fighter like you end up as a body-servant, of all things?"

"Long story," I said, making a face as she released me. After a moment of hesitation – I didn't want to be seen favoring the fae over humans, but it would be a useful way to get information – I added, "I'd be pleased to tell the tale over a meal sometime."

"I've enough chits saved up that we could do it over a drink, too," Stellaris said, her smile friendly. "Come by the outer garrison some night. I can introduce you to a few others."

"I accept." I gave her a little bow with my hand over my heart, far more surprised to be invited into the fae garrison than I would have been to get an invite to the human one. "For now, though, I'm going to go get this sore spot on the back of my skull checked out."

"Too early for alcohol, anyway," she said cheerfully, and slung an arm around one of her companions. "C'mon, Tjarrek. Let's hit the showers and make sure Marq doesn't crack his stubborn skull open on the tile floor if he keels over."

The other fae rolled his eyes, but flashed me a smile. "An interesting bout to observe, Isabela. I look forward to crossing blades with you." He gave me a deep nod before walking off with his arm around Stellaris' waist.

I cleared out of the ring, meandering back to Lianka and sprawling down on the bench next to her. "Hi."

She eyed me, looking amused, then set her fingers on my wrist. A moment later, the throbbing in my skull eased up, and with it the wooziness. Even a few other minor bruises from impacting the ground vanished, making me frown at her for the waste of healing power.

"You heard His Grace," she said, returning to her book. "Uninjured."

"Do tiny bruises really count?"

"Do you really want to find out?" she countered, turning the page. "Give the man a little compassion. He's clearly making an effort to let you have a life outside of being his possession, and he certainly doesn't have to." Lianka glanced over at me, looking me up and down. "I highly suggest you shower and change before you see him again."

"You don't think he'll like the blood?" I asked in a teasing voice, looking down at the red patch on my shirt. The thigh wasn't much better, and even though I knew it looked a lot worse than it really was, I didn't think draconic instinct would go much further than identifying gore.

"If you want to be kept within an arms-length of His Grace, by all means," she said drily. "But don't expect any sympathy from me."

I laughed, sprawling back with my arms across the back of the bench as I watched some of the humans take places in one of the rings, four-versus-one against a fae opponent. "Don't worry, I'll be good," I said, my lips twitching when she snorted. "Cross my heart." I drew an X over my heart, stretching my legs out. "Not interested in antagonizing the duke."

"Good." The sharp snap of a broken bone cut through the air, followed by a scream. The screaming didn't stop, merely turning into agonized sobs, and Lianka was on her feet in an instant, medical kit in hand. "Look lively, Bells, we're up."

I caught the kit as she lobbed it to me, following after her at a jog as the injured human shoved himself out of the ring, elbow bending the wrong way.

Just another day in the pit, I thought fleetingly, grabbing the man and hauling him backwards to safety as the combat continued. But that wasn't quite right, was it? Holding the man's upper arm in place so Lianka could set his elbow, I suddenly felt displaced, my old life intersecting with my new one in a way that left me dislocated.

An arena meant for fighting, rather than a chalk circle drawn on a concrete floor. Mirrors instead of walls of crates, and audiences excited for displays of skill instead of spurts of blood.

It could be like this. It could be like *this*, a combat-trained fae healer putting a human's elbow to rights in a minute flat, friends clapping him on the back, a fae soldier giving helpful commentary to the small squad of human soldiers he'd just defeated.

I'd known so much blood, and so much pain. Even knowing that places like this existed hadn't meant anything to me, because access was barred to people like me. But it didn't have to be that way, and that thought struck me breathless, as if a ball of ice had lodged in my chest. Was this what we were fighting for? Was this what *I* was fighting for?

I knew it wasn't. Not entirely. Shame made me blush as I took a seat again, watching people return to their training. I remembered looking at Varistan's wings and grimly imagining vengeance, those black wings broken and Nyx Shaeras burning in a small repayment for the gruesome fates of so many fallen people. Was that really victory, though?

There were fae who needed to be erased from the world—people who reveled in cruelty and who knowingly and remorselessly gained power and wealth from the suffering of others. Killing them didn't bother me. But there were plenty of others who weren't like that, no better and no worse than anybody else, and despite my discomfort with them, they ought to be a part of whatever future I was dreaming of.

I'd never really had a future to look forward to before. My whole life was steeped in pain and the anger that came along with it, cold practicality ruling me far more than any sort of hope or optimism. But sitting there, watching court fae and humans spar like compatriots, overlaying the sight with my memories of camaraderie with wildling fae, I could see a future worth having for the first time. I didn't know the way, but I wanted to find it.

Things can change, I thought, remembering stories Estarren had told me about how much worse things were for people like him now than they'd been even a century ago. They hadn't been good then, and they were worse now, but they didn't have to stay this way. There was a better future out there, and now that I'd seen it I wasn't going to forget.

Chapter Fourteen

UNDERBELLY

I presented myself to Varistan fifteen minutes before five, showered, uninjured, and blood-free. After that first night of seeing him go from tense,
tail-lashing pacing to smirking calm at my arrival, I decided that there wasn't
any reason to be late or unpresentable any time in the future. If I could rely on
anything about the duke, it was his possessiveness and temper. Provoking the
former and sparking the latter seemed... unpleasant. And unnecessary.

Things settled into a rhythm for me as I learned Varistan's patterns. Up at ten
in the morning, breakfast in his bedroom while he dealt with his personal correspondence, and then off to whatever the day called for—usually a great deal
of desk-work, but also trips to the shipyard, discussions with merchants, and
formal events like duels and feasts. Back at five to be changed into formalwear
for the events of the evening, and then awaiting his return in the hours after
midnight.

After that first night, Varistan had me help him with his pre-bed routine; he
did sleep in the nude, but those curls of his would turn into a frizzy snarl if he
slept on them too much, so each night he got a little bit of hair-oil scrunched
into the ends and everything loosely braided back and tucked away into a silk
wrap. To keep him from clawing himself or the bed open, I capped his claws
with cotton and put him in thin gloves to sleep, a process that never failed to
leave him unhappy and tense. At least he liked getting his hair tended.

He was quite the peacock so far as clothing and jewelry went, too, especially
in the evenings, and his hair-care, skin-care, and scale-care routines would
have put any professional courtesan to shame. Despite my putative duties,
Varistan did most of it himself, sometimes even going so far as to lock me out
of the bathroom while he groomed himself, and though he bathed daily, he
usually only washed his hair once a feast cycle, on the day before the feast-day.

Whatever. I didn't want to spend an hour a day polishing his scales or putting
serums on his skin, anyway.

While he went about his day, I took care of his wardrobe, bath, and jewelry, which mostly amounted to making sure the right things got cleaned, mended, or refilled. But none of that took a great deal of time or mental effort. It left me with a surprising amount of free time, and an equal quantity of freedom, at least on the days he spent in his office.

Once I managed to get my bearings, I put the time to good use. Rising days saw me sparring or assisting Lianka, resting days saw me exploring Nyx Shaeras on foot, and on the feast day I assisted with preparations for the day's evening event. I took invitations from the War Army and First Army garrisons, getting to know the various soldiers and guards, and I started making friends.

I spent less time with Varistan than I originally intended, but his life was a lot less interesting than I'd expected. He did occasionally host or attend events, but the summer social season was long past. Autumn apparently saw him mostly in his office, and I had better things to do than to refill his inkpot.

I didn't expect to be approached by anyone doing vermin control or in the wider resistance, at least not at first. I knew there were at least some people here that communicated with the people back home, but any new bondservant would need to be vetted before they were deemed safe. When nobody spoke to me after the first month, though, I started to wonder if perhaps I'd been deemed too dangerous to trust, given my close connection to human-despising Varistan and my budding friendships with Lianka and some of the fae I sparred with.

It would be lonely if I didn't have anyone I could speak freely to, but I couldn't begrudge anyone for not wanting to risk it. In their circumstances, I wouldn't have wanted to trust me, either.

There were still things I could do, though, and I did them: examining Varistan's correspondence when he left it out, memorizing the names on the envelopes he handed me in the morning to be sent off via flicker-bird or mounted courier, and shamelessly eavesdropping in the evenings when he brought people back to drink and game in his personal quarters. I even enjoyed the latter, marveling at the charisma that drew people to him as he flirted and smirked his way through the night.

None of them were companions of a softer sort. No one ever took up the offer of his casual flirtation, or asked for more. Even someone like me, untutored in politics, could read the distance people kept between themselves and the duke.

In a Court where even sky-called fae were looked upon with suspicion, if not outright hostility, Varistan occupied a liminal space. He was a duke, and he was almost as far from a court fae as it was possible to be. He hadn't been born aberrant or sky-called, so he couldn't be said to be a true wildling... but the only person who could make living amalgams was Ayre Xirangyl, the traitorous Raven Prince who had become the King of Windswept Court. Varistan had been made into an amalgam against his will, but he still *was* an amalgam, and it was impossible to see him and forget it.

From time to time, I even felt bad for him. Sometimes he came out of those late-night affairs visibly unhappy or full of restless energy, and I knew things hadn't gone well. That got added to my growing collection of information, too.

Intel was only useful if it made it to people who could do something about it, though, and I didn't exactly have free access to flicker-birds, whose every journey was tracked by their handlers to keep from exhausting them. But I did have a great deal of unscheduled time and an open invitation from the War Army barracks, populated entirely by humans. Surely someone in there worked vermin control.

The first note I "accidentally" left behind was a ledger of the different people he'd written to since I'd become his body-servant, with useful-sounding personal notes like "*stock more cream paper – almost out*" and "*needs the watermarked header*". I dropped the second eight days later, an unbound page from a journal written in English instead of Faery:

> ...really miss my rat terrier back home. The mouser who sleeps with me is a sweetheart and good at her job, but I'm a lot more social than a cat. It's kind of lonely being V's bondservant, even with my sparring friends. I'd rather keep down the vermin pop-ulation alongside the cat than brush the duke's hair, but I guess we can't pick our fates.
>
> Speaking of V, he got another note from Lord Zillvahris today that made him angry. Balled it up, threw it in the fireplace, & spat flame at it, and was a real pest about his clothing afterwards. 4 outfits before he was happy!!
>
> I poked around in the fireplace once he stalked off to his office, of course. Not much left, but he balled it up so tight the bits in the middle didn't burn. "expect the cut by", "time left to", "treat[ing? you?] well, as I learned", "your favor", and "our mutual endeavor in" were the bits I could decipher, in that order. My guess would be something to do with owing Z money, though I don't know why V would be mad at Z and not at the other bills.
>
> It made the morning interesting, at least. See how small my world is these days? One of these days I'm going to wax poetic about V's breakfast selections, and then you'll know it's time for me to

be put out of my misery. At least I've got access to his study and library, if I get bored of...

I was kind of proud of it, especially since I didn't actually keep a journal, and I thought the choice of language was a nice touch. Surely someone else in Nyx Shaeras could read English. Given the usefulness of communicating in a language most fae didn't know, my father had ensured that I learn to read and write the language, and I still had a little spoken Spanish from my mother. I knew Faery Sign from working full-moon nights in the pit, too. A regular polyglot.

Thankfully, someone took pity on me before I had to come up with some third plausible way to drop information. I was a soldier, not a spy, at least as far as either of those were positions in vermin control. While eating dinner in the servants' area of Nyx Shaeras one night, a handsome, light-skinned man in his early thirties joined me at the table, dressed in the same black-and-evergreen livery all the castle servants wore.

"Bells, is it?" he asked, flashing me a smile and holding out his hand.

I took it in the human fashion, gripping his hand instead of wrist. "To my friends."

A tiny smile touched his mouth as he gave my hand a firm shake. "Darius, to friends and foes." He sat back, crossing his arms over his chest. "How do you like Nyx Shaeras thus far?"

"It's a lovely place," I said, shrugging one shoulder. "Fewer rats than Lylvenore."

His smile grew, curling up at the corners. "Cities tend to attract vermin, though we have our own out here."

One corner of my mouth tilted up, appreciating the dance, and glad to finally be talking to someone else willing to step up. "I can't imagine the cats let that many mice roam in a place as small as this."

"Oh, I don't know," Darius said, dark eyes gleaming. "Sometimes it seems like they rule the place. Sure you haven't seen any in the duke's suite?"

"Do you honestly think the duke would tolerate the competition?" I asked with a smirk. Holding his eyes, I stabbed my fork into my slice of mutton and sawed off a piece. "He's too territorial."

Darius pursed his lips, setting his elbows on the table as he glanced to each side. When he met my eyes again, his expression was far more serious. "For a territorial man, he's allowed you a great deal of freedom."

I rested my chin on my hand, chewing my mutton as I regarded him. At last, I said, "He doesn't seem to like me much, and he surely doesn't trust me. Is it that surprising that he doesn't want me by his side all the time?"

"Hm." The corner of his mouth twitched—towards a smile or frown, I couldn't tell. "But you could be there if you chose, couldn't you?"

"Yeah," I said, searching his face. "I could."

He *hmm*ed again, leaning forward, his expression unreadable. "Do you want to be?"

There was more conversation happening here than I fully understood. My role in the pit wasn't people-forward, to say the least; Omari had done all of the interfacing for me. I was far more of a fighter—doing drops, throwing fights, and cleaning up vermin.

At least I knew I was out of my depth, though that was cold comfort.

"I'll stand where I need to," I said quietly. "I traded my life for my father's, but he knew the risks he took when he leveled his spear at a dragon." I took a deep breath, holding his dark gaze. "My loyalty belongs to the terriers, not their prey. I'm willing to do what's necessary."

The corner of his mouth twitched again. This time, I thought it might be towards a smile. "You take a lot of risks."

I shrugged, turning back to my dinner. "Life is a risk, Darius. 'Nothing ventured, nothing gained', right?" When he exhaled a soft laugh, I smiled, sharp and angry, stabbing my tough mutton. "I know where I stand, and what I stand next to. I don't give a shit about the feather bed or the cushy job description. I'd rather be stitching up wildlings in the shit lighting of an oil lamp, surrounded by crates." I flicked my eyes back up to his. "Omaxion put me elsewhere, and I won't challenge that. I know I'm not the most palatable, but you kinda gotta take it or leave it."

It wasn't quite true. I really, really liked the feather bed, even though I only got to share it with a cat.

He lifted a brow. "So you're a believer."

"You say that as if there's any question as to the existence of the fae gods," I said, leveling my gaze at him. "There's people who've seen and spoken to gods, and not all of them are fae. Hell, depending on who you ask, the Stag King might literally be the son of a god, and there were plenty of witnesses when his mother fucked Sarcaryn." I paused for a heartbeat, then added, "You may not like them, but we have to deal with them, one way or another."

"Honoring them isn't the only choice," Darius said, still with that aloof expression.

I leaned forward on my elbows, disliking the turn of the conversation. Sometimes I felt like I, too, occupied a liminal space, not unlike the duke—I was human, but native to Faery. My social mores and habits were far more fae than mortal (no matter my protests to the contrary), and it always left me feeling uncomfortable and displaced when I stumbled into one of the mismatches between what people expected of me, and who I actually was.

"Consider it a turn of phrase," I replied, keeping the words quiet so they wouldn't carry. "If Omaxion can pluck the strands of fate, I'm disinclined to be disrespectful. My father always said the gods are powerful enough that you don't want to anger them, and capricious enough that you don't want their attention." I fell silent as a pair of fae walked by, chattering to each other, then leaned back, tilting my head as I regarded him. "I'm not going to be conciliatory for acknowledging them."

A muscle on his cheek twitched. He held his shoulders square, his weight forward; I recognized a desire for battle when I saw it. If we'd been in the ring, I would have been circling, waiting for the attack.

But he didn't attack. He sighed, shaking his head. "I guess we all have to acknowledge them, one way or another," Darius said, sounding rueful. "By calendar, if nothing else."

I shrugged one shoulder; one corner of his mouth tilted up.

"Alpha wants to meet you, and you seem like the kind of woman with a fire in her gut. She might even like you." He flashed me the sort of gorgeous smile that probably melted most people he directed it at. "Interested?"

With an answering smile, I laced my fingers together and rested my chin on them. "Eager."

"Then you've another reason to anticipate the Feast of Ruekh," he said with a quick wink, naming the raven-god of battle and revelry. "Be in the Sea Room at the start of the fourth watch, and you'll get your conversation."

The gift of the sword is mortality. Ruekh's feast-day was thus the one time of the feast cycle when the barriers between fae and humanity came down, the future forgotten for the present. For one night, we would all be equals, humans mingling with fae in the wild revel and feasting side-by-side. Even Varistan wouldn't be able to stand aside from humanity. We were all ravens together, and his raven-black wings couldn't carry him away from our unkindness.

It was only a few weeks away, landing near the end of autumn this year. A generous amount of time for me to stew over the invitation—or for them to stew over me.

"I'll strive to be there," I said, my eyes narrowing when he rolled his.

Darius shook his head at me with a touch of condescension. "You're really halfway to fae, aren't you?"

I flushed, not liking the accusation from someone like him, no matter how true it was. "Caution doesn't make me fae. Can you see through glamor? You could be fae, coming to entrap me."

He flashed me that smile again. "I'd have plenty to trouble your duke already, even without an accidental promise as the cherry on top. Guess you'll have to trust me, Bells."

"Hardly," I said, leaning back in my chair. "I like to pick my risks."

"You like 'em more than I do," he said, getting up. "Ruekh's night. Don't forget."

"I'll strive not to." At his sour face from my fae turn of phrase, I bared my teeth in a feral smile. "Anything else?"

With a grunt, Darius flicked his fingers at me. "Just a message to keep better track of your papers, and to stay your hand until the feast. I'll tell Alpha to be prepared for your arrival."

I wiggled my fingers at him in farewell with a pert smile, leaning my chair back on two legs as he strode off. Probably I should have resisted the urge to be the raven tugging the eagle's tail, but I couldn't even manage to keep that impulse under control with Varistan. Surely Alpha wouldn't dismiss me out-of-hand for a little sass.

I hoped.

Chapter Fifteen

STORMS OFF THE SEA

Two days before the Feast of Ruekh, I presented myself at fifteen minutes before five to do my duty by the duke, and found his room vacant. I stood there dumbly for a solid thirty seconds, so stunned at not finding Varistan waiting for me that I didn't even notice the crisp piece of paper on his breakfast table at first, sitting there weighted down by a pair of silver bells.

Amused despite myself at the indicator of intended recipient, I freed the paper and flipped it open to reveal Varistan's handwriting, all bold, slashed lines.

> Isabela— I believe a true storm is coming in tonight, the first of winter. It's my intention to greet it as it arrives, so you need not await me tonight. If you have something delivered to my room for my supper when I return, I'll be content for the evening. —V

...Huh.

There was a lot that was strange about that, starting with the idea of greeting a storm and ending with his casual sign-off. It sparked my curiosity enough that, even once I'd gotten supper lined up for him, I couldn't stop thinking about what in the wilds he was doing.

Thunder rumbled, drawing my attention to the window. A smattering of rain pelted against the sill, not yet a downpour, but certainly a promise of one, especially if the darkness of the clouds had anything to say about it.

For a moment propriety warred with curiosity, but I'd never been very good with boredom, and I sincerely doubted that Varistan would take it amiss if I sought him out. It would be cold in the rain, but I had that invitation to warm myself on him, and it would be amusing to remind him of it. I still grabbed a heavy wool sweater on my way out, but if it wasn't enough, I had a draconic backup.

There was only way up onto the main tower of Nyx Shaeras, and though Varistan had wings and could very well be aloft, I suspected he'd come down to investigate me if he saw me. The door faced inland, away from the ocean's fury. I opened it with care so it wouldn't get snatched away from me by the wind, but the windbreak had been well-placed, and all that met me was the lashing precursor to the true teeth of the storm. Elation lit me from within, the wildness of a true storm putting me into the same heightened state of anticipation as I felt in the fighting ring.

Wind caught me as I came around the side of the windbreak, tearing at my hair as rain stung my face. Varistan stood near the edge of the tower, his head tilted back and wings half spread. Lightning flashed, giving me a brief sight of him: his rain-wet wings gleaming, his curls whipping in the wind, his white linen shirt plastered to his strong body, his tail lashing through the air.

Gods, he was so fucking beautiful.

I started walking towards him before I commanded my feet to do it, heart beating harder than it should have and breathing shallow. Lightning cracked through the air again, striking out over the sea in a fiery spectacle, illuminating Varistan's open-mouthed face of pleasure. He looked like I felt, a hunting-hound yearning towards the open fields, longing for the moment he was unleashed.

"Varistan," I breathed, unable to look away from him. How could someone like him even exist? It was like Sarcaryn had created him specifically to torment me.

His lashes parted, and he looked sidelong at me with the hint of a smile. "Isabela," he said, his rough voice caressing my name like a lover. Those crimson eyes lifted to the heavens, a shiver running down the long length of his spine. "It's almost here."

Lightning flashed again. *One... two...* Thunder cracked through the air, anticipation making my arms prickle. It almost felt as if my bones were trembling, the same sensation of awe and numinous elation that makes people feel as if they're in the presence of a god.

Varistan settled into a fighting stance, angling his wings into the wind. He rolled one shoulder like a cat getting ready to pounce. "Here we go," he crooned, eagerness in every line of his body, watching the line of pouring rain race across the waters of the ocean towards us.

A *BOOM!* slammed into us as lightning struck the metal rod affixed to the leeward side of the tower, casting Varistan's face in relief and making me freeze like a startled rabbit. Varistan started laughing as the wall of rain hit us, cutting us off from the world as visibility reduced to nothing. The rain soaked through my clothing in moments, the wool sweater going heavy and sodden and water sheeting down my body.

With a wild grin, Varistan turned toward me, his shirt all but transparent where it clung to the powerful lines of his body. "Come with me," he said, holding out one clawed hand.

It wasn't a command. It was an invitation, given without hesitation or restraint, and I responded in kind. I put my hand in that of a fae duke, and let him sweep me into the skies.

In one smooth motion, Varistan stepped forward and lifted me up. My arms went around his neck and my legs around his waist automatically as he leapt skyward. His wings snapped open with a *crack* like the thunder, flinging us into the raging storm. Pouring rain lashed us in waves, frigid and tasting of ice, but it was the warmth of his hand on the underside of my thigh that commanded my attention, matched only by the heat of the dragonfire in his chest.

The power of the winds commanded Varistan's wings, sweeping us inland from Nyx Shaeras. Updrafts flung us hundreds of feet into the air and downdrafts made us plummet, leaving my stomach behind. But Varistan moved through the storm with utter confidence, wide wings taming the wildness of the storm and long tail singing through the air, steering us higher and higher.

The ground vanished, roiling clouds surrounding us, lit only by lightning and the strangled light of the moon. This was the world: stinging rain in the night and a dragon's heat against my chest, my heart beating in tandem with his. There was nothing else. I didn't *want* anything else. It felt like I was at the edge of a precipice, yearning for the void and finding glass at my fingertips.

I belonged here, freedom in my wings—but they weren't mine. I could only claim this taste, so I took it to the hilt, reveling in the wildness of the open sky and the ocean's wrath.

As the rage of the storm battered itself to death against the coast, the winds became more predictable, and Varistan starting zig-zagging into the headwind. The rain mellowed to a steady soak, and though the winds rose and fell, the pattern of his flight shifted from a dance led by the storm to one controlled by his wings. Not long after, we dropped low enough in the storm to see the ground again, the saltwood forest reaching towards us and the distant lights of Nyx Shaeras beckoning us home.

Breathing hard, Varistan shifted his hold on me, easing the pressure of his arms against me enough that his wingbeats moved us against each other. I suddenly became very aware of the way I was pressed against him, heat that was far more than that of his body flaring where we touched. My stomach against his flat abs, my breasts against his powerful chest, my arms around his neck, feeling the flex of those strong muscles as he flew. My legs holding my core pressed up against his hips, every downsweep of his wings driving his groin up against mine—

"Fuck," he groaned in a pleasured voice, a tremor running through his body. "Didn't mean to do that." Varistan hoisted me up higher on his body, tightening his hold on me so we stopped grinding in countermovement against each other. His cheek ran against my face as he made a low sound, only audible because his throat was so close to my ear. "Hard to forget where you are now."

I started laughing, unable to do much else to relieve the tension. Like a cat, I rubbed my cheek against his, my smile broadening when he made a small whine of protest. "Long flight to Nyx Shaeras."

"Taking... a side trip," Varistan said, the words punctuated by his heavy breaths.

My eyebrows shot up as he listed to the side, the wind catching his broad wings and sending us shooting at speed towards the south. He danced across the breath of the storm, using his wingbeats to throw us into different wind-currents. It was like he had a sixth sense for the patterns of the sky, moving with the same confidence of a falcon.

I moved with him, the slight shift of his muscles and the tension of his fingers where he held me giving me all the information I needed to understand his movements. The pattern of his flight felt as natural to me as pattern-dances for the spear, as if I'd been flying with him for my entire life, an intuitive connection that made me never want to leave the skies.

But flying the storm while carrying me must have fully exhausted Varistan, because after not too many minutes more, he tightened his hold and folded his wings, dropping into a stooping dive. The wind whipped my hair against my face with stinging pain, the raindrops striking me from below as we out-raced its fall.

The trees stretched towards us like pikes towards a charging cavalry, and terror grabbed me by the throat. "Varis— *Varis— VARIS!!*"

He laughed, a wild sound heard through my chest, and didn't pull up.

I shrieked as we hit the canopy line, clutching at Varistan. Branches whistled past, coming within inches of my skin. Varistan's wings snapped out, my weight flung against his arms as a vertical dive turned to horizontal flight. He juked through the branches, tiny movements of his wings and tail sending us whipping through the understory between the massive trunks of the trees.

"You *ass!*" I screeched as Varistan veered between two trees, cutting so close pieces of moss went flying off in our wake. "Motherfucker!"

Seconds later, he backwinged, landing heavily in a small clearing. With a catlike expression, the duke leaned forward—and let go of me.

I wasn't expecting to be fucking *dropped*. I fell on my ass in the duff of the forest floor, yelping like a puppy, and ended up flailing my way onto my

STORMS OFF THE SEA

feet, wild-eyed and full of adrenaline. "Varistan Yllaxira! What in the wilds was that?!"

He smirked at me, stretching his arms over his head and spreading his wings like a bird. "A change in mood," he replied, still wearing the expression of a naughty schoolboy. "I don't have it in me to carry you all the way back to Nyx Shaeras tonight, but I *did* have enough stamina left to show you a little fancy flying."

"Fancy—! You fucking *madcap!* You're an audacious sonuvabitch! If you think that was *fun*—"

"You have quite the tongue on you," he said, clearly amused. Varistan sauntered past me, flicking me with one wing as he passed. "Come along, Isabela. You might catch a cold out in the rain without my fire to warm you."

Oh, I wanted to *bite* him. It wasn't like he was *wrong*, but he didn't have to be such a smug, arrogant bastard about it—

"Coming?" he asked from the doorway of the waystation, exhaling a curl of flame to reveal his rakish expression.

Cold day in hell when I come for you, I thought, recalling the first time he'd used that word as an innuendo. I still stalked over, though, unwilling to stand out in the fat drips of rain beneath the giant saltwood trees in the dark. There were worse things than feigning compliance.

Chapter Sixteen

COHABITATION

T he small building was pitch-black when Varistan closed the door behind me, and it hadn't been much better before. He moved through the darkness with surprising confidence while I waited for my eyes to figure out the deep dark, and before I felt comfortable enough to inch through the building, he breathed fire into a wood-burning stove and set a pile of logs aflame.

That was convenient. No tinder needed, let alone a flint and steel.

The light revealed a simple, one-room building, with a single bed, a counter atop a set of cupboards, and a copper basin with a faucet over it. There was not, I noted, any other door aside from the one we'd come through. Outdoor privy, then. That would be fun with the rain.

Varistan stood and stretched again, wincing as he leaned to each side. "Undress me?" he said, tacking a question mark onto the command instead of giving it in his usual imperious way. "My clothing is wet enough that I suspect it will still be damp in the morning, but I'd like to get it as dry as possible."

"Morning?" I asked, a bit unhappily. I didn't really want to share a bed with him, let alone sleep on the floor.

He made a rueful face. "I have excellent endurance, but as I said, I don't have it in me to get us back to Nyx Shaeras tonight. It's not the first time I've misjudged my flight capacity, so no one is likely to send out a rescue party, if that's what's concerning you."

"Your dinner's going to get awfully cold," I said, coming over to strip him naked with a sigh.

"There's generally supplies in these harvest waystations, but I've never truly needed to learn how to cook..." Varistan said, sounding hopeful as I peeled his essentially transparent shirt off of him.

That was a leading statement if ever I'd heard one. "I can cook, though I make no promises about the end results." I fought with the laces of his pants, the leather swollen. "Any dietary restrictions?"

Varistan grunted as I yanked his pants open, helping me get them off by wiggling his hips in time to my tugs. "Not familiar with my preferences yet, Bells?"

"I don't feed you," I pointed out, a bit amused. "I deal with the outside, not the inside."

"Well, true enough," he said with a laugh, tousling my wet hair. "Most everything except leafy greens is good, as long as it's cooked. Nothing raw. Oh, and no vanilla or pine sugar. I'm allergic to vanillin."

I draped his sopping-wet pants over the back of a wooden chair, raising my brows at him. "Vanilla? That's odd."

"Vanill*in*," he corrected, shrugging his wings. "It's an uncommon allergy, and I don't think you're likely to find anything with it out here, but I'd rather not spend the evening rasping for breath with a full-body rash." Varistan rubbed at his shoulders with a wince, clearly sore from the flight. "Do you need help with your clothing?"

"Oh. Um." I looked down at myself, and at the puddle I was making on the floor. "I don't... think so." I wasn't sure I wanted the duke helping me undress, even if it would be annoying to get out of my wet clothing on my own. He was far too attractive for me not to enjoy the process, and I didn't need more reasons to think about his long-fingered hands or the wickedness in his smile. "Not that eager to cook in the nude, though."

He breathed a soft laugh, looking amused. "Nor to be swanning about in the nude, I would imagine. You humans are so awkward about bodies." The duke moseyed over towards a dresser and started rustling around. "Let me see if I can find you something to shield your skin from my untoward gaze."

That made me laugh outright, starting to peel myself out of my wet clothing so I could wring it out to dry overnight. "More to the point, it's fucking cold, your grace," I said, wriggling out of my wet pants. "I grew up in Faery, if you'll recall. Public nudity isn't exactly new to me."

"Do I get to admire, then?" Varistan asked, glancing over with a raised brow as I squeezed water out of my sweater into the copper basin.

"When have you ever chosen not to admire?" I retorted. My shirt and breast-band got draped over the basin, followed shortly thereafter by my panties. It wasn't as if the wet cloth was doing anything to obscure details, anyway. "You ogle my cleavage any time it's on display."

I found him smirking at me when I turned, his wings held partway out to dry and a towel across his shoulders. "You *are* mine," he said, as if demurring a compliment, and tossed a bundle of cloth at me.

I caught it, shaking it out to discover a folded sheet wrapped inside a terrycloth towel. With Varistan leaning against the dresser watching me from half-lidded eyes, I scrubbed myself dry, then wrapped my hair in the towel and used the sheet like a sarong. With a flippant expression, I posed for him, knowing full well I looked ridiculous, then turned to dig through the cupboards for something easy to make.

Varistan made a slight sound of amusement and flopped onto the bed on his stomach, limbs akimbo.

He didn't make any commentary while I put together a utilitarian meal. The waystation had been set up for one or two people to stay at for maybe up to a week, and the cupboards contained primarily dry goods, with some cured and canned. The aluminum cans were clearly from the mortal world, which I noted with some dark satisfaction. Even Varistan had to admit that some human technologies were superior—after all, he wore human-made underthings and used human-made food preservation for his waystations.

The duke barely reacted to being fed a beige casserole made of rehydrated potatoes, canned tuna, and peas. He just ate it, putting away a shocking quantity of food—enough that I got up halfway through my own plate to fry up two cans of mystery meat, which Varistan accepted with a look of exhausted gratitude. By the time I'd finished washing the dishes, he was flat on his stomach again, eyes closed and body limp.

"Would you like a shoulder rub, your grace?" I ventured, eyeing him.

Varistan cracked open one eye, regarding me with wariness. "I believe that's the first time you've offered to care for me outside of your stated duties. What price ought I be concerned about?"

"None," I said, a bit surprised. I was his bondservant, after all. "You took me flying in a storm, and now you're sore. Easing your pain seems like the least I can do to show my appreciation."

"Oh." His brows drew together as he examined me. He flopped back down, one arm curled over his head. "I suppose I'll accept, then. Are you any good at it?"

"You tell me." I hopped up onto the bed next to him, then shrugged and straddled his waist, kneeling over him with my knees under his wings.

The duke shuddered, his shoulders rounding and wings spreading. I decided to ignore that particular physical reaction, making sure I had enough sheet tucked between my naked skin and the scales of his lower back that I could pretend to any amount of propriety before pressing the heels of my hands down against the scales at the top of his spine.

Varistan groaned, a low sound of pleasure that vibrated up my arms and made my core clench. I tried not to pay attention to the sounds he made as I worked my way down his back, getting a feel for where the muscles of his wings lay. He wasn't built like a human (of course), and I hadn't ever massaged anyone with wings, but I'd done enough prep with moon-called fighters on full-moon nights that I was pretty used to figuring out unusual anatomy on the fly.

It only took a few minutes to figure out that the vast majority of his flying muscles were actually on his front and sides, but I still spent a solid half-hour working on his back and the lower part of his wings as the fire slowly died. He grew quieter and quieter as his muscles relaxed, until he was only letting out sharp breaths when I hit something good.

Smiling with satisfaction, I ran my hands up his back to his shoulders, then sat up. "Roll over, your grace," I said in a breathy murmur, pleased with myself.

He made a soft thrum of sound, shifting his wings. "Can't," Varistan said, sounding half-asleep. "You're in the way."

I glanced down at his wings, lips twitching, but got off of him and scooted backwards before patting him on the calf. "And now?"

"Mmn." Varistan didn't move for a long moment, then sighed heavily and pushed himself up to flop down onto his back.

I got back on top of him, realizing only after I moved that I'd put myself in the most compromising possible position, dressed only in a sheet as I straddled the naked duke. By the smirk on his face as he sprawled out underneath me, the implications hadn't escaped his notice, either.

Moving now would be worse than pretending there was nothing to acknowledge, so I acted as if it was a totally normal thing to be doing as I set my hands on his chest and started working on the tension in his pectorals. Varistan gasped, his head tilting back and lashes fluttering, mouth opening in a raw expression that made me want to lick his skin.

"Harder?" he panted out, lashes parting for a moment in a pleading expression.

I gave it to him, because I absolutely could not have Varistan looking at me with those hazed ruby eyes while my fucking *bare pussy* was six inches from his hips. He groaned, head falling back until his horns rested against the mattress, his whole body going limp with pleasure from the pressure of my hands.

I had to keep my eyes focused on my hands and hope like hell that any... *humidity*... that Varistan detected would be attributed to the rain and general moistness of the air, because with his brow creased in bliss and lips parted enough to show the white of his teeth, there was no escaping the fact that Varistan was the most attractive man I'd ever met. He'd earned the name "Flame of Facry" fair and square, and his face was no less beautiful for belonging to the Duke of Nyx Shaeras.

The heat of his body radiated against me, warming my hands and my thighs. His stupid, perfect body felt like it had been sculpted for my sake, plucked out of the depths of my psyche and splayed out beneath me. I could find every knot and sore spot without thinking, my fingers running down the strength of his muscles with a sixth sense for where he'd hold his tension. I knew I looked at him a lot, but I hadn't realized the level of intuition I'd developed about his body—

My thumbs swept across his nipples as I ran my fingers along the grooves between his ribs. Heat flooded my veins when Varistan *moaned*, his back arching up off the bed and his hands going to my thighs, claws digging into my skin.

"Fuck," he got out, his voice shaking. His dark lashes parted, pupils so wide the red of his irises showed only in a narrow ring. "That's... perhaps enough."

I had to swallow, salivating at the sight of the duke in such a state of disarray, let alone from the feel of him gripping my thighs like he wanted to drag my pussy flush to his groin. "Yeah, okay," I managed to say, trying to act casual as I clambered off of him, the afterimpression of his hands feeling cold without his heat against my skin. "Feel any better?"

Varistan made a low sound of amusement, running one hand across his chest in a way that dragged my eyes along with it. "I may be inclined to take you flying more often, if it comes with such dedicated... aftercare."

My cheeks heated at the caress he put on the last word. "I'm going to make a final bathroom run," I said, trying to maintain any amount of dignity. "Don't take up the whole bed while I'm gone."

A slow smile spread across his face. "Joining me, then, Bells?"

"You gonna make me sleep naked on the floor?" I asked. "I might freeze to death."

"Gods forfend," he crooned back. "I'll warm your bed for you. Do dry off before you climb in."

I sniffed at the command, but I didn't complain. I just shucked the sheet at the door and made my awkward way to the privy, nearly tripped over my own feet on the way back in the pitch dark, and toweled myself dry upon my return.

In the dim light of the dying fire, I could see Varistan lying on his side, with the near half of the bed left open in invitation. I hesitated for a moment, shivering a little from the residual cold of the rain, and decided not to make a big deal out of it. He was fae, after all; I didn't have anything to fear from him. And it wasn't like I could see him well enough to want to stare at him in the dark.

I slipped into bed, scooting backwards until I could feel the duke's heat along my back. In a fit of pique, I didn't resist the urge to warm my cold feet on his legs, nor did I warn him. I simply stuck them against the scales of his shin, shivering as his dragon's warmth drove out the iciness of the outdoors.

Varistan stiffened for a moment, then laughed, his tail sweeping up along my leg. "How forward of you, Isabela."

"You never rescinded the offer," I said, shivering again when he combed my damp hair away from my face with the fingers of his wing. "And you're too warm to resist when I'm this cold."

"Too warm to resist, hmm?" he said in a low purr. "Is that an admission of interest I hear?"

"You wouldn't even know what to do with me," I retorted, trying to ignore the knowledge of the naked duke lying alongside me. It wasn't easy when he kept talking to me.

"Oh, I know very well what to do with a naked woman in my bed." Varistan leaned close enough that I could feel his chest brushing my shoulders. "Even with fingers tipped in claws, I think I could crack that aplomb of yours," he said, his voice dropping deeper. "Shall I make the attempt?"

"Tch. I dare you," I said, trying to belie the throbbing wet between my legs. If I kept it light, if I didn't let him know how turned on I was by having his naked body lined up with mine—

His low chuckle sent tingles down my spine and along my skin, gooseprickles rising on my arms. "That's not a 'yes'," he purred into my ear, his breath hot and lips brushing my skin. "I'm not going to play that game with you tonight. Tell me 'yes', or go without."

"You don't even like me," I said, my voice hitching as his tail brushed along my calf.

"Don't I?" he asked with a purr. After another pounding heartbeat, he made a low sound of satisfaction. "That's what I thought—"

I grabbed his wrist as he went to pull away.

Varistan froze.

"Yes," I said, my heart racing and breath shallow. Fuck, this was stupid, but I wasn't about to let him win.

"What?" Breathy. Startled.

"Yes," I said again. "I don't play games, either, and I'm telling you 'yes'."

The duke settled up against my back, his bare chest resting against my shoulders and his hips fitted to mine, the scales of his thigh against the underside of my leg. "Is this what you want, then, little mortal?" he asked, the words hungry and his heartbeat thudding against my spine. "The desire of a fae duke, hot against your pale skin?"

Varistan's hand gripped my waist, his talons barely prickling me. He slid his palm up along my side, fingers splaying across my ribs as he wrapped his other arm underneath me. It left me on fire, my hips tilting into his touch, clit begging for his fingertips, every thought swept away by the touch of his hands. His heated skin left a tingling wake behind as he caressed me, one hand drifting across my stomach to tease my pubic curls and the other cupping my breast.

I made a tiny noise, unable to help it as his thumb ran across my stiff nipple, the sword-calluses of his hands rough against my sensitive skin. All my muscles felt tense and trembly, my pulse throbbing between my legs and every part of my body demanding to be sated. Holy *fuck*, it wasn't enough to have his hands skimming across me. I wanted him to grab me, to bite me, to drive his cock into me and make me scream his name, and I wanted it *now*.

Even the sharpness of that desire couldn't erase the knowledge of who was rousing me—of the absolute *danger* I'd chosen to flirt with. This was *Varistan* with his hands on me, the fucking Duke of Nyx Shaeras, the nephew of the Raven King. He was awful, a beautiful waste of space, not worth my time at all—

"Bells." Varistan leaned his mouth against my ear, his dragon's heat stinging my skin with every harsh breath. "Do you think I'm an idiot?"

I almost couldn't parse the question, the words so unexpected that I could only lie there in befuddlement.

He sighed, extricating himself and rolling onto his other side, leaving me with only the glancing contact of his tail against the heel of my foot. "I'm quite familiar with the distaste of women, and the way someone feels under your hands when she doesn't want your touch," he said in a conversational tone, but with a dangerous edge to the words. "You seem a bold woman, the kind who hates to retreat from a challenge, but I'm not that interested in being the challenge you fuck for the sake of proving to yourself you won't back down."

My skin felt cold everywhere he'd touched me, remembering the heat of a dragon with shivering loss.

I swallowed, desire throbbing in my core and disgust at myself wrapped around my throat. "I wouldn't," I said, my voice wobbling. "I wouldn't do that to either of us."

The bed shifted as he relaxed, some of the tension leaving his frame. "I don't appreciate it being done even to my hands." Varistan sounded vulnerable, the unhappiness he carried with him everywhere breaking through the surface.

Guilt joined the tumult of my emotions, an uncomfortable feeling that left my stomach twisting. "I... apologize," I said, the word almost getting stuck in my throat, for all that it wasn't possible for me to owe anything more to Varistan than I already did. I scooted back enough that my shoulders brushed against his wings, putting enough strength into the contact that he would know it wasn't accidental. "I got... caught up. You're very good at..." I made a face, hating the admission, "...baiting me."

He made a low sound, something akin to amusement, and curled his tail around my ankle in an answering touch. "Apology accepted," he said in a grave voice. "I suppose both of us ought to improve at not teasing the other with things we don't truly want to give."

I wiggled a little, pressing my thighs together. If it was just the sex... but it wasn't. Plus, with those words, Varistan had all but said that he had no actual interest in having sex with me, just in getting a rise out of me. It was a game of chicken, with too much risk of ending in tragedy to keep playing without at least acknowledging that we were both doing it.

"Yeah," I said, instead of vocalizing any of that. "Especially while, um..."

"Naked in bed together?" he asked, with a lilt of humor.

My cheeks heated. "Something like that."

Varistan huffed a laugh, shifting into a more comfortable position. "All alone in the wilderness, no one but us to know what happens," he said in a sing-song. I could hear the wry amusement in his voice as he added in a more conversational tone, "Of course, we'd have to know. I'm not certain I could act unperturbed in front of even one of the fae while carrying the knowledge of having fucked a human."

"Good thing I'm not interested, then," I shot back, a bit waspishly. My damp thighs told a different story, but since Varistan wasn't asking them, he didn't get to know any differently.

His tail squeezed my ankle before relaxing, his breathing slowing. "Good thing," he murmured, the warmth of his body radiating against mine, driving off the cold of the night. "Think of how troublesome that would be."

"I like trouble," I said without thinking, earning a low sound of amusement from Varistan.

His wings relaxed down, resting against my back. "Do you even enjoy me from time to time, then?" he asked, flicking the tip of his tail across my foot.

There was hesitance in the words, despite the humor with which they were spoken. I could have said something snarky... but he'd carried me through a storm with no reward, and he was talking to me like I was something more than his slave.

"Yeah," I said quietly. "Against my better judgment, sometimes I do."

"I think I'll count that as a compliment." He huffed a soft laugh, brushing his wing back against me. "Sleep well, Isabela."

"Sleep well," I whispered back, staring into the dark of the room as if I could fall into the night, and never have to return to the real world.

Chapter Seventeen

SUNSHINE

F alling asleep, I'd briefly had the rueful thought that I'd probably wake up with touch-hungry Varistan plastered against me. If anyone was going to be a nocturnal cuddler, surely it would be the man who confessed to having never wanted to be put down as a child and to loving having someone rest on him.

I did not, however, wake up with the duke wrapped around me.

I woke up wrapped around *him*.

The sunlight roused me later than usual, feeling utterly comfortable and warmer than I usually slept these days, despite being naked and only under a single thin blanket. With every breath, I drew in the heady scent of musk and rain, and the warmth beneath me felt so good I didn't want to ever move.

That warmth was breathing, I realized with a start. It had a heartbeat. And scales.

Aw, fuck.

Somehow, in the night, I'd managed to get Varistan flat on his back, and then proceeded to climb on top of him. I had him completely held down, too; I was holding hands with one of his wings, had his tail trapped under me and one of my legs hooked around his, and was keeping his head immobilized via hanging on to one of his horns. My breasts pressed against the bare skin of his chest. One of his arms rested heavily across my lower back. I was straight-up straddling his thigh, my clit and curls pressed against him.

Gods, at least he can't feel that through the scales—

"Ah, Isabela," the duke said in a sensual croon. "How did you sleep?"

I froze. Fuck. He never woke up before me.

"You're... awake," I croaked out.

He chuckled, the vibration focusing my attention even more keenly on his body. "A bit difficult not to be, when I met the dawn with you running your tongue up my throat."

"No," I said, my eyes widening.

"Oh, yes," Varistan crooned, with a great deal of wicked amusement. "Let's see, what was it you said..."

"No," I said again, halfway to desperation. I did *not* want to know.

He ignored my protest, reaching up and taking my hand off his horn. "Ah, I remember," he said, as if he hadn't been lying there waiting to say it as soon as I woke up. "'Love you a million, *mi cielo*.' I'm not sure what the endearment means, but you said it quite... affectionately."

Aghast, I peeled myself off of him, trying to extricate myself from the situation. I'd left a fucking damp spot on his thigh, and had just as clearly drooled on his neck. I shoved the sheets between us to hide the evidence, praying that he wouldn't notice.

"It means 'my sky,'" I said, scrambling for something to wrap around myself, as if that would make Varistan forget the feel of my naked body sprawled against his. "That's my mother's language."

"A fitting endearment," Varistan said, sounding thoughtful. He pushed himself up as I cocooned myself in the muddy sheet I'd used to clean off my feet the night before, smirking at me. "Developing some modesty, Bells?"

"It's cold. I'm going outside," I said, the words clipped and my face so heated I knew I had to be bright red.

I followed up the words with action, zipping outside and dashing my way across the frigid, wet ground to the privy. The temperature didn't encourage lingering, and by the time I managed to make it inside again, any traces of ardor had been thoroughly scoured by the chill. To my relief, Varistan had moseyed out of bed and lit the fire for me, and was rustling around through the cupboards.

"Trying your hand at cooking breakfast?" I asked, pulling on my clothing with no regard for their temperature. Thankfully they'd dried enough during the night that the remaining dampness was only enough to make them clammy, and as soon as I plopped myself in front of the fire the heat of the flames chased even that away.

Varistan set a pot of water on top of the stove. "Not at all," he said with a bright smile. "I don't like to eat before flying. I'm trying my hand at making tea."

"How bold of you," I said, amused despite myself. I rotated to put my back to the fire, warming myself back up. "Feeling up to carrying me back to Nyx Shaeras?"

He shrugged his wings, sprawling down into a chair. "Once I get aloft, certainly. I'm in much better shape than I would have been without your assistance last night, but given the trees we'll likely need to find an overlook for the launch." He wrinkled his nose, looking away with an expression of mild embarrassment. "I didn't consider the difficult takeoff when selecting a landing location last night."

My lips twitched, recalling that landing. In the light of day, it was far more amusing than it had been in the black of night, and I did appreciate the skill he'd displayed. "Not a problem. I don't mind hiking," I said, hauling myself up and going over to the cupboards to see what I could find to feed myself.

By the time I put together a peanut butter sandwich for myself, Varistan's water had started boiling, and he was standing next to it with a jar of tea leaves in one hand, looking bewildered. I leaned against the cupboard in the kitchenette, chewing a bite of my sandwich as I watched him try to decide what to do.

At last, he looked over towards me with a pleading expression. "I've discovered that I have little intuition as to how this is done," he said, sounding mournful. "I request your assistance."

I smirked, but he'd requested instead of commanding, and I was inclined to reward him for the good behavior. "Do you want more than one cup?"

"One would be sufficient," he said, one corner of his mouth lifting. He picked up the pot by the sides, immune to the heat. "Fetch me a mug?"

The question mark felt tacked-on, but I did appreciate the effort. I pulled one of the tall ceramics out of the cupboard for him to pour the water into, and found a strainer for him to pour through. "Put a small palmful of leaves in here, then pour the water over," I told him, setting the strainer over the mug. "You like yours black, right?"

Varistan glanced sidelong at me, a small smile hovering on his lips. "Didn't you say you tended the outside, not the inside?"

"You eat breakfast in front of me on the daily, your grace," I said with a grin. "I'd have to be a lot less observant to not know you like your tea black, that you prefer floral teas to smoked, and that you'd rather have it half-frozen than hot."

He wrapped his tail around my hips, dragging me up against him and dropping his wing around my shoulder as he poured. "That's my sharp-eyed Bells," he said, with more fondness than I'd anticipated. "How long do I leave this in?"

"Until you like the color," I said, leaning my head against his shoulder since I couldn't really go anywhere else. "No way to cool it off unless you want to leave it outside for an hour, though, so I'm afraid you'll have to drink it hot."

"Such tribulation." He lifted the strainer out of the water, frowned, and dunked it back in. He glanced over at me again. "You know, I truly despise the scent of peanuts."

Smirking, I blew a breath up into his face.

Varistan made a sound of disgust, removing me from his vicinity with his tail. "Stop that."

"Stop what?" I asked in my most innocent voice. "Eating? I'll die."

He grimaced, checking his tea again. "If there are mints, I would like you to eat some of those before we fly."

"Well, since you asked nicely, I suppose I can do that," I said, popping the last bite of the sandwich into my mouth.

"Good." He dumped the tea leaves into the sink, took a sip of his tea, and gave me a long-suffering look. "Bells, this tastes akin to shoe leather."

"Drink it fast," I suggested cheerfully. "Everyone's first cup of tea tastes like shoe leather. Bottoms up, your grace!"

With a disgruntled look, Varistan obeyed, chugging the steaming-hot tea. With a *faugh!* sound of disgust, he set the empty mug back onto the counter and gave a dramatic shudder. "I think that's enough domesticity for me today," he said, lifting his lip. "Dress me, and we may go."

Resigned to playing maid – there was no way the duke knew his way around a broom or sink – I started picking up the mess we'd made. "Do you want your clothes warmed, or do you prefer them damp and chilly?" I asked, dumping our towels and my muddy sheet onto the bed before setting to stripping it.

"Warm. What in the wilds are you doing?"

"What, do you think remote outposts clean themselves?" I sniped back, moving the chairs with his clothing draped over them next to the wood-burning stove. "I'm cleaning up so the next poor sods to end up out here don't think vagrants have been living here."

"Oh." He looked a little taken aback. "I didn't consider that."

I bundled the linens into the laundry hamper with a shrug and set to re-making the bed. "Why would you?" I asked, giving myself a mental shake. There was no reason to get angry with him for having been born into wealth. "It won't take long. I know how to keep house."

"I... appreciate that," he said with a touch of hesitance, eyeing the few dishes in the basin before setting his mug in amongst them. "I'm afraid I've left such disrepair in my wake more than once."

I barked a laugh before I could stop myself, tucking the blanket down tight to ward off any daring insects. "Yes, I'm sure you have, your grace," I said, joining him at the basin to wash and rack the dishes. "You pay people to clean up after yourself, after all. But I'm used to needing to be thoughtful about who might use things after me, and a little bit of consideration can go a long way."

Varistan leaned up against the wall, arm over his head in a pose that emphasized the powerful lines of his very naked body. His tail flirted with my ankles as he watched me, teasing me with contact. "That seems to be a mortal attitude."

"I am mortal, your grace, in case you forgot." I set the pot on the drying rack, pausing for a moment to eye him. "It doesn't really seem that mortal, though. I thought fae liked to indebt others to them."

"Mm." He swept his gaze down along my body in what looked like an idle scan. "We're not all the same, Bells. When it comes to behavior, I generally believe that there's exceptions to every rule." He sighed, pushing off the wall and sauntering over towards the fire. "What I meant, though, was that regarding the world as a place of cooperation is far more of a mortal viewpoint than a faery one. You're social animals. We're..." Varistan trailed off, sounding moody.

"Predators?" I asked, setting the last dish on the rack to dry.

His mouth twitched back into a rueful smile. "I suppose that's as good a word as any."

The duke was unusually pensive as I dressed him, moving without me needing to tell him what to do next. When I'd done up the last button on his pants and tied the last knot for his shirt, Varistan tilted my chin up with the wrist of his wing. I raised my brows at him; he merely observed me for a moment before stepping away.

"After you," he said, holding the door for me.

In the crisp clean air after the storm, the saltwood forest was too cold for standing around in, but a beautiful place for a hike. The towering trees soared overhead, pale late-autumn sunlight filtering down through the evergreen branches, and the dense duff of the forest floor swallowed the sound of our footsteps. Everywhere in the underbrush, the bushes were holding on to the last of their fruits, vivid red and lapis blue orbs dangling from their stems.

Varistan noticed me looking at the plants and started identifying them for me: tall stems of whipgrass, which were so long and pliable in the summer that you could pluck one and use it for a horsewhip; the small blue fruits of cenoth shrubs; young snowspear saplings, so named for their near-black bark that stained the snow red for inches around their trunks; tart edible hawkberries. The last of those he offered me with a smirk, the pink berry pierced with one of his talons and vibrant crimson juice running down the black of his claw.

I ate it off his fingertip, holding his gaze as I licked the berry juice off his talon, the sensation of the sharp point of his claw dragging against my tongue making the hairs on my arms stand in reckless anticipation.

He watched me, lips parted and eyes half-lidded, and didn't offer again.

It took about an hour to reach a bluff. I hesitated, looking across the vista before turning towards him. "About this morning..."

Shaking his head with a smile, Varistan held out his hand to me. "If anyone can give understanding for dreams rising too close to the surface, surely it's me," he said, warmth in his garnet eyes. "I appreciate the knowledge that I'm not alone in such trials, and I carry no offense from it."

"Oh," I said, a small sound, almost involuntary. I set my hand in his, the warmth of his fingers making me shiver. "You're being kinder than I expected."

He laughed, tugging me closer to him. "I'm not *always* terrible, Bells."

"Could've fooled me, your grace," I said with an answering laugh as he picked me up. My arms went around his neck automatically, my body settling against his as if I belonged there.

With another bright laugh, Varistan threw us into the sky, and turned towards home.

CHAPTER EIGHTEEN

REVELRY

The Feast of Ruekh was a highly anticipated part of the feast cycle for mortals. There were more than three years to each feast cycle, so we humans had a long time to look forward to the one day where we got to be on even footing with the fae, and as a result people tended to go all-out in their revelry. Though I was a bondservant and hadn't had nearly enough time to accumulate the resources to outfit myself for a revel, Varistan apparently didn't want me embarrassing him, because he'd provided me with the sort of clothing a noblewoman might wear.

The floor-length dress was in an ancient style, made for and by warrior fae. Its woven bodice would turn a blade, the ivory stays in the corset made for support and protection instead of constriction. The loose sleeves were built to conceal blades. The burgundy spider-silk skirt flowed like water and had a slit up to my hip with a matching thigh-sheath for an ornamental blade. Varistan had provided a dagger, too, a whisper-sharp blade hilted in black brass with an enormous pigeon's-blood ruby for a pommel.

I'd never set eyes on that sort of decadent luxury before. It was ruinously expensive, and aggressively coordinated with the duke's own outfit of black lacquered armor. It was also, quite obviously, a possessive staking of claim, right down to the ruby collar necklace.

I was still going to wear it.

Once I finished dressing him for the revel and sent him off to go await his grand entrance, I finally took advantage of his offer to allow me to use his amenities. I didn't quite luxuriate, but I definitely enjoyed the deep tub and nigh-infinite selection of scents and lotions to choose from. I arrived almost an hour late to the revel, but who cared about that? It would go until sunrise, and the nights were long.

I received a number of round-eyed stares when I entered the revel, and one fae noblewoman went ashen when she saw me dressed like I was Varistan's duchess instead of his body-servant. The whole revel and feast were full of a bewildering assortment of color and movement, though, and I didn't draw as much attention as I'd anticipated. Most people likely assumed that I was wearing glamor, as many others were—I saw raven wings, drifting smoke that always managed to obscure the most salacious details, and clothing that was either glued in place or painted on by magic.

High Court Feasts typically had the feast and the revel divided, but the duke either disliked the practice of formal feasts or had erased the divide between them purposefully, just like the divide between fae and mortals was erased for this one day. Knowing how much he liked to preen, I suspected the latter; he wouldn't get to sit at a high table without the formal feast.

In lieu of formal service, tables were set up in the rooms away from the dancing, with massive platters of food for people to serve themselves from. The fae love of misdirection showed itself in the food; the dishes were all crafted to fool the eyes, though with clever cooking instead of glamor. I mentally complimented the kitchen staff as I bit into a cut of fish to discover it was pastry, instead. They'd truly pulled out the stops for Raven Court's patron god.

I went to join the dancing after a light snack, intending to eat more later, but a hand wrapped around my wrist and jerked me back into the shadows. I stumbled, almost falling before I got my feet under me, trying and failing to yank my arm out of an iron grip.

A fae lord sneered down at me. "So, the pet cleans up nicely, does she?"

He was the one who had been in Lylvenore with Varistan, a cruel man known for working his bondservants until they dropped. His tousled chestnut hair offset his porcelain skin and pale blue eyes, the loose curls tamed by a silver filigree band. In any room aside from one with the Flame of Faery in it, he would have been beautiful, but to my eyes he looked coarse, as if an apprentice had tried to imitate the painting of a master.

He would look better with a spear through his chest, I thought sourly. I hadn't forgiven him for getting sexed up instead of impaled, the single domino that had led to the whole chain of events ending with me standing here dressed like a Queen.

"Lord Sairal," I said, giving him exactly the bow our statuses demanded, and nothing more. It was difficult with my wrist manacled by his hand, but I managed. "What an unexpected pleasure."

His thin lips curled with distaste. "You don't deserve to be wearing that dress," he said, as if I hadn't spoken at all. "The woman who should have worn it hasn't set foot in Nyx Shaeras in decades. He ought to have burned it before giving it to you."

Fuck. He must have had this made for his "dearest", whoever she was. No wonder that fae lady blanched.

Even though it sounded like she'd never worn it, the fae nobles obviously knew of its existence, and didn't like me wearing it. I wasn't sure *I* liked wearing it, knowing that. It was far more than a mark of possessiveness. It marked me as important; someone he viewed like an extension of himself.

That could get me in a lot of trouble, if I wasn't careful.

"Do you like it?" I asked, giving him the prettiest smile I could muster. "It makes me feel like a lady."

"You're no lady," Lord Sairal sneered. "You're a weakness. The pathetic indulgence of a lonely monster." He dragged me closer and grabbed my chin with his other hand. "Pretty little thing, though. Is he fucking you?"

Rage flamed inside of me, my free hand going to my dagger with automatic temper—but I didn't need to defend myself, because Varistan did.

A line of steel flashed between me and Lord Sairal as heat warmed my back. The duke's tail lashed out and grabbed the lord by the arm as blood bloomed on his silk shirt.

"Who I'm fucking is none of your business," Varistan said, his voice as cold as the kiss of his blade. "And you're touching something that's mine. Let her go."

The lord's fingers tightened on my wrist. "Have you forgotten—"

With a sound like a tree branch snapping, the duke broke his lord's arm, throwing the man down to the floor with his tail and following him with the tip of his sword. His expression was flat, eyes glittering like the rubies he wore and ears pinned back in fury. "You should have let go of her when you had the chance."

Lord Sairal panted in the growing circle of silence around us, his body shaking from the pain of Varistan's grip on his broken forearm. "Let me— Let me *go*—"

Varistan dragged him back up by those broken bones, then flung him backwards. "Get out."

The lord staggered away, cradling his arm against his bloodied chest. "You... You..." He panted, shoulders moving with every ragged breath. "You'll surely regret this—"

"Take it up with your master," Varistan snarled, taking one deadly step forward. "Leave. *Now*. And don't *fucking* come back." His wings mantled behind him, tail lashing. "If I see you on my lands again—"

I grabbed his hand, not wanting this to escalate any further.

Varistan's attention snapped to me, his ears leaning forward and body turning towards me. It was like he forgot the entire world, from the injured, angry lord to the stunned onlookers. His eyes were on mine, and nothing else seemed to matter to him.

"Bells. Are you hurt?" he asked with focused attention.

"I'm fine," I said, staring back at him with wide eyes as I rubbed my wrist. "Did you... did you just *banish* Lord Sairal?"

His ears pinned back and his tail wrapped around my calf as he looked back towards where he'd flung the man. Lord Sairal had, quite intelligently, made his escape.

"He laid hands on you," Varistan growled, expression hard.

"Var— Your Grace, he's a *lord*," I said, aghast.

"And I'm a duke." He wiped the other fae's blood off his sword with a linen, then sheathed it, stepping backwards into the light.

"And I'm *human*." Had he seriously banished a lord from his duchy for the crime of manhandling me? That was... outrageous. Way more outrageous than putting me in an apparently-infamous dress.

What the fuck?

"And you're mine," Varistan said with a rakish grin. "Now that we have all those facts laid down, come dance with me."

I raised my brows, looking him up and down. I'd put him into that clothing, and it didn't really seem like the sort of thing one danced in. Armored pauldrons and bracers that mimicked the scales of his tail and legs over clingy silk sleeves, a long burgundy loincloth a shade darker than my dress, and a bare chest and back decorated with slender body-chains... It wasn't exactly made for draping a woman across.

I still can't believe he had Lianka give him nipple piercings for those chains.

"Seriously?" I asked.

He held out his hand, smirking at me. "I wasn't asking," he said, looking very self-satisfied. "Come dance."

"I'm terrible at dancing," I said, though I did step forward and take his hand.

The duke tugged me forward, setting my hand on his upper arm and pulling me flush to his body. "I'm an excellent dancer, though." He ran his mouth against my ear. "Let's see how well we dance together."

The vibration of his rumbling voice made my skin tingle and my heart beat faster, and with the rising swell of the music, His Grace Varistan Yllaxira swept me into the revel.

I'd attended revels, of course. I'd even *danced* at revels. But for all of my ability to move with grace and power in the fighting ring, I'd never mastered the ability to move on the dance floor. I got too far into my head, and unlike with fighting, I didn't have the thousands of hours of practice that gave me the muscle memory to override my desire to think about what I was doing.

The song ended, and Varistan didn't let me go. Three songs in, he started grinning, and by the fourth, he started laughing.

"Gods and monsters, Isabela," he said, his voice bright with amusement. "You're so *stiff*."

"I told you," I said, my voice as stiff as my body. "You can stop embarrassing me if you want."

He made a thoughtful sound, wheeling us to a stop in the middle of the dance floor. Varistan took my arm and shook it. "Relax," he said, settling his wings behind him. "Stop thinking so much."

"I can't help it—"

"Yes, you can," he said, cutting me off. "You moved with me beautifully in the air, and I've heard that you fight with the same perfection of body. So do that here."

I flushed, feeling like everyone was staring at us. "I don't know how."

"Mm." He settled our bodies together again, adjusting the position of my arms. "Imagine we're in battle," he said in a low croon. "Not dancing. Not in beautiful clothes. Move away from the pressure of my hand as if it's holding my sword. Follow my chest as if you have your spear pointed at my heart."

"I don't—"

"Try it," he said, not taking no for an answer. "Avoid my strikes. Make me retreat." His hot breath stirred my hair as he leaned closer and murmured into my ear, "You started out wanting to kill me. Have you fallen in love with me so soon?"

Outrage spiked, my spine going straight, but Varistan didn't give me an opportunity to snap back a retort. He stepped back into a dance, moving with total confidence in his body.

My first steps were even more awkward than before, but I had no interest in being dragged around on a tour of the dance floor until dawn, and I'd be *damned* before I let Varistan spend the rest of the night laughing at me. His hand shifted on my back, pressing towards my spine, and I stepped away from it, moving closer to him as he turned away from me.

"Better," he purred. "But I can tell you're still thinking."

I gritted my teeth, thought about thunderstorms and swords, and dropped into the anticipatory moment of standing across the ring from my opponent.

He growled, a low sound of hungry pleasure, and moved into the dance.

It was better than fighting, and better than flying. In a battle, there's always disjunction that requires readjustment. In the air, I was merely a passenger. But this...

He moved, and I moved with him. When I offered a variation, he answered me, played off of me, led me into it and through it. The world fell away into music and movement, my eyes closed and my lips parted as we stepped across the slick wood of the floor. His hand drifted lower on my back, his warmth soaking into me.

His thigh between mine. His hand on my spine. His heat and his heartbeat pressing against my chest.

My whole body followed Varistan's lead, stepping away from his hand and moving towards him—and stepping away from him as he moved towards me, maintaining the distance even as that distance grew smaller and smaller, with no friction between us.

As the song drew to a close, Varistan lowered me into a deep backwards dip, taking my full weight. A small smile hovered on his lips, his expression soft. "You're a beautiful dancer when you let yourself simply be in my arms," he said, pitching his voice beneath the music, quiet enough that only I would hear it. He pulled me back to my feet and stepped back, bowing over one of my hands. "And now that you've satisfied my curiosity as to our partnership on the dance floor, I'll release you from such embarrassment." A smirk touched his lips as he added, "For now, at least."

"I, um... appreciate it," I said, trying to form some semblance of words. We'd danced. I'd been dancing. With the fucking Duke of Nyx Shaeras. In front of *everyone.*

It's not like you had a choice, I tried to tell myself, though that wasn't much of an excuse, and it wasn't like dancing was the only thing people would be talking about. He'd fucking banished a lord for touching me, *and* given him an iron wound, even if it was only a fingersbreadth deep. The possessiveness, recklessness, and passion of the Flame of Faery was on full display tonight.

I only hoped it wouldn't hurt my standing with the people I was actually here for.

CHAPTER NINETEEN

ALPHA

V aristan wasn't the only one to claim a dance from me, but he certainly was the best dancer among them, and after having my foot stepped on by the third human soldier in a row, I found myself thinking longingly of having Varistan's arm wrapped around me and the shadow of his wings falling over me. He was so self-possessed, moving exactly as he should, without wasted energy or awkwardness. Everything, down to the tilt of his shoulders and the angle of his tail, was right where it was supposed to be.

I extricated myself before I started limping and had to deal with Varistan impaling someone else for causing me minor physical injury, and drifted towards the edges of the revel. It was harder than I'd expected to slip away; I had enough friends that people kept talking to me, and Varistan seemed to always have part of his attention on me, his body turned towards mine or his eyes glancing in my direction as I moved.

It wasn't until a human woman I didn't know walked right up to Varistan and asked him for a dance that I had a chance to escape. I almost missed slipping away, so delighted at the sight of the duke looking completely poleaxed that I wanted to stay and see how it played out.

I hope you have to dance with every mortal woman there, I thought to myself cheerfully, sauntering towards the Sea Room with ten minutes to spare before the fourth watch. That would serve him right for making a spectacle of me tonight: the rest of us human women could make a spectacle out of him.

A cluster of humans loitered near the entrance to the Sea Room, the sort of gathering that would look natural to the casual eye, yet was anything but. Darius wasn't one of them; I hoped that wasn't a bad sign. He'd been Alpha's envoy, after all.

The door was unlocked, and the room almost empty. It was one of the more stunning places in the castle, designed as a naval war room overlooking the sea, with massive windows of clear glass as thick as my wrist set directly into the stone. They must have been built into the castle when it had been raised, and they'd survived all this time. Maybe they were enchanted.

One figure stood at the frontmost window, like a captain at the prow of a ship. She was small, the sort of slip of a woman who can escape notice by merely remaining silent, her black hair cropped to chin-length and her plain clothing obviously of fine tailoring.

Alpha didn't look over as I walked up to her and joined her at the window. She just stood there, gripping one wrist behind her back, as quiet and still as the moon that shone down on us.

"You wanted to see me, Alpha?" I asked, keeping my voice hushed. It didn't seem right to talk at a normal volume in the moonlit room.

"Have you ever seen a chimera?" she asked in reply. "A true one, not your duke."

I hesitated, not sure how to answer that, or what she was really asking. "Only a dead one," I said at last. At least it was true.

"They're much worse alive," she said, her voice calm. "Creatures caught between worlds, half faery and half... something else. They shift, constantly, like their bodies are at war with themselves." Alpha fell silent for a moment, then glanced sidelong at me. "Do you even know what side you want to be on, Isabela?"

My chin came up and my spine went stiff. I didn't like the implication that I would side with the vermin instead of the hunters. "I'm on the side of freedom, Alpha," I said, my tone going frosty despite my best efforts. "Freedom for *everyone*, even the court fae. It doesn't have to be us versus them." It felt strange to say, but the longer I stayed in Nyx Shaeras, the more true it felt. My tolerance for collateral damage seemed to fade with every day.

She made a low sound of amusement, returning her gaze to the ocean. "My daughter is a court fae." Her voice hadn't changed, as calm as if I'd answered exactly as she'd expected. Maybe I had. "Every human in Faery is caught between worlds. Whatever lives we had on Earth are gone now, and whatever life we have here is faery, but we're still treated differently because we're mortal. But you never had a life on Earth."

"That doesn't make me fae," I said cautiously.

"No, it doesn't." Alpha turned and looked up at me, tilting her head to the side in a way that reminded me of a curious raven trying to decide if a morsel was edible. "Is he your lover?"

My eyes narrowed. "You're the second person to ask me that tonight."

"It's not an unreasonable question," she said, unruffled. "He's flirtatious, charismatic, and publicly unattached. The only woman he's consistently seen with is you, and he seems..." She trailed off.

"Possessive," I said, supplying the word before she could say something more dangerous. I couldn't forget the feel of his hands on me while we lay naked in bed together, or the way he'd danced with me in front of everyone, but that didn't make us lovers, and it didn't make us friends. I didn't know *what* it made us, but for the moment we weren't either of those things.

"That's one way to put it."

"He's half-dragon. It's accurate," I said, crossing my arms over my chest. "I'm sure you've been keeping an eye on me, Alpha, and I don't imagine that if you thought I was under the duke's thrall that we'd be having this conversation. So what are you actually asking?"

She smiled, an almost motherly expression on a woman who felt far more like a predator than a friend. "Would you kill him if I told you to?"

I stared at her. That wasn't the sort of question a bondservant should be able to ask without coming very close to death.

Alpha didn't move, holding my gaze without any emotion in her eyes.

"No," I said at last, putting my shoulders back. "I'd kill him if I believed he needed to die, but I'm not a soldier, and even soldiers ought to believe that they're doing the right thing when they take a life."

"Why shouldn't he die?" she asked, tilting her head to the side again.

"Why should he?" I countered, my temper rising.

"You were going to kill him the night you met him." Alpha smiled again, the expression cutting. "Omari had such high praise for you. I wonder what he'd say to find out you've stayed your hand?"

"He'd fucking ask me why," I snapped. "Alpha."

"I did." Her expression didn't waver. I supposed she dealt with far more frightening things than a single angry woman.

She's trying to get a rise out of you, I realized belatedly.

She's succeeding, I told myself, with a mental scowl. I didn't like stepping into traps.

"You did, Alpha," I said, pretending to politeness again. "My answer is: this whole duchy relies on him, and I'm disinclined to throw Nyx Shaeras into chaos and garner the King's ire without understanding the situation. If you've communicated with Omari, you know that we anticipated Lord Sairal, *not* the duke." I shrugged one shoulder, turning to look out the window with feigned nonchalance. "A dragon has very little akin to simple vermin. We bit off more than we could chew."

Alpha made a thoughtful sound. "What would convince you?"

I glanced at her sidelong; she remained unreadable. "I don't think I'm going to answer that question," I said after a moment. "I'm not a knife in your hand. I was a nobody in Lylvenore, but I was still a person. Everyone in vermin control was part of the team."

"We don't do things like that out here," she said, her tone cool. "You have room in the city for blundering mistakes. If we did something as stupid as attacking the Duke of Nyx Shaeras without total assurance of success, it would be the end of us."

There was no way she was a bondservant—at least, not of Raven Court nor of Nyx Shaeras. That probably made her quite good at her job, but I definitely didn't like her.

"I'm not going to just *obey*," I said, the word leaving a bad taste on my tongue.

"You're alone, Isabela," Alpha said, the words sounding pitying. "One mortal girl, caught in the claws of a dragon. You'll find yourself with a leash attached to that pretty ruby collar before long, and none of us will lift a finger to help you."

Anger bloomed in my breast, my heart beating harder and blood heating. I knew how it had to look—the pretty young human, dressed in fae finery, dancing with the duke after he'd wounded a lord for touching her. A possession. A *pet*, getting pampered and given special treatment so she wouldn't protest when he demanded more.

The very idea made nausea roil in my gut. I knew Varistan had invested in the fighting rings in Lylvenore, and I knew he hated the interactions between fae and humans. But he wasn't like *that*. Not the sort of monster who would use someone like a toy, or regard lives lost as mere annoyances. The pain he remembered in his dreams, the joy when he'd taken me flying, the concern when he'd asked if I'd been hurt... those things had been real. He didn't hide his emotions, not from me.

He'd once told me he had no expectation of privacy from me. He didn't even try.

She thought I didn't see the danger of my position; that I'd wake up one day to realize I'd been lured into the spider's web. She didn't know him at all. I didn't think any of them did. But why would they? It wasn't as if I'd ever known the vicereine as anything but a shape, her political actions defining her for me.

But then, when has any sparrow cared about the secret sorrows of the hawk?

"You have a difficult task, Alpha," I said, keeping my voice quiet to hide the unease. "You don't have tens of thousands of people to vanish into, and I'm sure there's not that many of you—"

"More than you might think." She regarded me with half-lidded eyes, her expression lazy. "But go on."

I sighed, resting my elbows on the windowsill. "I wouldn't trust me if I were you, either," I said, feeling moody. "I don't want to be alone, but if my choices are loneliness or becoming a mindless killer, I'll choose loneliness any day of the year. Aren't there any other roads we can walk?"

She didn't answer at first, the silence filling the room. We weren't that far from the revel, but the only sounds of people I could hear were the faint, muffled voices of those just outside the doors. I supposed that made sense; the

Sea Room was a war room, after all, built to keep those within safe and their words secret.

"It's not vermin control out here," Alpha said at last. "We use a lot of the same language, but that's only because there's more people in the cities, and their collective voices tend to be louder. We don't take stabs at the masters, because on their own land, a fae noble has absolute power, and if you fail, sometimes they'll simply kill until they feel the debt is satisfied." She exhaled, almost a sigh. "We try to save people. Get them out when they need to run."

"You're saying that your priorities are different. That I'm not useful to you, after all." My shoulders slumped, cheeks warming. I'd been so confident that I was helping—that I could *be* helpful. That being in Varistan's shadow made me powerful, not weak.

Alpha made a low sound, *hmm*, almost sympathetic. "I'm saying that the shape of the world is different from what you were led to believe in Lylvenore," she said. "Everything's connected, and not always in ways we can see. Killing monsters might improve the world, but it might rouse sleeping beasts we didn't know existed. Tell me," she said, her voice level. "How many people died because Yllaxira was attacked?"

"Only those who fought him. He didn't even tell the vicereine," I said quietly. "He was within his rights to have everyone I knew slaughtered. Every person at the pits. She would have turned the city upside-down to find the people who'd dared to coordinate an attack on the King's nephew." I swallowed, remembering the flickering flame of the burning spear and the last moments of people I'd counted among my friends. "But he didn't do it."

Varistan had implied he didn't want others to know he'd been funding illegal fights—had made it sound like I was doing him a favor by stitching him up. But he'd let my father live because I'd pleaded with him. Because I'd given myself to him. He'd taken the opportunity to repay the debt without more bloodshed.

He'd said he hadn't wanted to kill anyone. Even bleeding from an iron wound, Varistan had said that. He'd proven it, too, leaving a man alive who could condemn him simply because he didn't want to kill the father of a stranger.

Alpha turned to look at me. I could see her examining me in my peripheral vision, but I didn't move from my position, keeping my eyes fixed on the moonlight glinting off the dark waves of the sea.

"Nyx Shaeras is one of the safest holdings in Raven Court." Alpha shook her head, looking away from me. "The duke is hot-headed and bigoted, yet fiercely protective of everyone under his aegis. He may hate us, but he won't let anyone harm us. There's worse places to be, and worse people to have to live under. I don't want him dead, and I would have had you killed if I thought you were a danger to him."

She fell silent again, and I didn't try to hasten her along. There were hours left before dawn, and I didn't mind spending them watching the sea.

I'd never thought anyone in the resistance would want to protect *Varistan* from *me*.

Minutes passed before Alpha spoke again.

"You passed the test, Isabela. I don't think you need to be controlled or removed, and I'm willing to let you have access to us. Darius will be your contact," she said with calm finality. She joined me at the window, the slope of her shoulders looking tired. "We don't need information about the duke more than we need safety, and he's focused enough on you that having you try to help us would put us in grave danger." Alpha sighed, tilting her head back. "But if something happens, and you need help..."

I raised a brow, looking over at her. "I thought you wouldn't lift a finger."

"There's other roads," she said, one corner of her mouth lifting. "Stand back from us, and dance with the duke. Maybe he'll discover humans aren't quite the plague he imagines. But if not..." She shrugged.

"Whatever you're thinking, no," I said, smiling at her. "He'll hunt me down if I run away. He has a dragon's instincts." I took in a breath and sighed it out, almost laughing. "I suppose I'm alone after all. I won't put you in harm's way."

"Then I suppose you'll always be with the duke, even if he's got you on a leash," Alpha said, glancing sidelong at me. "Is that a price you're willing to pay to keep people safe?"

"It's not what I expected when I came to meet you," I said, shaking my head with a rueful expression. "I like action, and I don't want to be a pet. But when it comes down to it..." I trailed off, thinking of Estarren and my father, and all the other people in Lylvenore I loved and missed.

There was a better world out there. I could almost feel it at my fingertips, like a yearning itch under my skin.

"The world's bigger than just me," I said at last. "Once I would have happily run the duke through, but not anymore. If what you need is for me to stay at his side and remember that the people I love are safe in the shadow of his wings, I can do that. I'll even protect him for you."

"Even if he turns out to be far worse than you ever imagined?" she asked, regarding me with warm consideration in her eyes.

"Even then," I said, starting to smile again. "If things change, you know where to find me. Until then..." I flashed her a grin. "I guess I'll dance with him, instead."

Chapter Twenty

BEDTIME RITUALS

T he revel went through dawn, with little diminution. I left before Varistan did; as the host, he had to see it through until his guests left – at least the important ones – but my duty was to him, not to his guests, and I didn't want to have to prepare him for bed while wearing a spider-silk dress.

Even though it wasn't really mine, and had never been meant to be mine, I felt a sense of loss when I set it aside to be cleaned. For one night, I'd been a Someone, even if only by dint of being dressed like one. But Ruekh's night was over, and I wasn't Varistan's equal anymore. I wasn't anything special; just one more mortal bondservant, doing her duty.

Luckily for me, Varistan arrived not long after I'd changed into something simple and gotten the rack set up to put his decorative armor on, so I didn't have time to brood about it. He didn't offer any commentary, merely moseying over and presenting himself to be undressed for bed, and I got to work.

I couldn't stop thinking about the beautiful dress, though, nor about the reaction the fae nobility had shown. Maybe Lianka would tell me... but what if she didn't know the details? Would anyone, aside from Varistan himself?

Buck up, Bells, I scolded myself. *You have a captive audience. Just ask.* Out loud, I said, "May I ask a question?"

He made a soft sound of amusement. "You just did. But, yes, you may ask another."

My cheeks warmed as I blushed. "That... dress," I said, not really sure if I wanted the answer. "Who was it... made for? And, um..."

Varistan raised one brow as I paused, my fingers stilling. "Yes?"

Nothing for it.

"Well... why did you give it to me?" I bit my lip, staring at the clasps under my fingers. "It made a bit of a... splash."

He exhaled a laugh, tilting his head back as I returned to the task of freeing him from his armor. "It wasn't intended for another, if that's your concern," he said, sounding relaxed and content. "It's quite old, actually. Enchanted against decay. I bought it only a few decades after I'd been given Nyx Shaeras, imagining I might give it to whoever I chose to make my duchess, assuming it fit her and she liked it."

When I stopped dead again, staring at him in blank shock, he only laughed and ruffled my hair.

"Don't look so appalled, Isabela. If nearly dying taught me anything, it's that there's little reason to deny oneself the small pleasures of life." Varistan rolled his shoulders once I lifted off the weight of his ornamental armor, stretching his wings. "It gave me no enjoyment while it hung entombed in a wardrobe, and it amused me to put a spitfire mortal in a dress suitable for a fae warrior-Queen, especially on Ruekh's night." He glanced sidelong at me, with a flirtatious smirk. "And you looked spectacular in it, which I also appreciated."

I flushed again, cheeks hot. "I suppose that makes sense," I said, trying not to react to his appreciation of my appearance. Varistan's brush with mortality had given him a view into how easily life could end; I understood wanting to enjoy life to the hilt in the face of that. It was still an outrageous thing to do... but it wasn't as if luxury was any good when packed away in a box.

Though I suppose it would have to go back into its box, now that the fun had been had.

I came back over to undo the ties on his sleeves. "Who do I return it to? Your steward?"

"There ought to be enough space in your wardrobe for it," Varistan said, sounding amused. "No need to make Sintuviel lock it up again."

I almost choked on my tongue at that. "You— You can't mean— Varistan, you could *sell* it!" I stammered out, tightening the knot I'd been trying to untie. "It has to be worth a *fortune!*"

"It is," he said blithely, apparently unbothered. "The dagger, too. But they've been mine for a long time, and I don't wish to part from them." The duke smiled at me, stretching again as I hauled the rest of his clothing over to the rack. "As you're mine, too, and as I much prefer seeing you in a dress to wearing one myself, I'm pleased for it to be yours."

I set his clothing onto the rack, lingering at the task, with no idea of how to respond. It didn't seem out-of-character for Varistan to be extravagant or demonstrative, but I couldn't keep circling back to the fact that I was human. He didn't *like* people like me. He didn't want us in Faery at all. How could he look at me and say something like that, as if I'd be standing by his side for the rest of eternity?

"I didn't intend to cause you unhappiness," he said in a soft voice. When I turned to look at him, he'd sprawled out on his bed, propping his head up on his knuckles. Varistan gave me a lazy smile. "Trouble, perhaps, but you told me you like trouble."

"Well, you certainly caused trouble," I said, keeping my voice dry as I hopped onto the bed behind him and started separating his hair to braid it for the night. "Might I suggest reconciling with Lord Sairal?"

Varistan snarled, the sound raising gooseprickles up my arms with a feeling of anticipatory desire, like watching a predator preparing to attack. "He's getting what he deserves."

I rolled my eyes, though privately I was glad I never had to see the man again. "He grabbed me by the wrist and said a few mean words."

"He accosted you in my home," Varistan said, clipping the edges of the words in his anger. "I may have to tolerate the cruelties bandied behind my back, but I *will not* tolerate that disrespect being leveled at *you*."

"Varistan—"

"No." He turned his head to flash a smile at me, as if trying to take the sting out of the denial. "I'm allowed to choose to be protective of what's mine. I've protected my people for as long as I've had them, and I certainly won't stop when it comes to you."

I remembered Alpha saying, *"He may hate us, but he won't let anyone harm us."*

Varistan didn't hate me, though. I wasn't sure what he felt about me, aside from possessiveness and an enjoyment of playing with me, but he certainly didn't hate me. If he defended those he loathed against all harm, how much more someone like me?

I knew a losing battle when I saw one.

"If you say so," I said, tying off his hair and tucking it away into a silk hair-wrap. I scooted around him and picked up his warm hand to blunt his claws with cotton. "I suppose I can be glad that you didn't immolate him on the spot."

He burst out laughing, a bright sound that made me grin. "I honestly didn't consider it," he admitted, tipping my chin up with the side of one finger to show me his own broad smile. "My instinct when leaping to someone's defense is to draw my sword, as I've had a sword for far longer than dragonfire. Besides," Varistan added, with a bit of a smirk. "Think of what a shame it would have been to scorch that lovely dress."

I shook my head, putting his gloves on him. "It is a very lovely dress, though I have no idea when I'll ever have a chance to wear it again."

"Next feast cycle, of course." Varistan flopped down onto his back, one leg bent and one arm over his head in a position that made me want to drag my eyes down his powerful body, and then maybe to drag my tongue up it. "If you're nice to me, maybe I'll even dance with you at the revel."

"If you're nice to *me*, maybe you can get another dance before then," I said, shaking my head as I tidied up.

He smiled at me, slow and full of wickedness. "How nice?"

"Whatever you're thinking?" I told him as I sauntered towards my bedroom. "*Not* that."

CHAPTER TWENTY-ONE

DEEP WATERS

Any hope I'd cherished that people would overlook Varistan's behavior at the Feast of Ruekh went out the window as soon as I walked into the training grounds that afternoon. Every eye turned towards me, one of the pairs of duelists even stopping their match to watch me.

I scowled at them and stomped over to the bench where Lianka waited, crossing my arms as people started whispering. "I'm not fucking him," I snapped at them all, irritated. "I had no idea the dress had a whole damn history. And he's a fucking *war-dragon*, for Ruekh's sake; of course he's going to fight anyone who messes with his property. Any other questions I can head off at the pass?"

Tjarrek started laughing, resting his elbow on his sparring partner. "Wake up on the wrong side of the duke's bed, Bells?"

"I can and will beat the shit out of you," I said, still wearing my scowl. "I'm not the duke's play-pretty, and I'm not his pet. There's no big secret. So you can all go back to whacking each other with swords."

Lianka elbowed me, grinning when I snapped her a sharp look. "Lighten up, sourpuss. Better yet, go stab someone with a spear." She turned her attention back out to the training grounds, raising her voice. "Any volunteers to get the shit beaten out of them by the duke's favorite mortal?"

That got a few more laughs, and people started returning to their activities, apparently satisfied. A pair of fae glanced at each other before raising their hands.

"Up for two-on-one?" one asked.

Two-on-one was pretty brutal at the best of times, let alone when it was two fae on one mortal. What the hell, though. It would get my blood moving.

"Sure," I said, relaxing a little as the familiar sounds of the training grounds started up again. "Why not?"

Several hours later and a decent amount of blood lighter, I headed back up to the duke's suite for my usual duties. Varistan seemed more stressed than usual, not even bothering to flirt with me. It was a bit of a shock to find out I *missed* the flirtation, feeling almost like a girl who'd been snubbed by her beau. I supposed it was nice to get looked at like I was worth admiring, even by a fae nobleman. Not a lot of people looked at me like that, these days.

When I asked about what was troubling him, he brushed me off, his voice clipped and ears pinned back. It wasn't worth the battle, and while I had a sneaking suspicion there was more fallout to his little display of pique the night before than simply people wanting to stare at me, Varistan obviously didn't want to share.

That was fine with me. My job was no longer to try to gather information about the political circles the duke walked in, but to willingly stay at his side. He'd surely weathered political storms before, and I suspected my usefulness in the realm of fae politics would be worse than none.

His temper didn't improve over the course of the next fortnight, which was a lot more troubling than one evening of unhappiness. But every attempt to get him to tell me anything got a waspish response at best, and nobody else I knew in Nyx Shaeras seemed to know what was getting under his skin—let alone how to get him to stop being such a pain in my ass.

Sixteen days in, I was on the verge of snapping. Varistan spent nearly two hours trying on and rejecting outfits, then had the gall to get pissed at *me* for the fact that he'd be late to the dextral moon dinner he was having with a visiting lord. I put away his clothing while entertaining fantasies of stabbing him in the night, then decided I was done being his whipping girl.

Whatever was going on had started after the Feast of Ruekh, which meant it was obviously connected to me, and almost certainly to him stabbing and banishing Lord Sairal. He wouldn't talk to me, and he seemed determined to deal with the aftermath himself, but at the very least I wanted to know what he was dealing with. I probably wouldn't be able to help, but I would *know*, and that might make it more bearable to weather his temper, night after night.

He's anxious, my thoughts whispered to me as I picked the lock to his office. *You saw what he's like when he's angry. Varistan's scared.*

All the more reason to find out what's happening, I told my worries, shutting the door behind me and padding over to his desk.

The thing was massive; an ancient roll-top made of dark wood, the grain so fine that you almost couldn't tell it was wood. It was also locked, but the age of the desk worked against it, and I had the latch open almost before I'd put the picks in.

There were benefits to living in the underbelly of the world before getting dumped into a duke's lap. I had all sorts of interesting skills, and I doubted it would even occur to Varistan that I knew how to pick locks.

I'd never been allowed into Varistan's office before, but everything about it felt like him. The walls were lined with old bookcases that had glass doors protecting the gilded covers of the books, and the windows looked out across the courtyard of the castle, a view that I was willing to bet he loved. The pictures on the walls were all naturalistic, in varying styles, and I recognized many of the plants in them, no doubt depicting places in his beloved Nyx Shaeras.

But his desk was where his personality really shone.

It resembled the hoard of a museum curator, with small, valuable objects arranged with exacting care and his supplies and papers set into the nooks of the desk like regimented soldiers. A vial of perfume sat next to a carved stone lotus, with little holes in the center of the flower that showed traces of the liquid. Several books were set in place with silk ribbons between their pages, and he had arranged everything so that he could access anything he needed without moving from his seat.

He was vain, passionate, intelligent, and possessive. I knew Varistan was meticulous, too; the care he took with his appearance told me that, as did the attention to the details of the inner workings of his duchy. He'd turned his desk into a microcosm of the world he loved, filling it with sensuous beauty and setting everything he needed exactly where he wanted it.

Three picture frames caught my eye. They sat in the left corner of the desk; a portrait of himself before the war that showed him leaning against a stone wall with his hand resting on the hilt of his sword, an oil painting of the castle of Nyx Shaeras, and an old-looking gilded frame with only a black piece of paper in it.

I picked up the portrait to study it for a moment, a window into the life he'd once had. It was a beautiful painting, and obviously done well into his adulthood, but the self-possessed man in the picture looked oddly unfinished to me. It was like looking at a photograph of a familiar friend as a child, seeing the person they'd become in the soft-cheeked youth they'd once been. His face was the same, save for the horns, and that flirtatious smirk hadn't changed one bit, but the lean swordsman looking out of the frame at me still seemed incomplete without his wings and claws.

One day, I hope you get another portrait painted, I thought, surprising myself with compassion for the duke. He was clinging to a past he could never have again, and it would only make his life worse in the end. You can't find joy in the clean streets after a storm if all you can think of are the chalk drawings that were washed away.

Maybe it was a good thing he'd given me that dress, after all. At least it was movement towards a different future than the one he'd once dreamed of.

I set the portrait back in place and squashed an impish desire to set it askew, instead spending a few minutes memorizing the placement of everything. If I messed with something, it needed to go back *exactly* where he'd left it, or he would know someone had been in his things. Only once I was fairly sure that I could leave his desk in order did I start going through things.

Very quickly, I learned that Varistan wasn't wasting his time when he locked himself in his office. My human friends had told me stories of instantaneous communication in the mortal world, with machines that let you see each other's faces from thousands of miles away and the ability to write and send letters across the world in seconds, but fae communication was done primarily via handwritten documents. Smaller ones could be sent via flicker-bird, but longer communiques were sent via ground messengers, and often took days or weeks to arrive at their intended destination.

Varistan had at least two dozen conversations ongoing, each with its own folder, annotations, and table of contents listing the dates and two-line summary of the letter in question. At a skim, most of them looked to be economic in nature, which didn't surprise me, but some of them were slow negotiations of favors and social interactions. In several places, Varistan had refused to exchange land for anything, maintaining his duchy despite needing to take a lesser position in the dealings.

One was a drawn-out negotiation of political marriage, with the first letter dated almost a decade ago. An independently wealthy merchant family with no bloodline connections to the nobility, looking for the chance to capitalize on Varistan's loss of fortune to tie themselves to the royal family—and Varistan had been considering it. The last missive from the family had arrived six days after Varistan had brought me to Nyx Shaeras.

He hadn't yet replied.

I set it aside, feeling troubled. Varistan was selling himself instead of his duchy, sacrificing his autonomy and future so that Nyx Shaeras would survive. I didn't like the thought of him being trapped in a marriage with someone who didn't care about anything besides his bloodline. What would it be like for a man like him to be devoted to someone who only wanted to take advantage of him?

I knew how Raven Court treated wildling fae. Had heard the things people said about the Flame of Faery. Would she wash his hair for him? Protect the duchy he loved alongside him?

Would she even touch him?

Not your problem, Bells, I told the roiling in my gut, pulling out the next folder. *You shouldn't even care.*

I forced myself to focus on the papers instead of thinking about Varistan. These ones were annotated in some sort of shorthand or code, but the missives themselves were still written in Faery, though I struggled to parse the dense double-speak being used. The handwriting looked familiar, as did the name—*Xilvaris*. Where did I...

I flipped the page to a document written in Varistan's hand, and remembered, suddenly, poking through the ashes of a letter he'd burned. I'd even summarized it in my fake "journal" page for the human resistance, not yet knowing they didn't want me to do anything of the sort. Xilvaris was a difficult name to transliterate to English, and I'd probably done a bad job, but I remembered thinking that Varistan owed the lord money—

The sound of voices in the hallway cut through my thoughts. I froze, trying to discern if they were a risk to me, and caught the sound of Varistan saying, *"this way, my lord."*

Shit.

I put the file back as quickly as I could, hearing a key slide into the lock on the door of the office. Trying not to make noise, I pulled the roll-top of the desk down, grimacing when I didn't hear the latch click. I didn't have time to lock it; I'd have to hope that Varistan didn't intend to open the damn thing.

Behind me, the doorknob turned.

I dashed across the room to the door of what had to be a supply closet and yanked it open, blessing the gods that it was unlocked. It was full of books and paper supplies, but I managed to wedge myself inside and get the door shut before a beautifully-dressed fae walked in with Varistan at his right shoulder.

I peered through the crack of the door at them, my heart hammering and sweat prickling under my arms. I didn't recognize the lord, though that didn't mean much; I wasn't really one to walk in the circles of the nobility, after all. He was a plain man, his skin a few shades lighter than Varistan's and his mousey brown hair braided back from the sort of average face that fades into the background. The only thing of note was a silvery scar on his cheek, something that looked like a blade-mark from a duel fought with live steel.

"Pretty," he said as he looked out the window, his voice deeper than I expected from such a slight man. "Not as excellent as the ocean view, of course, but not an unpleasant vista."

Varistan's tail lashed. "There's no need for pretending towards affection, my lord," he said, his shoulders tense. "You may speak freely here."

"Oh, may I?" The lord sounded amused, almost mocking; when he turned away from the window, he was smirking. "Let's get right down to business, then. You publicly insulted my representative. Rescind his banishment and welcome him back to Nyx Shaeras. Eat with him at the high table, perhaps."

Varistan stood with his back to me, but I saw his chin lift and wings tuck tighter. "No."

The lord's eyes went hard. "No?" he asked, with a silken edge to the word.

"No, my lord," Varistan said, as if the honorific was physically painful to speak. "Lord Sairal accosted a woman under my protection, insulted me in my own home, and refused to release her when I took offense. Welcoming him back as if all is forgiven would be..." His hands fisted. "...displaying weakness. Surely you wouldn't want that."

The other fae stalked closer. Varistan took a step *back*, as if he was afraid. I'd never imagined that I would see him retreat in the face of anything.

"Perhaps we can reach a different agreement," the lord said, his expression as emotionless as a snake's. "I have other representatives, and other ways to collect what I desire. I've heard dockworkers make good fighters—"

"They're *mine*—" Varistan started.

"Silence that forked tongue of yours," the lord said, voice dripping with disdain. "Stop acting like a war-dragon and act like a man. You took my gold so you didn't have to sell your duchy acre by acre, and you owe me."

Varistan didn't say anything, standing there trembling with rage.

The lord smirked, his body language changing to desultory as he sprawled down in Varistan's desk chair. "You left three dead bodies in Lylvenore, and now the vicereine has her attention where I never wanted it. You ought to be appreciative that I'm not choosing to regard that as a breach in our agreement, given that you were supposed to be managing my affairs there." He licked his lips like a hungry animal, his tongue red and darting. "How much interest do you think I should charge you on my lost income?"

"You would have lost more if I'd died," Varistan said, his hands closing tighter. "Your representative's vices and your commands left me with few options. The risks were yours, Lord Xilvaris, but I'm the one who shed blood for them."

"So shed someone else's blood instead," the lord said airily, waving one hand. "It doesn't even need to be here at the castle, if you dislike it so much. Northport, perhaps—"

"I will *not* pay my debts with the blood of my people," Varistan snarled, his wings mantling. "Keep your filthy bloodsports out of Nyx Shaeras."

Lord Xilvaris stopped moving, his expression going flat. A muscle on his cheek jumped, and he held Varistan's gaze as he stood, eyes cold. "Have you forgotten where you stand in this relationship, Vee?"

Varistan flinched at the casual nickname, the flared spade of his tail flattening. "I have not, my lord," he said, his words clipped.

The lord walked up to him, and with careful deliberation, wrapped his hand around Varistan's throat.

My duke let him do it.

"You knew what I was when you asked me for the coin you needed to keep your *people* fed," Lord Xilvaris said with a sneer. "You sold yourself like a whore, but you keep trying to act like a free man." The slim man leaned forward while my hands shook with anger and fear, heart racing as I watched his fingertips dig into Varistan's skin. "You owe me gold. You owe me recompense. You owe me a *favor*, and I intend to collect."

Varistan just *stood* there, his tail lying on the ground and his wings folded behind him.

Lord Xilvaris released him with a scornful sound. "Pay in gold or pay in blood, Vee," he said, with a dismissive flick of his fingers. "You have until the spring thaw to make things right, or you'll find out just how tightly all those promises bind you." An ugly smile cut across his face. "Say, 'yes, my lord.'"

Varistan's wings furled tightly against his back. "Yes, my lord." He spoke the words like they were physically painful, torn out of his throat because he had no other options.

I wanted to tear out *Xilvaris'* throat. Would have, if it wouldn't have gotten me killed.

If it wouldn't have gotten Varis killed.

"There we go," the lord said, like Varistan was a well-trained dog. "No need to see me out. I know the way." He turned away from Varistan to saunter out the door, his back to a man who surely hated him with no fear that he would be harmed.

I narrowly refrained from leaping out of the closet to stab Lord Xilvaris to death with my belt-knife. Throwing myself at him wouldn't help anyone, let alone Varistan. Surely the lord had documentation of all of this—of whatever debts my duke had put himself into to keep his duchy safe. Killing him wouldn't solve anything.

And Varistan can't want me to know about this, I told myself as Lord Xilvaris walked out of my narrow field of vision. *He's so proud.*

It still made my gut churn to stand there helplessly, knowing that slimy monster was walking away. I made myself look at Varistan, instead, watching as his shoulders drooped and hands uncurled.

His claws were tipped with his own blood.

CHAPTER TWENTY-TWO

COMPASSION

"He's gone, so you can come out," Varistan said, sounding tired. He didn't move from his position, standing facing the door with his wings hanging and tail lying flat on the floor.

I flushed crimson, but there was no point in pretending I was a stack of paper if he already knew I was there. Attempting to look casual instead of guilty, I opened the closet door and stepped out, one arm wrapped around my chest. "I... I didn't mean to... eavesdrop," I said, knowing he had to hate that I'd seen this. "How did you... know?"

Varistan lifted his left hand, one corner of his mouth lifting up into a momentary smile as the golden signet ring he always wore caught the light. "Landed nobility, dukes included, are generally granted seals tied to their land. My connection to Nyx Shaeras isn't nearly as strong as that of the King to the Court, but it's certainly strong enough to know when someone's hiding in a closet next to me."

My cheeks grew hotter, enough that I pressed the backs of my fingers to them to try to cool my embarrassed blaze. "I didn't want to get caught. I was... snooping."

He barked a sharp laugh as he turned towards me, one without any humor in it. The fingerprints of Lord Xilvaris were coming up purple on his throat, dark enough that they had to be bruises. "I'm well aware, Bells."

Even the usual caress on my nickname was gone, his voice exhausted as he took a seat in his desk chair. Varistan lowered his face to his hands, his shoulders hunched. I recognized the pose. I'd seen it on fighters before.

It was the first time I'd seen Varistan Yllaxira, the Duke of Nyx Shaeras, Flame of Faery and royal son, look defeated.

Quietly, I walked over to him and brushed my fingers across the bruises darkening his skin. "Would you like a healer, or cosmetics?" I asked, keeping my voice gentle and running my thumb along his neck. "Nobody else needs to see how he treats you."

Varistan looked up at me with a searching expression, his brows drawn together and lips parted. "Does it matter?"

"Of course it matters," I said, sliding my fingers into his hair.

His eyelashes fluttered as I started rubbing my fingers against his scalp, and Varistan leaned the smallest fraction into my touch with a soft sound of pleasure—almost a whimper. "You need not comfort me," he said at a whisper, even as his expression softened and tail curled around my feet. "I've survived far worse alone."

"Do you want to survive this alone?" I took out the pins in his hair and combed my fingers through his loose curls, careful not to yank but not shying away from letting him feel the movement of my hands.

"No," he said, striking eyes closing as he put an arm around my waist. Varistan tugged me close, his warmth soaking into my side, and shuddered when he turned and rested his face against my stomach. "Gods," he whispered, his whole body slumped. "I would have rather you not known anything about this, but it's such a mercy to have you here in the aftermath."

That startled me; I wouldn't have expected him to be at all glad to have me nosing around his affairs, let alone seeing someone abuse him without punishment. But maybe it was just the comfort of having someone – anyone – to share the burden with, after years of silent endurance. Even the greatest of mountains are worn down by the rain.

"Any port in a storm, your grace?" I asked, looking down at him.

He only wrapped his other arm around me in an embrace, tail curved in an arc on the floor around my feet and wings limp.

I could feel him trembling. I recognized that, too—the viciousness of an adrenaline drop, leaving you shaky and anxious, with weariness pressing in on you from every direction. I'd faced down terrifying foes before, but I'd always been armed and prepared. No one had ever cornered me in my home, or gloated in the fact that they could do whatever they wanted to me.

That oil-slick voice, saying, *You owe me a favor, and I intend to collect.* Fingers on his neck. Varistan, the man I'd seen fight with the beauty and brutality of an ermine, standing there with the same despair as one facing execution.

"How would you feel about a bath?" I ventured, feeling my cheeks warm at the boldness of the suggestion, no matter that it was literally my job.

His arms tightened on me. "I prefer this to being alone with my thoughts," he said, voice muffled by my clothing. "You won't get rid of me so easily."

I smiled at that, both at his misunderstanding and at his utter lack of subtlety. Maybe some of that was simply because he didn't care to pussyfoot around with me, or because he could simply command me to stand here and let him hug me, but it still amused me. If I'd been the sort of person to fake physical affection for the sake of manipulation, I could have had him wrapped around my fingers with ease.

"I'm offering to bathe you, your grace, not to stick you in a cold tub and leave you there." My amusement came out in my voice, and Varistan stilled.

"Wh-wha— W-what—" he started, going stiff as he stuttered, his tail tightening around my ankles. Varistan pulled back enough to look up at me, shocked and tense. "You d—don't like that—"

Smiling, I ruffled his hair. "It's cute when that stutter comes out to play," I said, but relented when his skin darkened and he looked away with obvious shame. "There's no need for unhappiness," I said, returning to stroking my fingers through his maroon curls. "I meant it as an honest compliment, your grace. I enjoy the times when you're more like a person than a duke."

His fingers tightened on me, claws pricking me through my clothing. He didn't look back up at me. "It took me a great many years to ta—tame it," Varistan said with care, flinching when he still got caught on the word. "I still... struggle... when I'm... upset, or startled."

"I always seem to like the parts of you that you dislike, don't I?" I mused, not really expecting an answer. Then I shook my head, looking back down at him, and at my pale olive skin against the dark red of his hair. No human ever born had hair like that, rich true red, and I could almost imagine the fingers I pulled through those striking curls were fae. It unsettled, but less than it once had. I wasn't sure if that was good or bad.

Varistan didn't say anything and he didn't move, holding me with arms and tail, his breath making a warm patch on my belly.

"Come away," I said at last. "Sprawl in some water that's slightly less cold than you prefer, and make salacious comments while I bathe you."

He barked another laugh at that, pressing his face against me for a moment before rolling his head to the side and looking up at me through his dark lashes. "It won't be... unpleasant... for you?" he asked, sounding wary.

"No," I said, a little surprised that it was true. But I felt badly for him, and I'd mostly gotten used to having his naked body on display. It couldn't be as bad as sleeping naked next to him. "I'd like to."

"I will surely want to luxuriate," he warned, starting to disentangle himself from me.

"If you luxuriate long enough, maybe your bathwater will be warm enough that I'll use it after you," I said, smirking at him.

His eyes flashed, ears lifting and tilting forward in pointed interest. "Don't tempt me." Varistan stood up, wings mantling as he leaned towards me, with barely inches between us. He ran his fingers down along my jaw, examining me with a predator's focus. "I suspect I would do a great deal to have my scent and claim on you in such a way."

I raised my brows, not moving away from him.

With a sultry smile, Varistan lowered his face towards mine, eyes half-lidded and breath hot. "My sense of smell may only be a little better than yours, but I know your scent, and I know mine," he said with the edge of a masculine growl. "And I am *possessive*."

I leaned into the halo of his heat until my breasts brushed against his chest, the thrill of danger shivering across my skin as I bared my neck for him. "Are you going to mark me, then?" I asked, my pulse racing. "Rub your scent on me like a cat marking his territory? I'll let you."

Varistan's expression sharpened, nostrils flaring, but instead of taking the invitation he straightened, looking down at me with what looked like anxiety tensing his face. "You, you, you—" He stopped, gritting his teeth. "You're playing with me."

Wearing a grin, I stepped back and held out my hand to him. "And you're all bark and no bite," I said with smug satisfaction. "Come on, your grace. Save the byplay for when you're naked and I'm more easily flustered."

"I've been known to bite," he said, a little sulkily, though he took my hand and let me lead him out of his office. "Both when overwrought and for the sake of passion. I could bite you if I desired it."

He sounded so childish and petulant that I had to laugh, shaking my head with amusement as I drew him up the stairs. "'Can' and 'will' are very different things, as I'm sure you're well aware. I'm not at all frightened of your fangs, your grace."

He followed me with a disgruntled sound; I could hear his wings rustling as he resettled them. The duke didn't complain, though, and I brought us up to his suite along familiar paths. It took until I turned into my room for me to realize that I'd brought him up the servant's stair without thinking, but Varistan didn't give me any commentary. He walked at my right shoulder, his warm fingers laced through mine and his footsteps steady, acting as comfortable as if we'd gone up the grand staircases he usually trod.

Maybe he thought I'd done it on purpose, in order to keep him out of the public eye, or maybe he was simply too interested in our destination to risk irritating me. Either way, I appreciated the silence in the face of my blunder. No matter how many times I reminded myself that Varistan was a fae duke and I was a human bondservant, I couldn't shake my ease around him. It was so comfortable to be in his presence, even though I knew better. Sometimes I felt like I'd known him forever.

When we stepped into his bathroom, Varistan sighed and let my fingers slip out of his. "I keep feeling as if I should check again that this isn't an imposition," he said, sounding embarrassed. "It's been a long time since someone has offered me kindness when they couldn't use it against me later."

"Benefit of having a bondservant, I suppose," I replied, bending over to turn on the water to hide the way that quiet statement made my heart pound. "How warm can I run it before it won't be pleasant anymore?"

"As long as it feels cool for you, I think it will still feel comfortable for me." He came up beside me, his fingers trailing up my spine as he started looking through his bath oils.

The light touch sent a silvery feeling through me, almost enough to make me shiver. My pulse picked up, my cheeks warming. It didn't mean anything—but filling a bath for a man while he stood next to me with his hand resting casually on the back of my neck still *felt* like it should mean something.

Varistan pulled two bottles off the rack and poured a little of each into the bathwater before bending down and dipping his fingers into the water. I thought he was testing the temperature until he tilted my head to the side and ran his wet fingers up along my throat to behind my ears.

"There," he said in a low voice rough with desire, dragging his fingers through the sheen of oil on the water again before running them up the other side of my neck. "You may not be sharing my bathwater, but for tonight we'll share the same scent." His hot breath fanned against my face, his mouth close enough to mine that I could have leaned up to kiss him. The crimson of his eyes narrowed as his pupils dilated and eyes dropped to my parted lips. "I have *some* bite."

I had to swallow, my traitorous body salivating from that look on his face. "I'll believe it when I feel it."

He chuckled, a warm sound, running his thumb across my cheek. "While I certainly could bite you, given how very much I won't want to stop at that, unless you're inviting far more than a taste I think I'll refrain."

Heat thudded between my legs, my pulse suddenly a demanding presence. There was no hope of hiding my reaction from Varistan, either; he was far too socially adept and my cheeks far too hot for him to miss the effect his words had.

"Are you interested, Bells?" he asked with a smirk, all but rumbling the words. "Or are you merely... reactive?"

"Not as reactive as you, your grace," I said, snatching at my dignity and making myself stand. "Recall why you have a human body-servant, and not fae."

Varistan dragged his gaze up along my body before he stood, running his forked tongue along one of his long canines. "Because I claimed her," he purred at me, heat in his eyes. "Because she's *mine*." He leaned towards me, breathing hard, his wings mantling. "Because I wanted her here with me."

I hummed at that, his possessiveness far easier for me to deal with than him acting like a lover. If he'd meant to keep me off-balance, he'd misjudged the situation.

Holding his gaze with a smirk, I started undoing the buttons on his doublet, letting my fingers brush against his chest. "I'm sure you'll agree that I'm very obedient, your grace," I said in a placid voice, grinning when he snorted. "Can't you think of any other reasons?"

"None that I prefer," Varistan said, closing his eyes and tilting his head back with a soft smile as I took off his shirt, clearly enjoying being taken care of. "Human or not, it pleases me to have you here."

A dragon and his hoard, I thought, with a touch of humor. Though Varistan had never tried to control my interactions with other people, I knew he coveted my time and attention. That would probably only get worse—but, despite everything, I didn't mind. It wasn't as if our lives were likely to diverge until my death, so what was the harm in a little possessiveness?

Besides, it meant I could snoop in his office with relative impunity. I ought to be glad for that. But looking up at my duke as he relaxed under my hands, I couldn't help the twist of guilt in my gut. He wasn't innocent, but neither was he the monster I'd originally imagined. Did he deserve the bruises on his neck? The loneliness of his cold bed?

Had he earned any of this?

I didn't know. But there was more to the Duke of Nyx Shaeras than beauty and dragonfire, and I wanted to learn it all.

Chapter Twenty-Three

RELAXATION

I 'd never dared to tease the duke with sex right before bathing him. I knew his touch-sensitivity made such a game rather more dangerous—and not because I feared him losing control. I was prone to making stupid decisions when it came to gorgeous, deadly people who wanted to kiss me, even when they were otherwise terrible. That went doubly so when the sum total of my orgasms came from my own fingers, and I hadn't had sex since coming to Nyx Shaeras, and a good distance before.

So pulling off Varistan's underthings to discover that an aroused male dragon – even one with his cock firmly inside his body – had slick to rival a woman... well, it was all I could do to keep the immediate fantasy of running my tongue up his wet slit within the realm of my imagination.

Gods, I could fucking *smell* him, the warm musk and sharp copper of his natural scent laced with a brighter tone, something almost like saffron. The Flame of Faery, wet from scent-marking me, my face close enough to his groin that all I would have to do would be to sit up a little on my knees to taste him. If he wanted to have me—

But he doesn't, I told myself, grabbing hold of my runaway sex drive like a kennel-master scruffing an unruly puppy. *He just likes playing the game. Even if he actually did, he's a prejudiced, arrogant ass who benefits from the suffering of people like you.*

And yet, here I was trying to comfort him, and not for any selfish reason. I'd seen enough of him to know that there was something else there than his political reputation, and I suspected he had the potential to become more than what he'd shown the world thus far. I wasn't inclined to take it upon myself to try to fix him, but if he was willing to do the work on his own, I didn't mind giving him opportunities.

Varistan didn't seem to notice my lack of aplomb, stepping out of his under-things and into the bath. His tail brushed along my side as he settled into the water, the spade flaring against my arm for a moment before he used it to turn off the water.

The sudden silence, broken only by the small splashes as Varistan got comfortable, made the pounding of my heart seem audible. A moment later, his fingers brushed my shoulder, and I jumped guiltily, dropping his boxer-briefs onto the floor. I felt him flinch back, my face growing hot.

"You need not do this," he said, sounding the way dogs look when they cringe away from a cruel master. "I will... be alright. Eventually."

Taking a deep breath, I turned, trying to smile for him. He met my eyes with nervousness in his, an answering smile tugging at one corner of his mouth hopefully.

"I haven't done this before," I admitted, a far preferable confession to telling him that I was currently fantasizing about licking his slick off his underwear. The last thing in the world I needed was for Varistan to know how ridiculously horny I got when I didn't have anyone to burn off the sexual energy with. He would have far too much fun playing with me.

Varistan tucked a curling strand of hair behind his ear, looking self-conscious. "Bathed someone?"

"Yeah," I said, making myself laugh. "Not even children. I admit to a measure of nervousness."

"You need not—"

"—do it, I know," I finished, tugging off my shirt to force myself to move. I chucked it to the side and draped myself on the bathmat next to the tub, reaching over Varistan to grab his loofah sponge.

His eyes skimmed down the line of my throat to my breasts, resting there for a moment before flicking back up to my face. "Are you planning on joining me, Bells?"

"I'm planning on not getting my clothes wet," I said, regaining a bit of my aplomb. "Do you have a scent preference for the soap?"

Varistan settled lower into the water, his lashes drifting down over his eyes as he relaxed. "Surprise me," he murmured, reaching up to brush the scaled backs of his fingers along my arm. "I believe that I could use a short respite where I don't have to be the one making the decisions."

"I could give you that," I offered, skimming down the apothecary labels of his extensive collection. "I think I know your tastes well enough to pick out your clothing, as long as I know the event. Baths, too."

A smile touched the corners of his mouth. "Perhaps I'll take you up on that sometime."

My fingers drifted to a vial of oil with the label for saltwood resin, thinking about the way Varistan had stood in the storm, as wild as the lands he'd been given. After a moment, I added spruce and musk, lathering the scents between two bars of soap before scrubbing the loofah across them. The mixture wasn't quite the same as the scent in the forest, but it reminded me of it, and I hoped it would remind Varistan of the things he loved, and the reasons why he endured.

His body softened under my touch as I started lathering his skin. Even though I'd never bathed someone else before, it wasn't difficult to figure out, and it gave me the chance to explore Varistan's body with more than my eyes. His arms were strong, the muscles defined—not with the bulk of a laborer, but with the streamlined perfection of a world-class fencer. Those long-fingered hands were a pleasure to touch, the scales along the backs of his hands re-minding me of gauntlets and his obsidian-sharp claws gleaming and beautiful.

Varistan started breathing faster as I washed his chest, his back arching to press himself harder against my hands and a line appearing between his brows. It made me want to run my hands down those tense abs, feel the steely strength of his body and the tempting expanse of his smooth skin. The pace of my breathing picked up with his as I washed slow circles down his body, luxuriating in touching him.

It was my job, after all. Surely no one could take me to task for doing my *job*, no matter that it made my nipples tingle or my pulse pound between my legs.

He let out a panting breath as I dragged the sponge back up his midline to his shoulders. Before I could start on his back, Varistan grabbed my wrist, his face tensed with the battle between pleasure and discomfort. "Maybe you should... stop," he said in a rough voice, sounding reluctant. He looked up at me, his expression hazed and wanting. "I... I may be too touch-sensitive for this. It's been... a long time," Varistan added, sounding shamefaced.

"Stop for my sake, or for yours?" I asked, blushing slightly as he looked at me like he wanted me to give him oblivion.

"Yours." He swallowed, looking away. "I don't know that I'll be able to keep my reactions to physical enjoyment dampened, and I don't want to upset you. And... and mine," he said, his skin darkening with embarrassment. "I get a great deal of comfort from touch, but I also have a great deal of greed for it. I suspect if you finish bathing me, I'm going to want to get out of this tub and crawl into bed with you to be held, and that's..." Varistan broke off, his whole face flashing into unhappiness. "I've been told that's the behavior of a child."

I sat back on my heels, regarding him. Whoever had told him that had said it often enough to make it a wall around his heart, but he clearly didn't believe it enough to state it as bald fact. It wrenched at my emotions. What was it about the world that made gentle things such targets for malevolence? Why do we always have to wear armor around those who hold us closest?

"As long as you don't injure me, I don't think I'm going to be upset by you feeling nice," I said at last, thinking about Lianka telling me that his fae body-servants had found his physicality intolerable. "And, given that you're wearing bruises on your neck for refusing to force your people into blood-sports, if what you'd like after is to lie in bed being held, we can do that, too."

His garnet eyes darted across my face, searching my expression. "You don't think it's childish?"

"I don't, but who cares if it is?" I asked, resting my arms on the edge of the tub. "There's enough misery in the world that it's worth claiming joy where you can find it. I like blowing soap-bubbles and I sleep with the same stuffed animal my mom gave me when I was three." I flashed him a grin. "If anything's childish, it's having people boss you around. You're a three-thousand-year-old duke. It's high time you stopped being so docile."

Varistan burst out laughing at the absurdity of that statement, pushing himself up to look me in the eyes. "'Docile'? I think you may have the wrong duke in mind, Bells."

I booped him on the nose with one finger, smirking at the look of indignation it sparked. "Tamest duke I've ever met."

He exhaled a curl of flame, his lips turning up into a playful smile. "As I believe I'm the only duke you've ever met, would that not also make me the wildest one?"

Playful was a great deal better than despair or self-consciousness. I approved of it. "Let me bathe you, your grace. We'll see how wild you are."

"Is that not bossing me around?" he asked, leaning forward so that he was bare inches away, his breath warming my skin. "Perhaps I should bathe you, instead."

My eyebrows shot up in disbelief, a startled laugh escaping my lips. "You'd make a worse bondservant than *me*, and that's saying something."

Varistan wrapped a strand of my hair around his wet fingers and gave it a tug, a very self-satisfied expression settling onto his face. "That suggests wildness more than docility, does it not?" he asked. Running his tongue along the tip of his canine, the duke swept his gaze down my body, lingering on my curves and the flat planes of my stomach. "I would enjoy seeing you unclad again, and running my hands down a woman's body is a pleasure I greatly miss, even for platonic pursuits. I could insist."

I blessed my bra for hiding my hardening nipples as I tipped his face back up to mine, my skin tingling with anticipatory desire. Those warm, sword-strong hands, skimming down my body again before sliding between my thighs, his dragon-hot breath stirring my hair, lips brushing my ear—

Gods and monsters, Bells, pull yourself together.

"If you want to see me naked, all you have to do is join us on rising days for some sparring. I shower with the soldiers, and it's about as sexy as getting scrubbed down by a healer," I informed him, struggling to maintain my stern expression in the face of the pure wickedness dancing in Varistan's eyes. "You don't need to prove to me that you're capable of being naughty. Believe me, I'm quite aware of that fact."

He laughed again, sitting back up and turning to put his back to me. "Wash my wings for me. If you're untroubled by my reactions to that, I suspect you won't desire to flee my presence for anything else a typical bath might spark."

"As you desire, your grace," I said, shaking my head with a smile.

Varistan leaned forward, resting his head on his folded arms, with his arms on top of his bent knees. I started scrubbing the scales of his back, working my way out along his shoulders and down his spine. They were almost plates of armor along his spine, with barely any flex, but the others shifted atop his muscles with more fluidity.

"How much can you feel through these?" I asked, daring to run my finger down along his spine.

"More than you might imagine," he said in a thick voice, shivering as I reached his hips. "Not the sort of sensations skin possesses, but dragonscale is sensitive to the pressure of air and to changes in temperature. I can feel—" Varistan panted as I stroked my hand back up along his spine. "I can feel it when the storms come in, or when someone moves behind me." His tail snaked over the edge of the bath, flared enough that I could see a hint of the secondary spade. "I can feel your heat and the pressure of your hand when you touch me."

"Do you like it?" I asked, not that I needed an answer.

"Very much," Varistan said, the words husky.

"Hand me the soap, then," I said with a smile.

He did, passing it to me with a shaky hand. "What are you going to do with that?"

"I'm going to wash your wings." I ran the bar of soap down along the arm of his wing, following it with my other hand to serve as a gentle scrub.

Varistan gasped out a soft *"oh"*, his wing spreading out across the tub. His breathing grew more labored as I washed his limb by hand, a process that left my skin tingling and flushed. Slowly, not wanting to startle him, I stroked the soap out along the membrane of his wing, running my hand down along the other side to give me something to put pressure against.

His back arched, head falling back and mouth open with pleasure as he panted, long canine teeth bared. Trembling from the sensation of having my slippery hands running along his skin, he shifted his wing for me, spreading each section of membrane so I could wash it. There was a lot of skin to wash; Varistan had a remarkable wingspan, and those beautiful broad wings didn't fit in a tub.

"If you stand, I'll be able to do the bottom of your wings," I said in a low murmur.

"I don't know that—*oh, oh*—don't know that I—can," Varistan got out, moaning as I ran my fingers down the outer edge of his wing. He held up one hand, showing me how shaky he was. "Feels too—good."

I smiled at that, feeling rather pleased with myself. It didn't really matter that anyone doing this would have had the same response. None of them had been willing to, and I was. "On your knees, then."

He jerked his chin down into a nod and wobbled his way up onto his knees, bracing himself against the back wall. His tail, no longer constrained, wrapped around my waist and thigh, the fully-flared spade caressing my leg.

"S-s-s-sorry," he said in a breathy moan, even as his tail tightened on me, water dripping down my bare skin and soaking through my pants. "Can't—can't—can't—"

"Shh, it's okay," I said, working my slow way down the lower half of his wings, my pulse pounding and a demanding fantasy of closing my thighs around his tail and rubbing myself off against his scales intruding on my thoughts. "I don't mind. Guess I'm getting my clothes wet, after all." *In more ways than one.*

Varistan held himself there, breathing hard with his claws slowly gouging lines into the tiles on the back wall. It didn't even necessarily seem sexual for him. He simply was touch-sensitive, the raw tactile pleasure of having the delicate skin of his wings hand-washed leaving him a panting, needy mess. That was hot as dragonfire for me, but he reminded me of nothing so much as a cat receiving such a good petting that he drew blood kneading the lap of the person providing him enjoyment.

"Are you drooling yet?" I teased as I ran my hand across his wing.

"Not... yet," he moaned out, back arching and head hanging. His tail-spade flattened and flared in a brief rhythm against me before wrapping around my ankle like ivy.

"Oh, too bad," I said, still with a lilt of a tease. "I thought I was making you fall apart here." I kept washing him with the same slow care, framing one of the ribs of his wing with two fingers as I slowly stroked down along it.

"S-s-stroke my tail, *gods*, if that's the de—sire—" He whimpered, his wings shaking, unable to continue speaking as I kept touching him. His stupid tail slid up between my legs, a movement that brought his scales so close to my core that I could feel his warmth radiating through my pants.

"I've been warned against that," I said with heat, struggling not to tilt my hips the tiny fraction it would take to press my clit against the powerful muscle of his tail. "I have a whole list of wicked things never to do to my touch-sensitive duke."

"Good, or... bad...?" Varistan said between tiny sounds of pleasure.

I grinned at his back. He wasn't at all keeping his aplomb, but I liked that he was still trying to play with me. "Unclear. I think the assumption was that pissing you off and turning you on were both equally bad." I finished his wing and tousled his hair in a friendly gesture. "Wings done, your grace, and I think we've come through unscathed. Shall I do your legs and tail, and you can rinse off with a quick shower?"

He lowered himself down to sit on his heels, thighs visibly shaking, loosening his grasp on me as he did. "Do you think... that?" he asked, still breathing hard. Varistan turned to look over his shoulder at me, self-consciousness tensing the skin around his eyes. "That... that my interest is as unpleasant as my ire?"

My expression softened at the sight of the unhappiness in his. "No, of course not," I said, trying to be gentle with him. "But things that arouse you should really only be done with your permission, don't you think?"

The past eighty years couldn't have been easy for him, though a great deal of that was the company he surrounded himself with. He always had to know that he was disposable—the one acceptable aberration in a company of so-called purebloods, and only there on sufferance.

His solution had been distancing himself from the people Lord Xilvaris and his ilk wanted eradicated, turning himself into their enforcer. Mine was a great deal different.

Varistan sprawled back down into the tub, keeping his eyes on mine. "I think I would gladly welcome such violence for the proof that I was still desirable," he said, pain flickering across his face. "I loved being beautiful. Reveled in it. Sarcaryn's grace rested lightly on my shoulders, and I stepped through so many of the doors it opened without caring for those who couldn't follow." His lips twitched downwards, deep unhappiness showing itself for a heartbeat. "I suppose that speaks poorly of me."

I tried to smile, the expression coming out pitying. "That speaks poorly of the world, your grace. Having an 'acceptable' appearance shouldn't be what lets someone move through society."

He heaved a sigh, closing his eyes as I started scrubbing his foot with the loofah. "I didn't question it when I had it," he said, sounding as if he was talking to himself. "Of course I was desired. Of course people strove to gain my interest, no matter the circumstances. I took pleasure in being unattainable." Varistan shivered as I moved up his leg, his tail shifting underwater. "'The Flame of Faery'," he said, with an edge of disgust. "I didn't understand what I possessed until it was lost forever."

"I think a lot of the benefits of our birth are like that." I rested my hand on his knee, looking into his face. "It's easy to think you've earned what you gained from being born. After all, every peacock spends hours preening his tail for display. Surely the sparrows just need to work a little harder." I looked down at my hands, unpleasant memories settling in my gut like mud. "Even us sparrows judge each other for the drabness of our feathers."

"You're not a sparrow, Bells." When I raised my brow at him for that, Varistan flashed me a smile. "If I'm a peacock, surely you're at least a peahen," he said, sounding amused. "You may be a bit more drab than I," he added, tugging on a strand of his blood-red hair, "but you're certainly loud enough to join me among the peafowl."

"Hah!" I shook my head, laughing despite myself. "Whatever you say, your grace. Shall I wash your thighs and groin, or would you prefer I not?"

A shiver ran down Varistan's body, his hips tilting and head turning to the side to bare his neck. "You may," he said, his voice dropping to a lower register, "but I suspect I'll enjoy it more thoroughly than you intend."

"Is this a biting situation, then?" I asked, running my eyes down along the tense muscle of his thigh.

His tail curled, the tip breaking the surface. Studs stood up down the length of it for at least two handspans. I recognized them from when I'd yanked his hair that first night and had to swallow, desire making my skin tingle. That tail told me everything I needed to know about where his thoughts had turned. And he was lying here naked, sprawled on his back with his legs spread—

"I've never had sex with a human," Varistan said shakily, sliding one hand between his legs to cover his slit. "And I— I haven't at all, not since... this." He looked at me, lust warring with disgust on his face, his pupils dilated and face drawn with desire. "I want it, and I... don't." Varistan licked his lips, expression tormented. "But it feels very good to be desired again."

I regarded him for a moment, my own desire cut off at the knees by pity, then patted him on his leg. "Turn around, your grace, and give me your other leg. I can appreciate your beauty without being a predator."

He obeyed, moving with reluctant grace. "Even if I give you permission?"

"Even with permission," I said, picking up his other foot. "Remember the millennia set in front of you, and don't allow the longings of the present steal them from you." I looked down at the gleaming black scales under my hands, a dragon's body given to a man, and sorrow for him tugged at my heart. Even though there was nothing wrong with the body he had, it wasn't any easier for him to come to terms with it than any other amputee. "You don't have to live for today."

His warm hand covered mine, fingers curling around my palm, and I looked back into his crimson eyes in surprise.

Varistan smiled at me, his eyes soft and a resigned smile touching the corners of his mouth. "Today isn't so terrible."

I set my other hand atop his, running my thumb along the edge of his scales. "Could be better, though."

"Could be better," he agreed with a laugh, giving my hand a squeeze before lying back again, his fingers slipping out of my grasp. "If we're not indulging my self-destructiveness tonight, you should wash my hair and leave the rest of me be."

"Alright," I said, smiling at him. "It's a deal."

CHAPTER TWENTY-FOUR

CONSIDERATION

V aristan didn't have any fight left in him by the time I got his hair washed, scrunched dry, and wrapped up for bed. He made it to the bed, hauled me down next to him, and passed out within a minute. I almost couldn't believe how quickly he fell asleep, dropping like a shot bird. Maybe that made sense, though. Varistan confessed to being greedy for touch, but I thought that would be the reaction of anyone who'd been denied it, let alone someone who'd always loved it. He was probably more relaxed than he'd been in decades.

I couldn't fathom going without the comfort of touch for eighty years. I was a tactile person by nature; I liked cuddling up with friends, and up until I'd come to Nyx Shaeras I'd slept in the same bed as two other people. Only the cat who'd elected to sleep with me was keeping me from seriously considering asking to sleep next to Varistan again—but if my options were the Duke of Nyx Shaeras or a cat, the cat seemed like a much safer option.

I stayed with him for a while, watching him sleep. Maybe for the first time since he'd claimed me, he looked truly content, his body relaxed and the faintest touch of a smile in the corners of his mouth as he slept. Eventually, he fell asleep deeply enough that I felt comfortable extricating myself, leaving him alone to sleep despite the early hour. It wouldn't kill him to get to bed before two in the morning.

Varistan hadn't agreed to a healer, but I went and fetched Lianka anyway. She looked troubled when I said where he'd been bruised, but despite her love of gossip I trusted her professionalism. She wouldn't tell anyone—especially not about something like that.

He didn't wake when she touched her fingers to his throat, the bruises dissolving away as she did the work of days in a matter of seconds. When she was done, she tilted her head towards my room. I didn't have any reservations, letting her in and flopping back onto my bed.

Lianka perched on my desk, wearing a pensive expression. "That wasn't you, was it?"

I shoved myself up, indignant. "Of course not! What in the wilds gave you that idea?!"

She held up one hand palm-out in front of her chest in a warding gesture. "Don't bite," she said, giving me a lopsided smile. "You're the one with the greatest physical access to him, and I think he would allow a great deal from you if you demanded it." She chewed on one of her fingernails in what looked like an idle habit. "If you wanted to be his lover, I doubt it would be difficult to convince him."

"We *are* talking about His Grace Varistan Yllaxira, the Duke of Nyx Shaeras, are we not?" I said, damning my traitor cheeks as I turned crimson. That was far too close to the truth – that Varistan would have sex with me for the sake of feeling wanted, even though it wasn't something he really desired – than I wanted her to step. "The one who openly despises fae-human relationships?"

Lianka smirked at me with one brow raised, obviously amused at my embarrassment. "Indeed," she said. "The duke who keeps a human woman by his side, and who is currently passed out in bed looking thoroughly pleasured, with traces of her touch on most of his body. He has more nuance than you're giving him credit for."

Apparently healers could tell when someone had recently touched someone else, and where. I hadn't known that, and I filed it away with some trepidation.

"I don't know that nuance matters too much," I said with a sigh, pressing the backs of my fingers against my cheeks to cool them. "Even if he was interested, I'm not going to stand next to a man who views humans as a detriment to Faery, and pretend I'm honored to be the exception." I sighed, rubbing at my face. "There's always pressure to prove that you deserve the honor, and I'm not interested in turning on the people I love so I can be the one good human in his world."

"Maybe he just needs someone to show him there's nothing wrong with mortality?" she offered with an apologetic grimace. "His Grace would probably tell you his reasons if you asked. I know there was some sort of scandal around him regarding mortals when he was younger. Perhaps he overcompensated."

"'Overcompensated'?" I said, with an aggrieved laugh. "Good gods, Lianka. The man literally wants all humans expelled from Faery, and can't stand to be in the same room as the tamest of the sky-called fae." I shook my head, dropping back onto the bed with a groan. "He's not a complete waste of space, and I feel badly for the situation he's in, but that's a great deal different from wanting to be his lover."

Lianka sighed; I heard her hop down off the desk, and a moment later she dropped down onto the bed next to me.

"I've heard people call his mother a corpse-fucker for her fondness for human lovers," she said, sounding sad. "His Grace's father left her over it, as I understand it. To my knowledge, he hasn't spoken to either for longer than he's been a duke." She rolled onto her side, looking at me. "Having snowflake lovers is sometimes seen as all but bestiality, at least in the noble circles. He's had to deal with that his whole life."

"Sad backstory, but it's no excuse for his piss-poor behavior," I said, my voice sharp. "I'm not going to... to *rehabilitate* the duke, and I'm *definitely* not going to do it by fucking the prejudice out of him. That's a recipe for disappointment."

She shrugged, looking thoughtful as she examined me. "You like him, though, don't you?" she asked at last, her mouth tugging to one side. "More than you think you should."

That made me sigh again, dropping my hands over my eyes. "Yeah," I said quietly. "He's an arrogant, entitled, hotheaded jerk, but he's also playful, passionate, and loyal. I just..." I closed my eyes, shaking my head. "It's just not enough, you know?" I said, looking back over at Lianka. "I can't overlook the fact that he's willing to throw half of Faery to the wolves so he can be at the top of the heap. One day it'll be my turn, and I'd have compromised my entire moral code to be his shameful secret."

"And yet," she said, reaching over and giving me a hug.

I clonked my head against hers with affection. "And yet," I sighed. "I don't know. I like him. I'm sure as hell attracted to him. He's the fucking Flame of Faery, and I have to see him naked every gods-damn day. But I can't just ignore all... that," I said, waving my hand at the door.

"I think I understand, though I don't think you need to ignore it." Lianka gave me another squeeze before rolling onto her back next to me. "He's... unhappy," she said, in the tone of one carefully thinking about how much she could reveal. "And he doesn't seem to... talk to people, not about those things. But..."

When she didn't continue, I rolled onto my side to look at her, raising one eyebrow.

Lianka made a face, sticking out her tongue. "When he's in a room with you, I think there's always part of his attention that's on you. His eyes often fall on you, even when he should be looking elsewhere. He turns towards you the way a compass turns north. You make him laugh." She pursed her lips, ears pulling back. "I hadn't ever heard him laugh, truly laugh, until that revel where he danced with you."

"He's starving for affection," I said quietly, sorrow and pity wrapping around my heart in a heavy embrace. "I'm just the first person in a long while who's given him any of it."

"More than that, Bells," Lianka said seriously. "You may be his bondservant, but he never did blood-bond you, did he?"

I frowned at that. "Well, no," I said, after a moment. "I suppose he knew the consequences of breaking our bargain was enough to keep me in line, even without it literally killing me."

"That may be one reason, but I doubt it's the main one."

When I raised my brow at her again, she grabbed my nose between two fingers and gave my head a friendly little shake.

"I don't know that he could, even if he wanted to," she said, smiling. "That draconic possessiveness of his isn't destructive. Dragons *hoard*. The moment you became his, you came under his protection, and that includes from his wrath." Whatever she saw on my face must have pleased her, because Lianka grinned at me, her dark eyes dancing with mischief. "You could leave him if you truly wanted to. That gives you agency, which means he can treat you like an equal, if he so desires. But you're also his bondservant, which suggests that you could only hurt him if you were willing to die. See what I'm aiming at?"

I wrinkled my nose at her. "You're saying that I'm the only person in the world who's safe enough to tell his secrets to, while still being person enough to interact with. The special-est snowflake in the great snow-drifts of humanity."

She laughed and pushed herself up. "Something like that," she said, looking very pleased with herself. "You don't have to do anything about it, and you certainly don't have to rehabilitate our duke, but if you *wanted* to give him another road to walk on, I think you could." Lianka shrugged one shoulder. "He's floundering. It's an opportunity, if you want to take it."

CHAPTER TWENTY-FIVE

ACCOUNTING

After that conversation, I started paying more attention. I counted the hours Varistan spent in his office and broke into his locked desk late at night to pore through pages of ledgers. From the years working the pit I had plenty of experience with tracking bets; I was an excellent hand at figuring, but the complexity of Nyx Shaeras' finances meant that I was often up past dawn reading things that had never been meant for my eyes.

At least I was used to late nights and midday naps from working the fights.

Varistan's record-keeping was immaculate. The leather-bound, gold-stamped tomes lining the walls of his study were *ledgers*, thousands of them, every gods-damned expenditure, income, and favor owed documented in his bold handwriting. Receipts were annotated and filed, and when I finally found the store-rooms dedicated to them on one three a.m. night, I had to sit down, stunned by the sheer quantity of information contained in the room.

My duke knew Nyx Shaeras to its every breath, and in row after row of neat black numbers he documented its demise.

Rising tariffs. Trade agreements allowed to lapse. Suppliers raising their prices, and buyers seeking their wares elsewhere. A death by a thousand cuts, starting slow and growing more vicious as the bitterness planted by the Annihilation War started bearing fruit.

The duchy was still solvent—but barely. I was honestly impressed by Varistan's cleverness in how he'd used his money, keeping obsessive track of the tastes of the wealthy and staying a step ahead of his competitors in luxury goods. Nyx Shaeras was still the only supplier of several coveted spices; those violet-lit greenhouses were the only place on the Western Continent anyone had successfully grown ghost-root or zephyrial in captivity, and those were hardly the only expensive plants raised in the heart of Nyx Shaeras.

But the phrase "Nyx Shaeras" didn't have the same cachet it once possessed. Its duke was still infamous, but when people thought of him – and of his duchy

– they no longer thought first of beauty. He was the dragon duke, a royal son fallen to the ranks of the beasts. People thought first of flame and the brutality of the Annihilation War, and only thereafter of softer things.

If Nyx Shaeras sold swords and soldiers, it would have been a great boon. But we made luxury goods, growing them or harvesting them from the wildlands before refining them into perfumes and medicines.

Maybe there's a way to use the infamy, I thought one early morning, sitting on Varistan's office floor with ledgers surrounding me. *People like to flirt with danger, as long it's never too close.*

Something about that niggled at me, a thought on the edge of my grasp. With a frown, I reached over and picked up one of Varistan's less-numerical records, one in which he documented various fluctuations in the luxury markets, his predictions as to outcomes, and the accuracy thereof. I flipped back in time, skimming the summary pages for each solar year and feast cycle until I found one that looked right.

And then there it was, in an account fifty-four years old: "*Haislik cut off route to Maestrizen, no warning. Barred two merchant vessels at the port! Last source of coldwater pearls, westron star-iron, silver rain. Someone will surely be rich tomorrow when word reaches the pearl markets.*"

Even I knew what coldwater pearls were. Often called aurora pearls, the only source was the coldwater reef stretching along the Courtless islands to the west of Raven Court, and they had long been one of the most coveted gemstones among the wealthy. I'd seen one, once, an orb of iridescent storm-gray with colorful streamers of light drifting around it as the lambent aura of the pearl interacted with the ambient wild magic. If there was ever anything that tied beasts to beauty, it would be the pearls that came from the city long known as a haven for wildling fae.

Nobody traded with Maestrizen anymore. Nobody wanted to risk the ire of the Raven King, who had lost three of his sons to the Annihilation War, and whose hatred for wildlings seemed to grow year by year, his bitterness curdling inside of him. "*It's only a matter of time,*" I'd heard people say. For a fae as ancient as our king, eighty years was an eyeblink. One day he'd rouse himself, and the sword would surely fall upon everyone who reminded him of the Beast of Phazikai and of the Traitor Prince.

But that day hadn't come yet. It might not come for centuries, or at all. And Varistan had a reputation for being brash and wild, a fearless man who loved to duel and whose temper was only rivaled by his dragonfire. He could play on that, if he wanted to. Dare the City of Beasts, defy those who thought he ought to fade away, and rely on his royal blood to protect him from the King.

It was an idea, at least.

I started paying more attention to Lianka, too, and the rest of the fae in Nyx Shaeras. The way she talked about things – Varistan, and humans, and society as a whole – wasn't what I anticipated from a fae as old as her. It was like she *wanted* me to change Varistan's mind, even by manipulating him—as if she disliked the system that put mages like her at the top of the food chain as much as I disliked being on the bottom of it.

Lianka was my friend, and she was fae. *Most* of my friends at Nyx Shaeras were fae, and those that weren't lived lives that interfaced closely with the fae of the duchy. I hadn't really thought deeply about the weirdness of that, given how fae-dominated my life was simply by being bound to Varistan, but the more I looked, the stranger it felt.

It went beyond intermingling with humans, too. In Lylvenore, there were very clear divisions between wildlings and court fae. I'd always seen it as a continuum: aberrant fae transitioning to sky-called, and sky-called to court, with mages in a class all of their own and humans shunted off to the side like automata. And maybe that was true, at least as far as the visible effects of wild magic went, but as far as a social structure went, it broke down in Nyx Shaeras.

There were places in the city where visibly wildling fae couldn't walk in the streets safely, and places where seeing a court fae was like catching a glimpse of a unicorn. I'd grown up being taught those routes, until I could navigate them without thinking. But Lylvenore was a city of more than fifty thousand, and though Nyx Shaeras was a sizable castle with a prosperous shipyard, the castle and nearby land could boast three thousand souls at most.

When you don't have options, you learn to keep your mouth shut about the baker's son sprouting claws on the full moon or the night guardsman's eyes reflecting the light. Nobody showed off their wild natures in front of the duke, but neither did anyone make a fuss about Tjarrek's tail in the showers. It was... unsettling, albeit in a good way.

It wasn't all good, of course, but even those little things were strange enough to catch my notice. I brought it up one evening with Stellaris, tossing a hard sausage and block of cheese back and forth as we snacked, our feet propped up on the table.

She snorted, tossing back her long mane of blonde hair. "All that shit really depends on where you go," she said, cutting off a piece of sausage with her knife before passing it back to me. "I can't say that most places are exactly *welcoming* of wildlings, leastwise around here, but there's better and worse places." Stellaris sounded moody, examining a piece of cheese as if it had personally offended her. "As I understand it, we lose people every year. West to Maestrizen, south to Vixen Court, even east into gods-damn Stag Court."

"You can't hardly blame them for wanting to leave," I pointed out, tossing the sausage back to her.

She caught it with one hand, not even looking. "Did I say I did?" she asked, laughing as she re-crossed her ankles. "They so often get treated like shit here, and there's greener pastures elsewhere, so to speak. Did you know that Stag Court is freeing *all* their bondservants?"

I blinked at that, almost fumbling the cheese when she lobbed it to me. "No shit. Really?"

"It's caused quite the uproar at the Winged Palace, or so my cousin says," Stellaris said with a laugh. "It's been scarcely a year since the Beast of Phazikai took the throne with his human soulmate by his side, but apparently the two of them are happy to throw their Court into chaos by upending things rather than making careful changes."

"Good for them, honestly," I said, cutting off a generous chunk of cheese. When I held the rest of it up, Stellaris shook her head, so I tossed it onto the table instead. "Even a year's a long time for us mortals. They're probably fending off assassins in the night from all the pissed-off fae nobles."

"Hah!" She swung her legs off the table, dropping her chair back down onto all fours. "I *fought* in that bloody war, if you'll recall. I've seen the Stag King in action. Assassins are probably enrichment for that particular Beast. It's almost a civil service. Someone ought to keep him from getting bored."

I rolled my eyes, snorting a laugh despite myself. "All that aside, there being a whole nation of free humans led by a moon-called fae and his human love is going to turn Raven Court into a tinderbox," I said, thinking about how bad things had been in Lylvenore even a season ago. "If there was a trickle of emigrants before, it's going to turn into a flood, or worse. Slavery only works when people don't know there's other options. Even bondservants can kill their masters if they're not afraid to die."

Stellaris rested her forearms on her legs, slapping the side of her knife against her wrist. "You ought to watch your back, Bells," she said quietly, her brown eyes serious. "I admire that you stand up for what you believe in, but remember that others may harm you for it. You've got allies, but from what I've seen, the people who don't like you *really* don't like you. If someone can figure out how to do it without thereafter being immolated by His Grace, *you* might be the one fending off assassins in the night."

"I'm just his body-servant," I said with a frown, not liking the sound of that. I'd been in danger before, of course – in the fighting ring, on vermin control, and even out and about in the city – but nobody had ever been targeting me, specifically.

"Uh-huh." Stellaris stabbed the cheese, hauling it to her side of the table. "Says His Grace's most coveted possession. If you had a few less scruples about you, I, too, might believe that you were a danger to him."

"I'm not."

"I know," she said, sliding the cheese back towards me and adding the remains of the sausage. "I'm one of the allies, Bells. But I don't think you're wrong about the tinderbox, and in that metaphor, he's the flint and you're the steel. So watch your back, and sharpen your spear." Stellaris sighed, leaning back with a groan. "Gods. Something has to give, but I'm afraid it's going to be an ugly thing before it's finished."

With a sigh of my own, I tossed the butt of the sausage to a loitering hunting-hound, then brushed my hands off on my pants. "It's already ugly," I pointed out. "It's just that all the ugliness is heaped up on the mortals and the aberrations, and the sky-called have to all but grovel to be let in out of the dark." I shook my head. "All the chaos and blood is just spreading the ugly out."

"Oh, but then *I* might have to suffer," Stellaris said with mock-horror, clutching at her chest. "How can you expect me to do *that*?"

I chucked a piece of cheese at her, sticking out my tongue.

She caught it in her mouth, snapping it out of the air like a hungry dog. "You ought to be less uptight," she said through her mouthful of cheese. "Have a little fun. Even the finest paladins should cut loose on occasion."

"I'm not a paladin," I said, making another face at her.

"Oh, yes, you are!" she laughed, her eyes dancing. "And I'm fae, so you know it's the truth."

"Your truth," I said with an answering laugh. "From where I stand, I'm doing the bare minimum."

"Paladin," came the sing-song rejoinder, her laughter following me out of the room.

Chapter Twenty-Six

LEARN TO SWIM

D espite my familiarity with accounting, there really weren't enough hours in the night to pore through sixteen hundred years of meticulous records. Overachiever Varistan had also put together massive summary ledgers (by year, decade, and century; by feast cycle, decadal, and central; and for extra credit, by the Llystaeon, Mistravel, *and* Incantes comet cycles), but while they were useful for broad patterns, I didn't know Nyx Shaeras or its economy well enough to make intuitive leaps.

The easiest way to get that sort of insight would be to go to the source himself, but I wasn't sure that plopping a chair down next to Varistan and starting to ask him suspiciously well-informed questions about his duchy was the best move. He did seem to like talking to me, though, and I thought that if I made myself present while he was working, he might tell me things.

Varistan had never invited me to join him in his study or office, and I'd never volunteered. I liked being active more than studying missives and numbers, and I was happy to spend my time in the practice courts or barracks. But I'd thought in the beginning that if I wanted to go anywhere with him, all I needed to do was follow him, and it was worth a try.

So one bright winter morning, I idled in Varistan's bedroom while he ate breakfast, taking my time putting away his rejected outfits, making his bed, and tidying up various things that didn't need tidying. He eyed me a couple times while eating, but his mind was clearly elsewhere, and it took him until he was sitting down in his office chair to realize I had followed him there.

The duke froze about a handspan off the chair in the eerie way fae did, then turned his head with the slow deliberation of an owl to stare at me. I waved my fingers at him, taking a seat in one of the mostly-decorative velvet armchairs near the door.

"Why are you... here?" he asked, sounding completely bewildered, and still with his ass a solid six inches away from the seat of the chair.

"Nowhere else to be," I said cheerfully, delighted at how easy it had been to get access. This was much easier than picking locks. I pulled out my weapons kit, unsheathed one of the half-dozen rapiers I'd brought with me to sharpen, and started examining the edge.

Varistan sat down in his chair with the slow tension of a frightened cat, still staring at me with an expression of total bafflement.

I closed one eye, peering down the blade. Gods, Varistan was hard on his swords. What had he been doing with it? Chopping trees? "It's rude to stare, your grace."

"Are you planning on... staying here?"

Without looking at him, I grinned, unable to restrain my good humor. "I am, yes. I like working around other people, and Lianka doesn't let me sharpen swords in the healer's ward. No iron dust allowed."

"But iron dust in my office isn't an issue?" he asked, with a touch of annoyance.

I pulled out a suede lap-cloth from my kit and laid it over my legs. "Brand new iron-catcher, your grace. Obviously I wouldn't want you to end up with iron-scald."

"'Obviously', she says," he muttered, turning towards his desk. Then he sighed, unlocking the roll-top and pushing it up. "Stay if you like. I doubt I'll provide much entertainment, but if it pleases you to be near me, I have little complaint."

Despite his tone of mild annoyance, I could hear the hopefulness creeping in. Whatever else he was, I knew Varistan was lonely. Having my company didn't seem like it was much of a hardship at all—even with my humanity taken into the equation.

We settled into our respective tasks. Varistan was a bit stilted at first; his ears kept turning towards me and he kept reshuffling his wings and changing the position of his tail as if knowing I might be looking at him was uncomfortable. But I didn't do anything but sit there sharpening his sword, careful to work over the iron-catcher, and after a while he relaxed.

To my surprise, he worked mainly in silence, only occasionally murmuring something to himself. It made him an easy companion to work near, the natural movement of a living creature combined with the small sounds of pens and papers making for a relaxing backdrop to the rhythm of weapon-sharpening. I liked it a great deal.

Several hours into his work day, Varistan let out a growl of frustration, planting his elbows on the scattered papers and dropping his face in his hand. His tail coiled around the leg of the chair with enough force that it looked like he might snap it off, and the muscles of his shoulders and back bunched with tension.

I paused in my work, regarding him with some concern. "Is everything alright?"

"Clearly not," he snapped, wings flaring as he dug his claws against his scalp. "Port Kairos isn't renewing our gods-damned trade agreements. She's tripling the fucking tariff, and she surely know we can't *fucking* well pay it!" He slammed his fist down on the desk, making everything rattle and knocking a cup of pencils right off the edge. But as if the flare of anger had consumed all of his strength, Varistan wilted, his shoulders dropping down.

"Gods," Varistan said, his voice dropping to a whisper. "I feel as if I'm dragging the duchy to oblivion with me, and yet like a drowning man and his rescuer, I cannot bear to let go and fall into the dark alone."

I set his sword aside with care, taking off my thin leather gloves before getting up and walking over to him. "So learn to swim," I said, hesitating for only a moment before setting my hands on his shoulders and starting to knead. "The world isn't what it was even a century ago. Try something different, and maybe you won't drown."

Varistan made a low sound of relief as I forced the tension out of his muscles, submitting to the strength of my hands. His tail uncurled from around the chair, twining around my leg instead, with a much kinder grasp.

"I'm all but a pariah." Varistan sounded defeated, his wings drooping until they touched the floor. "It doesn't seem to matter how much I distance myself from my damned cousin, nor emphasize how I never wanted to look like this. I hear the gossip and the cruelties, and I watch them edge further and further away. If I can't keep the things I already have, how can I ever hope to gain anything new?"

I slid one hand under the collar of his shirt to work at a knot along his shoulder blade, eliciting a soft moan of pleasure as my skin touched his scales. "If some people insist on seeing you as a monster-loving traitor, why bother trying to convince them otherwise? It seems like a losing bet."

His shoulders tensed up; I switched from my fingertips to my knuckles and bore down to force him to relax again.

He did, obeying the demand with a panting breath, his muscles loosening. "What are you suggesting?" he asked, sounding wary.

"Maestrizen."

"*Absolutely n—*"

I stuck my fingers into his mouth to stop him from completing the negative.

Varistan *bit* me, snapping his teeth down on my fingers hard enough that I scraped off skin when I yanked them away.

"You are *terrible* at acting like a bondservant," he snarled, pinning me with a hot glare.

"You'll surely be appreciative later," I snapped back, holding my injured digits with my other hand. "Don't fucking make wholesale declarations before you bother to think things through, you stupid fucking excuse for a duke. Let me *finish.*"

Varistan narrowed his eyes, then grabbed my wrist and shoved my hand back onto his shoulder before turning to face forward again. "Continue," he said, the word sharp and his shoulders tenser than they'd been before I'd begun.

I rolled my eyes but complied, returning to giving him a shoulder massage. "One, Maestrizen is a city without a Court, so you don't have to deal with the long annoyance of building an inter-Court trade agreement. Two, up until fifty years ago, Raven Court *was* trading with them, and it has to be easier to re-open routes than to make new ones. Three—"

"How many of these are there?" Varistan asked, interrupting me. He sounded annoyed, but at least he was listening.

I leaned forward, putting my mouth next to his ear. "If you listen, your grace, you'll find out."

He grumbled, but he still relaxed into my touch, especially when I switched from his shoulders to the tight muscle at the base of his neck.

I slid my fingers under his collar and made sure to hit the tense muscles along his spine with my thumbs, giving him skin-to-scale contact. "Three, I'm pretty sure Maestrizen trades across the Western since people used to import star-iron and silver rain from there, so they'll probably be interested in what we have to offer—"

"Which is?" Varistan asked sulkily, interrupting me again.

That was alright. Questions meant he wasn't dismissing the idea out-of-hand, which by itself was surprising. I decided to reward him for it, moving my fingers up his neck to start to give him a scalp massage.

He groaned with pleasure, leaning his head back into my hands to ask for more pressure.

I gave it to him with a smile. "Lumber, your grace. If you're clever about it, maybe even ships. You already have a good shipyard, and that tall, beautiful saltwood forest is the perfect place to find the sort of masts ships need for ocean voyages."

"Pinesap Court is the current dominant player in the lumber market for this region," he said, sounding like he was only just this side of moaning. "Even though we have a reputable shipyard for overwinter repairs, Nyx Shaeras has no particular standing either as a lumber supplier or a ship-builder. Resin, perfumes, and medicinals hardly put us on the map for coarser goods."

"So?" I countered, rubbing the small muscles behind his ears as he all but melted into my touch. "You can't tell me that Pinesap's going to risk the displeasure of Raven Court in order to add one city to their trade routes, let alone *that* one. Unless Maestrizen is poaching trees off the coast, they've got shit for lumber. They're probably still working to find a consistent import, and even if they have one, we're closer and saltwood is better than almost anything else for sailing."

Varistan made a sound of amusement, tipping his head far back enough that he could look up at me. "Marshaled your arguments, have you, Bells?"

"Four," I said, smirking down at him, "Coldwater pearls have been out of the import market for long enough that most buyers are priced out. A clever fae – say, one who was willing to play into popular imagination of himself as brash and wild to make trading with Maestrizen daring instead of dirty – could make a mint by selling aurora jewelry alongside his other luxury goods."

"We don't have a ready source of gold or silver, nor do I imagine Maestrizen does, and coldwater pearls can't be strung." Varistan leaned his chair back on two legs to get a more comfortable view of my face, balancing there with his long legs stretched out beneath the desk. "But I suppose you have a number five for that?"

"I don't, actually," I said with a shrug. "I'm not really up-to-date on fae fashion, but even if you're selling raw coldwater pearls, you'd still have a corner on the market. I've seen caged pearls made with spider-silk before, but if you wanted raw gold there's always Windswept Court—"

Varistan's face went hard, his eyes narrowing and ears pinning back. When he opened his mouth to spit out his refusal, I held two fingers up in a hook, which earned me a lifted lip and low growl. "If you stick your fingers in my mouth to silence me again, I'm going to bite them again."

"I wouldn't expect anything less," I said. I put my fingers back in his hair and started rubbing his scalp again, working my way up towards his horns while his lashes fluttered in helpless bliss. "I know you hate him for what he did to save you, and I know people call him a traitor, but I also know that Windswept Court has a productive gold mine, no ships, and no one to sell all that lovely raw gold to. But it's not really necessary, and put in perspective, Maestrizen's a lot less bad than making peace with your cousin, right?"

"You're making me feel good so I'll sit here and listen to your horrible words, aren't you?" Varistan asked, eyes closed and mouth parted in pleasure as I rubbed his temples and behind his ears at the same time.

I grinned down at him, quite pleased with myself. "I didn't expect to get the opportunity this soon, but I wasn't going to let it pass me by. Is it working?"

"Gods," he moaned. "Even though I know you're manipulating me, I want you to keep talking so you'll keep doing it."

I laughed and grabbed one of his horns, giving his head a little shake. "That's the spirit, your grace."

Varistan froze, his eyes flying open to stare at me with shock.

I froze, too, unsure what to do, or what line I'd crossed. He liked being touched. I knew he liked being touched. He'd just finished saying that he wanted me to keep touching him—

Slowly, he lifted his hand and took my hand off his horn. With the same slow care, Varistan set the feet of the chair back on the ground, then turned to look at me, still wearing that stunned expression.

"I didn't mean to distress you," I said, because I had to say something. I tucked my hands under my arms, shoulders hunching, waiting for him to snap at me.

He didn't do any such thing. He reached up and touched his horn, as if I could have injured him, and swallowed. "You... manhandled me."

"Um." I swallowed, too, feeling far more anxious than I had any right to. "Should I... not do that?"

"You may," he said, so quickly that I flinched backward. Varistan dropped his hand, wrapping his arm around his chest. "I... just..." He shook his head with a self-conscious laugh. "No one has ever... done that."

I stared at him. "In three thousand years, no one's manhandled you?"

Varistan laughed again with that same air of discomfort, dropping his eyes as he shook his head. "No, I meant... no one has ever... grabbed me by the horns." He made a face, looking back up at me. "I didn't anticipate something like that. It was... pleasant."

"Pleasant?" My shoulders started relaxing down out of my defensive posture, my anxiety dissipating.

"Yes," he said, his voice soft. "It's the first time since that day in Pelaimos that someone has acted fully comfortable with me in a way that made me recognize it." Varistan sighed, showing me a rueful smile. "A pity it was due to someone suggesting I make peace with the man who made me a monster."

"He saved your life, Varistan," I said, keeping my voice gentle and using his name to try to soften the words.

A bitter expression flickered across his face. "And such a life it is. Slowly watching everything I cared about crumble while trapped in a body I despise." He snarled, dragonfire glowing from behind his teeth. "That *fucking* war."

Before I could think better of it, I walked over and sat down in Varistan's lap. He went stiff with surprise, his flame dying, and when he opened his mouth to say something, I stuck two fingers between his teeth.

He froze, eyes widening.

"Stop it," I said softly. "What's done is done. All you can do is move forward." Varistan didn't try to bite through my fingers, so I just left them in his mouth, his tongue hot against my fingertips. I brushed his loose hair behind his ear with my free hand. "There's no joy in the grave, you know. No storms off the sea. No days where you can smell the pitch dripping down the pines. No songs, and no silver-lit nights." I cupped his face in my hand, running my thumb against his jaw. "And there's no touch."

Varistan scanned my face, his expression troubled. With a careful grasp, he took my fingers out of his mouth, examining them for a moment before nipping my fingertips and curling them closed. "Why do you even care?" he asked, his voice so quiet that he all but whispered the words. "You must have spent a great deal of time poring through records to put those pieces together, and more to tie it to me and mine. Why bother?"

"This is my home, too," I said, amused at the tiny bite he'd given me as my price for silencing him. "It doesn't really matter how it came about. My life is aligned with yours." When he only gazed up at me, I flashed him a smile. "You are, as they say, between a rock and a hard place. You've been holding Nyx Shaeras together with every tool that came to hand, which means these stones are mortared with the blood of my friends. But it doesn't have to stay that way."

He sighed, dropping his head back against the chair and regarding me from beneath lowered lashes. "I dislike the idea of lending legitimacy to the City of Beasts, let alone making an alliance with the monsters of Windswept Court."

Anger sparked in my veins, my disgust showing itself on my face. "Do as you like, then, your grace," I snapped, getting up off his lap. "Beggar your duchy, sell yourself body and soul, and court spears in the night. You're a monster in exactly the same ways as the people you keep grinding under your so-gracious heel, but at least they have some fucking *morals*."

The duke shoved himself up, his tail snapping behind him as he bared his teeth. "I didn't ask for *any* of this!"

"Oh, and you think they did?" I crossed my arms over my chest, meeting his hot red gaze without letting myself be intimidated, even as he loomed over me with his wings mantled. "Nobody asks to be born, your grace. You don't get to choose your body, and you damn well don't get to choose your parents. The people you call monsters are as fae as you are." I shook my head, disgusted. "You can't have your pretty, pure-blooded fae paradise without seas of blood."

CHAPTER TWENTY-SEVEN

INTO BATTLE

V aristan matched me glare-for-glare, his fingers curved in dangerous claws and ears pinned back in anger. I refused to budge, facing down the Duke of Nyx Shaeras like an opponent in the ring, no matter that I was technically his property and he could punish me thoroughly for my defiance.

At last, he snarled and turned away, stalking across the room to where he had some sort of amber liquor in a decanter. He unstoppered it with an angry movement, pouring himself a generous two fingers of alcohol and tossing it back.

"You may have been born in Faery, but you don't move through the same world I do, and you haven't lived through more than the briefest moment of history," Varistan said in a tight voice, pouring himself another glass. He pivoted on one foot to pin me with a hot-eyed glare, his ears shifting in high temper and his tail snaking behind him with dangerous aggression. "How can you understand the cost of your presence when you haven't seen more than a glimpse of time?"

"Educate me, then," I snapped. "*Convince* me. Because from where I stand, you're just another fucking bigot, *your grace.*"

He went tense, his jaw clenching and hand gripping the glass so hard that the tendons of his arm stood out. "You lived in the underbelly of Faery," he said, practically snarling the words. "You've seen the blood. Do you think it's an *accident?*" Varistan downed the alcohol, slamming the glass down on the table as flame lit the air in front of him. "This world wasn't made for mankind. I doubt it was even made for *fae.* We must constantly struggle for our footing, and the ground beneath us seems to get worse with each passing year. How are we supposed to live for an eternity if we can't keep the world from killing us?"

Varistan started pacing, his wings and spade-tail flared. "Wild magic is *every-where*, Bells. You humans can't feel it, but *we can.*" His tail cracked through the air like a whip, sending a breeze tumbling through the room, ruffling the papers on his desk. "It's like a contagion, except it's part of us and part of this world. It soaks into us, year after year, and we don't have any gods-damned idea of how to escape it."

I eyed him, a little warily. Varistan's hot temper was infamous, but I'd never seen him lose it. I had a feeling I was about to.

"Wild magic makes life," I said, narrowing my eyes as he splashed more alcohol into his glass.

"Wild magic makes *monsters*," he spat, the scent of heated metal filling the air as he flamed again with a sharp exhale. "They spawn in the gods-forsaken wilderness and in our gods-damned *wombs*. And *no one* seems to know how to fucking *stop* it!"

He stalked past me, tail clipping me in the thigh. He didn't seem to notice, too caught up in his tirade to pause. "We fend it off with *you*. We build our cities and fill them with mortals so the magic that leaches out of *everything* gets soaked up by your hungry blood. Fae society as it stands relies on humanity, and there's only one way to get more of you."

Taking bondservants from the mortal world, I thought, watching him pace. *It's not only labor they want from us.*

"We go gallivanting off into the mortal realm like fishing sloops, coming back with a fresh harvest time after time, as if such a thing could ever be sustainable." Varistan flicked his wings with disgust, raking his fiery gaze across me. "Your kind changes so damn fast. One day, we'll be caught, and what then? If we're not prepared to stand on our own, I doubt we'll stand at all."

"Fine," I said, cutting him off before he could keep ranting. "So you have reasons for disliking the practice of bargaining with the dead. I do, too. But what about the rest of it, hm?" I asked, my own temper rising. "Treating us like garbage once we're here doesn't solve anything. And exposing wildling children in the wilderness damn well doesn't, either!"

"I have *never* condemned a child to death for its shape," he snarled, fury twisting his face. "I may be disgusted with this body. I may hate what wild magic does to my kind. But I'm not a *murderer.*"

"When you deny people access to their basic needs, you might as well be," I snapped right back. "People are just as dead when they can't get fucking *medical care* or *food.*"

With a growl, Varistan resumed pacing, his claws leaving pale marks on the wood floor. "And how do you propose to repair the damage?" he asked, his words dripping with disdain. "Say you elevate humanity to the same status as the fae, mortality hand in hand with eternity. What will happen then? Shall we attack the Veil with iron and open the floodgates? Humanity is busily destroying its own world. Shall we let them into Faery to do the same?"

"We're already here, you ass!" My fingernails dug into my palm with the force of my anger.

"Not for long," Varistan sneered. He tossed back his drink for a third time and threw the glass onto his desk, where it skittered across the papers and fell, the remnants of whiskey spreading across an abandoned page.

I glared right back at him, my heart pounding and jaw clenched. "And the wildling fae?" I asked, my voice dangerous.

"Humans don't breed true in Faery," he said, fury twisting his face. "Wildlings, though? Pair two of *them* together, and you get something even more aberrant. Do it long enough, and what comes out isn't even *fae* anymore." He made a sharp gesture with one hand, sweeping it across the room as if it encompassed the entire world. "*Something* needs to be done about the future, or there won't be one."

"There's a present, too," I said, taking an angry step towards him. "We're all people and we're all part of Faery, no matter what we look like or how long we live. You can't have a future without dealing with the now." When he didn't answer, not even looking at me, I picked up a pencil and threw it at him.

It bounced off his wing, making him jerk. Varistan whipped around, stalking towards me with deadly menace.

I didn't care. I'd faced down far more frightening things than him before.

I crossed my arms over my chest again, matching him glare for glare. "You think you're the cleverest boy in the classroom, don't you, your grace?" I said, all but sneering the title. "Get rid of the symptoms of trouble, and you can pretend the problem is gone. But did you ever bother to stop and consider that if people who think like that get their way, *you're* going to end up castrated right along with the rest of the so-called 'monsters'?"

"Since nobody's clamoring to be my mate, who the *fuck* cares? Maybe it would make my life easier!" He snapped his wings, knocking the crystal decanter to the ground.

It shattered, alcohol and glass spraying across the floor. Varistan shied like a horse, flaming as his tail lashed behind him, and planted his foot on a shard of glass.

"Fuck!" He staggered a few steps back, blood spattering the floor. "Gods-*fucking*-damnit!"

"Sit down, Varistan," I said, pissed off at him but unwilling to leave him standing there bleeding.

Varistan glared at me as if I'd personally stabbed him, his red eyes all but glowing with anger. "You do *not* have the right to command me."

"Bleed all over the floor if you prefer," I said, rolling my eyes and walking over to the cupboard to grab some linen napkins. "It's your own damn fault. I'm just being nice about it."

He snarled, the sound purely draconic. Though it probably ought to have made the hairs on the back of my neck stand up, I knew he wouldn't hurt me, and so I dismissed his wrath. When I turned back to him, he'd stomped over to the desk chair and was digging through one of his drawers, blood dripping off his clawed foot onto the wool carpet. That was going to be a bitch to clean; luckily it wasn't my problem.

The duke, however, was.

Varistan only grunted when I pulled the shard of glass out of his sole, his foot flexing. I let it bleed for another few heartbeats, to flush any dirt out of the wound, but seeing as he could get it fixed as soon as I got him in front of a healer, I wasn't that worried. The linens were, thankfully, large enough that I could fold one up to use as a pad and tie another around his foot, making a crude (but serviceable) bandage.

I finished, tossing the shard of glass into his wastebin, and a moment later Varistan dragged out a half-finished bottle of scotch from his desk. He uncorked it and went to take a swig.

I grabbed his wrist.

The duke *hissed* at me like a snake, his wings mantling, but I didn't let go.

"Varis," I said, trying to gentle him out of his anger. "It's barely one in the afternoon. What are you doing?"

Shame flickered across his face, so quickly most people would have missed it. But I was used to his moods, and his expressions were as familiar as my own. "I can get drunk if I desire it. I'm the Duke of Nyx Shaeras. Who has the right to tell me otherwise?"

My brow furrowed as I considered him. "Of course you can, if that's what you want. But will you please give it to me anyway?"

His eyes snapped to mine, shock at hearing me offer him a debt putting tension into his expression. Almost as if in a daze, Varistan handed me the bottle. The moment his hand wasn't touching the glass, something in him seemed to break, his eyes closing in pain and his shoulders drooping. He dropped his face into his hands, resting his elbows on his thighs.

I could feel him trembling where I still touched him, the muscles of his thighs and back so tight they couldn't hold. "What's really going on?" I asked, worry making my throat tight. I'd seen him drinking during the daylight hours fairly frequently; I knew he preferred liquor to milder alcohols, and that he wasn't shy about it. I hadn't thought anything about it, even when he'd gotten thoroughly drunk on occasion. He had a hard life, and few outlets for stress. It seemed understandable.

But this... tossing back drink after drink, keeping liquor in his desk, the anger, the *shame*... that was more than an occasional outlet. That was more than even a habit. That was a well-worn road, and a pattern that he fell into with far too much ease.

"Varis," I said again, when he didn't answer, "what's wrong?"

"Lianka knows," he said, his voice cracking. "She... takes care of it. I..." Varistan swallowed, hard, the sound audible as his wings started shaking. "Fuck," he whispered. "Oblivion has been the greatest kindness I could find for decades. Can you truly blame me for returning to its well again and again?"

He didn't need to say any more.

I'd seen people turn to alcohol and drugs for relief before, and though I'd never joined them, there had been times when I'd been tempted to drown the horrors in the bottom of a beer bottle. Most of them didn't have a healer to purge the effects of overuse on the body, nor to remove the physical need that grew from such things. That Varistan had stepped into the same warm embrace again and again told me a lot about his life.

With a sigh, I hooked one arm around his leg and leaned my face against his arm. "Is it still the greatest kindness you have?"

"No," he said in a ragged voice. "Yet it still beckons to me. Oblivion is an escape from this life and this body that I find difficult to resist."

I reached over and pulled his tail onto my lap, stroking down along the smooth scales. "Tell me three things you like about your life."

Varis huffed a weary laugh, his tail curling around my hips in a warm embrace. "I like having you, and having Nyx Shaeras." He paused, some of the tension leaving his body as he thought. "I like that someone touches me without expectation of repayment for the favor."

"That's a start," I said, rubbing my cheek against his arm. I felt him shift; I thought maybe he was looking down at me. "What about your body?"

He flinched. "Must I?"

I tilted my head back to look up at him, smiling for him when I caught sight of his exhausted expression. "You don't have to do anything, your grace. You are, after all, the Duke of Nyx Shaeras, and no one here has the right to command you." I squeezed his leg in a hug, feeling his tail tighten around me. "But I think..." I hesitated, then sighed and plunged on. "I think maybe learning to appreciate being alive as you are is the first step to understanding why the rest of us are happy to be alive, too. That's important to me, so I'd like you to do it."

Varistan closed his eyes, the muscles of his temples jumping as he clenched his jaw, but he gave me a tight nod. He reached down and laced his fingers through mine, holding onto me as if he might fall into the void if he let go. "I like... flying," he said with a shudder. "So I suppose that means I like having wings." He cracked open one eye, looking down at me. "Does that count as one, or two?"

Smiling, I held up one finger.

He lifted his lip, but he didn't otherwise protest. "I..." Varistan sighed, slouching forward. "I like being all but impossible to burn, despite the irritation of occasionally scorching things I'd rather not. I can walk through a forest fire and come out unscathed." A weak smile touched his lips. "I've even done it. Unfortunately, my clothing is another story."

I gave his leg another squeeze, still petting his tail. "That's two."

He swallowed, his skin darkening as he blushed. "I like that you look at me as if I'm still beautiful," he said in a whisper, not looking at me. "That you expect me to look like this, and have never once flinched away from the sight." The corners of Varistan's mouth trembled, his hand tightening on mine. "Does that count?"

My heart pounded with sudden speed, my chest feeling too tight to breathe. I had to wet my mouth before answering, unable to take my eyes away from his face. "I like the way your scales gleam in the sunlight," I said through the tension in my throat. "I think your horns are elegant and your forked tongue a temptation worthy of Sarcaryn."

Varistan looked down at me with shock and quiet longing, his lips parted and brows slanted.

I took a deep breath, trying to quiet the emotions roiling inside of me. "I find the sharpness of your teeth and the danger in your flame alluring, and I like that you can grab hold of things with wings and tail when your hands are otherwise occupied." I breathed a quiet laugh, thinking about the great many things I liked about his body. "I like that you're always warm, even on the coldest nights."

"I think that should count," he whispered, closing his warm fingers against mine.

I stroked my fingers down along his tail, stopping before I reached the sensitive blades of his spade. "Yeah," I said softly, leaning my face against him. "It counts, your grace."

CHAPTER TWENTY-EIGHT

ANOTHER BARGAIN

W e didn't say anything for a while, sitting there as the minutes ticked past, my fingers tracing the patterns of his scales. Despite my dislike of idleness, I never felt bored in Varistan's presence. He was enough of a source of interest that I didn't have to fill my time with other things, even when he was silent or resting.

At last he sighed and let go of my hand, sprawling back in his chair. "I don't have a good answer," he admitted softly, staring up at the ceiling. "I thought I understood everything, once. That our reliance on human servitude made us weak, and that those who reveled in such things were worthy of disdain." Varistan let out another heavy breath, his tail curling around my forearm. "I was raised with disgust for people who have an appearance akin to mine, and never saw much need to shake it."

"And now?" I asked, when he fell silent.

He didn't say anything at first, the blades of his tail widening a fraction before relaxing back down. I gave his tail a pat, amused at the number of emotional tells he had.

Varistan made a disgruntled sound, stretching his legs out. "Now the greatest comfort in my life is a human woman, and I'm facing down the prospect of making a trade route with Maestrizen the cornerstone of my duchy's economy." He sounded rueful, with a hint of self-deprecation. "The gods seem to be enjoying making my life a meditation on extremes."

"Could be worse," I said in a chipper voice, tilting my head back to grin at him. "You could be a nobody making ends meet by whoring yourself out in brothels and fighting rings instead of a fancy duke."

"Feh," he said, tousling my hair with one hand. "You've already made your point, Isabela. The millennia ahead of me matter little if the present is in ruins, for today informs tomorrow." He left his hand on my head, his thumb rubbing back and forth through my hair. "I believe what I said still holds. Faery is terribly out-of-balance, and if we continue as we are, I fear our entire society will fall to ruins. But the mere existence of the City of Beasts isn't what will lead to that ruination." He huffed out a breath. "Nor, as much as it pains me to say it, is the existence of Windswept Court and my thrice-be-damned cousin. So."

My lips twitched. That was more of a concession than I'd expected to get out of him. It was nice to know that even when in high temper Varistan was paying attention to everything around him, the precise location of his body parts notwithstanding.

"The future doesn't have to look like the past, you know," I said, in a mock-lecturing tone. "The way to save it isn't to try to preserve some rose-tinted version of history. Change with the world, or be left behind."

"Yes, yes." Varistan squeezed me with his tail; then, apparently not content with that, scooped me up and dumped me on his lap, draping himself over my shoulders.

I squeaked, laughing at him as he made another grumbling noise. "So you're thinking about it?"

He sighed, settling his weight more firmly onto my shoulders. "Yes, I'm thinking about it. I was thinking about it before you picked a fight with me, even." When I opened my mouth to protest at that characterization, he stuck two of *his* fingers in my mouth.

I sputtered, jerking back in surprise, but his body was immovable.

Varistan put his mouth against my ear, close enough that I could feel him smiling. "You're the one who introduced this to our relationship, Bells," he purred, as smug as a cat in a songbird's cage. He did not remove his fingers from my mouth. "What's good for the peahen is good for the peacock."

My sound of outrage had no effect.

"Expressing dislike of an idea isn't the same as rejecting it," Varistan continued, in as casual a tone as if he didn't have two fingers pressing down on my tongue. "In another world, our conversation might then have carried on to discussing how to manage that dislike, for I am appallingly bad at forcing myself to do tasks that are wholly unpleasant, and I suspect you would like this to occur within a mortal span of days."

Being silent had already grown boring, and Varistan seemed to like a captive audience, so I doubted he was going to release me anytime soon. He could do far more damage with his claws than I could with my teeth, so I didn't bother to try biting through his scales. Instead, I closed my lips around his fingers, caressed his skin with my tongue, and sucked on them with the same sultry expression I would have worn giving him a blowjob.

Not that I had ever thought about that. Vividly. With my fingers on my clit.

Varistan reacted instantly, shuddering and tilting his hips so my ass rested directly on his slit, his legs spreading and hold on me tightening. "Fuck, Bells," he said in a shaky voice, pulling his fingers out of my mouth with reluctance and shifting me onto his thighs instead of his groin. "That's fighting dirty."

"Do you honestly expect a pit fighter to fight any other way?" I asked, keeping my voice light to try to mask the way all my skin had gone hypersensitive and the desire making itself known between my legs. It was a good thing for me that Varistan didn't fuck humans, because if he'd offered just then I would have been hard-pressed to say no.

He draped his arms over my shoulders again, sighing out a hot breath against my hair. "Not really, no," he admitted, running his tail along my thigh. "Can we talk about Maestrizen, though?"

That tail was *not* helping my state of arousal, but I wasn't about to let Varistan in on that information. He was bad enough already.

"It's not my job to manage you and your dislikes, especially when they're stupid," I pointed out, resting my head on his shoulder and looking up at him.

"It's not," he said in an agreeable tone. "Nothing mandates that you offer me assistance of your own volition, and I would get little pleasure from commanding it from you." Varistan glanced sidelong at me, one corner of his mouth lifting and his ear tilting towards me. "Yet I thought that perhaps you would enjoy having another tool to bend me to your will. Was I wrong?"

I tried to keep a serious face, but Varistan could read people well, and as soon as my lips twitched he smirked, his tail coiling down around my leg. So I gave up and just laughed, sitting there on the duke's lap with him wrapped around me like a python.

"You weren't wrong," I said, shaking my head. "Gods. Put that way, you make me sound like some sort of evil mastermind."

"Not evil," he said, smiling at me with genuine warmth. "Possibly a mastermind, but I think I'll wait until the conclusion of these affairs to make a final call on that front. Will you bargain with me, Isabela Keris?"

I reached up and buried my fingers in his blood-red curls, rubbing my fingers along his scalp. "I'll seek a bargain with you, Varistan Yllaxira," I replied, using the formal wording. "Tell me your desires."

His lashes fluttered, his lips parting in an expression of pleasure. "This," he said softly, his wings dropping down to wrap around my chest in an embrace. "Platonic physical affection, given without reservation."

"Doesn't bargaining for that defeat the purpose?" I asked, setting my hands down over the hands of his wings.

"I ask only for the shape that it takes." Varistan nuzzled me, his nose running along my scalp. "Sleep in the same bed as me, in whatever aspect and dress pleases you. You're the only person who cannot use promises stolen in my sleep against me, and having had it once, lying alone in the night is now a quiet torment for me."

Formal bargaining was a dance between fae—a story woven with half-truths and misdirection. Each wanted something specific, and knew the other would try to escape paying it. But Varis wasn't playing the game. He was baring his soul, his face pressed to my hair and his heart beating too hard against my spine. I could hurt him so badly with the knowledge of the depths of his loneliness, stepping into his life with a smile on my lips and a dagger in my hand.

Once, I would have. But now...

"Every day that you make progress towards trade agreements with Maestrizen, or any other new partner you would otherwise dismiss due to their wildling appearance, I'll sleep alongside you," I said, giving him the same generosity in my bargaining. It left me open to him making only the slimmest margin of progress each day in order to keep me alongside him for longer, but he wanted my freely-given affection. Making himself my antagonist would be in direct opposition to that goal. "And if it makes it easier, I'll offer you touch while you take those steps, whether it's rubbing your shoulders while you draft letters or holding your hand under the table at a formal dinner with emissaries."

Varistan barked a laugh, hugging me closer for a moment. "Generous terms, Bells," he said, sounding relieved. "I accept. As embarrassing and childish as it may be, I may even take you up on the hand-holding. I'm not very good at being political."

"No?" I asked, trying to sound surprised but unable to suppress the laughter in my voice.

He nipped me on the neck in protest—then froze, all his limbs locking in place. "That wasn't intentional," he said, his voice strained. "You're very comfortable for me to be around. It makes it difficult to recall that I shouldn't be... biting you."

"I don't really mind," I said, amused at him. An understatement; being nipped on the neck gave me a great deal of interest in being bitten more thoroughly, both there and elsewhere.

"Nevertheless." Varistan relaxed his hold on me, settling his wings behind him again and loosening his tail's strangle-hold on my leg. "You allow me to take a great many physical liberties with you, well beyond what could be said to be expected of a bondservant. I appreciate it a great deal, but I would dislike stepping beyond your comfort by indulging mine."

"It really doesn't bother me—" I started.

"Bells," he said, his voice gentle as he nuzzled my hair. "Just as you didn't want to take advantage of my longing for sexual admiration without my full desire for what would follow, I have little interest in taking advantage of your willingness to be... bitten... without your eager consent." His tail tightened around my ankle. "As much as I would like to. As amazing as it would feel." He shivered underneath me, breath heating. "You're not a toy, Isabela, nor a slave," he said, breathing the words against my neck. "Until and unless you express your open desire to have my mouth pressed to your pale throat, I ought to refrain."

"But I'm human," I said, my heart pounding and pussy throbbing. Was he... was he *inviting* me to seduce him? Did he... want me to?

"Do you think that matters much to me anymore?" Varistan asked softly. "You're..." he hesitated, his hard swallow audible as he rested his forehead against my hair. "You're one of the few good things in my life. This isn't the life I wanted, and I don't know what it means for me that I cannot bear to let you go, but you're..." He gave a sharp laugh, one tinged with despair. "...my most treasured possession."

My chest was so tight it felt like my ribs had frozen, the bars of bone constricting the beating of my heart. I was *human.* He wouldn't have me forever, and he had to know it—and there was no way he would ever consent to raise me to his level. He saw me as his possession. Something he *owned.*

He's a dragon, I tried to tell myself, not wanting to bristle when Varistan was so clearly on the edge of falling apart. *Of course he sees me as part of his hoard.*

It wasn't very comforting.

"What do you want from me?" I asked through a throat gone tight, every hammering beat of my heart hurting.

"Do you truly want to know?" He said it with quiet caution, in a way that made me think that if I asked again he would tell me the raw truth.

"No." I said the word before I could consider doing otherwise, but once I'd said it I didn't want to take it back.

I wasn't even sure Varistan knew what he wanted. It seemed like it changed day by day, and I didn't want to poison... whatever this was... by giving it strict boundaries. I laced my fingers through his when he flinched back, holding his hands so that he couldn't simply dump me off his lap and make his escape.

"I don't want to know because I don't think *you* really know," I said, leaning back against his broad chest.

He tucked me a little closer to his body, curling around me. "Then why did you ask?"

"Consider it a rhetorical question." I gave his hand a squeeze, smiling even though I knew he couldn't see me. "I don't know what this is, which is... strange for me. Usually everything in my relationships is very explicit, but you don't really play by the rules."

"Are there rules you'd like me to obey?" he asked, a touch of amusement in his voice. "I'm willing to keep bargaining."

"Nah," I said, leaning my head back against him so I could look up into his face, the tension easing as we slipped away from serious conversation back into the comfort of flirtatious banter. "I'm enjoying the process of discovery, your grace. You're an interesting diversion."

Varistan snorted at that, giving me a little nuzzle before releasing me from his hold. "More than a simple diversion, I hope," he said, sprawling back in his chair with a lazy smile when I got up. "I don't know that my ego could survive the blow of being a mere... *aberration* in your routine."

My eyebrows shot up as I started laughing in astonished disbelief at the joke, earning myself a very smug look of pleasure from the duke as his tail flirted with my ankles. "*Really?*"

The corners of his eyes crinkled, with his sharp canines showing as he smiled. "Am I the cleverest boy in the classroom now?"

I shook my head, still laughing as I crossed my arms over my chest. "What you are is a menace, your grace. Do you want me to go, I don't know, drag Lianka up here to fix your foot? Maybe get someone to clean your carpet while you write the Duchess of Kairos a politely-worded 'fuck you'?"

"Will you come back and sharpen swords after?" Varistan asked, his rakish expression softening into a wistful one.

"If you like," I said, a small smile touching the corners of my mouth.

"I would," he said, looking up at me like I was giving him the world.

CHAPTER TWENTY-NINE

SILVER-LIT NIGHTS

Given the strength of his desire not to have to sleep alone, I probably shouldn't have been surprised by Varistan's dedication to the task of forging an alliance with Maestrizen. He really wasn't very good at doing things that were unpleasant tasks, but with me in the room and with the lure of comfort in the night at his fingertips, he got initial missives drafted, edited, and sent off. Other tasks would be easier – figuring out what he could offer in trade, setting up forestry, and shuffling the work of the duchy to make new trade routes possible – but there was a lot to do, and I suspected Varistan would make sure he had something to do every day.

That night, Varistan was as awkward as a teenager getting laid for the first time. He almost couldn't look me in the eyes, flicking his tail like a nervous cat and changing his body position as if he didn't know where to put his hands or wings. I'd taken his clothing off a hundred times by now, but he acted like no one had ever undressed him before, his skin rouging and his pulse visible in his throat.

I put my hands on my hips as he delicately sat on the bed after brushing his teeth, bemused by how nervous he was. "Is this actually going to be nice for you?" I asked, softening my voice when he flinched. "You don't have to jump into the deep water, Varistan," I said, smiling when he looked over at me with anxiety in his eyes. "Would you like something different?"

"Could I... wear something?" he asked, sounding embarrassed. "I... I know we've slept in the nude alongside each other, but..."

"Yes, of course," I said, surprised that he thought he had to ask. "Just under-things, or would you like a shirt, too?"

"Underthings would do," Varistan said, rubbing his knuckles against his cheek. "I..." He exhaled sharply, hunching his shoulders. "I'm male, with every-thing that goes along with that. Sometimes I wake up... hard. And I don't... want..."

"You don't have to justify yourself to me, your grace," I said, kneeling down in front of him to help him into a pair of boxer-briefs. "You're allowed to simply want things. I'm not going to take you to task for changing wanting to sleep in something more than your own skin."

I couldn't hide the blush at the thought of waking up with Varistan sporting a morning erection. If I was as cuddly as I'd been last time, or he a little more so, he'd be pressed up against me, his bare cock against my skin, the Flame of Faery *exactly* where I wanted him...

I raked my fingers through my hair as I stood, trying to clear my thoughts. "Anything else?" I asked, meeting his crimson eyes with my own hazel ones.

He breathed a soft laugh, face tilted up towards mine, all the tension draining away. "Just you."

That made my cheeks go even hotter, which earned me a self-satisfied smile from the duke. "I'll go get ready for bed, then," I said, all but darting away into my own room.

With a door between us, I took a moment to really stop and dwell on how preposterous this was. I was trading a fae duke – trading *Varistan fucking Yllaxira* – my service as a platonic bedmate so that he would strike up trade agreements with one of Raven Court's most despised neighbors. Windswept Court only still existed because its King was in the same bloodline as the Raven King, and they literally couldn't go to war without the instigator being killed by Court magic. Maestrizen was mostly tolerated because it was too much of an annoyance to be rid of them.

I was going to get into bed with the Flame of Faery. I was going to do it for months – maybe *years* – and with our mutual love of touch, there was no way we'd end up on opposite sides of the bed. He was gorgeous, flirtatious, and undeniably trouble... and my pussy was already throbbing at the thought of being sprawled in bed with him, every beat of my heart sending a spike of lust through me.

Fuck, I was going to *combust*.

I glanced at the door, chewing on my lip. Varistan didn't know what my bedtime routine was. Maybe he thought I was as much of a fusspot as he was. And it wasn't like getting off while thinking about Varistan *wasn't* a part of what I usually did before bed...

I was on my bed with my hand down my pants before I could really decide not to do that, clenching down on myself as I drove my fingertips against my clit. The thrill of knowing Varistan was just past the door, waiting for me to come to bed, made it even hotter to imagine what I could do to him. Just run my hands down that gorgeous body, rub my fingers against his slit as he roused for me, maybe slip them inside of his heat to meet the hardening length of his cock...

Fuck, it felt so good to imagine it, my pussy aching and clit singing with pleasure. I bet he fucked like it was his job, that he could throw me on my back and shove his cock into me and make me come with nothing more than that. Pinning my hands over my head with his wings, his callused hands massaging my breasts, that tail of his teasing my clit while he slammed his cock into me again and again and *again*—

I muffled myself with one hand as I came, my core closing down with waves of pleasure that ebbed away into tingling bliss. Slowly, I pulled my hand out of my pants, breathing hard, embarrassed at how fast I'd come even though nobody had been there to see.

I was such an idiot. This had been such a bad habit to get into. But after that first night in bed with him, I'd just kinda... started, and I'd never stopped.

You're so fucked, Bells.

After a few moments of recovery, I crawled off my bed and stripped, washing my hands and groin with the basin of water in my room so that I wouldn't so obviously smell like sex. Varistan was wearing underthings, and if I was naked it was going to go poorly for me, so I pulled on a nightshift and a pair of panties, grimacing at the way my nipples pushed up the thin fabric. But it wasn't as if I could wear a sweater to bed – especially not with Varistan in that bed, given his body heat – so this was as good as it was going to get.

Varistan had shielded the lambence-lamps while I'd been occupied, leaving only the small light next to his bed glowing. He was curled up under the sheets, tucked around a pillow with his wings furled tightly against his back.

He hasn't slept next to anyone for a thousand years, I reminded myself, the length of time those simple words encompassed staggering me. *Of course he's nervous. He's had all day to anticipate how badly this could go.*

"I'll be right back," I said, pitching my voice low before stepping into his bathroom. It was faster than going to use the servants' amenities—and I thought Varistan would appreciate me using his things. I was his, after all, one of the few things that belonged only to him, and he liked to be reminded of it.

After a moment of hesitation, I used the same toothpaste he liked instead of what I'd brought over, and ran one of the combs that still gleamed with traces of his hair-oil through my tresses. It might make him relax for me to smell like him, and the familiar scent soothed in a way I hadn't expected, as if I might find Varistan draping himself across my shoulders.

When had *that* become something I liked? I'd never expected the Duke of Nyx Shaeras to be anything other than my enemy, let alone a comfort.

Varistan was, if anything, even more tense when I re-emerged, his tail wrapped around his own legs and his breathing too measured to be natural. I didn't point it out, simply hopping onto the opposite side of the bed and getting under the covers with him. He cringed away from me, wings hunching up.

I regarded him for a moment, my mouthing tugging to the side in sympathy. "C'mere," I said softly, scooting close enough to him that it would be easy. "Let go of that pillow and come cuddle me, instead."

He went absolutely still, not even breathing, the same sort of frozen posture of a startled cat.

"What?" he whispered, voice shaking.

"C'mere," I said again, starting to smile. "You look like you're worried I'm going to slit your throat in the night if you accidentally touch me. Don't you remember how cozy I was with you that one night?" When he didn't move or answer, I ran my fingers down along his wing, and added, "Come curl up with me, *mi cielo.*"

That got him to move, my duke rolling over to face me. "What— Why would you call me that?" he asked, eyes darting across my face. "You were... weren't you dreaming when you said that to me?"

"Probably," I said, glad that the darkness would hide my blush. "It's a pretty common endearment, though I've never actually called anyone by it before you. I can't say I love you a million, but..." I shrugged one shoulder, reaching over to tuck an errant strand of hair behind his pointed ear. "You're the only one who's ever given me the sky."

"It's yours, if you want it," he said, sounding like his heart was in his throat. "I'll lend you my wings."

"And I'll accept that gift with pleasure." I ran my fingers down the smooth line of his jaw, so unlike the rough mortal masculinity I was used to. Varistan was so beautiful, almost unreal in his perfection, but every line of his body felt right to me. I wouldn't change anything about him. "But tonight I'd like you to come sleep next to me." I smiled at him when he didn't move, returning my touch to the edge of his sharp-tipped fae ear. "The nights are cold in Nyx Shaeras. Will you warm my bed for me?"

He wrapped his gloved hand around mine, his grip awkward from the cotton blunting his claws, and rested the backs of my fingers against his lips. "You'll enjoy it?" he asked, the words hesitant. "You're not... not doing it because you know I will?"

"I didn't ever sleep alone until you brought me here, and it's been just me and a cat since. You asked me for a price I wanted anyway, Varis." At his raised brow, my cheeks went hot again. "Er. Your grace."

Varistan huffed a laugh, shifting closer. "Do you think of me by that name?"

"Sometimes," I muttered, rolling onto my other side so I didn't have to look at that expression of arch amusement anymore.

"How charming," he said in a low murmur, fitting his body to mine. "I've always preferred it to 'Vee', but you're the first to call me that without being told to do so." His tail curled around me, the tip resting against my arms. "Is this comfortable for you?"

"Mhm," I said, my eyes drifting closed and my body relaxing from the comfort of having someone lying alongside me, even when that someone was the Duke of Nyx Shaeras himself. "You're good at cuddling."

"I love it," Varis said softly, his warm breath stirring my hair. "I should probably apologize in advance for how very much I'm surely going to chase you across the bed, now that I have an invitation."

"Why do you do that?"

"Hmm?" he asked, sounding sleepy.

"Apologize," I said, lacing my fingers through his to tuck his arm up against my chest. "You're the only fae I've ever met who does."

Varistan nuzzled me, inhaling against my hair. "Because I can, with you. You can't claim anything from me for it." I felt his lips turn up. "It feels good to... relax."

"I guess that makes sense," I murmured back, half-asleep already. It didn't, really – the fae I'd talked to described forgiving debts as deeply unpleasant, and I couldn't imagine wanting to toy with that sensation – but I was too sleepy to pursue it. "G'night, Varis."

He pressed his face a little closer to me. "Sleep well, Bells."

Despite his advance apology and my concerns, Varistan and I didn't wake up in a tangle that next morning, or any morning thereafter. Apparently falling asleep spooning each other satisfied both of our desires for bedtime snuggling, because we usually woke up sprawled in such a fashion as to use every available inch of the bed—but always with his tail wrapped around some part of me, as if he needed to be assured that I was still there.

He never woke me up in the night from his nocturnal shifting, and when I got out of bed hours before he woke up, he never roused. I'd never had such a perfect bed-companion before, and though I was eager to see progress made on the trade deals, I was loathe to give it up. The one night in those two weeks that Varistan didn't have anything to work on related to either Maestrizen or Windswept Court, both of us slept like shit, and I found myself as dedicated as he was to find something every day for him to do.

Our schedules started diverging from their usual patterns as a result of his new pursuits; Varistan had to leave the castle more, and mostly on the wing. He brought me along, once, but even with his body heat I was shivering when we landed, and the troubled looks people gave him for the sin of carrying his bondservant weren't worth the pleasure of flying.

I tried to keep track of when he'd be returning so I could do my usual duties, but it wasn't always easy, especially when his itineraries changed. I finally mis-timed things a little over a fortnight into our new schedule, staying at the War Army garrison for longer than I'd intended and not able to make up the time by jogging back. Windswept and preparing my excuses in advance

– Varistan was going to be an anxious wreck with me being more than thirty minutes late – I raked my hair back and ducked into his room.

CHAPTER THIRTY

STUCK IN A RUT

I did not receive a sharp inquiry as to my tardiness from my duke. I received a spectacular vista of him bent over the bed thrusting against a pillow, shirtless and disheveled. I'd seen him naked a hundred times and knew his powerful body by sight and touch, but I was unprepared for the sight of him rutting it out with slow desperation.

The strong muscles of his back bunched and shifted, his wings half-spread and his tail lashing. Sweat ran down his spine and darkened his hair. For some unknown reason he still wore pants, but they were tight and I could see the tension in his thighs as he pumped his hips.

I could imagine the look on his face as if I looked him full in the eyes, hazed and tortured with desire, the black wells of his pupils all but swallowing his crimson irises.

His room was warmer than mine, heated by the dragon within it. The rich scent of his body twined through the air, musk and saffron mixed with a heady smell that made my mouth water and my pulse throb between my legs. I'd crossed half the room towards him before I realized I was walking, catching myself mid-step as my heart pounded.

Oh, fuck. Varistan's in heat.

He moaned, his shoulders hunching as his head dropped down, hips rolling with steady force. A shudder ran down his long spine, leaving tension behind.

"Your—" I started. My voice cracked, and I had to swallow to moisten my throat. "Your grace."

He shuddered again, his visible hand digging into the bed, claws tearing rents in the quilt. "Fuck," he groaned, drawing the word out in his lust-soaked voice. "I lost track of time."

Varistan did not stop thrusting, each slow roll of his hips paired with a panting breath. I didn't manage to stop staring at him, either, watching the muscles of his thighs and back flex as he moved. Gods, what must it be like to get fucked like that? All that strength directed towards pleasure with dedicated, relentless patience, drawing it out until the cataclysmic end? Sweat dripping down his chest, his red eyes never leaving my face, his hot breath fanning against my bare skin...

I shook my head, a sharp motion, trying to drag my mind out of the gutter before I did something stupid, like going up behind my duke and running my hands up his strong sides, my mouth against his skin, the fucking delicious scent of his body filling my lungs—

I managed to arrest myself maybe three steps away from him, my panties soaked and nipples aching where they pressed against my bra. "Do you need anything," I said, not managing to put a question mark at the end of the sentence. The words came out mechanically, like I was reading off a script, but at least I managed to say something instead of licking the sweat off Varistan's throat.

He laughed, a bitter sound, his tail snaking through the air. "Dragons go into winter rut," Varistan ground out, his voice harsh and thick with want. "My cousin didn't see fit to ensure that particular biological urge didn't affect me." His hips jerked hard against the bed, his back going stiff. "Fuck," he said again, biting the word off. "I'm so hard it *hurts*, and I can't fucking *come*."

"Maybe that's because you're humping a pillow with your pants on. You might consider actually touching yourself," I said, before I could even hope to leash my tongue. "Er, your grace," I added belatedly, my cheeks going hot.

"I had a very different cock for thousands of years," Varistan said, his claws digging deeper into the bed. "It's disgusting. I don't want to touch it. I don't want to *look* at it."

"You're not disgusting." I walked up to him when he didn't say anything, his motion halting as I tucked the sweat-damp curls of his hair behind his pointed ear. "I've seen you naked, Varistan," I said, trying to put gentleness into my voice. "Many times. There's nothing disgusting about your body."

Varistan turned to look at me, breathing hard, his mouth parted and lust heating his gaze. "You've never seen me like this. I suspect you'd change your mind if you saw me naked now." He shuddered, dropping his head, starting to roll his hips again with hopeless dedication. "Just go," he said, his voice full of unhappiness. "I'm going to be like this for days. Sometimes it's as long as a fortnight. Consider it a vacation."

I regarded him for a moment, then sighed. Varistan was obviously suffering, and despite everything, I didn't like seeing him hurting. Plus there was the little fact that I'd very much enjoy having him desperate and under my power for once. He was gorgeous, and in heat like this he smelled like a fucking incubus. Maybe I could enjoy that body I'd fantasized about so often, and get to count it as... as a civil service.

"Let me do it," I said.

He froze, his wings tensing and flaring out. "What."

"I'll blindfold you if you want, but you're miserable, and I'm not going to leave you like this for a fortnight." I took a deep breath, trying not to look too eager for the chance to take him to pieces. "You won't have to look, you won't have to touch, and you'll get to come. Let me do it."

"It will only help for a little while," Varistan said, the words growing rougher as his voice dropped. "I don't need to eat and I get very little sleep in rut. Getting me off once won't fix anything."

"Then I'll do it more than once," I said, biting my lip as I considered what I might be getting myself into. "Isn't it my job to take care of your physical needs?"

He groaned, back bowing as he held himself in place. "That doesn't include sex, no matter how much my body wants it, and I know you know that. I won't ever command you to do such a thing."

"Which is why I'm offering. You're insufferable, but there's no reason for you to suffer like this." I did my best to keep my voice level and reasonable, but *gods* it was difficult to do with a sexually desperate Varistan talking in that lustful bedroom voice, all deep and rumbling.

"Gods, I know I am," he said with a shudder, the words halfway to a moan. "If... if you're determined to do this..." Varistan fell silent for a moment, audibly swallowing. "Call me Varis. No titles. I don't want..." He lifted his face again to meet my eyes with raw neediness drawing his brows together. "You can say 'no,'" he said, not finishing his previous thought. "I won't— I can't make you. You can say 'no.'"

"Varis," I said, his nickname sounding more right on my tongue than his title ever had, "get on the bed."

Varistan stared at me for a heartbeat, then jerked his chin down into a nod and crawled onto the bed, his whole body tense and wings trembling.

I watched him for a moment longer – *am I seriously doing this?* – then made myself move, going over to one of his dressers and pulling out a black silk cravat. That would do for a blindfold. When I turned back to Varistan, I saw him on all fours, staring at me with equal parts desperation and lust. I hopped up onto the bed next to him, then reached up and laid the silk across his eyes, tying it behind his head.

He kept panting, his expression raw and breath hot. Gods, he was beautiful like this. It was better by far than his usual arrogance—better even than having him naked and lounging. I wanted him like this forever.

"Sit up," I said, putting a hand on his chest. His heat soaked into my palm, the dragonfire beneath his skin turning him into a furnace.

With a low sound, Varistan obeyed, leaning back as I pressed forward, his chest heaving as he panted. I dropped my eyes down his body to where his erection pressed against his pants, the shape a great deal wider than I'd anticipated. He must have been grinding against the bed for a while, because his precome had soaked through, the wet making a dark splotch on the charcoal cloth.

I swallowed, my core clenching down at the sight of Varistan like that. *Okay. Nothing for it.* Pulse pounding, I leaned forward and started unbuttoning his pants.

Varistan moaned as soon as my hands touched his pants, the firm shape beneath the cloth flexing and his hips bucking forward. My breath hitched, my heart rate picking up, but I made myself move smoothly. I'd undressed him a hundred times. I knew how to take off the duke's pants.

He moved for me as I pulled them off, tension lining his whole body as I dragged them down past his knees.

I stared at his groin, boggled. He had *two* cocks, red and slick, with thick bumps running down the outer sides of each of them. The inner sides were smooth enough that they could be pressed together without being uncomfortable for him, the heads flaring away from each other, and the upper shaft curved towards his navel in a way that promised delight.

Holy shit, he could make me forget my name with those—

"I told you," he said, his voice tight as he balled his hands into fists. "It's not a pretty sight—"

"Oh, shut the fuck up," I said, exasperated.

He jerked as if I'd struck him, and I took the opportunity to wrap my hands around his cocks and start stroking.

Varistan... fell apart. He moaned with every breath, back bowing as his legs started shaking, kneeling there on the bed with his cocks in my hands. I didn't stop, not as he groped for me and clung to me with his face against my neck, and not as he started thrusting into my hands. The power of it all thrilled through me, the Duke of Nyx Shaeras helpless for me.

"Oh, gods," he groaned, hips driving hard as he fucked himself through my grip. "Oh, fuck, Bells, you feel so good—don't stop, please don't stop." His pace picked up, his shafts flexing in my hands, all the arousal of being in rut focusing on me. "Gods, it feels so *good*, I want to come so badly, oh, please make me come   "

"Are you begging for it, Varis?" I asked, heated desire throbbing between my legs as I shifted my grip, twisting my hands with each thrust to increase the sensation. I nipped him on the neck when he didn't reply, the salt of his sweat goading me into it. "Answer me."

"Yes," Varistan gasped out. His clawed fingers buried themselves in my hair, and a moment later his mouth was on the bare skin of my neck, his hot breath almost searing. "Yes, gods, please make me come, you're perfect and *mine* and you can't hurt me for begging— Oh, fuck, oh, fuck, please, Bells, please don't stop—"

The way he said that – breathy and desperate and full of longing – had to mean something, but I didn't have the wherewithal to contemplate it. Instead, I leaned into the pleasure that lanced into me from the feel of his lips moving across my skin, my mouth watering as I tightened my grip on him.

"That's my good duke," I crooned to him, the words coming smoothly to my lips, rock-solid certainty settling into me that he wanted it like this—that Varistan wanted someone to take him apart at the seams, and that I was the one who could. "Now come for me, Varis."

His fingers tightened on me as he whimpered, claws digging into my side and hair pulling at my scalp. A heartbeat later he cried out, his back arching and hips driving hard into my hands. Varistan came with a belling scream of pleasure, cocks throbbing as his hot seed struck me on the chest, soaking into my shirt. He chased it, fucking himself through my hands as he came, wings fanning and hands closing down in spasms against me.

He kept doing it, a moan on the edge of every breath, thrusting through my grip even after he'd finished orgasming. "Fuck, Bells," he said in a tight whine. "Fuck, that felt incredible, do it again, please, I can come for you again—"

Those words shot heat through my veins to lodge between my legs in an aching throb. I could feel my pulse across my whole body, demanding that I see to the desire slicking my thighs, and the sharp smell of sex did nothing to soothe me. Fuck, I just wanted to shove Varistan down on his back, climb on top of him, and fuck myself with his cocks—wanted him exactly like this, disheveled and with his pants around his ankles, his chest gleaming with sweat. He was always so collected and arrogant, stalking through the world like he owned it, and that made it all the more rewarding to see him undone.

"You like this, don't you? You like having me take you in hand and telling you when to come," I crooned the words, punctuating them with a hard squeeze of my fingers that made him gasp as he nodded against my neck. "You're so tired of having to be His Grace, the Duke of Nyx Shaeras. You want somewhere you can stop thinking. Where you can just *exist*."

Every word felt like saying something I'd known forever, as if I could look through him and see into his soul.

"Yes," he whispered, his voice hoarse.

His canine hooked my throat for a moment, as if Varistan could barely keep himself from biting me while he rutted against my fingers. The bumps of his cocks slid through my hands with ease, slick with come and precome, my palms tingling from the texture.

I had to keep swallowing so I wouldn't drool on him, my clit throbbing and pussy aching. Gods, what I wouldn't have given for a spare hand to shove down my pants—but mine were occupied, and Varistan was in no state to help a girl out, moaning and shaking as I drove him towards orgasm.

Varistan shifted as he got closer to coming again, spreading his legs wider and putting his weight more forward, his wings flaring out for balance as he leaned forward against me, openly chasing orgasm. I braced myself, taking more of his weight. I didn't even have to slide my hands, resting my elbows on my hips and twisting my wrists as he thrust. It was so easy to pleasure him, like all I had to do was relax into it to get it exactly right. That ease translated to comfort, so that instead of worrying about what all of this meant all I could think about was that I had Varis exactly where I wanted him.

My duke would never want anyone else. I'd see to that.

Varistan seemed tireless, moving with perfect rhythm and an innate sense of how hard he could drive into me without hurting me. He didn't hold back. He fucked himself to the hilt, long thrusts that ran my palms against the entire length of his shafts. My fingers pressed against his slit and scales with every thrust, my skin kissing him before he pulled his hips back.

I could tell when he got close again, as he grew a fraction harder and his thrusts became more desperate. His hand crept down from my shoulder and slid under my shirt; he shuddered as his fingers walked up my ribs.

"Bells," he said, his voice wavering. "Gods, Bells, please say it again."

He said my nickname like someone might say the name of a goddess, petitioning me for his pleasure. It filled me with hunger, coiling through me like a serpent.

I turned my head and put my mouth next to his ear, breathing hard. "*Come for me.*"

He fucking *did*, crying out as he snapped his hips forward. Varistan fucked himself through it, his hot come soaking through my shirt and pants and his cocks jerking against my hands, panting out his pleasure with his claws digging into my skin. I rode it out with him, my core clenching down and my body on fire.

"That's good," I moaned into his ear, my lips touching his skin. "Just like that."

With a low whine, Varistan slowed his motion, then stilled. His thumb swept across my neck, a tiny caress, his body relaxing down against mine. I didn't let go of him, the heat of his shafts soaking into my hands. I could feel his pulse slowing as his breathing eased, the sensation drawing me down out of high arousal.

"Gods," he said, halfway to a groan. "That felt... amazing." He turned his face a fraction, touching his lips to my throat without kissing me, then sat back on his heels, drawing out of my hands. As soon as I wasn't touching him, Varistan seemed to wilt, sinking down onto the bed with his pants still tangled around his ankles.

I glanced down at myself and made a face at the mess as he used his tail to free his legs. He'd come all over me and on the torn quilt between my legs, so while Varistan hauled his pants off and chucked them across the room, I peeled off my shirt and pants and dumped them on the floor. If he was going to be in rut for days or weeks, I probably wouldn't want to bother with clothing for most of it, anyhow.

Varistan didn't move – he didn't look like he *could* move – so I scooted away from the wet spot and sprawled down next to him. After a moment, I pushed the blindfold off, dropping it on the other side of me. Smiling, I tucked his damp hair behind his ear, feeling quite pleased with myself. Reducing the Duke of Nyx Shaeras to a limp heap with a handjob definitely felt good. The only thing better about the moment was that I was going to get to do it again.

CHAPTER THIRTY-ONE

EIGHTEEN HUNDRED YEARS

H is eyes opened halfway, hazed with what looked rather like bliss, and focused slowly on my face. "Why did you stay?" he asked quietly, his eyes searching my expression.

I rolled my eyes at that. "Because you're in rut, and you're probably going to be desperate for it again before I could manage to finish taking a shower."

A smile twitched at the corner of his mouth and died. "I suspect you're correct," he said, still in that serious tone. "But I meant... when you saw me."

My brows drew together as I regarded him. "You mean when I saw your cocks."

Pain flickered across his face, but he didn't look away from me. "Yes."

"What made you so certain I was going to go fleeing for the hills?" I asked at last, not sure how to answer him without telling him my body was still pounding with desire.

"I had a life before I was like this. A paramour." His tail wrapped around my ankle as he took a breath. "You're not the first to see me like that."

I felt my eyes widening at the admission. But of course he'd had someone. He was wealthy and titled, the Flame of Faery, the sort of man people cultivated and wooed. Why wouldn't he have had a lover when he'd been injured? The surprise was that he hadn't had one since.

A harsh smile cut across his face before melting back away, eased out of his expression by longing and sorrow. "She tried," he said, his voice going dull. "We'd been together for eighteen hundred and thirty-three years, and it was all but miraculous that I'd survived long enough for Ayre to do... this. Keep me alive." He swallowed, his eyes closing. "People acted like she should have been delighted to have me back. That to leave because I was a disfigured monstrosity would be a cruelty." Pain crossed his face again, tension tightening the corners of his eyes as he looked into my face. "It was crueler that she stayed."

"Varis," I said, horror coloring the word.

He set one finger against my lips to silence me. "I wanted to believe it would work. That if I could endure the way she flinched when I came into a room or the way she always pulled away when I tried to touch her, she would get used to what had happened to me." His jaw clenched and his tail tightened on my ankle, an almost imperceptible shudder running through him at the memories. "She got better at hiding it, and I told myself that things were going to go back to the way they'd been. That love could conquer all, and that even a beast could be desired."

I could only stare at him, the unhealed wounds on his heart writing themselves across his face. Eighteen hundred years. I couldn't even imagine it.

"She tried to have sex with me on my birthday, ten months after I'd been hurt," he said, in that same dead, quiet voice. "She hadn't seen me naked. Didn't know that I was... like this. I hadn't... been hard. I didn't know how different I was, either, but neither did I think it would matter. She was kissing me for the first time since it had happened, putting her hands on me, and it felt like I was finally waking up out of the nightmare. I th-thought..." Varistan's whole body tensed as he stuttered across the word. He didn't close his eyes, the pain in his gaze boring into me. "I thought I was coming alive again. We would make love, I thought, and it would all be better."

"What did she do?" I asked, my voice cracking and my lips moving against his skin.

One tear fell from his unblinking eyes, dropping across the bridge of his nose to darken the pillow. "She left," he said, with simple finality. "'I can't do this, Vee.'" Varis imitated the disgusted voice of a woman with such perfection that I knew the words had to be burned into his soul—that he'd replayed them over and over again, unable to escape them. "'You surely can't expect me to want to touch that thing. Gods, you're like an animal now.'" He leaned forward, his agony radiating across his face. "'It would have been better if he'd castrated you.'"

Rage flared inside of me. My face twisted into a snarl, adrenaline spiking and sweat prickling along my skin. "Fuck that and fuck her," I spat, grabbing Varistan by the horn when it looked like he'd try to turn away.

His eyes snapped back to mine, desperation overtaking pain.

"You listen to me, Varistan Yllaxira," I said, putting all my force of will behind the words. "There's nothing wrong with your body, and there sure as hell is nothing wrong with your *cock*. You want to know why I stayed? It's because you're fucking *gorgeous*. There's women who would *kill* to be in this bed with you. If you'd get your head out of your ass and stop trying to prove yourself to the most bigoted fae you can find, maybe you wouldn't end up humping a gods-damned pillow instead of someone eager to have a man who can fuck her silly!"

Varistan stared at me as if he couldn't recognize me, his crimson eyes wide and mouth parted. The blades of his spade flared, gripping my ankle. I could see his pulse jumping in his throat.

"You... enjoyed that?" he asked, his voice strained. His eyes darted down between us, along his own body. "...Me?"

"I would've thought that was pretty fucking obvious," I said, rolling my eyes. "You gloat about me looking at you enough."

"Well... I..." He swallowed, eyes darting across my face. "I thought you were... playing with me. Teasing me with... with what I couldn't have, like I'd done to you. And I'm not entirely... changed. I still have an attractive face and chest—"

"You have an attractive everything," I said, cutting him off. "Do you honestly think I could feign being unable to peel my eyes off you? I can't even feign being polite. You're like someone took the idea of sexual attraction and made it a man. It's a real problem for my self-control."

His lashes fluttered, eyes not quite blinking closed. "She was my partner for nearly two millennia, and she couldn't even bear to look at me in the end."

"You're such a fucking idiot." I made myself let go of his horn and got out of his face, rolling onto my back and putting my hands over my own face. "You don't have to live the rest of your fucking life by one woman's awful opinion, and especially not your *ex's* opinion. Dear gods, Varistan, have you seriously not even *masturbated* for the past eighty years?"

He didn't answer me at first, but I didn't really expect him to. There was a pretty big difference between being so horny it hurt and letting your bond-servant boss you through a couple orgasms, and getting yelled at by that same bondservant for being stupid. He tolerated a lot of sass from me, but I still suspected that I was going to be doing a lot of "your grace"-ing once he was done being in heat.

"Shall I assume you're not including humping pillows while in rut under 'masturbation'?" he asked in a suspiciously calm voice.

I looked at him sidelong through my fingers. He only watched me, his expression bland. His tail slid higher up my leg, wrapping around my calf with the tip running along the back of my knee.

"I am not," I said, trying not to let him see how that touch woke all of the quiescent sexual desire. I didn't forget the darkness of his words—but with his focus on me like a hawk, it was hard to cling to sorrow.

"Then, yes," he said, pushing himself up from the bed. "I have not even masturbated for the past eighty years." Varistan rolled his shoulder, then shifted his weight, moving to frame my body with his, blocking out the light with his mantled wings. "It seems to me that you'd like that to change."

"Might make you less unbearable if you weren't constantly sexually frustrated." I managed to keep the words from sounding like I wanted him to kiss me silent through a herculean force of will. The jig would be up if he so much as raked his gaze down my body; my nipples were definitely showing through my thin bra, and my panties were soaked through from getting him off. Having him naked and on all fours above me wasn't helping the state of things; my whole body throbbed from how much I wanted him to be touching me.

Even as I thought that, his eyes flickered down between us, then back up to my face as I flushed. "Is it the pheromones?" he asked, far too casually. Varistan's fingers wrapped around my wrist, his gaze sharpening as he set my hand on his hardening cocks, the pair of them held close together as they emerged from his slit. "Or is it truly this?"

I made a tiny whimper of desire as the slick heat of him touched my skin, my fingers closing automatically around his shafts, holding them together.

Varistan shuddered at my touch, his lashes fluttering and mouth parting. He rocked his hips against my hand before lowering himself towards me, heat in his gaze. "I can't do anything about the rut pheromones but bathe," he said, the words dripping with lust. "And I certainly can't make what's in your hand anything other than what it is. But if you're truly enjoying what I have to offer, I'm willing to make a bargain with you."

I had to swallow to call enough moisture to my mouth to speak. "What bargain?"

He started thrusting as his cocks grew fully hard, the pair of them too large for me to fully close my hand around. "I'll masturbate for you during this rut, as long as I can have my tongue between your legs while I do so." When I didn't immediately answer, shocked by him, a reckless smile spread across his face. "You don't need to agree. But if you do, know that I will greatly enjoy learning your flavor and hearing you moan my name as you come for me."

"Feeling pretty confident in your abilities?" I managed to get out, despite my whole body screaming at me to just say yes already. "Eighty years rusty."

Varistan rolled his shoulders like a cat about to pounce and lowered his mouth to my ear. "Eighty years rusty, and with a forked tongue instead of a fae one," he said in an agreeable tone of voice. "But though she may have left Raven Court to escape me, I kept a woman thoroughly pleasured for more than eighteen hundred years. I suspect I've forgotten more about how to devour a woman than most human men learn in their lifetimes."

I slid a finger between his cocks as I stroked him, holding them together against it to make him growl out his pleasure. "As long as you haven't forgotten it all, I'm willing," I said, not quite managing to sound nonchalant. "Don't you dare burn my vagina."

He chuckled, low and full of wicked promise. "Don't worry, Bells," he said, halfway to a croon. "I have no desire to burn you. I'm hoping that if I please you well enough, you might consent to allow me to attempt to, hm, fuck you silly."

"O-oh," I stammered out as he drove his hips forward. "You're really, really in rut, aren't you?"

"Yes," he purred into my ear. "I am really, really in rut. I'm going to be like this for days, and you're probably going to tire of it far sooner than I desire." Varistan's fingertips traced down my stomach before he ran two down between my legs, pressing down on my clit through my wet panties. "It's my intention to enjoy you until then," he said, his voice going deeper and his tail wrapping up onto my bare thigh. "I'd rather have you here than anyone else, and since you're determined to have me, perhaps you'll indulge my eagerness to have you in return."

I canted my hips against his fingers, the contact sending sharp pleasure radiating into me, making my core clench and pussy throb. "You just like that I've got my hand on your cocks."

His answering snarl shot heat through me, goosebumps rising on my arms. "No, Isabela," Varistan said with ferocity, his breath heating. "I like that you're *mine*. I like that you *see* me, and that you don't treat me like a monster for what you find. I like that I can beg you, and that I can tease you, and that you refuse to be intimidated by me." His voice softened as he spoke, until the words held nothing but lustful affection.

His fingers started circling on my clit, rubbing in time to his slow thrusts. "I like that you're a clever, ferocious, domineering woman who enjoyed walking in on me desperate and needy. And, yes, I very much like that your hand is wrapped around me. But it's hardly the only thing I like about you."

"I didn't realize you liked me that much," I said, the words far breathier than I intended, with his fingers touching me like he knew exactly how to do it. Gods, eighteen hundred years of keeping the same woman satisfied. He was going to make *me* come to pieces.

He planted a hot kiss on my neck, sliding his tail under my panties with the same motion. I gasped from the contact, my back arching and hips lifting. Varistan took the opportunity to drag my panties off of me, his fingers slipping on my skin from how gods-damn wet I was. My breath hitched as he pushed himself up, running his tongue along his sharp canine.

"Allow me to rectify that," Varistan said. He held my wet panties up to his face with his tail, looking at me sidelong while he inhaled with every appearance of enjoyment. With deliberate care, he ran his tongue up along them, giving me a show as he shuddered with pleasure. "It's my desire to make you come until you're wrung dry. Are you amenable?"

"I don't know that it works that way for human women," I panted out, fixated on the movement of his mouth.

A very wicked smile spread across his face. "Let's find out."

CHAPTER THIRTY-TWO

SKILL VERSUS ENDURANCE

V aristan moved like a predator as he settled into place between my legs, his wings and tail shifting. He looked up along my body with sultry heat in his eyes, and reached between his legs to stroke himself.

His hand stopped as if he'd hit a wall, whole body tensing and ears pinning back. He stayed there, his eyes on mine and his hand six inches from his cock, fighting himself. Then he snarled, turning away and slamming his hand down against the bed. "Fuck!" Varistan's tail snapped through the air, the blades flaring. He looked back to me, panting in frustration. "I thought this would be easier with such an alluring reward set before me."

I pushed myself up onto my elbows, regarding him with concern. He didn't shift his position, wings half-mantled and tail swinging like an angry cat's, tension lining his whole body.

"You had a very different cock for thousands of years," I said at last, getting a sharp look in return. I scooted underneath him and picked up his hand, running my thumb along his palm as Varistan let himself be manhandled. "But while you may have two, now, you can still treat them like one." I wrapped his hand around the base of his cocks so that he held them against each other. "You can't change how it feels, but you don't have to change what you do. One new thing at a time."

Pleasure made his eyelashes flutter as I moved his hand along his shafts, holding his fingers closed with mine. Varistan held my gaze, lust softening his expression as his eyes hazed and mouth parted.

I lightened my touch on his hand, then let my fingers fall away. Varistan kept stroking himself, his face dropping towards mine.

"That's my good Varis," I crooned to him. "Do you want what you bargained for?"

"I'm fae," he said, heat coming into his expression again. "If you want me to keep doing this, you have to give me what I bargained for."

I didn't need any more encouragement. I slid back out from under him and spread my legs, watching his expression like a hawk as I framed my sex with two fingers. "Come and take it, then."

He shivered with anticipation, and did.

The Flame of Faery ran his tongue up my center with demand, his breath hot and gaze smoldering. Eighty years of possessing a forked tongue apparently gave him enough knowledge of how to control it that he didn't hesitate to use it to his advantage. Varis caressed my folds, the forks of his tongue gripping me as he massaged my pussy. The heat of his touch left throbbing tension in his wake, my body responding to having a dragon at the door with reckless need.

I grabbed one of his horns without planning on it, but as soon as I did, I wanted more. With as much demand as him, I wrapped my other hand around his second horn and tilted his head to give me more pressure.

Varistan growled his pleasure, the vibration shivering through my body. He ran his tongue directly along my entrance with slow satisfaction—then flicked the tip up and grabbed my clit between the forks of his tongue.

Lightning-strike pleasure lanced into me from the sudden pressure. I jerked his face towards me, hunting for more, and Varis gave me everything I could have asked for. He ate me relentlessly, his skill unparalleled by anyone else I'd ever had between my legs. Varistan seemed to know exactly how to move to draw me toward climax, increasing his pressure and speed without needing any direction from the hands on his horns. Heat coiled inside of me, building like embers in the heart of a campfire, my core aching for more.

He set his fingertips against my entrance for a moment, the tips of his claws pricking my delicate skin. I had a sharp moment of panic – under no circumstances would that feel good – but Varistan growled again and took them away, leaving me unsatisfied. I gripped down on myself, wanting to have him inside me despite the danger, tilting my hips up against his face to drive away the need with the force of his tongue pressing against me.

As if he could read my mind, Varistan's fingers ran along my folds again, framing my entrance. A heartbeat later, the tip of his tail settled into the notch of his fingers, and without giving me a chance to protest, he slid it into me.

My back came off the bed from how fucking *good* he felt inside me. Nothing I'd imagined could compare. The fleshy blades of his spade radiated heat, pressing out against the walls of my channel in waves, and the slick scales offered a hard contrast to his suede-soft spade. I bucked my hips against him and was rewarded with a flare of his spade-tail and a deep rumble of pleasure.

Pressure sang out through me, spreading me wider as the nubs hardened along his tail. I could feel them coming up as I fucked myself on his tail, the texture making me gasp with pleasure as it pushed up against my g-spot and down against the lower wall of my pussy. My pussy closed down with a flash of pressure, a whimper escaping my throat from the feel of his tail filling me.

Varistan apparently appreciated the sensation as much as I did, because he came, *hard*, groaning with pleasure as his wings fanned the air. He looked up at me with hazed crimson eyes as his orgasm shook him, his hot tongue pressed against my clit, and didn't for one second pause in devouring me.

His lashes fluttered closed as I clenched down on his tail again, eyes just about rolling back in an expression of ecstatic bliss. Varis moaned again, taking his hand off his cocks to drag my thighs wider, starting to fuck me with his tail in earnest. That skilled tongue massaged my clit, rubbing me on all sides, making the tension inside of me build into unbearable need.

"Varis—" I gasped out, getting a pleased moan in return. "Gods, Varis, just—"

But I didn't have to tell him what to do to get me off—that the smooth slide of his tongue wouldn't be enough. He surged forward as my hands spasmed on his horns, the ivory lengths of his canines pressing hard against me as he sucked on my clit, forked tongue still gripping me.

The sudden sensation shocked through me, a flare of brilliant pleasure that threw me into orgasm. The pressure inside me shattered, my body slamming down on his tail and my hands jerking his face even closer to my skin. Liquid fire pulsed through my core, my blood feeling molten as ecstasy wiped away all other sensation. Every wave of pleasure made my hips buck against him, chasing more of it, the feel of his tail thrusting into me blinding me to the world.

Bliss washed through me as I came down, my fingers going lax and slipping off Varistan's horns. I fell back against the bed, breathing hard. Holy gods. Someone had given this up? Had given *him* up?

Her loss, holy fuck.

I moaned as he slid his tail out of me, back arching and hips lifting involuntarily from the sensation. Varis made a low sound, sliding his hands up my thighs until his fingers framed my mound.

"Good?" he asked, as if he needed me to tell him.

"I've had... better," I panted out, not giving him the satisfaction.

"Oh, *have* you?" Varis asked, sounding delighted. He shoved himself up and got off the bed, sauntering over to his dressing table.

A solid eight inches of his tail gleamed with wet, still flared and nubbed with arousal. Gods, he must have had it folded inside of me, pushed in so deep it curled around. I started blushing as I stared at it, pressing my thighs together and squirming a little bit. His tail wasn't all that slender at the tip. He had to have figured out that I liked getting filled and stretched, and he had the equipment to do exactly that.

Fuck, eighteen hundred years of experience. You don't stand a chance, Bells.

Varistan rustled around and came up with a pair of nail clippers and a metal file, then turned and leaned his hip against the edge of the table. Smirking at me as he made eye contact, Varis slid the talon of his left index finger between the blades of the clippers, and cut the tip off.

"That was my first time fucking someone with my tail, so perhaps it wasn't the best demonstration of my abilities," he said in a conciliatory tone, his eyes gleaming with avarice like garnets in the sun. He slid his middle talon between the blades. "I would hate for this encounter to end with you comparing my tongue disfavorably to another's. I shall endeavor to do better."

Varis licked his lips and clipped his second nail.

He examined his shortened claws with interest before flicking his eyes back to mine. With great deliberation, he clipped one a little shorter, and started filing down the sharp edges. "I've heard it said that skills long neglected can bloom back to life with only a little effort. I should like to find out if that holds true with... linguistics."

I had to stop staring at him like a deer caught by a poacher's light—couldn't just lie sprawled here with my pulse throbbing between my legs as he cut his claws for me. Even thinking that, though, I bit my lip as he ran his tongue across his blunted talons to test the edges, my skin tingling and nipples aching.

"Gonna— Gonna practice on me?" I managed to get out, cursing myself for stammering. Gods, he'd never believe I was holding my own like this.

"Practice?" A slow smile spread across his face. Varistan sauntered back towards me, wings trailing behind him like a cloak. "Oh, Bells," he crooned, his voice dropping deeper on my name. "I have so very much more in mind for you."

"And what's that?" I asked, pushing myself up on my side to look at him, dropping my knee to emphasize the curve of my hips.

My duke paused at the edge of the bed, tension flickering into his expression despite his bold words. He took a deep breath, his ruby gaze intense, and started rubbing two fingers along his wet slit. His wings flared, face softening with pleasure and tail snaking behind him. "My desire is to be the best lover you've ever had," he crooned, spreading his fingers to frame his cocks as they slid out. "For you to crave my... c—cock," he said, flinching as he stuttered on the word. "To crave... me. This." Varis took a deep breath. "Us. At least for one night."

"Varis," I whispered in surprise, my eyes widening and mouth parting.

He bit his lower lip, expression determined. Slowly, he wrapped his hand around his cocks, stroking up along the lengths. "Still willing?" he asked, with an edge of nervousness to the question, as if I might turn him down.

My eyes fell to his groin, drawn to the motion of his hand. I dragged my eyes back up along his body, appreciating the strong lines of his torso and the stark black of his scales. Meeting his eyes again, I licked my lips, smiling as his eyes flashed. "More than willing," I said, anticipation throbbing under my skin. "Eager."

A shiver ran down his spine, his wings mantling and tail snapping. "For my tongue? Or for something else?"

"Depends," I said, smirking at him as he leaned towards me. "Would you rather have me sit on your face or your cock?"

Varistan got onto the bed, moving like a prowling beast as he crawled towards me. "So you want me on my back, do you?" he asked, his voice low and wanting. "Am I a tool to be used for your pleasure?"

"You could be," I replied, pushing myself up and sliding my fingers into his hair.

He shivered, tilting his head back in silent request.

With a slow smile, I tightened my fingers in his hair and gave it a light tug, eliciting a whimper of pleasure. Biting my lip, I yanked harder, making him arch his back in pleasure, the blades of his tail flaring and the white arcs of his canines showing. "You get your pick, Varis. How shall I use you?"

With a hungry expression, Varis reached up and took my hand out of his hair, running his mouth against my palm. He closed his eyes, looking like he was steeling himself, then lowered my hand to his cocks.

Breathing harder with stress, he met my gaze with tension in his face. "I would much rather offer you a fae cock than what I possess," he said, ears pulling back and lip lifting in what looked like disgust. "But if you're willing to take a dragon to bed, I desperately want even these lengths buried in your heat."

I lowered my lashes, regarding him, and wrapped my hand around his shafts. "I've never had any desire to take a dragon to bed," I said, moving forward to force him to lie down. "So it's a good thing there's not one in bed with me."

Varis obeyed the silent command, lowering himself down slowly, keeping his body within a handspan of mine as I took him down to the bed. He looked stressed, the focus and need of rut leaving him panting with desire and his personal struggle with his body putting fear on his beautiful face.

"Varis," I crooned. "You're fae. Your body is fae. Your wings. Your flame." I stroked his cocks, reveling in the heat of his body and the slickness of his desire. "Your *cock*."

"Bells," he whispered, breathing hard and staring up at me with what looked like longing.

"Fae blood pumps through your veins. It's fae desire that has you sprawled naked beneath me." I settled closer to him, my pulse throbbing between my legs. "There's a fae duke in my bed, and I want him to fuck me with his fae cock." I almost couldn't believe I was saying the words, even while reckless want gripped me and a feral smile overtook my expression. "Are you amenable?"

"Gods, yes," Varistan said, his voice throaty with desire. "Far more than amenable. Three orgasms in and I've not yet begun to be sated. I feel like a hound who has at last caught the scent of a hare." His hands settled onto my hips even as he reached up with his wings, caressing my shoulders with his wing-thumbs. "I want you."

"Good." I punctuated the word with a squeeze of my hand that made his back arch with pleasure, his hands and wings digging into me. "Tell me how."

A bemused expression settled onto his face, his mouth quirking up into a smile. Varistan rolled his hips, thrusting his cocks up through my grip. "You seemed so certain you knew what you had in your hand. Do you need instruction on how to use it?"

I grinned at him, pleased by the humor in his voice. "I have plenty of experience, and rather more imagination," I assured him. "But I want to hear you call your cock fae, and since you don't get what you want until you do..."

His expression sharpened as my voice trailed off, gaze going intense. "I can't say what I don't believe."

"Believe it, then." I let go of him, sitting up and shifting so I could drop my hips down against his.

The feel of his hot shaft against my pussy made me moan, my core tensing in a flash of pleasure that shocked through me, tension coiling inside me. With slow deliberation, I rocked my hips, pressing down and tilting my pelvis so that the bumps of his cock hit my clit. I could feel his claws digging into my skin, eight sharp and two dull, and the thought of what he might do with those newly-blunted talons made my core tense again.

"Say it, Varis," I said, starting to grind against him in slow rhythm. "I can come like this, but I'll make sure you don't."

He whined, bucking his hips up into my motion. His tail wrapped loosely around my hips, the tip brushing against my ass.

"Say it," I said again, letting him drag my hips harder against him. I leaned forward, framing his body with mine. "Say 'I want to fuck you with my fae cock, Bells.' I want to hear you say it."

Varistan's throat worked. "I— I w-want to fuck you wi-wi-with—," he got out, the combined strain of being in heat and forcing himself to say something as fact that he didn't fully believe making him struggle with the words. "*Gods*, I want to fuck you, I want to fuck you, please just let me fuck you—"

As hot as it was to hear Varis beg to fuck me, and as badly as I wanted it, I wouldn't let him off the hook that easily.

"What do you want to fuck me with?" I asked, reaching between us to stroke his upper cock while I rubbed myself along the lower one. "Your tail? Your tongue?" I licked my lips, enjoying the lust painted across his face. "Those fingers you so thoughtfully blunted?"

"You know what I want inside you," he said, halfway to a whine. "Bells, you already know—"

Fae can't lie. That doesn't mean they have some secret line to the universe, and everything they say is factually true. Fae can be mistaken, or misled. But they have to *believe* what they say is true when they say it, and Varis had kept his body divided in two, deep inside his heart.

If being in rut was what it took to undo that for him, I would use it mercilessly.

"I know you believe you're fae," I said, the words fierce as I leaned closer to him, breathing hard as pleasure soared into me with every drive of his hips against me. "You told me you were fae the first day we met. That you were still *Varistan.*"

"I am, gods, I am, please just *fuck* me—"

"If you're fae, then your body is fae." I couldn't keep my movement slow, picking up the pace, the heat of his shafts making my clit even more sensitive. Every slide of my hips across his textured cock sent bright sparks down my veins, fanning desire into a conflagration. *Fuck, I really might come from just this.* "Even if you can't believe that, you have to know this cock is yours."

Varistan whimpered, his flared tail rubbing against my ass as he matched my pace with his thrusts. "—It's mine," he said, the look in his eyes becoming desperate. "It's my... cock. And I'm... f—fae. I'm fae." He whimpered again as I let the head of his cock run against my folds. "I'm fae, and it's my cock, and I want to fuck you with it— Please, can that be enough?"

I didn't want to break him, and *gods* did I ever want to take him. *Good enough.*

"That's my good duke," I purred, guiding his lower shaft to my entrance. "Now you can fuck me."

He cried out in pleasure as he thrust into me, practically a shout, his back coming off the bed and tail hauling me down against him.

The sensation all but blinded me to the world, my body suddenly filled and his draconic heat melting me from within. I pressed the other half of his cock against me, the smoothness of its underside a contrast to the textured bumps I'd been grinding against. Half a heartbeat later, Varistan had his fingertips against my clit and his wing replacing his hand on my hip, holding me in place as he rutted up into me.

"Oh, black night," he gasped out, looking up at me through hazed eyes. "Oh, gods, Bells, I'm so sensitive, you feel so good, I don't think I can last for you at all—"

I made some sort of *yuh-huh* sound, completely unable to focus in the face of the onslaught of sensation. My pussy spasmed against him with a shock of pleasure, his clever fingers relentless and his cock filling me like he'd been made for me. I could feel my pulse throbbing in my nipples and throat and core, every beat of my heart matching the strong thrusts of the man between my legs.

Varis cried out, his eyes closing and mouth dropping open into the expression of ecstasy. Heat flooded me as he slammed his fucking *fae cock* into my depths, and the radiating pleasure of that thrust combined with the press of his fingers against my sensitized clit threw me into orgasm alongside him.

My back bowed, fingernails digging into the bedding as my whole body shook. My pussy clenched down on him in waves, each flash of tension wiping all thought away, leaving nothing behind but mindless bliss. I ground down against him, chasing that sensation, and when Varis lifted me off his cock I snarled at him like an animal.

He snarled back, his voice so much more dangerous than mine, and drove his other shaft into me instead.

CHAPTER THIRTY-THREE

SIX DAYS LATER

M y thighs shook as I held myself in place, both my hands braced on the bed. Varistan watched me with hazed contentment as he massaged my clit with his tongue in languid strokes, his hand moving slowly along his cocks. I met his gaze, panting while my legs tried to collapse, barely functional enough to focus on his face.

"Your turn to do the work," I moaned, my left thigh shaking so hard I had to rest most of my weight on his face.

He made a low sound, pleasure and amusement blending together. His hands settled on my hips, and with smooth strength Varistan laid me down on my side on the bed. "I'd like to try something," he said, sounding almost sleepy. He fetched the bottle of oil with his tail and poured some into his palm while I lay there, not really capable of moving. "How would you feel about having a sword in each sheath?"

My body closed down with a flash of pleasure before going lax again, warmth suffusing me. "Sounds nice," I said, my eyes closing. I almost could have fallen asleep, as thoroughly fucked as it was possible to be. "You should do that."

Varistan made another low hum, sliding his slick fingers between my legs. He rubbed his fingertips against my ass, and I was so gods-damned tired that I couldn't do anything but relax into it, heat coiling through me with ease. With care, he slid one finger into me, warming up my body. It had been a long time since I'd done anal, but he seemed to know exactly how slowly to go, and by the time he was finger-fucking me with two fingers I was practically squirming for it, making little moans with every thrust.

He pulled his fingers out of me and dropped a kiss on my thigh, with more affection than I'd anticipated. Varistan sprawled down in front of me, draping my thigh over his hips and lining up his cocks with my entrances, then stroked my hair out of my face with a soft smile. "My beautiful Isabela," he murmured as he started rocking himself into me. "Do you think I was made for this?"

I moaned as his cocks spread me open, the pressure driving out thought. I didn't have enough energy left to chase anything, or even to clench down around him. I could only surrender to him, letting Varistan sink further into me with each thrust, my body throbbing. The pleasure soaked into my core, pressure and heat building and spreading deep inside me.

It didn't feel like getting fucked. It felt like Varistan was making love to me, using his body solely to please me, with no regard for chasing his own pleasure. He rolled his hips with slow care, one hand painting delicate tracery across my skin while the other found my clit, circling in time with his smooth thrusts. He leaned forward, nuzzling my neck and dropping a warm kiss at the join of my jaw.

"You're not in rut anymore," I said between soft moans.

"I'm not." Varistan said it with lazy ease, inhaling with his mouth against my skin. "Would you like me to stop?"

"No," I moaned. "You feel amazing."

"And you intoxicate me." He paired the words with a sharp drive of his hips, making me gasp with pleasure as he hilted himself in me.

Everything felt so good, building on itself. The texture of his shafts meant that each slow thrust became a series of sensations, the pressure rising and falling as each hard bump slid through me. His draconic body heat soaked into me, easing my tired muscles into lax bliss and leaving me with the feeling of growing tension despite the total relaxation. I couldn't even move to meet him, the slow, relentless motion of his body becoming my entire world.

Even the needy sounds I was making faded away as my whole self centered on the building heat inside of me. Varistan's fingers moved against me with perfect confidence, knowing just how to touch me as he slowly fucked me into oblivion. His hot mouth pressed soft kisses down my throat, achingly sweet and full of possessive affection.

"Bells," he said softly, almost whispering it, "come for me."

He knew exactly when to say it—knew the moment when everything would break. Orgasm crashed into me, my body throbbing with release as I gasped for breath, blinded by the pleasure that flooded through my veins. My body closed down around him in waves, each clench of my orgasm sending ecstasy streaking up my spine and into my belly.

Varistan gasped out his pleasure against me, his breath coming in hard pants and his hips stuttering against mine as he followed me over the edge. His cocks flexed inside of me as he came from the demand of my core gripping him, his fingers pressing hard against my clit, sending white pleasure through me with lightning-strike force. The heat of his come spread down the lengths of the shafts buried deep inside me, the sensation commanding all my attention.

Without thinking, I buried my fingers in his hair and kissed him, putting my tongue in his open mouth with wanton demand. He answered me, the forks of his tongue gripping me as he claimed my taste, kissing me like he was desperate for it. Varis moaned into my mouth as my fingers tightened in his hair, shuddering with pleasure. He lost himself in me, and I never wanted him to find his way back.

We came down together, panting with our open mouths touching, staring into each other's eyes. He was buried inside me, his tail coiled around my thigh and his fingers on my clit, his red eyes full of longing. I was wrapped around him, my fingers gripping his hair so tightly it had to hurt, his come dripping out of me.

I let go first, releasing him and falling back onto the bed, dazed. Varistan moved with obvious reluctance, sliding out of me and replacing his hips with one of the much-abused towels. I didn't even have the wherewithal to use it; I simply lay there, breathing hard, staring at the wall.

Almost hesitantly, as if he wasn't sure it would still be allowed, Varistan shifted so he could spoon me from behind, settling his arm around me and resting his face against my sweaty hair. With the fingers of his wing, he drew the loose strands of my hair away from my face, tucking them behind my ear. "How do you feel?" he asked in a low murmur.

"Like I'm ruined for human men," I answered, the words dragging as I made myself focus on thinking again. "You?"

I felt his lips turn up into a smile against my hair. "As if being shaped this way isn't quite as terrible as I believed." Varistan nuzzled me, his breath warm against my skin. "Any regrets?"

"We should've tried that one sooner."

He barked a laugh, tucking me closer to his chest and settling his wing over me. "You could perhaps convince me to try it again, if you ask nicely."

I let myself melt against the strong wall of his body. Probably I should have gotten up, taken a hot shower, and collapsed into my own bed again at long last, but my legs weren't up to it and I liked having Varis curled around me too much to leave. That was a rather troubling observation; I decided not to think about it. "What if I ask meanly?"

"That, too," Varis said in an agreeable voice. "Though perhaps wait a little while before making the attempt. It's likely that I'm going to sleep for the next several days before waking up extremely hungry and cranky," he added, sounding nervous about it. "The aftermath of rut has typically been such, but I've never actually... rutted... for it. I don't know how my body will respond."

"You're always cranky when you're hungry, and you haven't eaten in days. You're going to be a huge pain in the ass. Er, your grace," I tacked on, realizing belatedly that now that he was out of rut, I probably would have to go back to pretending to treat him like my superior.

"Varis," he said, pressing his warm mouth against my neck for a moment. "While I'd appreciate the honorific in public, it seems foolish to pretend that our relationship isn't fundamentally different than it was a week ago."

"I'm not going to be your mistress," I said, my voice wavering as I thought about it. I couldn't imagine being his dutiful bondservant in public and doing this in private. "I won't let you make me into your dirty little secret."

He flinched, his arm tightening across my chest. "It wasn't an offer with strings attached," he said quietly. "You don't have to be my lover to call me by my name. You deserve far more than such a thing."

"The sex was that good, huh?" I asked, trying to keep myself awake when my whole body was ready for collapse.

"Sleep, Isabela," he said, not answering me. Varis kissed me again, a soft touch of his lips to my pulse. "You can chide me for my many shortcomings when you awaken."

"Mkay," I said, my breathing slowing without me telling it to. I wanted to say something else snarky, but sleep came on the heels of permission, and I passed out in Varistan's arms before I could think of anything to say.

Chapter Thirty-Four

PROBLEMATIC

I woke up in my own bed with sore legs, a dehydration headache, and a raging UTI. Aside from the location, all of that should have been a predictable result of a multi-day fuck session that ended in collapse, but it was an unpleasant way to awaken. I whimpered my way through peeing, took a hot shower while sitting on the shower floor, then hauled myself down to Varistan's healers to get fixed up.

Lianka took one look at me and started laughing, one hand over her mouth while her dark eyes danced with mirth.

I gave her a longsuffering look and plopped myself down on the examination table. "Go on, get it all out," I said with a sigh. "I can take it."

She smirked at me, getting her mirth under control. "That's quite a few marks on your neck, Isabela. Change your mind about what you'd do if the duke offered you his sword?"

I narrowly avoided saying "swords" – Varistan would *not* want that to be common knowledge – and grimaced, my hand going to my neck. "Nobody told me he goes into fucking *rut*," I complained as she raised one eyebrow at me. "How was I supposed to resist the fucking Flame of Faery eager to please for once in his life?"

Her lips twitched, but Lianka came over, tilting my chin to look at my spectacular collection of hickeys. "It's not like any of us have spent it with him," she pointed out as she started running her thumbs slowly down my throat to erase all of Varistan's hard work. "Historically, he's locked himself in his rooms and ridden it out alone. The main evidence has been the laundry and his bad temper."

"Well, I suspect he'll be in mildly better temper than usual when he wakes up this time, though whoever gets the short straw for the laundry has my sympathies," I said, shifting to give her access to the other side of my neck. "I'd appreciate it if you fixed my lady parts. The aftermath of this particular fuckfest is deeply uncomfortable."

She laughed again at that, a bright peal of sound. "Gods, I love how you put things," Lianka said, shaking her head. "Yes, I'll deal with that infection for you. Are the love-bites just on the neck, or was he more creative?"

My cheeks went hot as I flushed crimson, dropping my eyes. "I've got them on my thighs, and one on my tit," I muttered. "His Grace was pretty motivated."

"Want me to clean them up?" she asked with levity, her voice lilting.

I grumbled, but I pulled off my shirt and flipped my skirt up to show her the damage.

Her brows shot up, and Lianka gave me a look of humorous disbelief. "'Motivated' is one way to put it," she said, rubbing her fingers over the bruise on my breast, the mild ache subsiding as the bruise cleared. She tapped on one of the actual bites on my thigh, with four distinct marks for his canines. "I heard it sounded like he was devouring you, but it looks like he actually made an attempt to do so."

"Oh, gods," I groaned, putting one hand over my face as she healed my bruises. "Absolutely everyone in the castle knows, don't they?"

"Probably," Lianka said, her lips twitching. "You weren't very sly about it. The two of you vanished into his rooms for six days, you had his guards bring you food and a suspicious quantity of oil, and from what I've heard, neither of you were particularly quiet about your pleasure."

"He may be terrible, but he knows his way around a pussy," I said, wrinkling my nose at her.

She grinned at me, then settled her fingers in a triangle below my navel. "Uh-huh. Give me a moment to clean this up. Do you need a contraceptive?"

"Nah," I said, shaking my head. "One of the healers in Lylvenore had a neat trick for turning off human menstrual cycling, so I'm good to go on that front."

"Mm." Her eyes went unfocused, the discomfort of the UTI fading as she healed the consequences of passing out directly after being fucked. When she finished, Lianka exhaled, then crossed her arms over her chest and gave me a meaningful look. "In the future, might I suggest visiting the lavatory after sex?" she said in an arch tone.

I made another face at her, earning myself another smirk. "Yeah, yeah," I said, tugging my shirt back on. "In my defense, I was a good girl up until the very end."

"That's not how I'd describe those bite marks," Lianka retorted with a smirk.

I blushed again, my memory helpfully replaying the hungry light in Varistan's eyes when he'd sunk his teeth into my thigh with that dangerous growl, his fingers buried in me and his thumb pressing against my clit. Gods. He really might have ruined me for human men. "There are many ways to be good," I said, despite the heat on my cheeks. "Though, um, since I asked for it, I think probably he was the one being good, there."

A slow smile spread across her face, full of wicked delight. "Do you command His Grace now, Isabela?"

"Doubtful," I said with a laugh, shaking my skirt out. "Given the context, I think pretty much all of His Grace's compliance can be chalked up to being in rut. I'm certainly not expecting anything else."

But even as I said the words, doubts came creeping in. I couldn't forget the way Varis had made love to me at the very end, his slow care and the affection in his kisses. He'd talked to me like we were friends and lovers—as if all the arrogance and armor had been stripped away, and the man underneath was one who wanted to cuddle after sex and be kissed awake in the morning. He'd offered to have sex with me again, and not in a rakish way, but like he wanted the affection that could come with it.

He put me in my own bed to sleep, I reminded myself, feeling foolish. He'd kept to the letter of our bargain instead of keeping me with him. Varistan being affectionate after six days of almost nonstop sex shouldn't come as a surprise, and it didn't mean anything, whether or not he'd told me to call him by his name. After all those orgasms, who wouldn't be affectionate? He was going to wake up hungry and cranky and with a great deal of regret over those gentle words and sweet kisses, and that would be that.

"Well," she said, giving me a thoughtful look, "he's known for being a very loyal mate. His last paramour was demanding and petty, but His Grace didn't brook any ill words towards her, and by all appearances he was dedicated to her happiness. You may find him more attached to you than you anticipated."

I crossed my arms over my chest as I leaned against the doorframe, trying to look casual despite the topic of conversation. "One rut's worth of sex does not a paramour make."

"Nah, but it's a good start," Lianka said, laughing. "Be realistic, Bells. Do you honestly think he's going to be any *less* greedy for your time now that you've allowed him to thoroughly ravish you?"

My cheeks grew hot as I blushed, with far too many salacious memories from the past days to even begin to protest that description of events. "Possessiveness is all well and good, but it doesn't make for a particular satisfying relationship if I'm still a second-class citizen," I said with a sigh, looking away. "Even if he *does* decide I'm his equal, can you honestly imagine him risking his social standing by having a human paramour?"

Hurt tightened my chest at the picture I painted, my mouth almost trembling. Stupid; I had no right to feel upset about things I'd always known about Varistan. He'd never claimed to be otherwise. Fucking me didn't change the rest of the world. I'd gone in of my own free will, and he hadn't promised me anything.

"I won't be his shameful secret, even if the reasons are good," I said at last, when Lianka only gave me a sympathetic look. "It'll just make me hate him, in the end."

"Not very secret, but I take your point." Lianka heaved a sigh of her own, turning to lean flat against the wall. "You're my friend, and I'd like to think you claimed some happiness this past week. But if what you want is to step away from His Grace, I'll support you in that." She looked over at me with a half-smile. "I'll admit I'm a bit jealous, though. Even with the scales, His Grace is rather attractive, and you wobbled in here looking as if you'd been riding Sarcaryn."

"Hah!" The stag-god of sex and beauty was known to take fae and mortal lovers from time to time, but I was pretty sure Varistan had been more dedicated to sex than even Sarcaryn would have been. "You're welcome to ask His Grace for a ride. He might even say 'yes'." Jealousy twisted in my gut even as I said the words, a possessive desire for my duke that made me want to see off all comers at the tip of a spear.

Lianka waggled her eyebrows at me before heading back over to her desk. "Given that look on your face, I think not," she said with an impish smile. "Go wobble back upstairs. I'll have someone bring food up for you."

I stuck my tongue out at her, appreciating her willingness to leaven the tone and getting a grin in return. "Much appreciated," I said. I turned to head back out, then paused, looking back over my shoulder at her. "Er... what day is it?"

She burst out laughing, tossing her head back. "Oh, dear gods," she said, looking delighted. "It's the fourteenth, Bells, and before you ask, it's around one in the afternoon. Now shoo; I have work."

"Yes, ma'am," I said in a chipper voice, heading back upstairs with her laughter following behind me.

I heard Varistan before I'd even gotten halfway up the servant's stairway. I supposed I'd seen enough of him over the past months that I could recognize even the muffled cadence of his voice, because before I'd even consciously identified that he was enraged I was sprinting up the stairs. My legs screamed at me as I flung open the door and darted into the hallway, Varistan's furious voice slicing through the air.

"Where is she?! If she's been hurt I'll fucking kill you—"

I rounded the corner to see a stark naked Varistan holding a guard up against the wall by the throat. Flame lit the hallway, flickering as the duke snarled, licking at the sweating, purpling face of the poor man he had in his grasp.

"Varis!" I snapped, before I could think not to. "Let him go!"

He dropped the guard and whirled towards me, his flame dying as the feral stress went out of him. The guard collapsed onto the ground, coughing as he shoved himself backwards with his feet, desperate to get away from Varistan.

"Bells." Varistan wavered on his feet, his eyes going unfocused. "You're here."

I walked slowly towards him, holding out my hands, trying to keep my eyes from flickering down to the injured guard. "Yes, I'm here," I said, keeping my voice calm. "You're not supposed to be awake yet, your grace."

"Varis," he said, taking a heavy step forward to meet me. Half his weight dropped onto my shoulders as he draped himself over me. "I'm not your grace. You're mine."

"Okay," I said soothingly. I caught the guard's eyes and mouthed, *"go"*.

He didn't need any more reason to leave, nodding and scrambling to his feet.

I turned my attention back to Varis, wrapping my arm around his waist and turning to help him back into his suite. He'd broken the gods-damned door off the hinges and singed the doorframe, but at least nothing was actively on fire. "You should still be sleeping," I said again, leading him into his bedroom. He'd completely destroyed the bed, too; there were feathers everywhere, and the mattress was flipped off the frame. "What woke you up?"

"You were gone," he said in a plaintive voice, drooping against me. "You should've been in our bed, and you were— you were— you were—" Varis tripped, almost taking both of us to the ground. "Why did you leave?" he asked, sounding like he might cry.

Gods. Apparently spending the rut with me meant his mostly-asleep post-rut self expected me to be passed out next to him, which I supposed would have made sense if we both had draconic physical cycles.

I made a snap decision and steered him towards my adjoining room, figuring it would be easiest to deal with him if I had a place to lay him down. "You're the one who put me in my own bed, sweetheart," I replied, falling into the endearment in an attempt to soothe. "I didn't leave."

"Oh," he said, tripping again as I hauled him through the doorway. "That was really stupid of me."

"Lots of that going around," I muttered, mostly to myself.

I managed to tip him into bed, though Varistan dragged me down with him. I ended up flat on my back with him halfway on top of me, one heavy thigh slung across my hips and an arm and wing across my chest. His tail slid under my knees and wrapped around my legs, weaving itself into a knot that ended up with the end of his tail lying in the crease between my thigh and hip.

He kissed me on the mouth, as uncoordinated as a drunk, then smiled and settled up close against me, his breathing easing. "I like our other bed better. This one is too small."

"You wrecked your bed, so you're going to have to make do with mine," I informed him, not dignifying that "our" with recognition. "If you wanted a nicer back-up bed, you should have given me something more comfortable."

"Bells," he said in a warm, sleepy voice that made it sound like I'd said something silly. "They're all your beds."

"I'll hold you to that," I said, trying not to laugh. "Promises still count if you're mostly non-functional."

With a low sound, Varis pressed his warm mouth to my pulse. "You're mine," he said, as if the words relieved some enormous burden. "You can't hurt me like that."

Resigning myself to being trapped in bed, I stroked Varistan's hair back, tucking the tangled strands behind his pointed ear. "Why're you so worried I might?"

"She liked to," he said, his voice fading towards sleep. "Fae shouldn't trust like I do. Said she had to... punish me." He kissed me again, then ran his tongue along my skin in a slow caress that shocked heat down my spine even as my blood ran cold at his admission. "Don't know why I keep... doing it. Maybe it's my... mortal... blood." He fell silent, his breathing slowing as he lay there. His thumb swept across my shoulder, then stilled.

"Varis?" I asked when he didn't continue, my heart still pounding.

His tail tightened on my leg. "She didn't... love me, did... she?" he asked, almost too quietly to hear, his words coming slower and slower. "Do you think anyone... ever... will...?"

I couldn't respond at first, struck silent by the naked pain in those words. But by the time I'd managed to unstick my tongue from the roof of my mouth, Varis was snoring softly against my shoulder, and it was far too late to give him an answer.

CHAPTER THIRTY-FIVE

THE MORNING AFTER

Within an hour, pretty much everyone in Nyx Shaeras knew that six days of sex had rendered Varistan an overprotective, unconscious heap lying directly on top of me. I had reason to be grateful for Lianka sending me lunch, because once word got out that the duke was liable to burn the castle down if he woke up without me, leaving the room wasn't really an option. I still had bodily functions to tend to, of course, but aside from zipping to and from the bathroom, I was consigned to lying in bed with Varistan wrapped around me.

If it hadn't been such a spectacle, it would have been really enjoyable. Cuddling with Varis all day left me as contented as a cat in the sun, his body heat radiating into me and his musk-and-copper scent warming the air. He must have had the energy to rinse himself off before collapsing into bed, because he neither smelled like days-old sex or rut pheromones. He only smelled like himself, a heady aroma that left me wanting to run my nose against his skin.

I could always tell when he was dreaming, because he often made faint expressions or murmured in his sleep. Most of it was nonsense, or little snips of dream-conversations that didn't make much sense out-of-context, but occasionally he'd say something that made me smirk. The best of those was a grumbling admission of, *"don't be mean, Bells; you know I like being pretty."* It was hardly the only time he used my nickname, though I supposed that made sense. We'd fucked our way through his rut and he was plastered against me; of course I'd be on the mind.

Varis followed me across the bed whenever I shifted, fitting himself to my body with a sixth sense for where I was in space. Sometimes he'd nuzzle me, but more often his tail would coil around one or more of my limbs. When I gave in to curiosity and fondled the blades of his tail-spade, he flared them and moaned, rolling his hips against me. After that, I kept my idle petting to his hair and arms, though any time his tail slid along my bare skin I had to fight temptation.

Of course, it also *was* a spectacle, and mostly at my expense. People didn't exactly troop past to ogle the naked duke sprawled on top of his bondservant, but almost every meal had someone new bringing it to me, and more than a few of my sparring buddies dropped in to "keep me company." Even Lianka came by to give the duke a post-rut physical once-over, telling me with a wink that he must have been sheathing his sword somewhere better than usual, given the lack of friction burns.

I refrained both from giving her salacious details and telling her that the friction burns came courtesy of pants and pillows, but it was a bit of a battle.

For Varistan's sake, I tried to keep him mostly under blankets, but given how domestic it looked for him to be under a patchwork quilt while obviously naked, I wasn't sure it was much of an upgrade. I was sure people could keep their mouths shut in front of him, especially about something as likely to earn them a flame-eyed glare as *that*, but for the two-and-a-half days I spent in bed with the unconscious duke, they sure enjoyed the sight.

Varistan finally woke up for real in the early morning of the seventeenth. I'd taken far too many naps in the previous days to sleep through the full night, so as luck had it, I'd woken with the dawn and was considering if I should try to wiggle out of his grasp to pee when he made a low sound and started shifting. His nose and mouth ran along my neck as his tail uncoiled from around my leg, sliding along my calf with languid strength.

"Bells," he murmured, inhaling with his nose buried in my hair. "You're here."

"It was be here or have you rampaging through the castle," I said, amused. "You were very insistent."

He stilled. "I was?"

"You wrecked your bedroom, broke down both your doors, and nearly strangled poor Maelin in your half-conscious unhappiness to discover me gone," I informed him. "Flattering, I guess, even though I'm pretty sure you're the one who put mc in my own bed."

"I did," Varis said, sounding embarrassed. "I assumed that would be your preference, and was... charmed, I suppose, to find you with me instead." He swallowed, the sound only audible because he was still nestled up next to me. "I didn't intend to cause trouble, or to force you to rest alongside me. This wasn't part of our bargain."

"Eh." I wiggled around to face him, grinning at his expression of consternation. "Easiest watch duty I've ever pulled. You weren't even that talkative in your sleep, your grace."

A wistful smile tugged at one corner of his mouth. Varis brushed my hair back, running his fingertips down along the curve of my ear. "Still 'your grace'?"

My eyes dropped down to his left hand as he lowered it, a blush warming my cheeks as I caught sight of the blunted claws of his index and middle fingers. Gods, everybody would know what *that* meant, and precisely why and for whom he'd cut them. "Force of habit, I guess," I said, dragging my eyes back up to his. "I'm still your bondservant, and you're still my master. Unless you're intending on forgiving that debt, our relationship is always going to have you on top."

His expression flashed into wickedness at that, and my light blush turned into a raging inferno at the implications of what I'd said.

"I don't remember being on top very often," Varis purred at me. "As I recall, you mostly had me on my knees, on my back, and being ridden like a prize stallion—"

I shoved him hard on the shoulder, earning a bright laugh and brilliant smile.

He picked up my hand and dropped a kiss onto my knuckles as if I was a courtier. He didn't let go of my hand, either, his thumb caressing my fingers as he set our hands on the bed. "As to our relationship..." One corner of Varistan's mouth twitched back towards unhappiness, his eyes dropping down to my hand. "You never owed me anything. I regret acting as I did, and claiming your service. The actions of a bondservant of Lylvenore could have been paid for by its vicereine."

"You're fae, Varis," I said quietly, examining him.

Varis looked back up at me, an emotion I couldn't identify in his beautiful garnet eyes.

When he didn't speak, I tried out a smile, though the image of him strangling my father by firelight flickered through my memories. "No matter the reason, attempted murder is the sort of insult and debt one of your folk can't ignore, and Her Excellency wasn't around to offer recompense. I know I'm not like you, but I grew up around fae, and I know what it's like." I squeezed his fingers where he still held my hand. "That level of imbalance demands immediate attention. I don't blame you for wanting him dead, and I'm not sorry to have made that bargain with you."

"I tend to like imbalance," he said, his mouth tugging to one side. "Not that much imbalance, perhaps, but some. I like to... forgive, and to be forgiven."

"Kinky," I said, raising one brow. Fae could physically feel debts, and most of them disliked the sensation of owing someone something and enjoyed extracting payment from others. That Varistan liked the opposite was unusual, to say the least.

"Very," he said with a huff of laughter. "It gets me into trouble more often than not. I have a very... mortal, shall we say, tendency towards forgetting that others will bind me to the implications of the things I say or offer." Varis shrugged one shoulder, not meeting my eyes. "I work hard not to relax into it, but I'm hardly perfect."

"You do have many flaws," I said agreeably, grinning when he smirked at me. "Is this all a lead-in to releasing me from this bond of ours?"

Varistan flinched, drawing his fingers out of mine and rolling onto his back. "No," he said, his voice soft. "I cannot absolve you of that."

"Hey." I moved to look down at him, framing his shoulders with mine and smiling at him with my loose hair cascading down to tangle with his. "I understand, Varis. Really. Even humans sometimes struggle to forgive. You don't need to be anything other than fae."

His face softened into longing, heartbreak writing itself across his expression. He reached up, sliding his fingers into my hair, looking tormented. "Bells, I—"

A sharp knock sounded on the door, followed immediately by the door opening. Varistan and I both jerked, our eyes going to the doorway, in which stood yet another in the long parade of people bringing me food. She wore a look of surprise, which rapidly changed into fear as Varistan's attention snapped from me to the tray in her hand.

He went tense, an almost feral expression coming onto his face as he started shoving me off of him with slow deliberation. I didn't make it easy for him, keeping my body between the half-dragon who hadn't eaten in almost ten days and the woman holding the food.

"I'll just... leave this here," she squeaked, setting the tray on the table and fleeing back into the servant's hallway.

Varistan managed to get me onto my back, clambering over me with no regard for where my body parts were, his state of nudity, or the fact that half the blankets were tangled around him. Several very uncomfortable seconds later, he was inhaling what was supposed to be my breakfast and most of my bed was on the floor, me included. I disentangled myself from the sheets and left him to it, getting dressed and emerging to get significantly more food delivered to the duke's quarters.

When I returned, I found Varistan prowling around in the nude and my plates literally licked clean, without even a crumb left behind. His eyes snapped to me as soon as I came in, though he seemed to relax as he saw me, some of the tension easing out of his shoulders.

"What day is it?" he asked, his tail flicking.

"The seventeenth. You were down for about three days."

"Damnit." He stalked over to one of his wardrobes and started digging around in it, growling to himself. "I was supposed to meet with that Maestrizen emissary days ago, but I suppose today will have to do, assuming they arrived. Run me a bath. Frankincense and cedarwood. I'm going to need to wear a fucking sword, too."

My cheek twitched. So much for a fundamental change to our relationship. "Yes, your grace."

His spine stiffened, wings and spade-tail flaring, but I didn't give him a chance to repent. I walked into the bathroom without a backwards glance, and turned on the water so the Duke of Nyx Shaeras could have his fucking bath.

Chapter Thirty-Six

UNRULY

I knew I had no right to be pissed about Varistan treating me like he always had. It wasn't a relationship of equals; he was the duke, and I was the bondservant. But it still rankled me to go from morning pillow-talk to *"run me a bath"*. If I'd been pettier, maybe I would have turned on the hot water, but I wasn't vindictive enough to make his life miserable for being the same person he'd always been.

I thought about it, though. Loudly.

"Bells."

My shoulders tensed at the sound of Varistan's voice, but I managed to plaster a polite expression onto my face before I turned. "Your bath will be ready in a few minutes, your grace," I said, keeping my tone as servile as possible.

He winced. "Please don't do that."

"Why shouldn't I?" I asked. "Your grace."

"I didn't mean to be... demanding," Varistan, his tail flicking like an anxious cat's. "Surely you know that I'm habitually imperious. I tend to speak my desires in commands instead of requests, but you may still refuse me, if you so choose."

"I really can't," I said, my brows drawing together as I regarded him. He looked uncomfortable, like there was something more distressing him than merely me being irritated. "We have a bargain, and it's not one I'm interested in breaking."

Varistan looked away, skin darkening with a blush as he resettled his wings. "You're mine whether or not you obey," he said quietly. "You need not be my slave to be at my side. I would far prefer that you weren't."

I crossed my arms across my chest, keeping an eye on the water level in the tub. "That's not how it used to be."

Pain crossed his face as he laughed, the sound harsh. "Of course it's not. Is anything how it used to be?" He crossed the short distance across the room to me, bending down to turn off the water. "You were my enemy, and you've stepped inside my guard and disarmed me. You could have done me great harm, but you've come alongside me to succor, instead." Varistan reached for me, hesitating for a moment before tucking a strand of my hair behind my ear. "Your defiance is *saving* me, Isabela. Can't you see that?"

My heart pounded, my eyes wide and lips parted as I stared up into his garnet eyes. Fae couldn't lie. They *couldn't lie*. Everything he said, he believed in its entirety.

"Saving you?" I asked, cursing myself for how small my voice sounded.

"Saving me," he said again, warm and sure, his expression softening as he held my gaze. "I didn't understand the gift I'd been given when I claimed you, and I'm sure I still don't have a full grasp of what I so unwillingly won, but my life is so much better for having you in it."

I had to wet my mouth to speak again, my chest tight and breath constricted. "I ran you a bath, but it's spruce and keskyr, not frankincense and cedarwood."

A slow smile spread across his face, calling an answering one to mine. "How wicked of you."

My lips twitched, my breathing still too shallow and skin too warm. "I could have run you a hot bath, instead. You didn't specify temperature."

Varistan ran two fingers up my throat to my chin, lifting my face towards his as his eyes dropped to my mouth. "You're being pert," he crooned, his tail curving around my ankle.

"And your bath is getting warm."

That look in his eyes made me want to throw caution to the wind—to grab him by the neck and kiss him like we really were lovers, and then maybe to get fucked on the bathroom counter. Lianka had healed all of the evidence of his affection, but he'd warned me about his interest in leaving his mark on me where everyone could see from the very beginning. Maybe he would bite me again, leave the impression of his teeth in my skin so the world would know...

Even if he did, though, it didn't change my status. It was one thing to flirt, or even to fuck me during his rut, but to make me his paramour? I couldn't imagine it, and I was sure I'd never be able to survive the pain of being his lover only in private. He meant far more to me than I'd ever expected. If it was different... but it wasn't, and *he* wasn't. I couldn't step into that future with him.

If he kissed me, I wouldn't be able to say no. I wanted it too badly to ever refuse him.

But all he did was brush his thumb across my lips with a wistful expression before getting in the tub, tilting his head back with a sigh. "Could you choose something for me to wear?" he asked, closing his eyes. "And I'm going to need a great deal more to eat if you want me to be at all capable of being polite to anyone aside from you, not that I'm doing an excellent job even at that."

"Second one's already taken care of," I said, my eyes skimming down his body before I tore my gaze away. "I'll find you something nice to wear."

"Thank you," he said, his voice soft. When I shot him a look, his lips curled up into a sultry smile, his lashes lowered. "I like imbalance, Bells," Varis purred, running his hands down his chest and onto his thighs as he arched his back with slow sensuality. "It feels... quite pleasurable."

My cheeks flamed hot, and I zipped out of the bathroom with his low chuckle chasing me.

Gods and monsters. He'd always liked playing with me, and now he had so much more ammunition. We'd had sex for six days straight, and it hadn't been exactly rote mating. Varistan knew a great deal more about me than he had two weeks ago, and my stupid face couldn't hide my emotions if my life depended on it.

Oh, fuck. We're going to be sleeping in the same bed tonight. How in the wilds am I going to keep from shoving his hand down my pants and begging for it?

I would... I would just have to display a little self-control. Surely I could keep myself from acting like a bitch in heat.

To at least keep myself from standing there thinking about it, I dug through his wardrobes until I found something that I thought would be decent for meeting an emissary from a foreign nation—and one where the relationship had historically been far from friendly. Varistan might have been the one to reach out, but that didn't bring any form of alliance with it. The Maestrizen envoy would almost certainly be wary, and Varistan would have to walk a fine line between displaying strength and aggression.

I wasn't exactly a connoisseur of clothing, but I did know a lot about presentation from the fights, and when I'd put Varistan into the clothing I'd chosen for him, I took a moment to admire, feeling smug. The cut of the doublet followed the lines of his body in a way that emphasized his perfection of form, obviously made after the war instead of being modified after he'd acquired his wings. The foggy gray-green and silver softened the inherent danger in his body, and with the combination of moonstone jewelry and the silver-hilted rapier hanging off his belt, the duke looked every inch the wealthy nobleman.

"Like the view?" he asked, his ears tilting forward.

"Always have," I said, giving him a quick wink. I glanced over at the plates he'd cleaned off while I'd been doing his hair. "Need anything more to eat?"

"Not at the moment, but I make no promises about an hour from now," Varis said, sounding a bit rueful. "Entering directly into tense political negotiations the same day I wake up from post-rut collapse leaves something to be desired, I'm afraid."

"You're less cranky than I expected, though," I said, smirking at him.

He snorted a laugh, one hand resting on the pommel of his sword and the thumb of the other hooked through a belt-loop. "Fucking my way through rut instead of begrudgingly grinding out orgasms seems to have done wonders for the aftermath. Who would have guessed?"

"Hm." My lips twitched as I fought off laughter. "Are you going to be less insufferable, now?"

"Almost certainly not," he said cheerfully, flashing me a sharp-toothed grin. "I suspect I'm far too avaricious of your attention to be anything less than a nuisance, even if I *am* somewhat less sexually frustrated." Varistan sauntered over to me and tipped my chin up with his wing, meeting my gaze with smoldering, half-lidded eyes. "Though given that I now know what I'll be missing, I can't even guarantee the frustration will be less."

I flushed and stepped away from his touch, my chest going tight as I looked away. "I didn't intend—"

"Bells," he said in a gentle voice, cutting me off.

My eyes darted back up to his, but all Varis did was smile, his expression soft.

"Do you want me to refrain from flirting with you, at least for a time?" he asked, ears leaning forward as he resettled his wing behind him. "You did me a great kindness, and it's not my desire to punish you for it by making you uncomfortable, or by demanding a closeness you didn't intend to maintain when you offered to take me in hand."

If anything, I blushed harder, my cheeks so tight it almost hurt.

"Bells," Varis said again, with an edge of concern. "Is it something I did?"

Something you won't do, I wanted to say, and didn't. Instead, I rubbed the back of my neck and gave him a self-conscious smile. "I'm not that great at... complicated relationships," I said, shrugging one shoulder. "I don't really know how to do this. The touching, the flirting, that's fine. It's just..."

"The sex," Varistan finished quietly.

I nodded, not meeting his eyes.

"Then I won't initiate sexually unless you give me leave to do so," he said. When my eyes shot back up to his, Varistan gave me a rakish smile. "I'm fae, Bells. I have no interest in sexual congress without the freely-given consent of my partners, and beyond that, I have no desire for you to leave my bed with enduring regrets." He sighed, turning away from me with his wings furled closed and his tail lying in a curve on the ground. "Besides," he added, the word almost inaudible. "I'm not certain I have the confidence to offer this body to you again without the relentless need of rut."

"You did once," I said, watching him.

One corner of his mouth twitched towards a smile that died as soon as it was born. "You were already there with me," Varistan said, his hand closing around the pommel of his sword. "The taste of your desire on my tongue and our scents so intermingled I could scarcely tell where each of us began. But to do it now? To bare a body I cannot help but see as misshapen and pray that I'll see desire instead of disgust in your eyes?" He shuddered, his ears shifting in the wary-animal way of a stressed fae.

He didn't finish the thought, standing there with his breathing careful and his face tense with unhappiness.

I watched him for a moment, then walked over and hugged him, nestling my face against his neck and wrapping my arms around his waist as I leaned against his chest. Varistan went stiff with surprise, the frozen startle response so common to the fae making me smile as I relaxed against him. Slowly, as if he were wary of my response, Varis returned the embrace, his breathing growing more labored as he rested his face against mine.

"It's not a question of desire," I murmured, my lips brushing against the skin of his throat. With gentle deliberation, I pressed a kiss to his pulse, nuzzling him when his breath hitched. "It's not even a question of affection, or alignment. But I didn't *do* complicated in Lylvenore, or anything approaching permanence. I expected to die young, and I didn't want to leave anyone behind the way that I got left behind."

Varistan's arms tightened, and I felt his tail wrap around my legs.

I kissed him again, the warmth of his skin inviting far more than that. "I also don't like pretending, and it's a pretty inescapable fact that there's a power imbalance here. The sex was incredible, and I don't regret spending the rut with you, but I don't like the idea of being your mistress, even if it's an open secret. Calling you 'Varis' in private and 'your grace' in public makes me feel..." I hesitated, resting my face against him. "It makes me feel used."

He sighed, some of the tension leaving his body. "Even Yesika called me 'your grace' in public."

"Yesika?" I asked, looking up at him.

"My former paramour," he said, the corners of his mouth twitching down in an expression of sorrow. "In noble circles, it's common even for spouses to call each other by their honorifics, at least in formal situations."

"I'm not your spouse," I pointed out.

Varis sighed again, resting his chin on my head. "No, you're not," he said. "But surely you understand why it would go badly were I to offer any position of openly egalitarian alliance."

I flinched; he inhaled against my hair before letting me go and stepping back. We looked at each other for a moment, the hazel of my human eyes meeting his fae crimson.

"I do," I said softly. "It's Raven Court, I'm human, and you're..." I trailed off, not sure of exactly what to say.

"You can say it." Varistan's tail snapped behind him. "I'm an amalgam in a Court that despises aberrant fae. My body ties me indelibly to the Windswept King and to the Annihilation War, and thus to the worst atrocities of recent memory. Few can look at me without thinking of it." He settled back into his posture of snooty aplomb, his lashes lowered and chin tilted up. "Stag Court and Windswept Court are both ruled by monsters and their human brides. How, then, would it appear to King and Court for this particular royal son to take a human paramour?"

I didn't say anything, simply watching him with my mouth tugging to the side in unhappiness. As far as reasons for not being willing to claim me openly went, avoiding the open hostility of others was a powerful one, especially when those others included the Raven King. Nyx Shaeras was only under Varistan's protection for as long as the Raven King believed Varistan served his interests.

I couldn't forget Alpha talking about how Nyx Shaeras was one of the safest places in Raven Court to be human or wildling, and as much as I wanted to burn down the system that made such a refuge necessary, the place to start was probably not the refuge itself. I still hated it, though. I wanted to be worth the fight—wanted him to care enough about me to refuse to allow me to have to live in his shadow.

I couldn't forget that decade of marriage negotiations, either. Varistan was well aware of the value of his hand, and with his dedication to his duchy, I doubted he would throw that away on me.

He drummed his claws against the hilt of his sword, looking away. "I care far more about Nyx Shaeras than my own happiness, Bells," he said, echoing my thoughts. "If the price of keeping security for my people is a cold bed, so be it. I've paid worse before."

"Your bed is never cold," I offered with a slight smile, trying to leaven the mood.

Varis' expression twisted, his ears pinning back. "And that's exactly the problem, isn't it? What I am is inescapable. If things were different—"

A sharp knock rang through the room, making both of us jump. Varistan recovered first, straightening his posture before calling, "Come in."

The door opened to reveal Sintuviel, Varistan's steward. He bowed with military perfection, his golden-blonde hair falling over his shoulder. "Your grace," he said, his crisp voice without emotion. "I was informed of your awakening. The emissary from Maestrizen arrived four days ago, and has remained, but seems restless. What is your desire?"

Varistan's jaw tensed, and the tip of his tail started to flick like a nervous cat's. "Is there time to set up an early luncheon? I suspect I'll need to... explain myself."

"Of course, your grace," the steward said, his eyes flicking over to me for a moment. "A private one?"

My duke gave a curt nod. "For myself and Isabela, and the emissary and whomever they choose to bring with them."

Sintuviel bowed again. "Very well, your grace. Where would you like to await my summons?"

"My office will do, but send Bells something appropriate to wear, first."

"As you will it." The steward cast a long, measuring look at me, then turned on his heel and left me alone with Varistan once more.

CHAPTER THIRTY-SEVEN

DRACONIC INSTINCTS

I furrowed my brow at Varistan, who only swished his tail, not looking at me. At last, I sighed, planting my hands on my hips. "I hardly think meeting the emissary with your bondservant in tow is going to make the right impression—"

"I don't care," he said, cutting me off. His ear tilted towards me in the way of an attentive animal, though he still stood there looking at the closed door, wearing a moody expression. "I'm better off post-rut than I think I would have been without you, but I'm also experiencing an entirely new set of instincts, and I'm disinclined to trust my behavior if I ignore them."

"And what instincts are those?" I demanded, frowning at him.

His ears pinned back. "I'd rather not say."

"And I'd rather not go swanning into a formal meeting like I'm either your duchess or your favorite pet, especially not without knowing why."

Varistan flinched, his shoulders hunching. He muttered something I didn't quite catch, and lifted his lip in a half-snarl when I flicked him on the wing.

"Don't be an ass, your grace," I said. "Just tell me."

"You promised to hold my hand," he said, still muttering the words.

"And I will," I said, with a little less antagonism. "But I still want to know why you need it."

He turned away from me, tucking his wings closer to his back. "A male war-dragon competes for females before and during rut," he said, the words tense. "A great deal of his success depends on his ability to impress his chosen female with his hoard, combat prowess, and, ah... sexual endurance. As you've... experienced." With a gusty sigh, he tilted his head back, the spade of his tail flaring as he did.

"A successful male then proceeds to dote on his mate until their chicks are old enough to leave the nest in the spring," Varistan continued, sounding embarrassed about it. "He'll hunt for her, bring her valuables to adorn their nest, and generally devote himself to being at her side in case she wants anything. Suffice it to say that I'm rather disinclined to be parted from you, and I suspect it will last through the winter. If you want an exhaustive description of precisely what biological drives I so unwillingly acquired, I have the treatise in my library."

I suppressed a laugh, not very successfully. When Varistan frowned at me sidelong, I flashed him a grin. "You're a bit of a bookish dork, aren't you?"

He made a disgruntled sound. "I looked it up after my first rut. That's not an unreasonable thing to do when confronted with the unknown. And where else would I put a book, aside from my library?"

"Not a bad thing, your grace," I said, amused both at the idea of Varistan bringing me shiny things like a jackdaw and at the fact that he had a book of dragon biology I could read. "So you're dealing with a bit more than greed, hm?"

"My current desires are along the lines of wanting to drape you with jewels, sprawl in bed with you, and feed you delicacies by hand while you tell me what an excellent provider I am," Varistan said, his skin reddening. "It's rather all-consuming, and if you make me leave your side for any other reason aside from fetching you something, I suspect I'm going to be too anxious and unhappy to be at all reasonable to deal with, even for people with whom I have established relationships. So."

"So you need me to hold your hand, and you'd like me dressed up." I smirked at him when he glanced back over at me, the intensity of his focus obvious now that I knew what to look for. "That's a bit outside our bargain, but I guess I can comply. You can channel that desire for dressing me in jewels towards acquiring coldwater pearls while I sit there looking pretty."

"You're the one who insisted on spending my rut with me," Varis grumbled, sounding sulky. "One could even say you took advantage of me. Now I'm entertaining fantasies of being your devoted pleasure-slave with little outlet for such things, and I'm not entirely sure when it's going to wear off."

"It was good for you," I said, attempting to keep my attention away from the temptation of his words by moseying towards the bathroom so I could freshen up slightly before needing to be seen by strangers.

"It certainly improved my desire to interact sexually, which is now entirely stymied," he said in a vexed tone. "I'm not certain that counts as good for me."

"Hardly entirely," I said as I opened the door to the bathroom, trying to keep my voice dry and instead managing to sound mildly antagonistic. "You've got hands, a prehensile tail, and a whole big continent of potential partners. There's surely women who'd be up for a tumble once you get your instincts straightened out."

Varistan shut the door behind us harder than necessary, almost slamming it closed. "Is that what you'd see me do?" he asked in a silken voice. "Throw the gates of Nyx Shaeras open to any woman willing to ride a dragon? Give them a quick fuck to tame my ardor before coming home to curl up in bed with you?" He flicked his wings in disgust, the tips whistling through the air. "I'm not a promiscuous man, Bells, and even if I was, I have little desire to experience the disappointment of you sending a rival woman off with a smile instead of putting her in the fucking *ground*."

"That is *not* the future I'm suggesting," I snapped back, scowling at him. There was far too much in that little tirade to unpack before we had to go be political, but I wasn't going to let it simply stand. "You might live *millions* of years, and in case you forgot, I'm mortal! This isn't going to last forever, so why in the wilds would you want me to kill your lovers?"

He snarled, flame flickering between his teeth. "Because the thought of you taking another to your bed makes *me* want to impale those shadow-lovers." Varistan turned his head and exhaled sharply, a plume of white-hot flame heating the air. "You're *mine*. Can't I hope for a little territoriality in return?"

I crossed my arms over my chest, narrowing my eyes at him. "Are you telling me I'm not allowed to decide who I have sex with?"

"No," he gritted out, wings mantled and tail lashing through the air hard enough that he smacked it against the side of the tub. "But I reserve the right to draw my sword if they cause you the least measure of harm."

"So if I got in a spat with a lover..."

"Stabbing," Varis said, the word clipped.

"Stepped on my foot at a dance," I said with a lifted brow, amused despite myself at his overprotectiveness.

"Stabbing," he said again, though the corner of his mouth twitched.

I gave him a pretty smile. "Left a bite mark?"

He wrapped his tail around my ankle. "I'm not sure what's so difficult to comprehend about my desires in this, Bells. That would *certainly* be courting stabbing. Possibly also immolation."

I laughed, the stress falling away as I tilted my head back to look up at the ceiling. "You're being ridiculous. You know that, right?"

He blew a curl of flame at me with a smirk. "I told you right from the beginning that I have a dragon's greed. Are you surprised to see it heightened after spending days tangled up with me?"

Lianka's words scrolled through my mind—*do you honestly think he's going to be any _less_ greedy for your time now that you've allowed him to thoroughly ravish you?*

How prescient of you, I thought at her, still smiling as I turned to the sink and started running the water so I could wash my face. "Is that part going to wear off when spring comes?"

With surprising gentleness, Varis stepped up behind me and combed the claws of his wing through my hair, running the scaled backs of his fingers down along the curve of my ear. "I hope not," he said, his voice softening as he looked down at me. "I'm not certain I could convey the full depths of my pleasure when the focus of my possessiveness turns towards me of her own desire and volition."

"Something else to like about your body?" I asked, looking up over my shoulder at him with a smile.

"Perhaps," he said, his full attention on me. "But only if this ends well, I think."

"What if it doesn't end?"

Varis tilted his head to the side, ears leaning forward. "What would make you say that?"

I smirked up at him. "You planning on becoming something other than possessive over me?"

"No," he said, those sharp-tipped ears of his pinning back. "But you could come to hate it, and me in turn."

"Do I look like I hate it?" I asked, feeling bold as I leaned my shoulders against his broad chest and ran my bare toes up along his scaled ankle.

His tail wrapped around my leg like a vine. "No," he said again, exhaling the word as he leaned towards me.

"Then don't borrow trouble, your grace." I flicked my tongue out at him for a moment, grinning at the flash of desire in his eyes. "And maybe let me get ready for our meeting."

"Very well." Varistan untangled his tail from my legs, running one knuckle down the line of my spine before he stepped away. "May I stay while you do?"

Desire sparkled along my skin at the words, the thought of having my duke watching me while I washed and changed my clothing making my nipples harden and breath quicken. Fuck, if I was naked in a room with him, I was very shortly thereafter going to want to have *him* naked—

Get it together, Bells, I scolded myself. *He's waiting for an answer.*

"Sure," I said, shrugging one shoulder as if it was no big deal. "Not like you haven't seen me naked before."

His answering chuckle seemed to fill the room, remembered fingers tracing up my inner thighs and down along my sides. I shivered without meaning to, my pulse pounding in my core.

Gods, Bells. You're so fucked.

So, so fucked.

CHAPTER THIRTY-EIGHT

FAERY SIGN

S hockingly, I made it all the way from fully dressed through naked and out the other side again without breaking down and shoving Varistan against the wall. Some of that was due to needing to move quickly to be presentable for what amounted to brunch with a foreign dignitary, but a lot of that was due to my duke's restraint. He watched me – he always watched me – but he didn't pair the eye-fucking with anything approaching verbal flirting, instead walking me through the sort of manners that accompanied initial meetings between potential trade partners.

Even Varistan forcing me to recite the formal greetings back to him couldn't fully take my mind off the movement of his hands as he painstakingly laced my corset for me. Nor did it save me when he leaned down, his hot breath stinging my skin, and told me that he'd thought I couldn't get any more beautiful than when I'd been sprawled ruined in his bed, but he was glad to be proven wrong.

The walk to the Sea Room was long enough that at least I wasn't reliving what it felt like to have the Flame of Faery's cock inside me when we arrived.

We stepped into the room like a pair, with me standing at Varistan's left hand. Despite Varistan's invitation for the envoy to bring a companion to this meeting, only one person was in the room, and he stood when we entered.

He didn't bow. Neither did Varistan.

Maestrizen hadn't told us who they would send as emissary, save for a name: Yncarin Byneros. I'd wondered if they would send a court fae in deference to Varistan's sensibilities, or if they'd shove it in his face precisely who he was inviting to his duchy. They'd apparently walked the line, because Yncarin was only barely an aberration, wearing a pair of ram's horns and a long, slender tail bearing macaw-bright feathers that stood in vivid contrast to his black clothing and deep brown skin.

He made a gesture, one I recognized as the sign for requesting that the other begin conversation. It was casual, like he'd done it a thousand times—like signing was more natural for him than speaking.

Next to me, Varistan cleared his throat and said, "Envoy Byneros, I presume. I invite you to partake of my hospitality."

Before he could say anything else, I booted him on the ankle and lifted my hands, flashing the sign for introduction before giving him my name-sign, the sign for bells.

He rocked back on his heels, all the feathers on his tail spreading wide as he signed, "I didn't expect a translator."

His signing was a slightly different variation than I was used to, but close enough that it wasn't difficult to read. I'd spent a lot of late nights signing with people who sometimes didn't have hands even approaching five-fingered, and I'd gotten used to the various ways Faery Sign could be modified.

I had to fight to keep the grin off my face as I signed back, "Duke V-Y wants to do business. He's willing to do it your way. May I have a name-sign for you?" I had to invent the most boring possible name-sign for Varistan on the fly, but that was fine. I could always change it later.

Gods, of *course* Maestrizen would use signing as their language of business. True wild fae sometimes couldn't speak at all, and a lot of sky-called fae didn't have voices friendly towards spoken language when they were shifted—but nearly everyone could sign, even if they had to use a modified version.

"Bells?" Varistan asked out of the side of his mouth, sounding stiff.

"One moment, your grace," I said in my most polite voice. "It takes a little longer to initiate conversation in sign."

The envoy gave me his name-sign, a combination of the sign for a quill pen and the letter Y.

I bowed to him and signed back, "I'm starting translation." I closed my eyes for a moment, settling into the mode of translation, then signed, "I assume you are Envoy Y-Quill. I offer you my hospitality."

Faery Sign didn't have the same syntax as spoken Faery, but anyone who used sign was used to that. I was willing to bet Yncarin could understand Varistan just fine—but using sign for the business part of the discussion was going to do wonders for our position in Maestrizen's eyes.

"I accept your hospitality, Duke," the envoy signed back, smiling at Varistan with what looked like the same irrepressible glee I was trying to smother. Oh, he had to be *loving* seeing the infamous Duke of Nyx Shaeras standing patiently next to his mortal translator while she talked to Maestrizen's aberrant envoy in a language he didn't understand. "I was surprised at the delay, but your hospitality is otherwise good." He signed the last word smaller than usual, which made me smirk.

"I accept your hospitality, your grace," I said, trying to keep my voice calm instead of bubbling with laughter. "I was surprised at the delay, but your hospitality has otherwise been acceptable."

Varistan's tail snapped behind us, but other than that little show of emotion, my duke kept it together. Though I was almost entirely certain he'd never needed to use a translator before – even bondservants spoke Faery, thanks to a common knowledge-transfer magic – apparently my behavior was cue enough, because he directed his attention to the envoy instead of to me.

"It's my hope that you're familiar with wild natures," Varistan said, sounding like he was trying not to choke on the words as he placed himself firmly in the category of wildling fae. "Unfortunately, mine isn't timed to the patterns of the sky, and I was in a deep sleep these past days. I only woke this morning. It wasn't my intention to make you wait, which is why I asked you to join me the morning I awoke."

Clever, I thought as I translated the words for Yncarin. Using the unavoidable delay as a way to build a sympathetic connection, instead of needing to give up any ground for the rudeness of leaving him loitering for days. Varistan might not consider himself political, but he'd been treading these grounds for literally thousands of years. He knew the dance.

The envoy looked contemplative, pausing for a moment before signing, "Even some sky-called have wild natures that don't obey the sky. I take no offense."

Varistan inclined his head towards Yncarin when I translated, some of the tension easing out of his shoulders. "As my guest, would you prefer to eat first, or conduct business?" he asked, his tail swishing behind him. "I, ah, imagine that it's not as simple to have formal conversations over a meal when one speaks with one's hands, and I would like my... translator... to be able to have a meal, as well."

Yncarin gave me a measuring look as I signed Varistan's words, his ears tilting forward in the fae display of pointed interest. "You're willing to have an informal meal with me?" he asked, emphasizing the sign for "informal" with a flash of his brightly-colored tail-feathers.

"You're willing to have an informal meal with me?" I translated for Varis. "With the emphasis on 'informal'." I had my suspicions about what that meant, and I wanted to make sure Varis knew what he might be agreeing to.

He tucked his wings closer together, the tips crossing behind him. "I am."

Yncarin lifted his chin, a very self-satisfied smile curving his full mouth. "I'd like to eat first." He met my eyes, with a challenging glint in his dark eyes. He gave me the sign indicating a spoken name, then said aloud, "Ynca."

Emphasis on informal, I thought, very amused at the level of antagonism it took to demand that the Duke of Nyx Shaeras sit down with an aberrant fae from Maestrizen for a meal where everyone would be calling each other by their most informal nicknames.

"My spoken-name is 'Bells,'" I signed, saying only my nickname aloud. "His spoken-name is 'Varis.'"

From Varistan's point of view, all he could understand was a smug aberration saying "*Ynca*", followed shortly thereafter by me saying "*Bells*" and "*Varis*". His spine went ramrod straight at the sound of his nickname, wings mantling and the spade of his tail flaring out in a display of aggression.

I kicked him on the ankle again.

He snapped his furious crimson gaze to mine, lip raised—then, via what looked like a supreme effort of will, folded his wings down and forced his face to relax. I could still see his pulse in the veins of his neck and feel the heat of his dragonfire radiating off of him, but at least he didn't look fully murderous.

"Shall we eat, then, Ynca?" he asked, the words carefully measured as he gestured towards the table.

"It would be my pleasure, Varis," the envoy replied, all but licking his chops.

What followed was by far the most stilted meal I had ever attended. Both men seemed to be working from the same master list of polite topics, which ranged from the expected winter weather to the latest fashions from Pinesap Court to the coming events in the feast cycle. Varistan visibly flinched every time the envoy used his nickname, which Yncarin did with comical regularity and a shark's smile. To his credit, Varistan didn't throw any barbs back, maintaining some semblance of aplomb as he ate his way through his third meal of the morning.

I sat at Varistan's right – convenient for hand-holding, given that he was left-handed and I was right-handed – and started out with my knee resting against his and his tail loosely coiled around my ankle. By the end of the meal, he was gripping my hand so hard that I was going to have to get Lianka to fix the ache, and every inch of Varistan's tail that could reach me was wrapped around my legs. He even had a solid twelve inches of his tail shoved up the cuff of my pants, the tip vibrating every time Yncarin spoke.

My feet started going numb about halfway through the luncheon.

I didn't mention it.

Once we'd well and truly exhausted every possible boring topic, Yncarin finally set his fork and knife down parallel, tines down on the plate. I'd been looking longingly for that signal almost since the meal had started; I had a lot less to say about the Pinesap fashions than they did, given that I'd never paid any attention to the fashions of the High Court.

The envoy showed his hands in a polite gesture, then signed, "Business?"

I had to peel Varistan's hand off of mine to free it, and stuck his hand between my thighs a little over halfway up from my knees, pressing my legs together to give him a little contact. With his claws pricking my inner thigh and his rapt attention on me, I gave Yncarin a polite smile and turned to look at Varistan. "Are you ready for business, your grace?"

He yanked his gaze off my mouth and looked at me as if he couldn't comprehend what I was saying, then blushed, his ears leaning back. "Oh. Right." His eyes dropped down to my lap before jerking back up to mine. "Business. Yes. Let's do that."

I couldn't suppress my smirk as I turned back to Yncarin, signing, "Duke V-Y is willing to come back to business."

If Varistan's hand crept a half-inch higher on my thigh, I pretended not to notice.

The envoy's eyes moved between me and Varistan. He raised one brow at me. "Don't translate this," he signed, meeting my eyes. "You're more than his words, yes?"

Pretty obvious, I supposed, given me kicking him multiple times and not-so-surreptitiously holding his hand under the table. "You could maybe call me his handler," I replied, pairing the last word with a modifier to indicate uncertainty, as well as giving him an expressive half-shrug. "He knows he's emotional and hot-tempered. He also wants this to work. I help ground him."

Yncarin tilted his head to the side in the way of a curious bird, his eyes half-lidded. "I'm impressed by both of you. Do you think you could do this under worse circumstances?"

"Bells?" Varistan asked quietly, sounding uncertain. "That looks like more than initiating a conversation."

"Give me a moment, your grace," I murmured back. To Yncarin, I signed, "Worse than being called his heart-name by a stranger?"

The envoy sat up a little straighter, his ears turning like those of a startled animal. "Heart-name?" he asked, his lips parted. "What spoken-name does he use with friends?"

"Varistan," I said aloud.

"Yes?" Varis said, looking at me.

I squeezed his hand with my thighs. "I'm just saying your name, your grace. We're having a conversation."

"I can see that," he said, with a touch of humor. "Do I get to know what about, aside from me?"

"Maybe later," I said, focusing on the envoy as he started signing again.

"I'm more impressed than before," he said with a slight smile. "I didn't mean to cause offense. I only use my full spoken-name in formal situations." After a moment, he added, "You may translate that."

"Envoy Byneros would like to say that he didn't intend to cause offense by using your private name, your grace," I said, trying and failing not to blush. "He only uses his full name in formal situations, which is why he gave his shortened name. It was my misstep."

Varistan swept his thumb across the top of my leg, looking back towards the envoy. "No offense claimed," he said, with a calmer voice than I'd expected. "From either of you," he added, looking at me with a wry smile.

I nodded, my cheeks still hot, and turned back to Yncarin. "Duke claims no offense from you," I signed to him, trying to look collected despite my no-doubt red cheeks. "We can do this under worse circumstances if we must. Why do you ask?"

Yncarin pursed his lips, then exhaled sharply through his nose. "Because Vicereine didn't give me her voice. She doesn't trust your duke," he signed, making a rueful expression. "I carry a message for Duke. You may translate."

Whatever he was going to say, I was pretty sure Varistan was going to hate it. But I still gave him a little nod, watching his hands.

"The words of Vicereine," he signed. "I will not bargain with you from across the sea. I will not set foot on your land before you set foot on mine. Come to my city, or leave me alone."

My eyebrows shot up, but he wasn't finished.

"My words. I am the Sword of Wild Sky," he signed. That had to be the name-sign used for the city, and though he'd used the same sign as the object for the word "Sword", he signed it with such sharp perfection I knew it must be a formal title. "I have the duty of protecting the city. It's my task to ensure that your duke won't bring death with him." Yncarin took a deep breath, looking into my eyes instead of Varistan's. "I will only allow him to come if he brings you."

I stared at him, my skin prickling with excitement. Darkest night, this was really happening. This was happening because of *me*.

With a growing, reckless smile, I turned back to a nervous-looking Varistan. "The Vicereine of Maestrizen has a message for you," I said, vivid delight brightening my voice. I was *important*. Alpha had thought my only purpose would be to be Varistan's tame pet—but it *wasn't*. "She won't bargain with you from across the sea, and she won't come here unless you set foot on her land first."

Varistan's eyes went wide, his ears pinning back as his wings hunched up.

"You have her invitation to come to Maestrizen, or to leave her alone," I said, and before he could cut me off, I held up two fingers in a hook, earning me a raised brow and a tiny snap of his teeth. "Envoy Byneros is also the Sword of Maestrizen, and charged with its protection. He says he came to ensure that you wouldn't bring death to the city, and," I added, straight up grinning at him, "he's decided that you're only allowed to go if you bring me."

He narrowed his eyes at me, flicking one ear. "You're enjoying this, aren't you."

"Really a lot," I confirmed. "I like being useful. Not that you wouldn't have brought me anyway, but..."

He sighed through his nose, closing his eyes for a long moment, the muscles in his temples jumping as he clenched and unclenched his jaw. "Every night at sea or in Maestrizen counts towards our bargain?" he asked, voice tense.

"Agreed," I said. "Nights waiting for a planned journey, as well, as long as preparations are being done with due haste."

"You're sometimes very kind to me," Varistan said in a low murmur. "Agreed." He took a deep breath, looking like he was steeling himself, then carefully unwove his tail from around my legs and took his hand off my thigh.

I followed him to my feet as he stood, balancing with care as my lower legs came back to screaming awareness, the pins-and-needles pain dominating my attention. I took careful breaths, not wanting to drag Varistan's focus onto the fact that I was hurting. It would pass soon enough.

"I accept your vicereine's invitation," Varistan said, sounding like he was calling for his own execution. "I will strive to meet her at the table." He swallowed, his hands closing into fists. "In Maestrizen."

CHAPTER THIRTY-NINE

CROSSED WIRES

I made it through the rest of the formal meeting as an ordinary translator, deciding the details of the journey and making the lengthy farewells required by fae tradition, and all but skipped my way back to Varistan's suite once we'd passed the information to Sintuviel.

When we got there, I hopped up onto his bed, sprawling across the center of it with an irrepressible grin. Holy *fuck*. We were going to *Maestrizen*, and I wasn't just Varistan's luggage. I was important—a critical piece of being able to forge an alliance with the city. Who would have thought all those late nights working the full-moon fights would pay off like *this*?

I dropped my head to the side to regard Varistan, who stood just inside the door in such an aspect of tense misery that I wanted to laugh at him. His worst fucking nightmare. We were going to *Maestrizen*. I couldn't stop gloating over it, turning it over and over in my mind. I was going to cherish every moment of this.

"Have any favorite necklaces?" I asked, grinning at him.

"...What?" he asked, sounding completely lost.

I stuck my tongue out, unable to stop smiling. "Necklaces, your grace. Shiny jewels," I said, putting a lilt on the words. "To drape across my wonderful, perfect self before you go and fetch me delicacies to feed me for dinner."

Varistan's expression snapped from woebegone to hungry focus in an instant, his wings flaring and eyes darkening as his pupils dilated. "Do you know what you're asking for?"

"For you to pay attention to me instead of where we're going next week," I said, flopping back down against the bed and wiggling with glee. "You're gonna be a wreck otherwise."

"You're asking for me to treat you like my *mate*," Varistan said with a masculine growl. He padded over and got onto the bed, crawling over to me on all fours with his wings cutting us off from the world. "To indulge in those desires.

To act as if I've won you, and as if you never want to leave the shadow of my wings." He licked his lips, his crimson gaze intense. "Is that what you want from me, Isabela? And don't say 'yes' unless the answer truly *is* 'yes'."

That look in his beautiful, inhuman eyes always made me want to throw sense to the winds, every particle of my being fixated on reckless want. "Is that something you can do for just one night?"

His face dropped a little closer to mine, his panting breath hot against my skin. "I don't know."

"Are you willing to try?" That expression was going to be the death of me. That raw look of want on the face of a man whose magnetic allure I'd never been able to ignore was more than I could ever hope to resist.

"Yes," he said, all but breathing the word. "Right now, I think I'd do anything for one more night with you."

"Dangerous words, fae duke," I crooned to him, my heart beating too hard.

"And you're a dangerous woman, Isabela," Varistan replied, saying my name like he savored every syllable, "but you're the only one in all of Faery who can't turn those words into shackles."

I reached up and hooked my fingers between the buttons of his doublet, tugging him closer to me, until the tips of my breasts pressed against his chest and our lips weren't even inches apart. "Watch me," I said, smirking as his eyes dropped to my mouth, pupils all but swallowing the red. With sensuous care, I ran my hands down his tense arms and wrapped my fingers around his wrists, holding him there. "If I wanted to literally shackle you to this bed and have my wicked way with you, there's no way you'd say 'no'."

A shudder ran down his body, a low groan escaping his throat as his back arched. "Don't torment me," he said, sounding strained as he held himself in place. "A promise is like a noose around the throat of my soul. I've given you my word not to initiate sexually without leave, but it doesn't change what I feel or desire. It... hurts... to have those yearnings and that promise drawn into such sharp conflict."

I let go of him immediately, my whole demeanor changing as I relaxed down against the bed, no longer teasing him with sex. "I'm so sorry, Varis," I said, my eyes wide as he shuddered again, his lashes fluttering with what looked like pleasure. "I had no idea. I thought fae enjoyed keeping promises."

He pushed himself up, his wings trembling, and gave a weak laugh as he closed his eyes. "I'm afraid I'm something of an exception when it comes to fae," Varis said ruefully. He heaved a sigh and pushed himself to the side, dropping down next to me with enough force that I bounced. "Whatever magic allows fae to feel debts and binds us to our words is..." His teeth clenched for a moment. "It's broken in me."

"You're not broken—" I started, turning towards him.

Varis rested two fingers against my lips with a smile that sat halfway between sad and nervous. "It's alright, Bells," he said softly. "I came to terms with it a long time ago. It feels good for most fae to complete bargains and hold true to their word. I've heard it described as coming home." His eyes searched my face, anxiety tensing his expression. "I like imbalance, but it's more than that. It's not not as gentle as coming home. It's like..." Varis squeezed his eyes closed, with a tiny shake of his head. "Is there something that feels good for you, every time? Like the first taste of water when you're dry with thirst, but over and over again?"

Touching you, I thought.

"Maybe stepping into the dueling circle," I said.

He nodded, visibly swallowing, then opened his eyes and looked unerringly into mine. "Making promises is supposed to feel uncomfortable; restricting. Apologies, like theft. Forgiveness? Even worse." Varistan's crimson eyes bored into mine, as if by the force of his will he could make me understand. "But for me?" he asked, his ears dropping down into a pose of self-consciousness I'd never seen him wear before.

"Making promises is like flying," Varis said, almost whispering the words. "I enjoy keeping them of my own will, like winging through a storm, but being forced to do so is like being yanked backwards on a leash, leaving me choking and wounded. Pleading and gratitude feel like perfection every time, never diminishing in their pleasure. And forgiveness?" He shivered, his tail curling across my legs. "To be released from a promise or a debt is better than any other high I've ever felt. It commands my whole soul with the same force as orgasm."

"Oh, wow," I said against his fingers, my eyes wide. That went so much further than merely kinky. He was built nearly the opposite of every other fae I knew, with his reactions to debt stoked like a bonfire on Midwinter.

He took his fingers away, running the backs of his claws against my cheek. "I don't generally tell people, because it's far too easy to entrap me when each step towards my doom is like a drug. Every few years – sometimes every few months   Yesika would yank the leash, and remind me of where I stood and of what I am, so that I'd stop relaxing into how good it felt." Varistan's lashes fluttered, distress flickering across his face. "It was horrible, and perhaps... necessary. After all, she was truly fae, and I'm..."

"You said you had mortal blood," I said quietly.

Varistan froze, face paling. "When did I say that?"

"Three days ago," I said. "When you woke up because I wasn't there. You told me Yesika liked to punish you for making foolish promises, and that you didn't know why you kept doing it, except for your mortal blood."

"Oh." He looked unhappy, and rather like he wanted to escape, but when I laced my fingers into his hair and started rubbing his skin with my fingertips,

Varistan's body relaxed and his breathing eased. He could never seem to manage to move away when I was offering him touch, and I used it now to keep him with me.

I didn't want him anywhere else. Just here, looking into my eyes, turning my world crimson and black. It was like looking into the heart of a volcano—*or the heart of a dragon*, I thought, wanting to lose myself in his naked soul.

"I won't tell anyone," I said, still keeping my voice soft. "You fight hard enough to keep your head above the water, and I know mortal-born fae have it harder than fae-born in Raven Court." I paused for a moment, then added, "You also don't have to tell me, if you don't want to."

"Do you know anything about my family?" Varistan asked, closing his eyes with a soft sigh.

I pursed my lips, but he didn't look tired, just comfortable, so I kept rubbing my fingers across his scalp. "I know your mother is infamous for her fondness for snowflake lovers, and that you haven't talked to her or your father for longer than you've been a duke. But that's all."

He nodded, not saying anything. I didn't push him, though. He'd had a difficult enough day already.

Eventually, Varistan exhaled heavily, then turned his head and kissed the pulse point of my wrist. The soft touch arrested me, my awareness of him blooming across my skin and frisson singing along my veins. There was nothing sexual about the contact. Nothing there but affection—and *trust*.

"My mother wanted a child very badly," he said like a secret. "She's far older than even the Raven King, with a great deal of wild magic in her blood and bones, and as such it's much harder for her to have offspring." Varistan ran his nose against my skin, inhaling slowly before brushing another gossamer kiss against my pulse. "It's generally easier for those with less magic – such as humans – to reproduce in Faery, and many of the oldest fae lack the more recent... prejudice, shall we say, against human lovers."

"You're one to talk," I murmured, a smile twitching at the corners of my mouth despite the breathlessness of having Varistan baring his soul for me.

His lashes parted, those brilliant garnet eyes capturing mine as a heart-stopping smile spread across his beautiful face. "I can admit when I've been wrong." Varistan brushed my hair behind my ear, running his fingers down along the curve. "And I was wrong to judge you for your mortality. You're the equal of any fae in Nyx Shaeras, and the better of many."

When I stared at him, Varistan flashed me an impish smile and draped his long tail along my body, the spade lying relaxed in a comma across my waist.

"My father didn't care that my mother had snowflake lovers, as long as he was still first in her life, and as long as he would be the sire of her children," he continued, quite as if he wasn't busily dismantling my understanding of him. "They were together for tens of thousands of years, each year diminishing her chance of having a child the next. Not removing, of course, for my uncle is still siring children," Varistan added with a shrug. "After all, Ayre is scarcely more than a century old, and Pelleas only reaching his first millennium."

"'Only'," I said, starting to grin.

"Mere children, compared to me," Varistan said, a wicked glint in his eyes.

"Oh, *really*," I said with a laugh. "Does that make me a babe-in-arms?"

"You're a deadly, beautiful woman," he purred back, leaning towards me with a hungry expression. "Age only truly matters when it comes to family. In all else, it's ability. And you, Bells," he said, brushing his fingers along my jaw, "are more than capable of matching me."

"Is this the draconic affection you warned me about? You're being very demonstrative," I said, not sure how else to respond to a declaration like that.

"Am I?" Varistan flashed me another smile, settling back against the bed. "As to the sordid tale, my mother grew tired of waiting. She sought out human men whose appearances were alike enough to her mate's that none would question the outcome." His expression went hard, jaw tensing and ears flattening. "She betrayed my father, and when she was at last successful, she kept the secret well. But not well enough."

He fell silent, jaw working and ears pinned back, but he seemed to recollect himself to the present, exhaling sharply before meeting my eyes again with a wary expression. "My mother was born long before the invention of notation, let alone writing. I don't know that it occurred to her that a youth she'd had taken from the mortal world for her pleasure could out-think her, nor that his words would outlive him by centuries."

Anger sparked inside me at the thought of an ancient fae capturing young men as pleasure-slaves, but I didn't take it out on Varistan. He'd had nothing to do with the circumstances of his birth, and it wasn't as if he was following in his mother's footsteps—more like the opposite.

The corners of his mouth twitched backwards towards sorrow. "I never met my sire," he said, without any emotions in the words. "I don't even know where he's buried, or if he has a grave at all. But I have the letters he wrote to the son he wasn't even supposed to know existed. I found them centuries later, secreted away beneath the slate floor in my childhood rooms." Varistan shook his head. "By the dates, I can only assume he placed them there long after I'd left, and not long before he died."

"You still have them?" I asked, surprised.

A smile touched his lips for a moment before fading away. "He etched them into thin lead sheets so they'd survive, and I..." Varistan took a deep breath. "I was less guarded, once. Furious at having an entire life stolen from me, and determined not to lose anything else. I confronted my mother, of course. She forbade me from saying anything, and I... obeyed. That might have been the end of it, except that my father was gored by a boar in the groin when I was in my tenth century, and needed healing."

He paused, holding my gaze, letting the tension build.

"My father is sterile, and he discovered so from the lips of a healer who felt she couldn't remain silent when she learned the truth."

"Oh, fuck," I whispered.

"Yes, 'fuck'," Varistan said, tilting his head back with a sigh. "And unlike me, forgiveness isn't part of his repertoire. He publicly disavowed my mother and disowned me, and told the world why. He had no proof that my sire was human, of course, but my mother's proclivities aren't a secret." He fell silent again, waiting a long moment before rubbing his face against my wrist. "I had a choice, Bells. To claim my long-dead sire and my mortal heritage, perhaps losing everything I had left in the process, or to disavow my mother and embrace being fae with single-minded dedication."

When I didn't offer commentary, Varis shrugged his wings. "You can surely guess how I chose, and why, but for the sake of history..." He huffed out a soft breath. "I cut ties with my mother and put myself under my uncle's aegis, and did a great deal to distance myself from mortality. I used my beauty and notoriety to court women who had the sort of impeccable social standing I lacked, and when I found one who would have me, I devoted myself to her happiness, and then to the duchy our partnership won for me." Pain flickered across his face as he added, "And then I lost it all anyway in Pelaimos."

"You didn't lose it all," I said, turning my head to kiss his wrist, in the sort of payback that earned me a yearning sound from deep in his throat and a shock of heat running down my spine to lodge between my legs. "You still have Nyx Shaeras. And your sire's letters."

"To my knowledge, aside from my mother and myself, you're the only one who knows about those letters," Varistan said in a serious tone. "I'd appreciate it if you didn't share. You're the first person I've told in more than two thousand years."

"Why me?" I asked, staggered by that span of time, and that level of trust.

He smiled, slow and easy. "Because when you see me hurting, your first instinct is compassion." Varistan drew his fingers through my hair, his claws skimming my skin, his smile spreading to show a line of white. "Because you apologized to me without considering the cost, and asked for nothing in return. And perhaps because we're sprawled in our bed together, and I can think of little else besides ensuring that you have everything you want, even if that's my secrets instead of my cock."

When I frowned at him, Varistan merely flashed his teeth at me, utterly unrepentant.

I opened my mouth to make a pert reply – *"What if I want your cock, too?"* – and thought better of it, pursing my lips as I regarded him. He'd liked the byplay before, but he'd leashed himself for me without hesitation, and it would be cruel to yank on that leash. Giving him a chance to lean into the pleasure of keeping a promise was one thing, but it didn't work that way for him, so I'd have to figure out a different way to interact with him.

"It's not initiation if I start it," I said.

He lifted one brow in a silent question.

"I don't want you to come onto me out of the blue, but if I start it..." I bit my lip, watching his focus dropping to my mouth. "Dance with me?"

"You're certain?" he asked, his voice rougher than it had been only heartbeats before.

"It might not end in sex—" I started.

"I truly don't care," Varistan said, one corner of his stupidly kissable mouth kicking up. "I would love to have sex with you again, of course, but I see little reason to require all-or-nothing in our interactions. If you want to dance... Well." He wrapped the end of his tail around my wrist, leaving the tip of his spade resting against my palm in heated temptation. "I'm an excellent dancer, Bells."

Chapter Forty

WINTER SEAS

W e spent eight days preparing for our journey. It wasn't that the trip itself was long; as the raven flew, Maestrizen was roughly a three-day's sail from Nyx Shaeras, and even though we'd be hugging the coast so as to avoid the risk of being caught in the sea by a winter storm, it would only take four or so days to arrive. But since this was a trading mission, Varistan wanted to bring not just the two of us, but several merchant vessels, and getting *them* prepared on such short notice was nothing short of miraculous.

The Maestrizen envoy left the same day we met him, sailing with the tide on a slick-looking ship that cut through the waves with the same precision as a porpoise. I was a bit sad to see him go, but I supposed that I'd probably get the chance to see him again. At least having the man off his land let Varistan relax a tiny fraction.

That wasn't to say that Varistan *relaxed*. Every day seemed to wind him tighter, the anticipation of traveling to the City of Beasts coming out in his waspish temper and his nightmares. To my surprise, those restless dreams never featured disgust. Varistan was afraid—of being surrounded by people who hated him, of being confronted with all the things he'd shunned for so many centuries, of going and failing and losing everything. He was even afraid of losing *me*, as if I might fall in love with Maestrizen and refuse to leave.

Maybe I would fall in love with Maestrizen, but that didn't necessitate staying. I'd told Alpha I would stay by Varistan's side to help protect everyone he shielded beneath those night-black wings, but even without that I wouldn't have left him.

All of the reasons for that were too dangerous to contemplate, so I locked them away and refused to think about them. I was mortal. He was fae. There was never going to be a future for him that had me in it, and I couldn't in good faith make myself the center of his world.

I wouldn't destroy him. He'd said I was saving him, and I was determined to do exactly that.

We started our journey on a bright winter's day, with the sunlight playing off the ocean and the icy breeze laden with the salt-scent of the water. The tides were friendly with the itinerary: we could leave on the departing tide in the early afternoon, which left plenty of time for us to have a lazy morning and extended luncheon before moseying up the gangplank onto Varistan's personal vessel.

It was a beautiful ship, with a stunning figurehead of a winged hippocamp on the prow and crimson sails that must have borne the same sort of enchantments my spider-silk dress did. But the beauty fell into the background as soon as I set foot on the ship, the movement of the planks beneath my feet leaving me queasy. That queasiness turned rapidly to horror once we sailed out of Nyx Shaeras' protected port and hit the true waves of the ocean.

Oh gods, I thought, white-knuckling the railing as the ship rose and fell beneath me. *I'm never going to survive four days of this.*

"Bells?" Varis asked, a moment before his hand settled onto my lower back. "Are you alright?"

I shook my head, which was the wrong thing to do, as only staring with grim focus at the horizon was keeping my poor confused body from completely losing track of its place in the world. I flung my torso out over the railing a heartbeat before I puked, hearing Varistan yelp *"Bells!"* in the split-second before I emptied my stomach of that lovely long luncheon we'd had.

He had his tail around my hips and his hands holding the escaped tendrils of my hair back from my face before I finished the first heave. Varis crooned to me, a sound I heard more than felt. "I'm sorry, Bells," he said, pitching his voice low. "I didn't even think about how seasick you'd be in all my worries."

I let out a sound of abject misery and puked again.

There was nothing left in my stomach before the castle had disappeared beneath the horizon, but I didn't move from the railing, panting from the nausea as I leaned on my forearms, the cold wind flirting with my hair. Once he'd found me something to rinse my mouth out with, Varistan stayed with me, rubbing my lower back under my heavy coat for a little bit of comfort.

"Come on," he said in a gentle voice. "Let's get you lying down in our cabin. I think you'll feel better if you sleep some of this off."

"I don't know that I can walk there," I said with a groan. "This is awful."

Varistan leaned down and dropped a soft kiss at the base of my jaw. "That's alright," he said softly, his warm breath scudding across my chilled skin. "You needn't walk. I can surely carry you there."

I glanced sidelong at him with a weary expression.

He grinned back at me, wickedness sparkling in his warm ruby eyes. "I'll admit, I didn't envision the chance to balance the ledger of you dealing with my nausea that first day, but I'm finding it rather rewarding."

I made a rude gesture and returned to hanging mournfully over the railing.

"Ah, none of that," Varistan said cheerfully. "Come along, Bells." He hoisted me up, ignoring my indignant yelp as he manhandled me into a bridal carry. With his wings half-cocked for balance, he strode across the deck of the ship as if he'd been born there, heading for the entrance belowdecks with absolute surety.

Most of the nausea actually abated as he carried me, his body compensating for the movement of the ocean enough that I could focus on him instead of the sea. I clonked my head against his shoulder and groaned again, making him chuckle as he ducked down into the dark entrance, heading down the steep stairs with perfect balance.

I expected him to put me in bed and leave me there to sleep, but Varis got onto the bed without putting me down, arraying himself in the middle of the mattress before draping me across him. At my questioning sound, he pressed an affectionate kiss to my hair.

"You slept best in the carriage when you were lying on me," he said by way of explanation. "Take off that coat and rest on me for a while. See if it helps."

Feeling self-conscious, I sat up on his lap, shucking off my heavy coat. Unlike me, Varistan was dressed only in a blousy shirt, the laces loose and his warm brown skin showing between them. If it wasn't for the fact that the cloth was of such fine quality, he could have been anyone, dressed for a casual summer day at sea.

Of course, he wasn't just anyone. He was His Grace Varistan Yllaxira, the Duke of Nyx Shaeras and scion of the Raven King. But he was looking up at me the way that prisoners look at the sky when they're finally freed, and for a moment it felt like maybe I could pretend otherwise.

"I'm always so jealous of that draconic heat," I told him, pausing in taking off my sweater as I looked at him.

He gave me a slow smile, the same rakish expression that always made me want to throw him up against a wall so I could wipe it off his face. "Come enjoy it, then," he purred at me, running his fingers down my side. "I'm yours for the taking."

His chin came up as my eyes flashed, his pulse visible in the hollow of his throat as it quickened. "What's that look for, Bells?" he asked, holding himself very still.

I was sitting on his lap. That was a dangerous place for me to be.

Fuck it.

I tugged my sweater the rest of the way off, shivering in the chill of the room even though I was wearing long sleeves. But the moment I sprawled down across his chest the cold of the air didn't matter, not with his warmth surrounding me. I nuzzled my face up against the column of his neck, basking on him like a cat in the sun with his copper-and-musk scent heating my lungs.

"I was admiring you," I murmured against his skin, running my nose up along his jaw as he started breathing harder. "Thinking about the way you look when you're so turned on you can't think about anything else."

Varis groaned low in his throat, his arm tightening around my waist as he shifted underneath me. "Is this an invitation to the dance floor?" he asked, sounding remarkably put-together in direct opposition to the way he was very clearly trying not to cant his hips up against my thigh.

My lips turned up into a wicked smile as I pressed a kiss to his pulse, following the touch with a short lick. "Mhm."

"Not nauseous?" he asked, with a little less aplomb.

"Mm-mm," I said, exhaling across his ear.

My duke let out a panting breath, leaning his face against mine as he draped his tail across me. "To what do I owe the invitation?"

I laughed, wiggling a little closer to him as he made a sound of pleasure, shifting his position so I could feel it against my thigh as his cocks slowly hardened, their lengths pressing against the fabric of his pants. "Hoping for a repeat later?"

"Trying to find a conversation topic so I don't grab you by the hips and grind myself against your thigh like a desperate adolescent," Varis said, running his hand down the back of my thigh before tugging me against his hips. "You're quite the temptation, Isabela."

"Three thousand years old, and you're that eager, hm?" I asked, tracing my fingers down his chest.

His cocks flexed against my leg, drawing my focused attention. "Eighty-one years of unwanted chastity will undo a great deal of self-discipline in a man," he said, sounding amused as he slid his warm palm back up my leg, leaving my skin tingling in his wake. "I come embarrassingly quickly now, but I'm hoping that will wear off before too long." Varis held my hips in place and rolled his slowly against mine, a sensual movement that showed off his total control of his body. "I've been practicing for you."

I shoved myself up to look down at him, laughing in disbelief. "Really? Your chosen flirtation is 'I come prematurely, but don't worry, I've been masturbating'?"

Varis looked not at all concerned, smirking up at me with his lashes lowered across his ruby gaze. "You're the one who demanded that of me," he purred at me, rocking his hips again with the same slow deliberation. "Aren't you pleased that I haven't managed to go a full day since waking without being... So. Overcome. That I have to take myself in hand to the memory of how you feel when you're coming on my cock?" he asked, punctuating the words with his movement.

Heat thudded between my legs at the admission. I rocked my hips against him without even thinking about it, and he ran his hands along my sides to grip me by the waist, his body rolling with the ocean beneath us as he used his tail to shift me so I was straddling him.

"Fuck," I half-moaned, the feel of his cocks pressing up between my legs commanding my attention. "I think you're better at this than I am."

He made a low sound of pleasure, smirking up at me. "Oh, don't be so certain of that. After all," he added as he rocked his hips against mine, "I'm the one driven so mad by the thought of you that I can't help but to dedicate my body to you each day."

"You're late out of the starting gate, your grace," I said with a reckless smile, walking my fingers up his chest. "I've been doing that for months."

Varis froze mid-thrust. His ears snapped forward into a pose of avid interest as his pupils contracted and claws dug into my sides. "You, you— What?" he asked, sounding strangled.

I sprawled down across him with an evil little laugh, very pleased with myself. "Ever since you took me flying. I couldn't get the feeling of your hands on me out of my mind, so I put my hands on myself instead," I said, licking my lips at his sound of protest. "I couldn't get over *who* was touching me, but, gods and monsters, you did it well."

"I wanted you *badly*," Varis said with a growl. "I would have spent the full night pleasuring you if you'd desired it of me, and damned the consequences. I would have even dared your disgust and let, let, let—" He closed his eyes, breathing hard. "Gods, I would have let you touch me," he said, whispering the words.

Gently, I leaned down and pressed a kiss to his warm mouth, smiling against his lips as I felt him relax underneath me. Varis kissed me carefully, cupping the back of my neck as his mouth slanted across mine, his hot breath fanning against me.

I pulled back, breaking the contact to look down at him, and at the expression that told me he'd been savoring every moment.

His dense lashes parted, those beautiful eyes taking a heartbeat to focus on mine. "You're being affectionate," he murmured, looking up at me with quiet focus.

"So are you," I said, smiling down at him. "Can we switch back to me passing out on top of you, though? I don't know that I have it in me to actually follow through on any of this. I feel like a wet rag."

"You're the lead in this dance," he said with amusement. "You need not ask."

"Well, maybe you'd rather give yourself an orgasm before having me collapse on you." I flashed him a grin, wiggling a little. "Or won't it trouble you to have me lying across your chest?"

Varistan barked a laugh, draping an arm across my lower back. "I have a bit more self-control than *that*, Bells. A little sensual grinding and one chaste kiss is hardly enough to break me."

I snuggled down onto him, completely at ease. I wasn't sure exactly when Varistan had become someone who felt like home, but it was hard to ignore. "What'll break you, then?"

"That's for me to know, and for you to find out," he murmured, dropping a kiss onto my hair as he folded his wings over me like a blanket. "Let me know when you'd like to experiment."

"'When'?" I asked, my smile in my voice.

"When," he said, with his usual aloof smugness. "You're surely far too curious of a woman to leave such an offer on the table."

"I do have a curated list to try out," I said, luxuriating in the heat of his body and the scent of his skin. If there had been a way to make it last forever, I would have claimed it in an instant.

He rumbled a laugh and set my hand over his heart. "If you ask nicely, perhaps I'll allow you to try them all."

"Promise?"

He shivered underneath me with what I knew was anticipated pleasure. "I promise."

Chapter Forty-One

CITY OF BEASTS

I t didn't take four days to get to Maestrizen. To my great sorrow, it took six.

I spent them primarily sleeping, and secondarily hanging over the railing like an abandoned dishrag. Varistan, in the throes of his post-rut desire to see me content and cared-for, therefore spent the entire time in a state of all-consuming unhappiness. There really wasn't much further I could get from content, though Varistan did try his best to take care of me.

He was terrible at it, of course – I was pretty sure that my duke had never once in his three millennia of life needed to nurse someone who couldn't keep anything down but broth and bread – but the one time someone dared to offer to help, he almost lit the ship on fire, which put an end to that. The possessiveness would have amused me more if I hadn't been so miserable, but one upside of his total focus on my sorry state was that he didn't have time to anticipate arriving at Maestrizen, and thus was merely upset instead of upset *and* anxious.

If I'd allowed it, he probably would have confined me to the cabin and spent every second by my side, but that was a bit smothering for me. I didn't mind him trailing me around like a woebegone bondservant, though. That was fine.

Honestly, I kind of liked it. There was something very rewarding about having the Flame of Faery at my beck and call.

I managed to pull myself together enough to be presentable once we got within striking distance of Maestrizen. There wasn't much to be done for the fact that I looked like a wrung-out cheesecloth, but at least I washed my face and hair and put on some nice clothing. As Varistan's translator and off-the-books handler, I needed to look like I could hold my own, and as if it would be reasonable for me to be standing at a duke's hand.

With nothing in my stomach, I had no reason to puke, so I managed to keep it together as the ship slid into dock, gripping the railing with one hand so I didn't simply fall over. Varistan stood behind me, very obviously brooding.

I supposed that was only to be expected. It would probably draw a decent amount of antagonism from the city folk we encountered, but that was going to happen, anyway. It wasn't as if Varistan wasn't already going to have a target painted on his back.

Maybe I should have brought my spear.

I made my escape from the ship as soon as the gangplank was down, striding down with Varis holding one of my hands so that I wouldn't wobble. The feel of the solid dock under my feet made me want to lie down on it and never get up again, but that would have been undignified, so I kept it together and followed Varistan down the broad wooden pathway towards the city itself.

The wood looked old—not collapsing-old, but definitely worn. How long did docks last, I wondered? There were enchantments against rot, but the mages who could cast them weren't loose on the ground. Maybe Maestrizen would need saltwood for more than their ships.

Movement caught my eye: a sable-furred creature atop a stack of crates, round ears turning and long silken guard-hairs catching the light as they observed us. Dressed in loose clothing and with a set of gleaming mother-of-pearl jewelry, they were obviously fae of some kind; either a day-called fae or a true wild fae.

I cracked a smile for the first time in days, a sense of wonder washing away the days of nauseous misery. Holy *fuck*. The fucking *City of Beasts*.

The sable fae abandoned their perch as we approached, winding down the boxes with the fluid ease of a squirrel. I wasn't sure Varistan even saw them, given that he was keeping his eyes trained straight ahead with what looked like an effort not to stare at the people we passed. He very nearly jumped out of his skin when the fae went from horizontal to vertical in front of us, shying backwards with a startled sound, complete with a curl of flame.

I stepped around his half-open wing with a bright smile, one that was matched by a great deal of bared, sharp teeth from the fae. "Duke Night-Flame and translator Bells," I signed in introduction. I'd chosen the name-sign for Varis, riffing off of the closest translation I knew for Nyx Shaeras: Lightning in the Night. It seemed fitting, and when I'd mentioned it to Varis, he hadn't seemed offended by the idea.

"Sunlight," the fae signed back, with a little flick of their fingers at the end of the sign that I tried to file into memory. "Spoken-name R-A-Y-L-I-E-N and gendered 'she.'"

Oh, that was a useful bit of introduction in a city where many fae wouldn't be visibly distinct as male or female, or anything else, and I liked the use of the alphabetical signs as a way of giving a translatable name. "Raylien?" I asked aloud, to a signed affirmative. In Faery Sign, I added, "Are you our guide?"

"Yes," she signed back. "If Duke agrees, my task is to show you Wild Sky."

"What's it... saying?" Varistan asked, sounding wary.

My spine went stiff with outrage, though Raylien merely flicked her ear dismissively. "Your Grace," I said through my smile, not looking at him. "If you insult our hosts again, I will personally stab you on their behalf." I saw his shadow jerk back from me as I signed, "If I had the authority to apologize for him, I would."

Raylien made a churring sound I took as laughter, given her general appearance of relaxation and the way her long whiskers tilted forward. "That isn't necessary," she signed back. "I expected him to be rude. But he came here. That's more than Vicereine thought her neighbor would ever do."

"He wants to be your ally," I replied with a shrug and a rueful smile. "He'll probably be poorly-mannered, but he *is* trying," I added, emphasizing the verb by pausing on the sign.

She tilted her head to the side, looking over my shoulder at my duke. "I see that."

"Bells?" Varistan asked, sounding plaintive. "I would appreciate any amount of translation."

I glanced over my shoulder, but he looked abashed enough that I relented. "This is our guide, Raylien. If you're agreeable, she's been tasked with showing us Maestrizen. And then I was making polite recompense for your unwise tongue."

His ears leaned backwards, but Varistan very carefully tucked his wings behind him and put on a measured expression. "I suppose you'd enjoy seeing the city?"

"Oh, definitely," I said, grinning at him. "Are you amenable?"

He exhaled through his nose, looking resigned. "It's the first time I've seen you smile in days. I'm amenable."

Raylien didn't even bother to wait for me to translate. Hauling the Duke of Nyx Shaeras through the City of Beasts was clearly far too great a lure to stand on ceremony for, and she led us into the city without further ado, moving on all fours with the slinky grace of a weasel.

Somewhere in the back of my mind, I'd filled in the blank space for Maestrizen with a copy of Lylvenore, the only fae city I'd ever seen—but Maestrizen was only similar to Lylvenore in the way a falcon is similar to a chicken. Both were densely-populated locations with cobblestone streets and multi-story buildings, but that was about as far as the resemblance could stretch.

Lylvenore was an ancient city, buildings built upon buildings built upon buildings for so many thousands of years that it sat on a hill of its own making, with winding, labyrinthine roads and enclaves that turned the city into a complex web of interconnected communities. It was full of stately manses, trees shaped over the course of centuries into fantastical forms, and the sort of continuous history that turned every building into a story.

Maestrizen was... alive. I didn't know how else to describe it. It felt like the city was in a constant state of becoming, with visible construction and places that looked raw and new. It wasn't that Maestrizen was young, because I knew it had existed for millennia. But while fae and their societies tended to be sedate and grounded in the ancient past, Maestrizen didn't seem to have any particular attachment to what had come before.

There were ancient places – Raylien showed us down holloway paths that were sunk easily eight feet into the ground from the tread of countless feet and to a tavern that had been open since the founding of the city – but they weren't kept *because* they were ancient. Rather, Maestrizen kept what it loved, and wasn't afraid to change the rest. History anchored the city, but it didn't bind it. It felt like a wedding of the best parts of mortality and eternity—as if this was the way it had always been meant to be.

I wondered if Varistan could see it, looking past his fears and the narrowed eyes that watched us. I wanted this for him. I wanted him to be able to remember where he'd come from, the good and the bad, without living his entire life chained to the experiences of his early life. He had so much time ahead of him. He could be so much more than even the Flame of Faery.

After six days of mostly not eating, I didn't have my usual stamina, but Raylien was a good host and clearly knew the city like the back of her furred hand. She paused frequently near interesting sights that had places to sit and little vendors for food, and when I ventured the question on what sort of payment people in Maestrizen preferred, she waved away the query and told me that, as guests of the city, the vicereine would reimburse vendors for any necessary expenditures on our part.

I appreciated the chance to eat—but I appreciated the fact that Varistan could be the one to acquire food for me more. He visibly relaxed when I took the first bite of solid food in days, and by the time the tour was winding down, he was almost acting normal.

Munching my way down a skewer of grilled scallops as we headed towards our lodgings – I'd grown quite fond of seafood since arriving at Nyx Shaeras – I voiced my surprise at how many court fae lived in the city. Raylien was far from the only wildling fae we saw, but at least ninety percent of the fae we saw weren't visibly wildling at all.

She only laughed, a sharp barking sound. "Only at most one in twenty are born wildling on the mainland. The majority of them are moon-called fae who shift very little," she pointed out, twirling the whiskers on her brows in what looked like an expression of amusement. "Even with the bias in who immigrates here, most aren't going to stand out from court fae." She shrugged, then added, "And Wild Sky doesn't even have enough magic to birth a Court. Most born here are court fae."

"Huh, that little magic, and you still have a birth rate?" I asked aloud, since my hands were occupied.

She shrugged again. "Mortal-born."

I translated for Varis, who made a thoughtful sound. "One of the things I like about Nyx Shaeras is the relative dearth of wild magic for such a small settlement," he said, his tail flicking. "The ocean is a hungry neighbor. I always assumed..." He trailed off, and when I looked up at him, he made a disparaging face. "Like many, I assumed the reason Maestrizen didn't have a Court was due to the lack of candidates suitable to the land as Monarch. I'm embarrassed to admit that I didn't even consider the effects of the sea, especially given that I live alongside it."

Raylien flicked her ear at him in a dismissive gesture. "Assumptions are a fool's prerogative."

My duke's ears pinned back when I translated, but he didn't snap at our guide. Perhaps the threat of getting stabbed by me was still holding sway. "I've been called many things, 'fool' among them," he said in a mild tone, keeping his eyes on me as he tucked a loose strand of hair behind my ear, his fingers lingering. "I've also been called reckless, temperamental, hot-blooded—"

"You going somewhere with this list, your grace?" I asked, smirking at him when he flicked his ear at me in the same gesture Raylien had used. He was just as fae as she was.

"Merely reminding our companion that one's history may mark one's future, but it hardly controls it," he said, one corner of his mouth lifting in a wry smile. "I've dueled lords for lesser insults, but instead I'm willing to re-think my long-held patterns, even in the face of antagonism." Varis ran his fingers along my jawline, wearing a look of raw affection for one warm moment before he turned back to Raylien, his expression shuttering as he met her dark eyes with his crimson. "I have little expectation of affection from you, Miss Raylien, but I would appreciate some modicum of polite attention. Even a veneer would do."

She tilted her head in a catlike expression of interest. "Why did you let her change you?" she asked, signing the words with thoughtful slowness.

He flushed faintly when I spoke the words, and his wings furled more tightly against his back. "My personal life is hardly what I envision for polite conversation with a guide to the city."

The sable fae made a soft *hm!* noise before shrugging one shoulder. "It seems politeness in Wild Sky differs from the mainland," she signed, her furred hands flashing through the signs again as she paused in walking to answer him. "We seek to show respect by striving to treat each other as equals, so that only duty divides us. If you prefer separation, I'm amenable."

She didn't wait for a response, diving back into the crowd with us trailing behind.

"I'd like the answer," I said, chucking my bare skewer into one of the public refuse bins as we strolled back towards the docks. "Why *did* you let me change you?"

Varistan gave me a pained expression. "Bells, you already know what I'm dealing with regarding your desires. Are you truly going to make me grant intimacy to a—" He stopped, mouth open to say something no-doubt offensive, then visibly reconsidered. "—stranger?"

"When in Maestrizen," I said with a grin, knowing there was no way he'd even recognize the allusion.

He looked away, swallowing, then sighed. "Because you're mine, and I can't bear for you to hate me for it," he said. "Because you look at me as if I'm valuable, when few others do. I feel I could name a thousand reasons, Bells. Must I list them all whilst already struggling to keep my balance?"

I hooked my arm through his and leaned my head on his shoulder. "Thank you," I murmured, so I could watch him shiver in pleasure. "I'm really impressed by how well you're keeping your balance, even though I do like tweaking your tail."

That tail brushed up against my leg in a way that suggested Varistan was narrowly restraining himself from accidentally tripping us by wrapping it around me. "I'd rather get it— *fuck*," he gritted out, going stiff as his promise caught him before he could say whatever flirtatious thing was on the tip of his tongue. "Sorry. I didn't mean—"

"You can say it," I said quickly, not wanting him to suffer even the glancing punishment of treading too close to the edge of a promise. "It's alright."

Varis shuddered, voicing a weak laugh, and laced his fingers through mine. "I'd rather get it stroked than tweaked," he said, sounding shamefaced. "But that's, ah, rather too explicit for the sort of flirtation I'm currently allowed."

"Are you wanting to be let off the leash, your grace?" I asked, giving him an impish smile.

He only lifted his lip, not answering.

Raylien, walking on all fours in front of us, wisely pretended not to hear any of our exchange. She bounded ahead of us to a handsome-looking stone building, rearing up on her hind legs and brushing off her hands. "Vicereine is providing this home to you for your residency in Wild Sky," she signed, her ears cocking forward. "An assistant is scheduled to come each morning and evening to prepare food and care for other needs. Your first meeting with Vicereine is scheduled for tomorrow at half past the tenth hour of the morning."

I translated as she signed, feeling Varistan's tail curling around my ankle.

"Your assistance is appreciated, as is the hospitality and generosity of the Vicereine of Maestrizen," Varistan said gravely, inclining his head towards her as I signed the words to add some formality to the exchange. "Will the assistant be providing the appropriate mode of conveyance to the vicereine's palace in the morning?"

Our guide made a chattering sound, which I thought might be a giggle, given the gleam in her dark eyes and the way her brow-whiskers twirled. "This housing is not intended as an insult, Duke," she signed, baring sharp teeth in a grin and signing with a bounciness that clearly meant amusement. "Vicereine lives in a house, not a palace. The meeting is to be held at the city" – she used a sign I didn't recognize – "and I am to guide you there."

I repeated the sign back to Raylien, giving her a confused expression and a query-sign.

Her ears flicked back, one at a time, then leaned forward again. "A large building meant for meetings," she clarified. "Meeting-house?" she added, signing the two words in rapid succession, with her own query-sign attached.

I pursed my lips, never having heard of such a thing, but translated for Varistan as best I could.

"Ah." The grip of his tail tightened around my ankle. "Then I bid you farewell until we meet again, tomorrow or thereafter."

She flashed us another grin and a quick sign of farewell, then dove down to all fours and bounded away down the cobblestone street, apparently uninterested in the extended dance of formal farewells.

"Well," Varistan said, sounding glum. "Let's see what our new home looks like."

CHAPTER FORTY-TWO

EAGER TO PLEASE

T he house was a great deal nicer than what I'd been used to in Lylvenore, but definitely quaint compared to the amenities of Nyx Shaeras. Varistan poked through it all wearing a sulky expression, as if the rustic decor had been chosen specifically to offend him. During our tour of Maestrizen, someone had brought our personal things to the house and stowed them; I could only assume that the vicereine had also provided something for our crew, though probably not as nice as this place.

They'd put my things in the small second bedroom. Without bothering to ask, I transferred them to the master suite, which at least perked Varis up a little. He still flopped facedown on the bed with a groan once we'd completed the explorations, lying there like a slain deer with his wings akimbo and tail flopped between his legs.

Well, that was fixable.

I scooped up his tail as I hopped onto the bed next to him, getting a sharp sound of surprise. "So," I said, tucking his tail around me like a sash with the spade lying in my lap. "You liked the tail play, did you?"

Varis rolled onto his side; though I didn't look at him, I figured he was probably staring at the back of my head. "...I, ah... yes?" he said, sounding baffled by the topic change. "I buried it in you often enough that I assumed that was obvious."

I smirked, walking my fingers down the scales of his tail towards the tip, watching the blades of his spade flaring out a fraction with each touch. "So we're up to five things you like about your body, hm?" I asked, sliding my fingertips slowly towards his suede-soft spade.

"Five?" he asked in reply, sounding a little bit strangled.

"Flight. Fire-walking. My admiration," I said, spreading my fingers so that they framed his spine, my callused fingertips running up along the heated skin of the base of the blades. "Possessive focus. And this," I said, sliding his spade between two fingers and stroking back up along it.

He let out a panting whine of sound, the studs along his tail hardening. "Six," he groaned out as I did it again on the other side. "I loved having both my cocks buried in you, too. I find dual-wielding iron swords a tedious exercise, but that was better than any other—oh, fucking black night, Bells, are you trying to kill me?"

Massaging his spade was clearly a winning move.

"Kill you?" I asked, all innocence. "Doesn't this feel nice?"

My duke groaned again, his hips grinding down against the bed as he writhed from the feel of my hands on his sensitive tail. "I made a promise—"

"—which I modified," I said, grinning as I skimmed my eyes down along his taut form. "Wouldn't you say I'm initiating?"

"I wish I knew *why*," he moaned, managing to sound plaintive despite the raw lust thickening his voice. "Are you... gods, are you... rewarding me for good behavior? I... I... ohh, *fuck*, if you are, it's fucking working, I'll be so good for you tomorrow if this is what I get after—"

With a pleased little sound, I ran the flat of my palm along his spade, pressing it against my thigh. "Do you think anyone back home would believe it if I told them about the Flame of Faery acting like my good little slut for the sake of a little tail-petting?"

His back arched when I wrapped my hand around his spade and started stroking, mouth falling open and the white lengths of his sharp canines showing. The spade flared hard against my grip, his skin hot, and then started rhythmically flexing and relaxing with the movement of my hand.

"Bells—" he gasped out, head thrown back.

"Is that what you are, Varis?" I asked, my nipples aching where they pressed against my bra and my panties absolutely soaked from the sight and sound of my duke letting me take him to pieces. "A good little slut?"

"If you want—want—want— Oh, fuck— *Fuck—!*" Varistan's voice cut off with a sobbing sound of pleasure. He drove his hips against the bed, his wings clawing at the air and the talons of one foot sinking into the quilt on the bed as he shoved himself forward. He breathed hard, almost hyperventilating, back bowed and his pulse throbbing against my hand.

I stopped stroking his tail, staring at him with my eyes wide and pussy clenching. Had he seriously just—

The tension in his spine lessened, and Varistan started laughing between panting breaths. "Fuck," he said again, sound half-parts embarrassed and amused. "I truly do need more practice."

That made me start laughing, too, loosening my grip on his tail enough that he could tug it out of my hand. "Really?" I asked, my cheeks warming as I grinned at him, eyebrows raised. "You came from that?"

Varis rolled over onto his back, making a face at me before framing his groin with forefinger and thumb, showing off both the bulge of his cocks and the wet of his come soaking through his light pants. "It hasn't been all that many days yet since you broke my fast," he said, his eyes sparkling with good humor. "As I recall, I outgrew my youthful, hm, *rapidity* earlier than my peers, so enjoy it while it lasts, Isabela. Once I've gotten more used to the sexual sensitivity of this body, I suspect I'll reacquire my former endurance with alacrity."

I flopped down on the bed next to him, propping up my chin on one hand, still grinning. "I'll believe it when I see it."

His lips twitched with amusement. "'When'?"

"If," I corrected, blushing. "We're in Maestrizen and I'm as much a part of this as you are, but it's not like this back home. Back in Nyx Shaeras, I mean, and Raven Court." I shrugged, feeling awkward as I looked away from his soft expression. "When I'm not seen as your equal, I don't think I can... do this."

He blew a curl of flame at me, the flare of light drawing my eyes back to his face. "I have no desire for you to do this, or anything like it, if you don't enjoy it," Varis said, brushing his tail down along my calf. "I enjoy it greatly, obviously," he said, gesturing to his groin with a wry expression, "and I'll surely be delighted if you change your mind about being my lover, but you needn't enter into such a relationship for my sake, and in truth, I would be horrified if you did." He reached over and twined a strand of my hair around the blunt-clawed fingers of his left hand. "I shall strive not to hold you to anything I read into your initiations while I'm bound by the promise I gave you regarding mine."

I leaned my face against his hand, a smile tugging at my lips. "You know, you're kind of charming when you're not busy being an ass."

Varis flashed his teeth at me in a lazy smile. "Did you think I won a paramour and a dukedom merely via Sarcaryn's grace? I'm fully capable of being charming when the opportunity presents itself. Given, of course," he added with a smirk, "that the reward is tantamount to the effort."

With a bright laugh, I shook my head at him. "You're terrible."

"At least I have a pretty face," he said, warmth in his garnet eyes.

"At least there's that," I said drily, pushing myself up. "Want some clean pants?"

"Please," he said, looking at me with such unsullied happiness that I could almost believe he loved me with more than the affection of a dragon.

Despite the early winter sunset, it was only the late afternoon, but six days of shipboard misery followed by a five-hour tour of a hilly city had really taken it out of me. I was well and truly wilting by the time our assistant – a plump, cheerful court fae man named Tessekh – arrived to cook and show us how to work the various amenities of the house.

Varistan watched me like a hawk through dinner, demurred a bath, and had me strip him down for bed before it was even eight in the evening. He insisted

I get into pajamas, threatening to undress me himself if I didn't obey (which perhaps wasn't the threat he meant it to be; I would have quite enjoyed that). Being in nightclothes completely broke my will to stay awake, though, which was doubly slain when Varis picked me up and put me in bed, snuffing all the lamps before clambering in himself.

"It's so early," I said, feeling like I should protest as he tucked me up against his body.

"I would have put you to bed earlier if I'd thought you would acquiesce," he said in reply, settling his wing around me. "This past week has been a misery, and bullying you into sleeping now that we're on solid ground again is one of the few things I can do to improve both your life and my temperament."

I huffed, but my heart wasn't in it. "Don't turn into a nursemaid on me."

He made a disgruntled noise, hooking the claws of his wing over the collar of my shirt. "Am I not allowed to feel unhappy when you've spent six days being, as you so eloquently put it, a 'soggy, moldering sack of potatoes'?"

"Gods," I said, stifling a laugh. "You're really put-out about the seasickness, huh?"

He grumbled some more, wrapping himself more firmly around me. "This is my first experience with draconic mate-affection, and it's going extremely poorly." Varistan set his chin on the top of my head. "Have a little pity on me. It's not entirely my fault that I'm a wreck. Thanks to your intervention, I'm now an obsessed, eager-to-please, submissive—"

"Yeah you are," I said with a giggle, interrupting him. "Never expected the Duke of Nyx Shaeras to tell me he'd be my good little slut, if only I'd keep stroking him off."

"*Bells*," he whined in protest, his tail wrapping around my ankle. "That is *not* what happened. Not... not precisely."

I giggled again, wiggling back up against him. "It was delightful."

Varis heaved a sigh, his hot breath stirring my hair. "I found it enjoyable, too," he admitted, though that had been rather obvious at the time. "As I've said, I appreciate both the imbalance of a power differential and the act of begging, and, given that I've surrendered the lead to you, submission is the natural extension of those particular troubles of mine."

"Mm," I said, closing my eyes and relaxing into his warm embrace. "I like how different you are from most fae. With the imbalance thing, I mean." I rubbed my cheek against his wing, then added, a little shyly, "Thank you for telling me."

A little shiver ran through him, his tail tightening on my ankle for a moment before he relaxed again. "I never expected anyone to use it solely for my pleasure," he said, sounding shy himself. "It has been a curse my entire life, but knowing you couldn't hurt me for it meant I could..." Varistan swallowed, the sound only audible because of his nearness. "I could... relax," he said, with relief tingeing his voice. "You let me discover a world I hadn't anticipated. It's so much easier to act as I must with others when I have somewhere I can be... like that. And when it feels as if you enjoy it, too."

"I do," I said in a low voice, too sleepy to feel nervous about the intimacy of the conversation, but knowing I would worry it into the ground in the morning. "Everyone ought to have a place where they don't have to pretend. Even you," I added with the lilt of a tease.

"Then there's hope for me yet?" he asked, sounding amused.

"Mhm. I'll keep you in line," I said, the words coming slowly as exhaustion enforced its will on me. "Just act like I'm the duke and you're the bondservant, and it'll all go perfect."

"Yes, your grace," he said, crooning the words like he meant them.

A smile touched my lips for a moment. "That's my good Varis," I murmured as I drifted off, letting his heartbeat lull me to sleep.

Chapter Forty-Three

NEGOTIATIONS

D espite the early hour we'd gone to bed, I slept in past dawn, only waking when our assistant Tessekh arrived to make breakfast. Varis was sprawled on his stomach next to me, an arm and a wing slung over my chest and his heavy thigh between mine; he'd gotten rather more clingy in his sleep since his rut. Probably that would wear off once winter ended, but given the general chill of the room, I appreciated having the built-in heater he provided.

With a sleepy smile, I tucked an escaped curl behind the sharp tip of his ear.

His brow creased, fear crossing his face. "Bells, don't— I couldn't— Didn't—" Another flicker of emotion tensed his face, one hand flexing.

"Shh, shh," I said, trying to soothe him. His bad dreams were nothing new to me at this point, though they'd never involved me before. "Wake up, Varis. It's alright."

He flinched backwards, eyes opening but not focusing on me. "Please," he said, his expression blank. "Don't leave. I can't, can't, don't—"

On instinct, I kissed him on the mouth, gripping him by the back of the neck and giving him the best reassurance I could think of in the moment—something that meant more than words. He made a sharp sound of relief, almost a sob, a shudder running down his body as he relaxed into the contact. A heartbeat later, his lashes fluttered and lips broke from mine, the laxity of his body going from the heaviness of sleep to something more controlled.

"Bells?" he asked, his eyes slowly focusing on mine. "You're... not..."

"It was only a nightmare," I said with a quick smile, pulling back so that it wouldn't look so much like I wanted to turn a single kiss into tangled heat. "I'm not going anywhere, your grace. You know that, right?"

He closed his eyes, trying to smile for me, unhappiness still tensing his face and pulling his brows together. But he still nodded, not looking at me as he did.

I ran my finger down between his brows. "Want to talk about it?"

Varistan's throat worked. "I don't... I don't think so. Not right now."

"Alright," I said, not pushing the topic. He was dealing with a lot of draconic emotions, which might explain everything, and there'd be time enough to unpack his turmoil when we were back in Nyx Shaeras. Right now, it seemed a lot more important to let him keep what emotional grounding he had, so he could deal with the Vicereine of Maestrizen and whatever antagonism got thrown his way in the negotiations. "Let's get ready for our day, then."

Varistan was unusually subdued as I dressed and coiffed him, not giving any opinions on clothing or adornment, nor even making any lascivious comments. He ate breakfast with the same quiet stoicism, even pouring himself a mug of my vanilla chai before I yanked it away from him, his mind clearly elsewhere.

"Must have been a really bad dream," I offered as I mopped up the spill with my napkin.

He shrugged one shoulder, but was saved from answering by a sharp knock on the door. "That's surely our guide," Varistan said, giving me a smile that didn't reach his eyes. "Shall we?"

Troubled, but unwilling to dredge for his sorrows, I smiled back. "Let's."

Raylien greeted us cheerfully and led us down a scenic route towards one of the denser centers of the city, bringing us into a large stone building adorned with bas-reliefs of fae and beasts living in harmony. The not-so-subtle symbology made me smile, but I appreciated the artistry, even if Varistan was too busy staring straight ahead to take in the sights.

I was pretty sure it wasn't simply a desire not to stare at the wildling fae that kept his gaze fixed on the middle distance. Given his nightmares, his general state of stress, and the metaphorical hourglass on repaying Lord Xilvaris running down, I thought Varistan was merely holding himself together via force of will, and didn't have the energy to spare for sightseeing. There wasn't really anything to do for that but to solve the problem, so that's what we'd do. The alternative – dismembering Nyx Shaeras – wasn't an option.

Guards took us through the austere stone halls to a pair of double doors, the dark wood carved with a bramble pattern. They opened the doors, and I walked in at Varistan's left hand.

You belong here, I told myself as I quailed from the stern eyes turned towards us. *This wouldn't be happening without you.*

I took a deep breath, held up my hands, and opened negotiations with the Vicereine of Maestrizen.

Faery negotiations had as much to do with social graces as business desires. The Duke of Nyx Shaeras and the Vicereine of Maestrizen both stood to gain a great deal from a trade route between their lands, but they were standing across a great social chasm, and that distance needed bridging. The first olive branch came from the vicereine: instead of the informal interactions we'd had thus far with her people, she entered the negotiations with the full formality that Varistan knew so well.

It took more than an hour to get through the dance of introductions, and at that point she gestured us out into the grand gardens of the meeting-house for a full luncheon fete. Despite our company, the comfort of the formal negotiations relaxed Varistan, so that by the time we'd concluded our first day of apparently getting nothing done except tiring out my arms he was sauntering down the street after Raylien with one hand resting on the hilt of his sword, a contented smile warming his face.

I kept shooting looks at him until he looked sidelong at me with a smirk. "Is something wrong, Bells?"

"You're *happy*," I said, the words accusatory.

His lips curled up higher. "Is that so?"

"We're in *Maestrizen*."

Varistan chuckled, stretching out his wings, his long tail curling behind him. "So we are," he said, as if only just noticing it. "Have you observed anything about how people are treating me in this city of pearls?"

I flattened my mouth at him, though I was charmed by his twist on Maestrizen's usual nickname. "Open antagonism? Wariness? Occasional looks that suggest a stabbing is in your future?"

"Almost like you did, little mortal," he said, flashing his teeth in a grin when I mock-growled at him. "But do you see how they feel about me?"

Varistan paused to give his farewells to Raylien, putting his hand over his heart and bowing to her as if she was a courtier. She chattered a laugh and imitated the gesture before bounding off, and Varistan turned back towards me with a smile.

"They hate you," I said.

He opened the door for me, sunnier than I'd seen him in a long time. "I believe they do, at least some of them," he said, following me, looking completely content. "I've certainly earned such antagonism, by reputation if nothing else. But do you notice what else is true?" When I merely raised a brow, Varistan draped himself across the couch with a satisfied smile. "When they're looking at me, they're only looking at *me*," he said, with a touch of marveling in the words. "Not the wings. Not the scales. A whole city of people who look at me the way you always have."

I blinked at him, my face laxening.

"If I'm seen as a monster by them, it's due to who I've been, and not what I am," Varistan said in a dreamy voice, almost murmuring the words. "Do you have any idea how incredible that feels? How freeing?" He sighed happily. "I think I like it here."

A smile tugged at one corner of my mouth as I perched on the couch next to him. "Worth the trip?"

"Surely," he replied, a line of white showing between his lips as he slowly smiled back. "But we have so much more to gain."

"Oh, definitely," I said, holding his gaze as ambition lit the space between us, feeling almost like a tether connecting our hearts. "I want to be adorned with aurora pearls, your grace," I said, licking my lips as that crimson gaze dropped to my mouth. "Will you get them for me?"

"It would be my pleasure," he purred.

We fell into a pattern over the ensuing weeks. On the rising and resting days of the feast week, we met the vicereine and her advisors at eleven—often at the meeting-house, but also at various businesses in the city, ranging from casual eateries to Maestrizen's shipyard. For some of those trips, we brought the various experts we'd brought across the sea with us, and those nights were usually late ones, as we pored over notes and hashed out how to proceed in the negotiations.

On the feast day, we were invited to a variety of gatherings, essentially all of which we went to, acting the role of visiting dignitaries. Some of those were formal events, but many were raucous gatherings of merchants and tradesmen, fae and mortal alike. Despite – or because of – the informality, they presented excellent opportunities for side bargains, and before we were a fortnight into our stay in Maestrizen, Varistan handed me a blood-sealed writ of authority in his handwriting.

"Don't spend it all in one place," he said with wickedness sparkling in his eyes, and left me to it.

I wasn't nobility, and I wasn't fae, but that played well with the humans as well as with the fae who were more than a little wary of approaching Varistan himself. All my historical negotiations had been done in back rooms regarding bloodshed and dirty bets, but I knew how to haggle, and I'd spent enough late nights with my nose in Nyx Shaeras' books to know what we had on offer—and I received enough compliments on the perfumes I wore that I knew I could sell them.

Varistan's shining pride when I presented him with my first signed trade deal was worth a great deal more to me than the silver it earned us.

Only once did our negotiations go obviously sideways, which had a great deal to do with Varistan having too much of the extremely alcoholic seaweed grog the night before. Lacking a healer to deal with the ensuing hangover and the desire for more that lurked in the patterns of his mind, he was a misery in the morning, and worse when we arrived at the meeting-house to do business. Waspish and imperious, he laid out a plan for the improvement of Maestrizen's shipyard, complete with the wages for the builders, then spread his hand in a gesture he'd picked up: *that's all I have.*

Her Excellency let him say it all, her expression pleasant, then made an exceptionally rude sign in response. I turned bright crimson as she turned her dark eyes on me. With a little smirk, she flicked her fingers at me as if to say, *go on.*

I cleared my throat and turned to Varistan, holding onto my polite expression despite the heat in my cheeks. "Her Excellency says that your offer is dogshit."

Varistan's ears dropped down, looking abashed. "Ah," he said, sounding a little strangled. "Perhaps I should consult my chief architect again."

I gave him a tight smile, turning back to the vicereine as I signed his words. "Might we call a short recess?" I asked, raising one of my brows at her.

She smirked, as smug as Varistan at his worst. "Agreed," she signed back, standing and stretching. "By the way, Miss Keris," she said aloud, glancing over at Varistan as he beelined for the water service. "My congratulations on your conquest."

"Oh, um, he's— He's not—" I stammered out, my blush coming back full force.

The vicereine laughed, the sound bright with delight. "My daughter," she said, her eyes crinkling in the corners as she smiled. "She's a wary woman, and fully expected for her time in your duke's company to be unpleasant, even though she volunteered for the position. But she likes you." The woman breathed a laugh, shaking her head. "Both of you."

My brows drew together before I realized who she was talking about. "Raylien," I said, my eyes going wide. "She's your daughter."

She inclined her head. "I left Minnow Court nearly as soon as she was born. There's little kindness for day-called on the mainland, and I wanted her to grow up well."

"She has," I said, glancing back at Varistan, who was visibly loitering, tension building in his spine.

"She's asked to join us for our excursion to the pearl market tomorrow," she said. "Are you amenable to her company?"

"Of course I am," I said, a little puzzled. "But why're you asking me instead of His Grace? And informally?"

A smile turned up the vicereine's full mouth. "Nyx Shareas belongs to its duke," she said, her gaze level and placid. "But this treaty is yours, Miss Keris, and we draw towards its birth. Your companions for that moment are yours to choose."

Oh, wow. I'd always known it was, but to have that recognized by the Vicereine of Mastrizen...

"My desire is to have her there," I said, starting to smile. "She met us on the docks and showed us your city's heart. She deserves to see this through."

"Very well," the vicereine said, inclining her head. "I will extend your invitation."

"Bells?" Varistan asked, sounding unhappy.

I bowed farewell to Her Excellency and turned back towards my duke, walking over with my hands extended. "C'mon, your grace," I said, smiling up at him with pride heating my blood. "Let's go figure out a slightly better offer."

CHAPTER FORTY-FOUR

AURORA PEARLS

M aestrizen's pearl market was impressive not in its style or overt luxury, but for the sheer casual volume of the outrageously expensive coldwater pearls. It wasn't just the pearls, either—there were jewelers working with the spun strands of spider-silk soaked in silver rain imported from across the ocean, carvings made of mother-of-pearl, and a glorious profusion of gleaming ebony-black coldwater coral. Everything was drenched in color, sound, and motion; a feast for every sense.

It was, unsurprisingly, adjacent to the seafood market, where the mussels that were the source of the pearls were shucked for food. The fishy smell was kept abated by the cold breeze off the sea, though, and I cheerfully munched on fried mussels as we browsed through the stalls. Since it was ostensibly a casual outing, Varistan and Her Excellency discussed various styles of jewelry aloud, with a variety of merchants and high-ranking people pitching in comments.

I trailed a little behind my duke, chatting with Raylien in sign about the pearl economy. People wore them in Maestrizen, of course, but while they were valuable, anyone could get one just by being persistent in reef diving. Many were traded across the ocean to the deep wilds, and there were some small buyers up and down the coast—but Nyx Shaeras was poised to become the primary export partner of the aurora pearl trade.

I walked through the market with unfamiliar avarice heating my veins. This wealth was going to be *ours*, I thought, looking over at Varistan to catch him watching me with a warm expression. I smiled back at him before returning to admiring the broad collar necklace of slices of mother-of-pearl that had grown rare attached pearls, the woven strands of silver-rain silk connecting the plates enhancing the natural auroras of the pearls. We were going to be filthy rich. I couldn't wait to see the face on that snake Xilvaris when he was forced to sign *"paid in full"* across Varistan's debts.

With one last wistful sigh, I set the beautiful necklace down and strolled after my duke, who'd split from the vicereine and was examining raw pearls, each of them set in a bed of cotton. I glanced after the departing vicereine, then back at Raylien. "Did I miss something?"

Her ears turned forward, the corners of her eyes crinkling. "It's nearly sunset," she signed. "Vicereine prefers to be home by sundown. I should go soon, too."

I blinked, then grinned. We hadn't once seen her after dark. "Night-called?"

Raylien bared her teeth at me. "I'm her daughter," she pointed out. "Is that so surprising?"

"Bells, come translate for me," Varistan called, with a playful whine to the words. "I can't haggle well like this."

"I'll be right there!" I called back, shaking my head as Raylien churred her laugh, her long whiskers sweeping forward.

"He's needy," she signed, smirking at me as she twisted the clusters of whiskers on her brows.

"He's greedy," I signed back with a grimace. "I'm talking to you instead of him, and now that he's not being political he wants my attention back."

She churred again, wiggling a little in amusement. "Despite your grumbling, you seem to like it as much as he does."

"*Pleeease*," Varistan said, pitching his voice to carry.

Raylien burst into laughter, barking the sounds. I flushed crimson as people in the market stared, looking between me and my duke with expressions ranging between shock and delight, with several people casting knowing looks my way.

"Fucker," I muttered, shaking my head as Raylien leaned against the wall, holding her chest as she kept laughing.

I stalked over, glaring at an unrepentant Varistan. He wrapped his tail around me as soon as I got within range, tugging me up against his side and draping an arm over my shoulders.

"Thank you," he crooned, toying with the laces of my coat. "Translate this shopkeeper's lovely inaudible words for me, will you?"

"You're making people think I'm some sort of dominatrix," I muttered at him as I signed a greeting to the shopkeeper, a rough-edged human who I was almost entirely certain could speak Faery, but no doubt appreciated the spectacle of making Varistan use Faery Sign instead.

He only smirked, and started negotiating with me as his intermediary.

Several gorgeous black pearls richer and a few slips of gold poorer, Varistan hooked his arm through mine and strolled down the street towards our home. "Where would you like to eat, your grace?" he said in a teasing voice, batting his eyelashes at me. "Dinner in, or something a bit more high-class, as suits your station?"

I scowled at him. "I'm going to kill you."

"I don't believe that for one moment," he replied with a smug expression as we cut through an alley towards the sounds of laughter. "You seem quite attached to my lovely self, not to mention my trade goods and good name. Don't think I didn't notice the times you've taken the words out of my mouth and prettied them up—"

"You're being a brat," I accused, shoving him up against the alley wall.

He went with a smirk, looking down at me from under his lowered lashes. "And if I am?" he asked, wrapping his tail around my hips. "What are you going to do about it?"

I grabbed his tail by the spade.

Varistan gasped with the shock of pleasure, lips parting and hips bucking forward as I started stroking his sensitive tail like a cock, holding the blades of his spade down as they flared out against my palm and fingers. He started panting, shoulders flat against the wall and head tilted back, making helpless sounds of pleasure.

"Any more smartass comments?" I asked, leaning forward.

"We're, we're, we're— People can see us," he got out, eyes hazed. "You—"

I grabbed his wrist as he reached out for me, smacking his hand back onto the brick wall. "Palms against the wall, your grace," I said in a croon. "Good dukes get to touch themselves, but you're gonna have to take what you're given."

"Fuck, *Bells*—" Varistan writhed up against the wall as I tightened my hold on his tail, the studs fully hard and his spade flaring in waves. His claws dug runnels in the brick, scraping along the red clay until they caught in the mortar.

"Tell me to stop, and I will," I said, using my free hand to undo my belt. "Otherwise..."

He only whined, holding himself in place against the wall with his stiffening cocks outlined against the cloth of his pants.

Smirking at him, I peeled his tail from around my hips, then slid it down the front of my pants. Varistan moaned as I guided the tip of his tail to my wet pussy, pushing his spade into me with same fervor as the first time he'd fucked me. I had to hold myself up against his chest, my pussy spasming down around him from the sensation of being spread open, the heat in his blood soaking into my core.

"Gods, I missed this." I closed my thighs against his tail, pushing the length up against my clit as I rubbed myself against him.

Varistan took the hint, pressing his tail against me and grinding the studs of it across my clit as he started thrusting into me. I braced myself against his shoulders with both hands, making him do all the work as I let myself focus on the pressure of his body inside mine and the slick movement of his scales on my sensitive nerves.

Watching his face, I clenched down on him, the flash of pleasure making me pant. He threw his head back, horns scraping against the brick as his hips bucked forward. "Oh, fuck, please don't make me come like this again," he said with a whimper, his cocks flexing against the constraint of his pants. "Please touch me—"

"You have your tail eight inches deep in my pussy, your grace," I said, panting with pleasure when his spade flared hard inside of me. "Seems like that should count, especially since it's gonna make you come."

"*Please*," he whined, with obvious desperation.

He took one hand off the wall; I grabbed him by the wrist and pinned his hand back down.

"*Behave.*"

His answering sob of pleasure made my pussy close down on him with a flash of bright sensation, my pulse throbbing in my core and every thrust of his tail making it harder and harder to think.

"Please, I can be good, I just, I just—" he got out before his thighs started shaking, pressing his ass against the wall and thrusting up into his taut pants for the friction.

"So you want me to touch your cock?" I asked, breathing hard.

"Yes, oh, fuck, please touch me—" His hips canted up, a hint of wet showing through his pants where the tips of his cocks pressed against the fabric.

"Want me to suck it, instead?" I asked, lowering my lashes as I admired the bulge his cocks made.

Varistan froze, his eyes flying open. "Wh-wh-what— You—"

"Ohh, I think that's a 'yes,'" I said, licking my lips as his cocks flexed. "What do you taste like, your grace? Will your slick be my new favorite flavor?" I asked as I sank to my knees, his tail still buried inside me and my eyes on his groin.

"I, I, I, I—"

"Poor baby," I crooned to him, rocking my hips against the hot press of his tail. I didn't give him the time for his tongue to catch up to his thoughts, enjoying taking him to pieces. "No wonder you're so needy. Eighty-one years since someone's wrapped her mouth around this gorgeous cock of yours. You might as well be a virgin." My fingers undid his laces with the ease of experience, yanking his pants open to free his shafts.

He whimpered again, talons chipping pieces out of the wall. "Huh-huh-hundred and four—"

I put another black mark in my mental ledger for his ex-paramour. Asshole. There was no way he hadn't gone down on her for twenty years. The man ate pussy like it was his last meal.

"Let's fix that," I said, and ran my tongue up his lower shaft.

CHAPTER FORTY-FIVE

TROUBLE

Varistan cried out as his taste bloomed on my tongue, as clean and crisp as mineral water. I clenched down on his tail and wrapped my hands around the base of his cocks, pleasuring all three of those sensitive lengths. It was hard to focus with the movement of his tail, but I was determined to make him come apart at the seams.

"Fuck," I moaned, licking across the tips of his cocks. "You taste as good as you look." Stroking his upper cock, I wrapped my lips around his lower shaft and sank onto him with purpose, flicking my eyes up to look at him.

My duke made little whining noises on the edge of every breath, his mouth open and garnet eyes fixed on me as I gave him his first blowjob in a century. He looked stunned, like he couldn't believe what was happening to him, his whole body shivering with tension. I moved my hips for him, riding his tail as I sucked his cock, every movement sending spikes of pleasure through me like sparks thrown up from a fire.

Hunger coiled through me, a searing need to see Varis undone. I pulled off his lower cock with a *pop!* as the suction broke, and pulled the other into my mouth, massaging him with my tongue. He cried out again, bucking his hips forward and flaring his tail, the warm taste of saffron flooding my mouth as more precome drooled out of his cock. I felt it dripping onto my chest from his other shaft, the grip of my hand around his length pumping it out of him, and greed flared inside me. There was no way I'd be able to swallow both shafts, but I could have both heads on my tongue, and not waste a single drop of his come.

His hips started moving more, helpless-seeming thrusts that shoved his cock deeper into my throat.

I pulled off of his cock and smacked him on the inner thigh, hard, instinct telling me that my touch-sensitive duke who fell apart from getting his hair yanked could be as much a slut for pain as he was for pleasure.

Varis cried out, cocks twitching hard in my grasp and a spurt of precome dripping over my fingers. His tail flared so hard inside me that I saw stars, the pressure of his tail against my g-spot such perfection that I almost tipped over the edge into orgasm.

I smacked him again when he bucked into my grasp, hard enough that my hand stung. "*Bad* duke," I said, my voice sharp and my attention fixed on him like a falcon on her prey. "Take what you're given, or get nothing. *No moving.*"

He whined, eyes closed and brows pulled together, but he nodded in desperation as his thighs shook and tail flared with his arousal and need.

My skin felt hot all over, greed and want combining into a lustful conflagration as I clenched down on his sensitive tail and wrapped both hands around his dripping cocks again. Varis had to brace himself against the wall as I started sucking on his cockheads, my hands pressing his lengths down next to each other so I could work the last three inches of his shafts with my tongue and stroke the rest.

My duke started making sobbing sounds of pleasure, his breathing ragged and whole body shaking. He kept his hips shoved against the wall, but his tail didn't stop moving, studs grinding down against my throbbing clit as the blades of his spade kept flaring in waves, pressing harder and harder against me as he got closer to coming.

I couldn't stop my legs from closing down against his tail, only the act of pleasuring him keeping me from coming to pieces. Gods, he felt so *good*—

But he knew it, damn him, and with a tight whine Varistan shoved his tail deeper and fucking *vibrated* it inside me. The sudden shock of pleasure threw me over the edge into cataclysmic ecstasy, my whole body tensing as my pussy slammed down onto his tail and as I moaned around his cocks.

With a guttural moan, Varis followed me into orgasm, his hips canting up and claws embedding deeper into the brick as both cocks jerked against my tongue. I swallowed, the taste of his hot come as sharply metallic as a sword, my throat working in the same rhythm as my pussy. Every clench of my body sent a vivid flash of delight through me, my whole soul focused on the places that joined us. I wanted it to last forever, even as the bliss flooded my veins and the throb between my legs eased from demand into glowing pleasure.

His body couldn't go straight from a doubled orgasm into more, though – at least, not outside of rut – and I reluctantly let go of my duke before I took him too far into oversensitivity. I pulled his tail out of my pussy with another moan and stood slowly, keeping my body close to his and dragging my wet fingers up his thighs.

"You made a mess, your grace," I crooned, tilting my head to bare the shine where his precome had dripped onto my skin.

With a whine on the edge of every breath, Varistan leaned forward and started licking it off, his breath searing and his claws still impaled in the wall.

He was almost hyperventilating, his breathing fast and shallow, and his wings shook.

"Hey," I said, voice gentle, and tugged his head away from my skin by his dense curls.

He went with a moan, eyes unfocused and the tip of his tongue still out, completely overwhelmed.

I'd taken him to pieces, exactly as I'd intended. Now it was my job to put him back together again.

"C'mere," I said, lifting his hands off the wall and tightening the laces of his pants enough that they wouldn't fall off. I buttoned mine, too, then took him by the hands and led him through the alley to a little patch of ground under a cypress tree.

He came, shakily, tripping over an uneven cobblestone and nearly falling. When I tugged him down to the ground he went without complaint, moving like he didn't know where the parts of his body started and ended.

The ground was cold, but I knew that wouldn't bother him, and Varistan would keep me warm enough. I snuggled close to him, face-to-face, with his leg hooked over mine and my arms around him. "Hey," I said again, nuzzling him as I stroked his hair. "Come back to me, Varis. You did so good for me. Now come back, sweetheart."

Varistan shivered, almost a shudder, and burrowed closer to me, his tail coiling around my leg and one hand wrapping around my arm. He said my name, his voice hoarse, and shuddered again.

"That's my good duke," I said, gentling him back down, my breath mingling with his and his warmth soaking into me.

I kept petting his hair, my arms wrapped around his shoulders and my forehead resting against his. I knew what it was like to be overwhelmed—to have surrendered completely to someone, and to need time to come back from that. It made my chest tight to think about, warmth flooding my veins. Varistan, going there for *me*. Who could ever have imagined something like that?

His breathing eased as we lay there together, the tension drifting out of his body so that his muscles stopped trembling with fatigue. "Bells," he said again, his lips brushing mine as he spoke.

"I have you, Varis," I said, trying to ignore the way my heartbeat picked up from the touch of his mouth. "I'm here."

He nodded, then breathed a laugh, stroking his fingers up my arm. "Gods," he said, just above a whisper. "That was..." He smiled for a moment, settling closer to me as he fully relaxed. "I'm fairly certain that's the best fellatio I've had in my life."

That made me laugh, and I rubbed my nose along his. "And I don't even have eighteen hundred years of experience."

"To be fair, neither did Yesika," Varis said, with a bit of a rueful smile. "But that's not surprising, given that it's not that pleasant for the giver. It was an indulgence, often for my decadals—"

"Hold up," I said, brows drawing together. "Who told you it's unpleasant? I love giving head."

Varis blinked, clearly taken aback. "I— What? Is that a human trait? None of my former paramours were particularly interested—"

"Ruekh's mercy," I muttered. I shook my head, frowning at him. "It's not a human trait; you just have terrible taste in women."

"Present company excepted?" he asked, smirking back at me.

"Present company included," I said, with an answering smile twitching at my lips. "I'm an aggressive, cantankerous mortal, and a bondservant, to boot. Completely unsuitable for the role of a duke's paramour."

"Conversely, you apparently enjoy pleasuring me with your tongue, which I find quite intriguing in a potential paramour." Varistan shifted, hooking his wing under my arm so he could drop it over me like a cloak, pulling me flush against the warm strength of his body. "Though, given that you've been fairly belligerent in your refusal to consider me as a potential romantic partner, does it truly matter if you don't suit what might traditionally come to mind for such a role?"

I frowned at him again, a line forming between my brows. "What're you talking about?"

He lifted a brow. "I recall being told quite firmly that you weren't interested in being my lover."

My frown deepened. "I don't want to be your mistress."

"It doesn't seem to me as if there's much of a difference."

I stared at him; he simply met my gaze, looking bemused.

"...Why would you think that?" I asked.

Varistan huffed a laugh. "At this point, I'm not quite certain what I think." He rubbed his nose against mine, smiling. "Given that you've engaged sexually with me multiple times since that conversation, including publicly, and that you're currently holding me like a lover, I admit to not understanding what you desire from me." His lips quirked up towards a smirk as I flushed, and he added in a pert tone, "Except, of course, that you *do* desire me."

"I..." I trailed off, not sure what to say. I'd thought *he* was the reason we weren't a pair. Even if we couldn't publicly be partners – drawing the ire of the Raven King seemed incredibly foolish – I'd thought he didn't want to bind himself to me in any formal way.

Varis brushed the knuckles of his wing against my cheek. "You need not know what you desire, and even if you know, you need not tell me," he said, his crimson eyes warm with affection. "Despite all evidence to the contrary, I do know how to be patient, and we still have time yet."

"You more than me," I said with a rueful smile. He would live a lot, lot longer than I would.

"Me exactly as much as you," he replied, voice gentle. "But that doesn't matter much at the present moment, and as much as I'm enjoying having your body alongside mine, the hard ground is growing rather unpleasant to lie upon. So shall we perhaps go find some dinner, as we were before you so demandingly changed our itinerary?"

"You liked it," I said, wrinkling my nose at him before I extricated myself from his embrace.

He rose gracefully to his feet and held out a hand, towing me upright when I accepted his assistance. "I did," he said in a genial tone of voice, his tail swaying behind him as I tied the laces of his pants closed. "I loved it, in fact. It's been..." Varistan fell silent, as if trying to count the years. "Centuries, I suppose, since I've felt that... wanted."

I paused in buckling my belt to look up at him. "You said you kept Yesika satisfied for your whole relationship. Did she not...?"

Varistan gave a slight shrug, looking away from me. "I dislike speaking ill of her," he said, a faint flicker of tension crossing his face. "She was my paramour for the lifetime of some mortal civilizations. But as you're no doubt well aware, when it comes to touch, I'm quite needy, and that applies to sex, as well." He shrugged again, crossing one arm over his chest in a self-conscious gesture. "It's hardly reasonable to expect anyone but a soulmated lover to be a perfect match for one's sexual desires. I don't blame her for becoming jaded with me."

I watched him for a moment longer, but Varis only stood there, looking melancholy. Pushing aside my hesitation, I finished tidying up my clothing, then took his hand, lacing my fingers through his like we really were a pair.

When he looked down at me in surprise, I smiled at him. "Your loyalty is admirable, if misplaced," I told him, then gave his hand a squeeze. "And you're not needy. Your needs were different from hers, that's all."

One corner of his mouth lifted into a soft smile. "If you keep saying things like that, I may start to think you actually like me."

Far worse than that, I thought, my heartbeat stuttering as he looked at me like he might fall in love with me. I couldn't imagine my life without him anymore—but he was fae, and I was mortal. Fae called human partners "snowflake lovers" for a reason. A snowflake may be beautiful, but it doesn't last long, melting in the sunlight or at the touch of a hand. What would life be like when I started aging? When I became gray and stooped?

When I died?

How could he – a man who looked into the millennia ahead with every expectation of seeing them – ever deal with my mortality? How could I watch my lifespan break his eternal heart?

"I do like you, Varis," I said at last, putting on a smirk so he wouldn't see my sorrow. "You're a troublesome pain in my ass, but," I added with a flash of my brows, "I like trouble."

He laughed, the sound bright and beautiful, and slung a wing across my shoulders. "Then let's go make a little."

CHAPTER FORTY-SIX
VICTORY

W e signed the trade agreements with Maestrizen on a bright late-winter morning, the skies scoured clean by the storm of the prior night. Varistan signed his name with bold lines and sealed it with blood—then turned and passed me the quill and silver knife.

My hands closed around them slowly, my lips parted and eyes wide.

"It's your treaty," he said, ears tilted forward and pride in his eyes. "You deserve to have your name on it."

And so the last ink on the treaty was mine: "Isabela Keris", written in clean script and sealed with my mortal blood.

In true fae style, the conclusion of business came with revelry, the sort of party that started with brunch and started getting its legs at about five in the afternoon, as the genteel celebration began to anticipate the freedom of the night. The vicereine and Raylien both vanished around sundown—and returned once full dark had settled across the island, Raylien as a curvy fae woman in a shimmering green gown that showed off her dark skin and the vicereine as a nine-foot-tall wildling with night-black fur, clad in a vividly-patterned sarong.

Varistan didn't even bat an eye, lifting his glass of goldenbloom tea in a salute when they re-entered before tossing it back.

I didn't touch the stuff, of course. For a fae, it was the sort of pleasant drug that made one mellow and eased the discomfort of conceding ground in bargains. For mortals... well. Without an innate defense against debts, we became eager slaves. I was a little surprised Varis could drink it, but when he looked down at me, all but beaming, he didn't have the glassy-eyed look of a mortal under the influence of heartflower. Apparently even his broken debt-sense was defense enough.

The first bars of dancing music sang out across the vaulted ballroom of the meeting-house, and Varis pursed his lips as he turned towards me. "How nice, precisely, do I have to be to get another dance before Ruekh's night?"

I held out my hands, smiling as his warm fingers wrapped around mine. "Tell me I'm beautiful," I said, feeling lost in his eyes.

"You're beautiful," he said, setting my left hand on his shoulder and wrapping his arm around my waist.

"Tell me I'm the best thing that's ever happened to you," I said, smirking up at him.

"Oh, that's how it is?" Varistan ran one tip of his forked tongue along the sharp point of his canine, his dark lashes lowering across his ruby gaze. "You're the best thing that has ever happened to me, Isabela Keris," he crooned, without so much as a moment of hesitation.

My breath hitched, warmth scudding across my skin as Varis tugged me up against him.

"Anything else you want me to say?" he asked, sounding very pleased with himself. "Three is the traditional number for such demands, after all."

"Tell me you're mine," I whispered, my heart pounding against the cage of my ribs as if it could escape.

His tail ran up the back of my calf, soft and warm. "I'm yours," he said in a low voice, the world seeming to vanish around us. It was like we were caught in a whirlpool together as we gazed into each other's eyes, my mortal hazel matched to his fae garnet. Caught up together and yet divided by eternity, with no way out.

It was enough to break any heart. It was certainly breaking mine.

"Dance with me, Bells," Varis murmured, and stepped into the song with my body against his.

The revel went until dawn, and I spent most of the night in Varistan's arms. I knew it was only one night, time stolen from an uncaring future, but I was mortal, and I'd grown up knowing that life could be cut short in a single moment. I chose to forget the future – that I would have to go back to his beloved Nyx Shaeras, and to go back to standing in his shadow – and lived this one night where we could be something together, our names sealed next to each other on a treaty that could only have happened because of the two of us, allied together.

The vicereine and her daughter vanished before dawn, of course, and Varistan and I were free to change out of our finery and mosey through the rousing city to watch the sunrise over the ocean while our ship was prepared. I sighed, leaning back against his warmth as the sky brightened.

"We did it," I said in a soft exhale, still barely believing it.

"We did." Varistan reached up with his tail and pulled something out of his belt-pouch, holding it out to me. "This is for you. A token of my appreciation."

I looked up at him with my brows raised, then unfolded the black cloth. Colored streamers of light started drifting up before I'd even finished opening the parcel. "Varis," I said, shocked, as I stared down at the wildly expensive necklace I'd been so enamored of in the pearl market. "We can't afford this."

He made a pleased sound, the low thrum vibrating against my spine. "We can, actually, thanks to you," he murmured, tucking my hair behind my ear with his wing. "But I asked for it from Her Excellency as her trade-gift for the closing of our bargain, and she agreed." Varistan hesitated for a moment, then added, "May I put it on you?"

"Do you know what you're asking for?" I asked, looking back up at him with a sleepy smile, hearkening back to when I'd first asked him to put a necklace on me.

Varis smiled back down at me, his eyes still lined with kohl from the revel and his ears tilted towards me in total focus. "You asked me to adorn you with aurora pearls," he said softly, sidestepping the question. "You argued with me. Convinced me. Stood beside me and held my hand." My duke picked the necklace up out of my hands and rested his face against my hair, inhaling slowly. "I didn't deserve that intercession, and I don't have any idea how to proceed from here. But will you allow me to start by giving you one of the many things you've always deserved?"

"It's going to be different in Nyx Shaeras," I said, not sure what to do with Varistan holding me like he'd never wanted anything else.

"I know." He nuzzled my hair. "Will you let me do it anyway?"

He'd asked three times. *The traditional count*, I thought. No matter what answer you've gotten from the first two questions, the third answer was always truest—and final. Ask a fae for something three times, and you never got to ask again.

"Yes," I said, barely above a whisper, my heart beating too hard and my throat tight. It felt like I was caught in a vise, flattened by a force I didn't understand, and when Varistan settled the necklace against my throat I almost couldn't breathe.

"Seven," Varis murmured.

"Seven?" I asked.

He laughed and scooped me up into his arms, sauntering down the dock towards our ship.

"Varis!" I yelped, throwing an arm around his neck in reflex.

"Seven things to like about my body," he said smugly, ignoring my protest. "Flight, fire-walking, your admiration, the rewards of possessiveness, tail play, dual-wielding, and the satisfaction of mate-bonding."

"I'm not your mate," I said with a touch of admonition. "I'm not even your paramour."

Varistan smirked. "Semantics, Bells. Our names are marked in blood as equals on a treaty we won together. You sleep in my bed. You take command of my body and pleasure with the confidence of one who knows she'll be answered with passion." He stretched his wings, the rising sun gleaming off his black scales. "Even if you're not my mistress, lover, paramour, mate, or whatever other word you choose to disdain, never think you don't hold a position of preeminence in my life."

I rolled my eyes, though my lips were twitching towards a smile. "And why, pray tell, are you carrying my preeminent self up the gangplank instead of letting me walk?" I asked, swinging my legs.

"Because I'm disinclined to spend the next four to six days watching you suffer," he said, as if explaining something obvious to a small child. "Once was more than enough of that particular experience for me."

"I'll just get seasick as soon as you put me down," I replied, amused at him. "It's not like you can carry me for the next week."

"Can't I?" he asked, flashing me a brilliant smile. "Try me."

I sputtered as he strode across the deck towards the stern of the ship, the various people aboard offering bows as we passed. "But that's— That's ridiculous! Varis!" I yelped as he crouched and leapt up to the higher deck rather than walking over to the stairs, one hard beat of his wings flinging us over the railing. "You can't just—"

"Can't I?" Varis asked again, folding his wings behind him and giving a nod to the captain before taking his ceremonial place at the stern of the ship. People yelled out commands, ropes being tossed back up onto deck and poles shoving the ship backwards from the docks. "I'm more than willing to trade a little bit of ridiculousness for your comfort, and that extends to fighting with you over this. Are you truly going to pick up the spear to defend your right to vomit over the railing?"

Grumbling, I subsided, crossing my arms over my chest. "No," I muttered.

"Good," he said, with a touch of his usual imperiousness, standing as solidly as the bedrock stone as the ocean's tide took hold of the ship beneath us.

Varistan kept his word. At no point during our four-day journey did my feet touch the planks of the ship. He put himself entirely at my disposal. If I wanted to go somewhere, Varis carried me there – including, to my embarrassment, to the head – and held me in his arms when I wanted to stay somewhere. I sat on his lap during meals I could actually keep down, and slept across his chest with his slow heartbeat setting the pace for mine.

Nobody said anything. They didn't dare. The one time someone opened her mouth to make a comment, Varistan's entire body went tense, his eyes glittering like rubies in the sun and his wings mantling in a dark shadow behind him.

She changed her mind before a word left her tongue.

We arrived at Nyx Shaeras late at night on the fourth day, and Varistan didn't bother waiting for the ship to dock. He took me up to the deck when the castle hove into view and threw us skyward. The heat of his dragonfire warmed me as he winged for home, a sharp contrast to the late-winter chill.

Home, I thought when Varis set my feet on the stone of the castle. It felt like I could sense the world around me—as if I was part of one living organism, spreading out in every direction from the castle's heart. Wind flirting with stone towers, a forest drowsing in the winter night, the hungry sea lapping at the shores, the vivid flame of the man standing to my back. I turned to him, smiling as that sense of being right where I belonged sank into my bones.

"Ready for bed?" I asked.

He ran the backs of his fingers along my jaw, his expression soft. "We're not at sea anymore," he said softly. "I've done nothing today to pursue a trade deal with wildling fae."

"So?" I asked, taking his hands and stepping backwards, tugging him after me. "It's cold. Be kind to me, and keep me warm tonight."

Varistan started smiling, following me across the roof towards the entrance of our home. "Are you asking as a favor?" he asked in reply, never looking away from my face. "Or would you like another bargain?"

Knowing exactly what I was doing, I smiled and said please.

CHAPTER FORTY-SEVEN

EVERYTHING

In the shadow of night, lying in bed with Varis, it was hard to muster the fortitude to push aside how much I simply *liked* him. He wasn't perfect—but who was? And he was trying, which was more than could be said for a lot of people. The habits of millennia could calcify around anyone, but Varis was shedding the weight of the years. He'd done so much already.

He'd done so much for *me*.

"Why are you looking at me like that, Bells?" he asked, his voice rough. Varistan brushed my hair back from my face, his fingers warm. "Did I finally do something right?"

Holding him at bay was stupid. I was a mortal bondservant, and he was my fae duke, but even the most socially inept person in the world wouldn't be able to miss the way his eyes followed me, or the absolute hunger he had for my approval and attention. It went far beyond any draconic greed. As Lianka had warned, he was a loyal lover, and he'd set his heart in the palm of my hand.

That heart would already break when my life ended. There was no reason to deny him the years of happiness we could have together. No reason to eschew joy for the anticipation of grief.

"You've done a lot of things right," I said, taking his hand before he could draw it away. With careful deliberation, holding his gaze, I set a kiss softly against his palm.

Varis made a yearning sound, his expression going soft and full of longing. His lips made the shape of my name, not even whispering the word.

"You made a bargain with Maestrizen," I murmured, lacing my fingers through his. "You've allied with those you saw as enemies, and you treat me like a partner. You're learning Faery Sign so you can talk to people you used to regard as monsters. Any one of those would have been unthinkable for you not so long ago."

One corner of his mouth flipped up into a wry smile. "It seems that I'm very easily won over with a little affection and nights I don't have to spend alone," he replied, his voice as soft as mine. "Might I request that, of your kindness, you not mention such to my truer enemies?"

I grinned, giving his hand a squeeze. "I have no intention of giving away my secrets so easily. It's delightful to be the one person who can change your mind." Gently, I ran my fingers up along his arm to his bare shoulder, then down along his side, painting delicate tracery on his warm skin.

"Bells..." he said with warning, shivering from the touch. Varis panted when I settled my hand on his hips with my fingertips beneath the band of his underthings, his tail sliding up my leg with demand. "Bells, if this isn't an invitation—"

"Who said it's not?" I shifted closer to him, luxuriating in his heat as I tangled my legs with his. I took his hand and set it on my thigh, dragging his palm up along my bare skin until I slid his hand under my nightshirt and onto my ribs. My pulse pounded between my legs, my breathing quickening and mouth going wet at the expression of naked desire on Varistan's face.

"I release you from your promise not to initiate, Varis," I said, watching with avarice as his back arched and face dropped into an expression of raw ecstasy. I could have simply given him permission, but this was so much more rewarding than completing the bargain.

"Bells—" he gasped out, shuddering from the intense pleasure of being freed from his promise, his beautifully broken debt-sense playing perfectly into my hands. His lashes fluttered as I dragged my palm back up his side, reveling in the feel of his tense muscles and the echoes of pleasure on his face.

Fuck, I could do that to him a thousand times, and only want to do it a thousand more. "Do you want me?"

"You, you, you, you—" He stopped himself, squeezing his eyes shut and swallowing as his fingers tightened on my side. "You didn't want to be my mistress."

"I didn't want to be your dirty secret," I corrected, pressing up against him as I buried my fingers in his curls. "But I'm not, and it's getting ridiculous to pretend otherwise." I ran my nose along his, panting from his nearness and the desire slicking my thighs. "I want to be your lover. Do you still want me, Varis?"

"Yes," he whispered, trembling from that want. "Yes, gods, please—please—please—"

I silenced him with a kiss, melting up against him with my mouth fitting to his in perfect harmony. Varis moaned against me, his hand sliding up under my shirt in a possessive caress and his flared tail pressing up between my legs.

I took my mouth away from his, admiring the longing in his eyes. "Then I'm going to kiss you," I said through the desire in my chest, my lips brushing against his as I spoke, and kissed him again.

His mouth moved against mine like an enchantment, his scent wrapped around me and his heat soaking into me. I parted my lips and Varis took the invitation without hesitation, nipping my lower lip before he offered me his tongue. His taste flooded my mouth as our tongues met, my core feeling molten as he rocked his hips against mine.

"And kiss you," I moaned when he broke away to breathe, lacing my fingers through his hair and dragging him back to me.

Varistan came with hunger, making low sounds of pleasure deep in his throat. He rolled me onto my back, following me with his mouth and body. His forked tongue caressed mine, spreading wide to grip me. He took his mouth away from mine to drag my nightshirt off of me, dropping back down to press his bare chest to mine.

"And kiss you," he said, his voice so thick I thought he might cry. But then the heat of his mouth was on mine again, his tongue twining with mine and his hands exploring my body, and I didn't have any time to wonder about the strength of his emotions.

Varis didn't rush past foreplay. With his skin against mine and my fingers in his hair, he seemed content to kiss me, and kiss me, and kiss me. I let myself melt into it, falling into the depths of affection he offered me without fear of drowning. The hard heat of his shafts pressed against my clit where he rocked against me, only the thin fabric of our underthings between us. His ankle hooked around mine, his scales smooth against my skin, and his tail rubbed between my legs with slow demand.

It was that tail of his that grew tired of slow kisses. It slid beneath my panties, Varistan shuddering with pleasure as he touched my wet skin with his sensitive spade, and a heartbeat later he flattened the blades and started pressing it into my pussy.

"Fuck," he moaned, shaking as his tail filled me. The studs along it fully hardened before he'd even gotten it halfway in, sending flares of sensation though me. Varis tensed, lifting his hips for a moment, and *shoved* his tail home, the spade flaring and relaxing in waves as it curled inside of me.

I cried out with him, my back arching off the bed as pleasure speared through my core. Need gripped me, my clit throbbing. I grabbed him by the hips and hauled him back to me, desperate for the feel of his cocks against me, even with his tail filling me.

He obliged, thrusting against me with his back bowed as he tail-fucked me. "Oh, gods, darling, I—"

Varistan froze, apparently not having meant to say the endearment, but I was having none of it. I grabbed his tail just above my pussy so he couldn't take it away and bucked up against him, determined to do the work if he wouldn't.

"Varis—" I said with an edge of need to the word, my clit throbbing and the tension inside me demanding attention.

"S—sorry," he got out, sounding almost frightened. He started thrusting against me again, sliding his fingers between us so he could rub circles on my clit. "I didn't intend—"

"Fuck *intentions.*" I reached up and grabbed for his hair, catching a handful of curls. I didn't even have to yank for him to moan, the Duke of Nyx Shaeras as wanton as I could ever have asked him to be. "Just *be.*"

He kissed me fiercely, thrusting his tongue into my mouth with the same demand as his tail. Before I could recover, Varis shoved himself down along my body and grabbed my panties with his teeth, pushing his fingers underneath. Flame lit the bedroom for one flickering moment, stinging heat washing across my delicate skin, but with Varistan's dragon-scaled hand between me and the flame, the only thing that burned was the cotton.

With a snarl, Varis dropped his scorching mouth to my pussy, his tongue licking my wet off his own tail before he focused on my clit. He knew my body too well, and he wanted me to come for him. Varistan ate me with hungry insistence, massaging my clit with his tongue while he closed his mouth against my skin, giving me waves of suction.

I had no hope of withstanding the onslaught, nor desire to do so. Pressure spiked inside of me, my pussy clenching down against his studded tail with flashes of pleasure. Raw need grew in my core, unbearable tension that seemed to spiral tighter and tighter, my thighs shaking and toes pointing.

Varistan growled like an animal, the vibration sending white-bright pleasure through me. At my whimper and the clutch of my hand against his hair, he did it again—and again, and again, until he was growling like a dragon guarding his hoard, and the shivering pleasure inside of me shattered into a flood of ecstasy.

I came screaming his name, hauling him against my pussy by one horn as waves of pleasure wracked me. My core closed down on him over and over, each clench of my body sending another blinding rush of pleasure through me. Varis drove me through it without mercy, his tongue and tail not easing up until I was nothing but a trembling wreck, panting with a whine on every breath.

Only then did Varis lift his face up from between my legs, his crimson eyes black in the darkness, gleaming from the faint moonlight illuminating the room. "Shall I give you more?" he asked, his voice low and dangerous.

"Yes," I said, whimpering when he growled again and flared his spade-tail inside of me. "I want your... cock," I panted out. "All of it."

"All of it?" he repeated, sliding his hands up along my thighs, leaving heat in his wake. "You may truly never wish another mortal man in your bed once you enjoy taking all of me."

"Isn't that... what you... want?" I asked between shallow breaths, reaching out towards him.

Varistan twisted his tail inside me, making me whimper. With an expression of feral lust, he slid his fingers into his mouth, running his tongue along them before sucking on them. He started to pump his tail in and out of me again, pressing into my depths with slow insistence.

"I would prefer you never take anyone but me to your bed again," Varis said, his voice intense as he folded his tail-spade down so he could slide his two fingers into me alongside it. "So if no one but I can slake your thirst...?" His thumb pressed against my clit as he started slowly flaring his tail again, spreading me wider. The movement pressed his fingers hard against my g-spot, two immovable bars of sensation that grew in intensity as he filled me. "All the better."

I didn't have a clever answer to that. I couldn't even really think, not with the growing tension inside of me. Gods, I loved this so much—how it felt impossible for me to be stretched any wider, until his blades pressed harder against the walls of my pussy, forcing my body to accommodate him. I whimpered, canting my hips so that the pressure of his fingertips rubbed against my throbbing g-spot, the promise of ecstasy a desperate ache in my core.

Varistan leaned down, his breath hot as he ran his mouth against my ear. "I'm going to fuck you with my *fae cock*, Bells," he purred. He flicked his tongue out, licking the curve of my ear as he started rocking his fingers against me. "Stretch you better than any mortal man can. And if we're very lucky, I'm going to fill you with my seed while both my shafts are buried to the hilt inside you."

I whined, my voice high and tight as I squirmed against him. "I want it, fuck, fuck—"

He shoved his fingers deeper inside of me, his blunted claws two points of vivid pleasure as they dragged against my channel. "Just it?" he asked in a croon. "Or *me?*"

His tail twisted inside of me, fingertips grinding hard against me, and I came apart. Pleasure slammed into me like a tidal wave, my whole body curling around the spear of sensation piercing my core. I gasped, vision whiting out as my body closed down against Varistan's immovable fingers, the tension spiking to apocalyptic heights.

The sharp perfection of orgasm turned to a flood of heat, my pussy unable to release the pressure any other way. Come rushed out of me with ecstatic relief, overwhelming bliss racing through my veins. Even the embarrassment of soaking Varistan's bed couldn't take me out of it, every grip of my pussy against his tail and fingers leaving me sobbing out my pleasure.

Varistan's warm mouth pressed against my jaw, his voice guiding me back to my body. "—that's my good girl, my wonderful Bells, let go for me—"

I whimpered as I came down, leaning my face against his. I couldn't seem to catch my breath, every movement of his tail sending aftershocks spiking through me, leaving me teetering on the edge of orgasm. I wanted more— Needed more— Fuck, the void was calling, and I wanted to leap into that echo of eternity with every fiber of my being.

He moved with smooth care, pulling his tail out of me and tugging off his underthings. Even dazed and needy, I could sense his control—and feel his desperate want in the way his wings trembled as he lined up his cocks with my pussy. "Tell me if it's too much," he said, voice wavering. Varis framed my body with his, face pressed against my neck, and started slowly driving his shafts into me.

Gods, he was so warm, the heat of a dragon melting me from within as he rocked his twin lengths deeper into me. All the strength of his body, used to conquer mine—the slow, inexorable press of his cocks into my core sending a radiating ache of unyielding pleasure through me. I panted, overwhelmed with the sensation of being stretched wider and deeper, my hands spasming against the slick scales of his back as he spread me open.

There was no room for thought—no room for anything but *him*. Varistan became my entire world: his wings my sky, his body my earth, his cock my soul. With every rock of his hips I thought I couldn't possibly take more, until he held me down and thrust a little harder, driving a fraction deeper into me. I clung to him, bucking my hips up against him, every movement dragging the studs of his cocks against my walls with vivid pleasure.

"Fuck, you're so tight," Varis moaned, sweat-damp tendrils of hair hanging down as he started moving with more vigor. "Just a little more—"

"Please," I gasped out, gripping his hips. "Everything—"

Varis slid his fingers into my hair, caressing my face. "As you desire," he said, his voice low and full of promise.

His tail wrapped around my left thigh as he hooked his arm under my right knee. I had only a heartbeat to anticipate before Varistan hauled my hips back against his, pairing the motion with a hard drive of his hips that slammed his cocks into my depths. I cried out, back arching from the spike of pleasure as he bottomed out in me, his scales kissing my pussy and his pulse throbbing in my core.

Panting with pleasure, Varistan took my hand and slid it below my navel. He held my palm against my belly as he drew back and thrust into me again, so I could feel the bulge of his cocks inside me as he moved. "You have me," he growled, starting to move with slow purpose. "Now I'll have *you*."

He didn't give me time to answer, wrapping his arm around me as his strokes became deeper and more powerful. My every ragged breath came out with the edge of a moan, my whole being reduced to the intense pleasure of Varistan fucking me, his shafts cleaving me open. With shaking hands, I grabbed him by the face, staring into his eyes in the darkness. A curl of flame lit the air between us, illuminating his beautiful eyes, the pupils all but swallowing the red.

"Varis," I whimpered, my thighs trembling and my whole body focusing in on the growing tension in my core. "Varis—" It was like I could feel his soul at my fingertips, the inexorable pull of the tides drawing me towards him. I wanted him so badly, wanted it, wanted it—

Purring a growl, Varistan moved his fingers to my clit, pressing down and circling. With his tail and other arm, he lifted my hips, angling my body so that every thrust slammed his shafts against my g-spot. I gasped out, pressure building inside of me, like water behind a dam. Oh, fuck, it was so good, *he* was so good— Why had I ever wanted anything else?

My legs started shaking, need wracking me, nothing mattering but the coiling tension in my depths. I felt like an animal, bucking my hips up against him to chase the spreading pleasure that built inside of me, as focused as a wolf chasing down a doe.

Varistan answered that need, increasing his speed and force. The heat of his harsh breaths fanned across my face, sweat dampening his curls and gleaming on his chest. I couldn't even focus on his face, my head dropping back as he claimed everything I had to offer. His cock drove against my g-spot with every thrust, that pressure in my depths becoming more and more and *more*—

Orgasm struck me like lightning, stealing my breath and arcing through my body. I gasped for air as ecstasy wracked me, my whole body dedicated to pleasure, gushing through me and out of me. Distantly, I heard Varis cry out my name, hilting his cocks in me as he came alongside me. Hot come filled me, the throbbing of his cocks pairing with the clench of my orgasm to wipe everything else away.

Bliss flushed my body as I came down from ecstasy, my muscles going limp as I sank down onto the bed. Varistan licked the sweat off my neck, nuzzling me with affection. I could have stayed like that forever, holding his body with mine and lost to pleasure, but he pulled out of me with slow care, murmuring something affectionate against my skin.

A low moan escaped my lips, my pussy closing down on nothing as he slipped out of me. The movement sent a wash of come sliding down my skin, the wet patch on the bed growing increasingly uncomfortable as it cooled. When Varis tucked my hair behind my ear with a gentle touch, I made some sort of incoherent sound, unable to think of words to say.

He chuckled at that, his voice low and pleased, and pressed a soft kiss to my lips. "If you give me a few moments to collect myself, I ought to be able to carry you to the lavatory," he said, running his fingers along my hair. "I suspect my legs will work before yours."

I wiggled my way up out of the wet spot I'd made, flushing as the movement made more come slide out of me. Varis made another sound of amusement, but he didn't leave me without assistance. He fished around on the floor for our clothing, coming back up with his boxer-briefs, and started carefully cleaning his come off of me with the cloth.

"You don't have to... do that," I said, feeling shy about being taken care of by him.

"I know," he said, his voice warm. Varis dropped a kiss onto my stomach, rubbing his nose along my skin before he returned to his self-appointed task. "There are many things I'm compelled to do, but caring for you is a pleasure, not a burden." He paused, his tail wrapping loosely around my foot. "I have some regrets about how poorly I've done that, but I'm..." He shook his head with a sigh. "I'm not sure how to undo the decisions I've made without undoing everything that stemmed from them."

I flopped over when he lay down next to me, dropping my arm and thigh across his body and shifting my head to his shoulder. I knew he was talking about making me his bondservant, but it had mostly ceased to bother me. If I didn't serve him, it would force him to claim my father's life instead, but I liked my life, and I liked him. And as Lianka had once pointed out, Varis had never blood-bonded me. Staying was my choice.

"We can't change the past," I said, loving the feel of his body against mine as I traced circles on his sweat-sheened chest. "We can only move forward."

Varistan huffed a laugh, setting his hand over mine. "Surely you cannot deny that the past informs the present, given that you've been terribly aggressive in forcing me to acknowledge the same about the present and the future," he said in a mock-lecturing voice. "I have a great deal of past to inform my present, and a vast expanse of time laid before me to contemplate."

"Mm, that's true." I rubbed my cheek against him like a cat, sleepiness settling on me like a comfortable blanket. "Let the actions of your near past define the present, and carry my wobbly-legged self to the bathroom so I don't get scolded by Lianka about post-sex hygiene again."

"Again?" he asked with laughter in his voice, scooping me into his strong arms as he sat up.

"Post-rut," I informed him, cuddling closer. "I was off and about because I woke up with the worst UTI I've ever had and made Lianka fix it for me. Not that interested in a repeat, either in the infection or the ensuing ducal rampage."

Varis laughed, scooting us to the edge of the bed and carrying me towards the bathroom without any appearance of strain. "I wasn't quite in my right mind, darling," he said, flinching as the endearment slipped out again, his hands tightening on me.

"Don't be afraid," I said, listening to his heartbeat quicken. "I'm not going to hate you for loving me."

If anything, he got more tense, stopping in the doorway of the bathroom, his wings mantled. "I don't deserve your affection," he said, voice tight. "I don't deserve any of this, and I'm starting to believe that the gods won't allow me to keep it."

"Varis..." I brushed my fingers across his cheek, wanting to talk about it, but Varis pecked a kiss onto my fingertips and set me on the floor.

"Do as you need to," he said, flashing me a smile that didn't reach his eyes. "I'll see what I can do about the aftermath."

"Alright," I said, my brows furrowing and a frown settling onto my mouth.

He tipped my face up towards his and kissed me on the mouth, with the soft focus of someone memorizing every moment. "I'll be waiting for you," he murmured, as if we were parting for years instead of minutes. "Don't tarry."

"I won't," I replied, not understanding.

Varis didn't give me an answer. He only smiled, looking at me as if he couldn't bear to lose the sight, and finally turned away.

Chapter Forty-Eight

DEBTS PAID

As usual, I woke up before Varistan. He was sleeping sprawled on his back, the pale light of the morning beautiful on his warm brown skin. The sheets were tangled across his legs, but even that couldn't disguise the shape of his morning erection, his shafts pressing up the creamy cloth.

With an admiring sound, I ran my hands up along his chest, biting my lip as he inhaled and his abs went tight, lashes fluttering as my touch roused him. Gods, Varistan was gorgeous. I couldn't believe it had taken me this long to lay claim to what he so badly wanted to give.

"What're you..." he asked sleepily, trailing off as I straddled him. His hands went to my thighs in what looked like an automatic gesture as his focus snapped to me, fully awake in a heartbeat.

"What does it look like?" I stretched, pressing my pussy down against him, smirking as his ruby gaze dropped to my bare breasts.

"But we... we just had sex last night..." Varis tilted his hips with a groan as I settled closer to him, the hard lengths of his cocks pressing up between my legs.

I wiggled on my perch, running my hands up along his strong arms. "Oh, are you not interested?" I asked, making like I'd get off of him. "We can get out of bed—"

"What? No!" Varis hauled my hips back down against his, bucking up against me with an expression of raw desire. "I only thought... I... You truly want to?" he asked, his eyes darting across my face.

That look of shocked eagerness made me grin, rocking myself against him with heat in my eyes. "Sweetheart, I have a sex drive worthy of Sarcaryn. I'll fuck you every day if you let me."

"*Let* you?" he asked with disbelief, a smile spreading across his face like the dawning sun. "Bells, I'd *beg* you for that."

"Don't make promises you're not excited to keep," I told him, lacing my fingers through my hair and rolling my hips to give him a show. "I like it when you beg."

"Then I'll beg, darling," Varis said, running his hands up my sides. A flash of the wickedness I loved so well lit his eyes before his expression melted into a needy one, brows lifted and ears dropped. "Please fuck me," he breathed out, dragging my hips down to seat my pussy firmly against his cock and thrusting up against my heat. "Please, Bells, I want it so badly. Make me your slut; I can be so good—"

I smacked him on the shoulder, getting a bright laugh in return.

Varis flipped me onto my back, grinning down at me with a feral light in his eyes. "I can be bad, too, little mortal," he purred. He ground down against me, reaching between us to line up one of his cocks with my entrance. "And I'm in the mood to take."

"Let's see it, fae duke," I said in challenge. "Make me forget my name."

He snarled his pleasure, and drove his cock home in reply.

We made it out of bed sometime around noon, ate a cold breakfast, retired to the luxurious bathroom to bathe and for Varistan to do his beauty regimen, and finally got interrupted around three in the afternoon by Sintuviel. I had to give credit to Varistan's steward: not only was he bold enough to simply walk into the room when nobody answered the knock on the door, but he managed to maintain a completely polite expression when he found his duke getting queened by his bondservant.

"Your grace," Sintuviel said in a grave tone.

Varistan growled his annoyance as I awkwardly clambered off of his face. "This had best be important."

One of Sintuviel's ears twitched. "It's Lord Xilvaris, your grace."

Both Varistan and I froze in place. He recovered first, shoving himself upright and wiping his mouth off with the back of his hand. "Xilvaris?" he asked, his voice strained.

His steward nodded, looking as if he'd bitten into a lemon. "He's here."

My duke hissed like an angry serpent. His tail wrapped around my wrist so tightly my hand started going numb. "Have him shown to the Sea Room," he said, words clipped. "Provide whatever refreshments you deem necessary for hospitality. Tell him we'll join him as soon as we may."

Sintuviel's eyes flickered over to me.

Varistan followed that gaze, looking over at me. A touch of the tension left his shoulders. "It's only through Isabela's intervention that I can pay what I must pay," he said quietly. "She ought to gain the satisfaction of seeing that debt cleared."

"Very well, your grace," Sintuviel said, his voice giving none of his thoughts away, and left.

I watched Varistan for a moment before sighing. "I don't need to be there," I said quietly. It would probably cause more problems, no matter how much I'd appreciate both seeing Xilvaris' defeat and being recognized as standing by Varistan's side.

"I need you there," he said, and that was that.

We got ready to face the Devil in silence. It hadn't exactly been a secret that we'd gone to Maestrizen, and Xilvaris surely had the means to have a spy or three in Nyx Shaeras, but that didn't make it feel any better to have him here, under the same roof as us, lying in wait for us. Even the fact that we could pay him didn't erase the unease.

Xilvaris had picked the time and place. We'd simply have to deal with it.

I put Varistan in an outfit that hearkened towards armor, a high-collared doublet with embossed brass plates across his chest and black-on-black brocade. It was a bit blatant as a message, but I adorned him like a prince: a series of gold cuffs on his horns with dangling amber drops, earrings in every one of his ear piercings, and a gold bar through his bridge piercing. Onto each of his obsidian talons, I clasped engraved brass claw-covers we'd picked up in Maestrizen, a clever invention that Varistan had embraced with a great deal of relief.

As a scion of the royal family, he was entitled to wear a circlet, and I picked one out that came down to a point on his forehead. Just to really rub the changed situation in, I dug through the small collection of aurora jewelry we'd put together from our trade in Maestrizen, and added a cuff with an inlaid pearl to each of his wings.

For my part, I dressed simply. Gone were the days of being regarded as Varistan's equal. No matter what we did in this room, to the rest of the world I needed to be merely his bondservant and pampered pet; nothing more dangerous than a favored possession. I didn't like it, but I'd come to understand the necessity. What worked in Maestrizen wouldn't go over well in Raven Court, and we were already flouting custom and social mores.

He took a deep breath at the door to his suite, his hand on the knob, then turned to me. "When this is done," he said, looking anxious and unhappy, "there's something you deserve to know."

My brows drew together, unease coiling in my chest like a restless serpent. "What're you talking about?"

His tail snapped behind him, his wings closing tighter against his back. "I suspect you'll be angry, so I'd prefer to tell you after dealing with Xilvaris."

"You realize that's only making me more concerned, right?" I asked, putting my hands on my hips.

Unhappiness flickered across Varistan's face. He didn't look at me. "Without something to force me to tell you, I don't know that I ever will," he said, sounding miserable. "I'm terrified of the consequences, but I have enough courage to..." He took a deep breath. "To say something that will compel me to say the rest."

I searched his expression, not liking getting put in the position of having to walk into the lion's den with a wolf snapping at my heels. But at last I shook my head, choosing to let him have the space he wanted. "Let's go."

We walked to the Sea Room without speaking, Varistan looking like he was walking towards execution and me walking a step behind him, standing to his left. It had once been an easy position to take, almost automatic; now it rankled. Maestrizen was mine, from start to finish; it had been my idea and it was my blood that provided the final seal on the treaty with the city. But all the other options were worse. This plan hinged on it becoming an established fact before the Raven King decided to take notice—and by it being palatable enough for him to swallow for the sake of his nephew when he did.

It had been by his command that Varistan had been given the wings and flame of a war-dragon. It had been his war against his disloyal betrothed that had gotten his sons killed, with Varistan caught in the crossfire. Surely that granted Varis some leeway... but even I couldn't make myself believe that it was enough leeway for him to make a mortal woman his formal paramour and get away with it.

He would never do anything to put Nyx Shaeras at risk. If I wanted to be with him, I had to do it in his shadow, even though I knew he regarded me as his equal. Time would tell if I could do it without coming to hate him for things that were out of his control.

Xilvaris had come dressed for war. His perfectly-tailored clothing was in the newest style of wealthy Pinesap Court (which I knew solely thanks to having to sit through that first meeting with Maestrizen's envoy), and the wire-wrapped hilt of his saber was one meant for fighting, not for show. He even wore a gold ring in the same style as the signet on Varistan's finger.

He sat sprawled in one of the comfortable chairs with his feet propped up on another, sipping from a glass of sparkling wine with his eyes focused on the door. Those eyes narrowed when Varistan stepped into the room, then slid over to land on me—and the small chest I carried.

"Brought your fucktoy, Vee?" he asked with a lazy sneer.

Varistan growled, a low and dangerous sound. "Isabela Keris is a valued member of my household, and I will not accept such words spoken against her," he said in a flat voice. "Isabela, if you will?" he asked, looking back at me.

I took a deep breath, meeting his eyes. For a heartbeat, I saw pleading in that so-familiar red gaze, before his expression shuttered again. I couldn't forget what he'd said – *"there's something you deserve to know"* – but now wasn't the time or place. I nodded, and turned to face Lord Xilvaris.

With my jaw clenched so I wouldn't say something stupid, I walked up to the man who'd bound my Varis with blood and debts. In silence, I set the chest on the table next to him, undid the clasp, and flung the lid open. Auroras poured out, gem after gem gleaming with eldritch light, making the shadows eel across the table.

"Even at half of current market value, I think you'll find that this satisfies all my monetary debts to you, my lord, including interest and a reasonable penalty for the events in Lylvenore," Varistan said silkily. "Will you accept payment in full now, or shall I pay in gold once I've cornered the aurora pearl market?"

Xilvaris sat with the stillness of a viper, his breathing controlled. He was furious, I realized with a start, feeling that rage like the ghost of an empathic sense. That careful expression covered over the snarling rage of a predator who'd had his prey snatched out of his jaws. Xilvaris was an upstart lord, born a nobody and gaining his position via debts, favors, and clever maneuvering. He'd risen as far as he could, titled and unlanded with no hope of gaining more.

He could never be a duke. But he could own one.

And now he didn't.

The lord blinked slowly, a lizard-like movement, then turned his face to regard the auroras of the coldwater pearls, the light gleaming off the shine of his eyes. His gaze traced up my arm to my face, expression sharpening. He regarded me for a long moment, calculation in those cold eyes. It felt like he could see through me—that this man who played with dukes like pieces on a chessboard could look at me and see things about me even I didn't recognize.

"Well?" Varistan asked, his voice harsh.

Xilvaris met my gaze with the hypnotism of a cobra, holding me there for a breathless span of time before he looked back over at Varistan. With the precision of an executioner drawing his sword, Xilvaris smiled.

"I accept your offer as recompense in full for your monetary debts." His red tongue flicked out, wetting his lips. "But why stop there, Vee? Let's put all our debts to rest." He reached out one slim-fingered hand and shut the casket of jewels, cutting off the light of auroras. Xilvaris leaned forward, his focus on Varistan like a stooping falcon on a dove. "Come down to the dueling grounds with me so you can discharge that little favor you owe, and escape my collar in truth."

CHAPTER FORTY-NINE

DUELING

We acquired a collection of people as we made our way to the formal dueling grounds. Two glamor-artists and Lianka, of course—but also curious onlookers. Though Varistan and I were both duelists, we'd never even been in the same room for matches. With the added intrigue of Lord Xilvaris as a combatant, it was an irresistible event.

"Well?" my duke asked, when we arrived. "I'm prepared to match you in the ring if that's your demand."

That same slick smile turned up Xilvaris' lips. "I have no interest in facing you across the dueling field, Vee," he said cuttingly. "I call your favor due. Duel Isabela Keris as if she is your true enemy."

Varistan went tense, his wings mantling and gaze going intense. "A duel takes two," he ground out. "I cannot be bound to that favor without her agreement. She must also consent."

"Is she not your bondservant?" he asked, his predator's eyes gleaming. "Can you not simply command her? A bondservant's consent is given to her master until the conclusion of their bargain."

"It's alright, your grace," I said, cutting him off before he could speak. I could already see the discomfort from trying to slip past Xilvaris' command, the compulsion of his promise dragging at him. "I'll join you in the ring."

Despair darkened his eyes, but Varis nodded. He took off his sword and handed it to one of the two glamor-artists. "The usual," he said, the words flat.

"Yes, your grace," he murmured, stepping over to the sidelines.

Varistan followed me as I walked to the other side of the ring, even as the glamor-artist started painting over his formal clothing with combat-suited garments. "Bells—" he started.

"As if she's your enemy, Vee," came Xilvaris' mocking voice.

Varistan's body went stiff, pain flickering across his face as the promise that bound him sank thorns into his soul.

Favors are the most expensive coin a fae can pay with. You can't pick how it's spent, and if your creditor dislikes you, the payment is almost guaranteed to hurt in ways you can't avoid, because a fae's word truly is his bond. If a fae breaks a promise, he dies in agony, his soul shredded by the wild magic at its core. The longer he fights against the promise binding him, the more likely he is to go fully feral, losing command over himself and doing anything he can to gnaw his way out of the trap.

My duke owed Xilvaris a favor, and Xilvaris had named it. There was nothing for it but for us to fight as if we were each other's most despised enemies. Anything less wouldn't just kill Varis.

It would destroy his soul.

He snarled at me, flame flickering in his breath, pain wracking him as he struggled against something he could never defeat. "Keep hold of your spear, little mortal," he said with a sneer, his voice cruel but the words still kind, using the same nickname he did when acting the aggressive fae duke in bed with me. "You've seen what I can do to people like you when I have their weapon in my grasp. Flame and blood, li-li-li-li—" He panted, taking a staggering step backwards, the pain turning to agony as he kept trying to help me—as he kept fighting against Faery itself.

He loved me. It was impossible to deny. Even faced with a force of magic that clawed at his very sanity, Varis couldn't bring himself to act like my enemy. Not really.

I couldn't watch him kill himself for me, not for something like this. I already knew the truth of his heart; did he truly think I could be fooled by a few harsh words and a cutthroat duel?

Cold necessity sank into my bones. If he couldn't bring himself to treat me like an enemy, I would do it for him. I wasn't about to watch him be consumed from within. If I needed to harry him until he snapped and attacked me with everything he had, I would do it.

I lowered my lashes and lifted my chin, giving him a supercilious look. "You've never even seen me fight, *Vee*," I said disdainfully. "Keep your advice to yourself. Go be a good boy and wait for me in the ring."

His lashes fluttered in relief, some of the killing power of Xilvaris' command easing as I played the part of his enemy. "You're not my better," he warned, taking a step backwards with his tail snapping behind him, a glassiness in his eyes I didn't like. "Don't forget."

I waved my hand at him as if shooing away a fly, and turned to the anxious-looking glamor artist to cut him off, my skin feeling cold. "I've got a few modifications for my usual gear, Maira."

Her eyes flicked up towards Varistan as my duke stalked away. "What can I do to assist?"

I took a deep breath, my spine prickling with sweat and palms hot. I didn't like any of this. What game was XIlvaris playing?

"He uses that tail as easily as he breathes, and he's surely going to flame," I said quietly, thinking fast and trying to imagine what Varistan would be like when he couldn't fight against his promise anymore. "Can you do spined greaves and vambraces?"

She nodded, her nervousness turning towards calculation. "Faux-iron, or another material? And are you thinking needles, or breakable barbs?"

"Faux-iron barbs," I said, putting away the twist of nausea in my gut for what I was going to have to do to Varis in order to survive this. "Do you have anything that amplifies pain to put on them?"

"Yes," she said, ears flattening as she cast a glance towards our duke. I knew without looking that he was pacing; he would never be able to stand there quietly while waiting for this. "Hawk-wasp venom."

I closed my eyes, breathing carefully so I wouldn't flinch. "Do it." I took another careful breath. "I'd like a dragonscale shield for my left arm. Dragonscale armor. A clear shield for my eyes. Spike on the butt of my spear." Another breath. My heart felt like a bird battering itself to death against an iron cage. *Keep it together, Bells.* "And coat the blade and butt of my spear with hawk-wasp venom, too."

Maira took my hand and gave it a friendly squeeze. When I looked at her, she smiled. "It's only a duel, my friend," she said kindly. "Do you truly need all this?"

I tried to smile back; by her expression, I knew it came out ghastly. "He has to fight me like I'm his enemy, and that promise will harry him until he does," I said, keeping my voice low. "He can light cold oak alight in an instant. What do you think that might do to mortal skin and bone? How long do you think I'll live if it's his claws that slash my jugular open instead of his sword? Long enough for Lianka to reach me?" I took a deep breath, settling myself into what I needed to do to stay alive. "Xilvaris is surely trying to punish him. What do you think it will do to him if he kills me? Or if I live, but maimed by his claws and flame?"

Understanding hardened her face, and the glamor-artist nodded, letting go of me. "He's faster and has more endurance than any of the other fae you've faced with my weapons," she said in a murmur, her lips barely murmured. Maira closed her eyes and held up her hands, a line forming between her brows as she focused. "But he's hot-headed even in fights. With a promise binding him, he may even cease thinking. Get him angry, Bells, and you may have an edge."

She opened her eyes as glamor weighed my limbs down, the dragonscale armor I'd asked for spreading across my body in gleaming ivory. My scalp warmed as a helm framed my skull, with a transparent shield protecting my eyes. The weight of the dragonscale shield settled onto my arm. My spear appeared in her hands, growing solid in the space of a heartbeat.

Her green eyes met mine. I reached out without speaking and took my spear, then turned to meet my duke in the ring for the first time.

Everything fell away as I stepped into the ring. It was so much more than the focus I usually felt when entering battle. The rest of the world didn't simply not matter; it might as well have not been there. There was nothing left but my despairing Varis, yoked by a promise he'd given to keep his people safe, his sword drawn and wings shaking, eyes focused on me despite his glazed expression.

He sank into a fighting stance. I matched him, my skin prickling with anticipation.

We both leapt into motion at the same moment, the sound marking the start of the match not even registering in my conscious mind. A snarl twisted his face, anguish flaring as he struck for me with the sort of speed I couldn't hope to match.

I dropped and pivoted, swinging my spear across his field of attack, hoping only to keep him from landing a killing blow—and felt the shock of his sword meeting my spear as I blocked his strike.

Perfectly.

We sprang back from each other with a screech of steel, my skin buzzing. Fluke, that had to be a fluke, couldn't trust that I could do that again—

Varis lunged forward, the expression on his face animalistic. I moved with him, falling back before his movement registered. The tip of my spear didn't drift from its aim. I caught the sharp blows of his sword on the metal-capped tip of the haft, the clang ringing in my ears.

Like dancing, I thought distantly. My body moved of its own accord. *Like flying.* I didn't have to think. Just moved, blocking strike after strike. It was so easy. Like breathing. Like being carried in his arms at sea, the movement of the world not mattering when I had his body to rely on.

The tip of my spear shrieked across his breastplate. Varis fell back, shaking his head like an animal trying to shake off flies. Blood flew.

Not blood I'd drawn. Blood from his ears, dripping down to splatter on his armored shoulders.

Idiot. He was still fighting that damn promise.

"I thought you were a duelist!" I called, circling him, trying to spur him into motion. He *had* to do this. I wouldn't let him die to refuse Xilvaris. "Where's the fire, Vee? I'm not even breathing hard!"

With a sharp cry, Varis attacked again. I defended, moving like a dancer's silks. My skin felt hot, all over, my body heating from the intensity of the fight. Fast, too fast, he was so fast—

His sword flashed, a flicker of flame lighting the air as Varistan started losing his grasp on himself. I pivoted with him, spear like an extension of my arm, meeting him in the middle.

I fell back, Varistan following me with the tip of his sword. So fast. Gods. He was so fast. I couldn't even think that fast, could barely *move* that fast. But I still met him, my body moving without my direct command. Sparks flew up as our blades squealed against each other.

I wasn't even *reacting*. There was no thought. Every move was perfectly matched, just like watching a duel between soulmates—

Soulmates.

Like watching *soulmates*.

It was always perfect. Flying. Dancing. Being carried across the sea. Sprawling in bed, and the way his body tangled with mine. It was so easy, everything exactly right, like I'd known him forever—since before forever.

He'd said it a thousand times: *You're mine. You're mine. You're mine.* And then he'd said it again: *I'm yours.*

Lying in bed, smiling at me like he loved me. *"You never owed me anything."*

Varistan Yllaxira, the Duke of Nyx Shaeras and Flame of Faery, was my *soulmate*.

He'd made me his *slave*.

With a scream of rage, I batted aside his sword, stabbing forward. He moved *with* me, as if I was leading a dance, the tip of my spear flashing within a hair's-breadth of him. It was like being in a staged fight, every move choreographed. Like *dancing*.

I was a terrible dancer. But *he* wasn't.

"You *bastard!*" The words tore themselves free of my chest, lacerating my throat like glass. "You fucking *coward!*"

He fell back, breathing hard, the knowledge of his damnation in his beautiful eyes. I held my spear level, the tip pointed at his heart.

"How could you?" I asked, my voice harsh. We circled each other, blood dripping down his face from his nostrils and ears. "Every day. While I *served* you. While I *saved* you. While I fucking *loved* you!"

I struck for him again, too hurt and too furious to hold back my strength. He blocked, easily, ears forward and expression halfway between ferality and despair. With a scream, I swung my spear in an arc, a stupid, brash move—and was forced to leap backwards when Varistan lunged into the gap as I made it, sword flashing.

Don't fight. You can't win like this. Just defend. Let him do it—

To defeat a fae, you must outlast him.

He led our dance, driving me across the ring. When he struck for me, I met him—or slipped past him, moving like a fish in the sea. I didn't have to think. There was only being: the feel of my body as I let him waste his strength, the raging inferno inside of me as his sword flashed through the air, the innate sense of him that had always been such a comfort turning him into nothing more than a target for my spear.

"Nothing to say? No clever defenses?" I shouted, tears cutting across my cheeks like acid. "Tell me I'm wrong. Tell me I'm not your *fucking soulmate!*"

His snarl made the hair on my arms lift, vicious elation scudding across me. He attacked, the force of his strikes making my hands tingle. *Shing!* sang his sword, skidding down the steel of my spear.

"Gonna kill me to shut me up?" I taunted, rage seething under my skin, my eyes hard and spear steady. "Think you can, you pathetic excuse of a duke? You can't even take a mortal on your own castle grounds. *Fuck* you!"

He lashed out at me, teeth bared and streaked with his own blood. He was still fucking *holding back*, fighting like we were in a gods-damned exhibition duel.

He wouldn't even fight me to save his own life. Fucking *fine.* Then I would hurt him until there was nothing left but pain—until he *had* to fight back. He deserved to feel every ounce of agony tearing at my soul.

"*Fight me!*" I screamed at him. "You fucker! You don't deserve anything I ever gave you! Pay it back in *blood!*"

Varis came at me with a tortured cry, talons digging into the sand and wings flared.

I let him get close. His tail lashed out for me, and I let him hit me, the sensitive length wrapping around my leg and yanking my feet out from under me. I moved with him, hitting the ground without losing my focus, and as he cried out from the searing pain of the venom flooding his veins, I slashed my spear in an arc across his unprotected wing.

He let go of me. Staggered back, his torn wing bleeding and trembling.

For one moment, I saw something new shining in his eyes.

Fear.

I was on my feet before his expression turned feral, throwing myself to the side to evade the blast of white-hot flame. It left my skin stinging; it filled the air with the scent of hot metal.

It left the sand *glassed.* Holy *fuck.*

Varistan came for me like the angel of death. He drove forward with the vicious speed of a feral wildling, his dragon's instincts coming to the fore with the pain I'd inflicted screaming through him. He finally, *finally* fought me the way he always should have.

Like my *enemy.*

It was easy. It shouldn't have been easy, but gods, it *was.* The bond between us removed his skill and speed from the equation, and I was the better soldier by far. He attacked and attacked, blinded by the pain. I led him, harrying him any time he tried to slow, pricking and insulting and giving him openings that left him with agonizing barbs of iron and venom embedded in his flesh.

His breathing grew labored, flame on every breath. Burns heated my skin, even the edges of his searing dragonfire leaving me feeling as if I'd been sunburnt beneath my armor. Blisters rose and burst at the joints of the dragonscale armor, leaving ragged flesh behind.

Sweat dripped down my face. Stung my eyes. Fogged my visor. I shook my head, trying to clear my vision, and with a howl of pain he threw himself into the air for one last desperate attack.

I didn't have time to think. I tore off my helmet so I could see and flung it blindly at him, dropping and rolling as flame scorched the air and left me gasping for oxygen.

"You should have known!" he cried. Varis hit the ground hard, his leg going out under him so that he skidded across the sand on all fours, leaving a smear of blood.

I lashed out, forcing him to rear up and stagger backwards, giving me time to find my feet.

The wing I'd wounded was torn nearly in half from that one wingbeat, hanging like a broken kite. Tears of blood tracked down his face, the venom coursing through his veins breaking the capillaries of his eyes.

"Bells." Varis fell to one knee, barely able to hold his sword up, his arms shaking. The accusation in his voice struck me like a viper's fangs. "How could you not know?"

"*Fuck you*," I snarled, my heart breaking all over again, and flung myself at him with everything I had left.

CHAPTER FIFTY

CONSEQUENCES

H e didn't yield. He had nothing left and he still didn't yield, despair breaking him before the tip of my spear did.

I didn't pull the blow, driven by grief and rage. Tears streamed down my face
as I drove my spear through his armor, through his heart, through the beautiful
scales of his back—

The glamor vanished. I slammed into Varis, my teeth clacking together from
the force as I flattened him, our bodies skidding across the sand together. Hot
pain radiated from my burned arms and thighs. My pulse roared in my ears, but
I could still hear him wheezing with every breath, the glamor gone but blood
still in his eyes, his lungs, his mouth.

Oh, black night. What had I done? What had *we* done?

I shoved myself away from him, scrambling backwards and thrusting myself
to my feet to stagger away. His wing, torn—*broken*, white bone showing and
blood staining the sand red. Red, so red, as red as his eyes, as red as my pain.
Blood on the sand, on his tail, on his *face*—and then Lianka was there, her skin
ashen and hands steady as she grabbed him by the throat and the hand and
saved his life.

I backed away, my vision widening as the world came crashing back in. They
were watching me, staring at me, all of them. Friends. Enemies. Stellaris, staring
at me in open shock. Darius, sitting on the ground, his face slack. Xilvaris,
smiling like a well-fed cat.

They were silent. They were all silent. There was only the sound of my
beating heart and the rasping of Varistan's breath.

They'd seen it all. Knew it all. What Varistan had done. What *I* had done—my
bloody, vicious, *public* revenge.

How many of them had known? Had seen what I hadn't?

Xilvaris had, and he'd only been in a room with us for a few minutes. Who
else? How many? How could I ever face them again?

"Bells," Varistan begged.

"You didn't tell her." Lianka, her voice full of horror. "You damn fool."

As if in a nightmare, I walked to Xilvaris, the victory in his eyes catching me like a hook in the mouth of a fish. The sand crunched underfoot. My arms burned with the memory of Varistan's flame.

"Your grace," he said, putting his hand over his heart and bowing, never looking away from my eyes.

"I trust that you consider your favor discharged." My voice didn't shake. There was no emotion in the words. Tears were drying on my face, and I sounded like I'd forgotten them.

"I do," he said. "Your debts are cleared to my satisfaction."

Everything soulmates possess belongs to each other. Their titles. Their power.

Their debts.

"Good." I held his gaze for another long moment, the cost to my body coming due as the distance of battle faded. Pain made itself known, a throbbing headache taking up residence and even the heat of my body agonizing against my burns. "Now go away, Xilvaris."

The corners of his mouth curved up like a scimitar. He kissed his fingertips, hunger in his eyes. "As her grace desires."

"Bells, *please*—"

I ignored Varistan's pleading and Lianka's command for him to stay down. I turned my back on them all and walked out of the room, my spine straight and my soulmate's blood dappling my skin, and I didn't look back.

I walked through Nyx Shaeras, a ripple of awareness spreading through me with each footstep. I hadn't noticed it when Varistan had first brought me to his duchy, but he and I were so much more in sync than we'd been then. The signet ring on his finger linked him to his land like a Monarch to his Court, and that power was mine as much as it was his. I ran my fingertips along the rough stone of the hallway, feeling the rooms beyond and the millennia of power that had soaked into the basalt.

A Monarch can draw on the power of her land. The ring on Varistan's finger made me the Duchess of Nyx Shaeras, and through the cold wrapped around my shattered heart, I reached for the magic in the stones of my castle. Nyx Shaeras answered me, that power soothing my burns and easing the trembling exhaustion in my muscles.

That's how you survived in Pelaimos, I thought distantly. *That's how a man survives a trebuchet stone and a blackened spine.* Nyx Shaeras' power had been shaped by the man who'd cared for it for sixteen hundred years, and it could heal. That meant that Varistan knew how, too.

Varistan wasn't a mage, but that didn't mean he completely lacked magical talent. All fae had wild magic in them, even if it only expressed itself in their immortality, debt-sense, and promises. I doubted he was a true healer, but regeneration was only a half-step beyond immortality. He could heal *himself*, and with his power at my fingertips, so could I. That ability had kept him alive when his body had been nearly destroyed, and as I walked up the wide staircases and down the fine carpets I'd been denied, it slowly healed the injuries he'd given me.

Even soulmated nemeses possessed everything that their soulmate did. That didn't extend to innate abilities – the soulmate of a mage wouldn't become a mage herself – but Nyx Shaeras wasn't a part of Varis. Its power was mine as much as his, and it knew its duke's soul.

He'd had so little power in Pelaimos, nothing more than the ambient wild magic that loved fae so well. Surely not enough for an observer to be able to tell the difference between slim chance and the sort of magical talent that could barely be called such. And when would he ever have been hurt badly enough in Nyx Shaeras to notice—to even think to lean into its power?

Tears stung my eyes as I stepped into Varistan's suite and walked across the beautiful carpet, past the wardrobes and the bed and the uncovered mirrors, to the door to the servant's room. I refused to let them fall as I closed it behind me, forcing myself to stay calm and quiet.

There were so few things to pack. I owned so little—had brought so little with me.

(*They're all your beds.*)

A few outfits. The grungy stuffed rabbit doll I always slept with. A battered book of childhood fables; a little carved lion.

An aurora pearl necklace wrapped in black satin.

I yanked open my wardrobe to escape the memory, and came face-to-face with the shimmering burgundy of the spider-silk dress. It almost broke me, the open proof of who I was to Varistan hanging there in silent accusation.

(*I imagined I might give it to whoever I chose to make my duchess.*)

(*You should have known.*)

I reached out to touch it on instinct—then flinched away, not wanting to sully the silk with my blood-freckled, soot-darkened hand. I remembered, suddenly, Alpha asking that night if I would stay by Varistan's side, even if he turned out to be far worse than I'd ever imagined. I'd promised her that I could, so certain of my strength and of his character.

I'd never imagined this. The cruelty of it. The *selfishness*.

An image of the future scrolled out in front of me: me taking my position behind Varistan's wings, pretending I forgave him, waiting and waiting until I found the chance to do to him what he'd done to me. Soulmates in one of the most brutal of balances, eternal betrayers in a dance of deception and treachery.

It would be easy. I could feel the void calling. I'd felt it over and over, moment after moment where we could have found a balance of affection, if only I'd known.

But I would rather die than see that look of hopeless pain on his face ever again. I'd kill myself first.

I heard movement to my left. Knew, instantly, that it was him.

"Bells," he said from the entrance to the servant's hall, his voice soft.

"Don't call me that," I said, not looking at him.

I heard him swallow. "Your grace, then."

(*Where would you like to eat, your grace? Dinner in, or something a bit more high-class, as suits your station?*)

(*It's common even for spouses to call each other by their honorifics.*)

(*You should have known.*)

(*You should have known.*)

(*How could you not know?*)

"I trusted you," I said quietly, my eyes flooded with burgundy and black. "That's why I didn't know." Slowly, I turned to look at him, my expression flat and my heart so broken I felt numb. "You're fae. You can feel debts, and soulmates can't ever be in debt to each other." I took a shaky breath. "No debts, and no forced bargains. I was never your bondservant, and you've always known."

"Bells—" he started.

"Don't. Call me. That," I ground out, anger flaring again. "I *trusted* you. You had a thousand chances to tell me, and you let me believe I was your slave when I should have been your *duchess*." My hands shook. I clenched them into fists to make them stop. "Does it feel good, Varis? The imbalance? Is that why?"

His eyes gleamed. "No." Varistan took a breath, his pulse visible in his throat. "It's not an imbalance. It's a lack of balance. It feels like..." He swallowed, lashes fluttering. "It feels like imminence; something just out of reach. It's driving me mad."

I tried to laugh. It came out almost as a sob, my chest wrenching and throat aching. "At least there's that. At least we're both suffering." I turned away, looking back at the dress, unable to keep looking at the heartbreak on his face. "Why didn't you just tell me?"

"You would have *left*," Varistan said, his torment heating the words. "Like you're leaving *now*. I have a dragon's instincts; I can't bear to let you leave—"

Fury stiffened my spine. "Shut up," I said, turning back towards him with cold eyes. "You're a man, not a dragon. It doesn't matter how strong those instincts are, because you still get to choose your actions. You're not like your *fucking* cousin. The dragon was *dead*, and the only one in charge of what you do is *you*."

He stared at me, brows pulled together and ears pinned back.

"You claim to love the future, but you're obsessed with the present," I continued mercilessly. "You decided you wanted me by your side, so you chose the sure thing. A free woman can leave, but a bondservant?" I laughed, bitterness harshening my voice. "You got exactly what you wanted, *your grace*. Someone who couldn't leave you, and who couldn't choose you. Did you seriously think we could find balance on a foundation of deception?"

Varistan took a deep breath, a shudder making his wings rustle. "No," he said quietly, all his fire gone. "I hoped... but I cannot truly say that I believed."

I shook my head, my eyes returning to the dress without seeing it. "You're such a coward," I said, barely voicing the words. "We had so many chances."

"I know." He let out a slow breath. "I know this is my fault. I know what we could have had, and what I cost us."

My shoulders lowered from their tense position, my eyes starting to sting again. I turned back towards him. "Varis..."

He got down onto his knees and held his hands up in the fae posture of submission and supplication. "I chose this for us, and my reasons don't excuse my behavior. I did you a great wrong. You deserved to know from the start, but I was selfish and afraid of what it meant, and then afraid of what I might lose." Varistan closed his eyes, a line between his brows as he carefully controlled his breathing before looking back up at me. "I want you to stay. Will you bargain with me for that, Isabela Keris?"

A bargain. From any other fae, an apology would have been far worse punishment, but bargains weren't comfortable for Varis. He'd bound me with deception and misdirection, and now he was offering to let me bind him in return.

There was only thing I could possibly ask for.

"It's always been Nyx Shaeras standing between us," I said, my words falling into the space between us like stones into a still pond. "You love this duchy with your whole heart, and you've always been afraid that my existence means you'll lose it. After all," I said, fighting back the tears, refusing to cry in front of him, "Windswept Court and Stag Court are both ruled by monsters and their mortal soulmates. What would your King think of yours?"

His eyes searched my face as he knelt there, waiting for me.

I knew he would refuse. No one can serve two masters, and Varistan had put his duchy before me, over and over. But I could make him be the one to say it.

I licked my lips. "One hundred thirty-nine days, Varis," I said. "That's how long you denied me what I was owed as your soulmate, and that's how much you owe me. Do to yourself what you did to me. Give me Nyx Shaeras, and make yourself my bondservant."

He looked up at me, his expression controlled. "One hundred thirty-nine days?"

"That's all you get," I said. "That's all the chance I'm willing to give you."

The corners of his mouth trembled. He held my gaze and slowly pulled the signet ring off of his finger. The skin beneath was almost as pale as mine, stark against his black scales and brown fingers.

Without asking, I knew he hadn't taken that ring off since he'd been given his duchy.

"I accept," he said, breathing hard as he held up the golden signet to me. "Your grace."

Chapter Fifty-One

On the Other Side

T he world seemed to shift sideways as I stared at Varistan. It was like being an ant scurrying along my scent trail, then getting picked up and put on a new path by some helpful person. I wobbled in place, disorientation settling in. He was... that was...

Not betrayers, I thought in stunned silence, staring at the golden ring. With one simple act, Varistan had refused an entire eternity. It was simply... gone.

In a daze, I reached out and took the signet from his hand. The sense of the castle around me grew as I held it, a pool of awareness around me for maybe a hundred feet in every direction. The sense of distance hovered on the edge of that awareness like a form of peripheral vision. All I had to do to see further would be to turn my attention towards it, to peer into the distance and have all of Nyx Shaeras laid out before me—

The ring was sized for Varistan's hand, but when I slipped it onto my thumb it settled into place like it had been made for me, still warm from my dragon's heat. For an endless moment of time, Nyx Shaeras sang to me, the whole duchy sprawled around me like a tapestry. Though I knew there were lines on the map that marked the edges of the land considered part of the duchy, the edges of my connection to the duchy were only cleanly demarcated along the ocean. Everywhere else it sort of... fuzzed, as if something was interfering with my reach.

Frustration tensed my brow as I tried to push against that fogginess, a headache taking up residence behind my eyes. Why couldn't I *see*?

"It's alright, your grace," Varistan said soothingly, still on his knees. "Let it pass. Raven Court isn't yours, and it can't be broken into sharp-edged pieces, so the deed you wear on your hand is as frayed cloth, not cut. You have to let the thirst for more abide, or you'll be forced to duel the King himself to claim what you desire."

Anger sparked, a possessive craving for what lay out of my reach that made me want to bare my teeth and claw for more. That was a shocking enough emotion that I jerked away from it, my control reasserting itself. "They're hungry," I said, unease twisting through me and gooseprickles rising on my arms at how easily it had caught me. I blinked, trying to focus on the room, even as my vision swam and Nyx Shaeras clamored for my attention. "The Courts. They're hungry."

"They are," Varistan said, still in that soothing tone, as if calming a snarling dog. "They're living things, and they can be as greedy as any other creature. Why do you think the birth of Windswept Court and the loss of the eastern hills to Stag Court was so painful for our King?"

I fumbled for a seat, collapsing down into one of the chairs, breathing harder than I had at the end of our duel. "I thought he was... was angry..." I shook my head to clear my vision, starting to get control over the clawing desire for *more* that buzzed underneath my skull. "Gods," I said, forcing my eyes to focus on Varis' face. "This is just a taste of it, isn't it? It must have been like having a piece of his soul torn off."

His brows pulled together for a moment into a yearning expression, his chin lifted and tension in the corners of his eyes, but Varistan took a breath and put on a measured expression. "Yes, I suspect it was, your grace. Monarchs of newborn Courts are often so land-tied that they cannot leave their Court for centuries, and Raven Court was born with our King. Even for those who inherit an established Court, losing land is like losing part of your body." He took another careful breath, then got to his feet, a wry smile tugging at his lips despite the sorrow that still showed on his face. "And I've lost both, so I feel uniquely qualified to make that comparison."

Guilt twisted my gut, followed immediately by a flare of anger. He didn't deserve my guilt. He deserved to suffer—to feel every ounce of pain he'd inflicted on me. But I still asked, "Does it hurt?"

The corners of his mouth trembled as he tried to smile. "No, your grace," he said, his breath hitching. "Through you, I can still feel Nyx Shaeras. It's simply..." He swallowed, pain crossing his face. "Distant. As if I'm... numbed."

I wrapped my hand around the signet ring, hiding it from view. I didn't know what to say to that.

He watched me for a moment, then dropped his eyes in a submissive gesture. "May I bring Lianka to you, your grace?" he asked quietly, looking down at the floor. "I know you were... hurt..." Varistan trailed off as he glanced back up at me, a look of confusion overtaking his face as he examined me for injury. "Weren't you?"

"Burned, mostly," I said, rolling up my sleeve to show the raw, blistered skin where the joints of my armor had been. "No direct hits, or I'd be missing more than skin. The near-misses were brutal enough."

Varistan cringed again, looking like I'd struck him. "I'll seek her," he said. "I'll— I'll return as soon as I may."

He fled, and I didn't try to stop him. I could have told him how much worse it had been – the way my very pulse had hurt, how the brush of cloth against my burned skin had felt like sandpaper – but he was already...

Broken, my heart supplied. *Defeated*, I snapped back, refusing to feel pity for him. He'd abused my trust for months. All my gratitude and sparkling feelings of pride at earning my place by his side were soured by the shadow of his duplicity.

He *should* feel guilty. He'd taken my ability to choose from me, and his deceit could have cost me my life. I had no illusions about my skill as a fighter. I was excellent, but I was still human. Matched against someone of Varistan's skill and stamina, I should have lost, and brutally. If we hadn't been soulmates, I would have died at first flame. If I'd known we were soulmates, we wouldn't even have had to fight, because Xilvaris couldn't bind me to Varistan's promises. If I hadn't discovered we were soulmates on the sands, if I hadn't been willing to flay his soul bare, if, if, if... Gods, everything could have been so different.

I snarled, angry at myself and angry at Varistan and this whole stupid, un-necessary, *agonizing* situation, and shoved myself to my feet. I stalked into Varistan's bedroom (*my bedroom*, I reminded myself), over to one of his (*my*) wardrobes, and flung it open. The sight of all of those familiar clothes clawed at me with rage and despair. That shirt had gotten worn at the shoulder, but served well under a doublet. That drape had to be pinned in place, lest the stain along the edge show. That coat didn't quite fit, but looked good open.

I'd learned it all. Memorized it for him, served him out of duty and affection, and it had all been a fucking *lie*.

With a sharp sound of anger and pain, I tore the clothes out of the wardrobe, throwing them onto the floor. I kicked them out of the way, heedless of the tears that started streaming down my cheeks again, and emptied the drawers of his underthings.

I was four wardrobes deep when a knock on the door startled me. I whirled, drawing my dagger, and caught sight of Lianka, her face lined with concern. Flushing, I looked down at the mess of clothing, then back down at my filthy hands and bared dagger. "He lied to me," I said, my voice cracking.

"He denied you the truth," she said in a gentle voice. "May I come in, your grace?"

A sob choked me, and I sheathed my dagger as I swiped at my face with my other hand. "I don't need that from you," I said miserably. "I just... I..." Another sob escaped, my throat and chest aching. "Gods, Lianka, what do I do now?" I asked, looking up at her with my eyes stinging from the tears.

She came over, holding her arms out, and I let her hug me. I all but fell against her chest, more silent tears spilling out of my eyes. Stupid. It was stupid to keep crying about this. It wouldn't fix anything.

Tingling warmth rolled through me as she healed the rest of my injuries. "Shh, shh," she murmured, kissing me on the temple like she was my mother. "He hurt you very badly, didn't he?"

I nodded against her chest, misery oozing out of the wounds on my heart. "Why did he do it?" I said, as plaintive as a child. "Why would he... I just don't..."

"You're wrung out, honey," Lianka said. "C'mon. You'll surely feel better for a bath and some sleep."

"It's not even dinner-time," I protested as she started towing me towards the bathroom.

"So?" she countered. "I can knock you out, if you like. It won't even be difficult."

"But—"

"Nah," she said, closing and locking the door behind us. "None of that." Lianka started stripping me out of my sweaty, soot-marked clothing without so much as a by-your-leave. "I've not seen you quite this close to the edge before, but I know how you get when you're done in. You'll surely regret it if you plant that dagger in someone's chest."

"Someone being Varistan," I said, scowling as she took it away from me.

"Someone being literally anyone who pushes your fragile self a little too much." She turned on the water before returning to undressing me, breaking the laces of my boots instead of untying them.

The shoes were ruined, the leather scorched and cracking to pieces. Small beads of glassed sand spattered the side of the right one. I hadn't realized I'd come that close to losing my foot.

She peeled off my pants, then pointed at the filling tub. "In."

I obeyed. It was too hard to keep fighting, and I trusted Lianka. She was a good healer, and a good friend. None of it was right, but would it ever be right again? All I wanted was for Varis to wash my hair like he had when I'd been seasick, to gentle me like I mattered to him, to pick me up and tuck me into bed and—

I cut off that line of thinking, with prejudice. Varistan had forfeited all rights to my heart every time he'd decided to claim my affection under false pretenses. He didn't deserve my longing. He'd chosen his own security and comfort above mine, and through flame and blood it had all come crashing down.

So it was Lianka who washed my hair while hot tears tracked down my face, and it was Lianka who helped towel me off and brushed my hair. She was the one who went out and brought me pajamas, and when I finally crept out of the bathroom she was the one who set my dinner in front of me and stayed to make sure I ate.

Sometime in the interim, the clothing I'd dumped on the ground had been removed, along with all of Varistan's personal effects. My few belongings would have looked pathetic in their place, but it wasn't only my things that had been put out. There was a full rack of jewelry I didn't recognize with a carved pair of stone lions framing them, my little wooden lion set in the center of the dresser like a talisman. A set of old-looking books spread across a shelf that had previously held a collection of gilded pottery. The rack for Varistan's swords was nowhere in sight; a new one held a set of ornamental daggers.

I didn't know who had done it, but I knew who must have made the choices. I hated how well he knew me; how much the things he'd chosen felt like they were mine. They *were* mine – had always been mine – but he knew what would appeal to me, and every detail I saw broke my heart a little more.

I might have simply sat there dully until exhaustion forced me to sleep, but as soon as I finished eating, Lianka raised one brow. She didn't have to bully me further. I dutifully brushed my teeth, crawled into bed, and let my friend send me into a deep and dreamless sleep.

CHAPTER FIFTY-TWO

THE DUCHESS OF NYX SHAERAS

I woke to the familiar sound of Varis moving in the room, and then to the pale winter-morning sunlight as he pulled back the drapes on the window overlooking the southern coast. For a few minutes, I simply lay there, not wanting to open my eyes and have to face the truth of the world: that Varistan was my soulmate, and that I was the spurned Duchess of Nyx Shaeras. But I couldn't lie there forever, and I forced myself to open my eyes, and then to sit up.

Nothing was better in the morning light, but it had congealed together instead of feeling like I'd swallowed a handful of broken glass. At least I could turn and look at Varis without wanting to howl out my pain like a wounded animal.

He looked like I felt, with shadows beneath his eyes and his lovely face stripped bare of any happiness. Even in the darkest days, I'd never seen him look like that—a man lost in the Tangle, harried by wolves.

"Good morning, your grace," he said, his voice grave and expression impassive. He'd dressed in some of his simplest clothing, nothing more than pants and a plain laced-up shirt, with his only ornamentation a set of the claw-covers we'd gotten in Maestrizen. "Do you have any preference as to your clothing today? Your grace doesn't have any scheduled events until the feast tomorrow, but given the circumstances, your steward has requested a meeting."

Everything felt slanted, the stark reversal of our roles making me feel as if I'd fallen into a parallel universe, one as wrong as the first day of my tenure in Nyx Shaeras. But this was what I was owed. I'd stepped boldly into Maestrizen with the same strength of character that had brought me through battle after battle, and I wouldn't let something as simple as grief sweep my feet out from under me. I'd survived watching my mother getting brutally killed for sport; I would survive this.

"What are my options?" I asked in a cool tone.

Pain tensed his eyes, but Varis only nodded, his wings tucked close to his back and his tail curling around his own ankle in an unhappy gesture. "I took the liberty of having all the fine women's clothing in storage that is likely to fit your grace taken out of storage. There isn't a great deal, and..." He hesitated, then took a deep breath and continued, "...much of it was owned or worn by my former paramour, Yesika Laeshant. Does that trouble your grace?"

I searched his expression, but Varistan kept hold of his aplomb, nothing showing on his face. At last, I sighed, turning away as I clambered out of bed. "It doesn't matter," I said, my emotional exhaustion coming out in the words. "Pick whatever's appropriate. Maybe if I dress like her, my soulmate will treat me as honorably as he did her."

"Bells, that's not—" he started, sounding hurt.

I whirled on him, anger covering over the sick weight of guilt in my gut. "*Absolutely* not," I snarled, balling my fists. "You gave up any right you had to familiarity when I had to find out I was your *soulmate* in the middle of a fucking *public duel*. You don't get to have our relationship in your back pocket. This time *I* get to decide."

He rocked back, ears pinned and wings clamped against his back. I half-expected him to snap at me, challenging me on my vitriol as I'd so often refused to tolerate his aggression. But he didn't. He only nodded, his expression tight. "It's a difficult habit to break, your grace, but I will attempt to do so if you desire such," Varistan said quietly, dropping his gaze to the floor. "I would appreciate standards for my behavior, so I can avoid offending your grace."

I'd teased him once, telling him he'd make a worse bondservant than I did. I hated having to learn that I'd been wrong. Varistan was treating his bargain with me with deadly seriousness—with more intensity than I'd approached preserving my father's life.

He never made himself small for others. He stepped into the world with bravado and determination, but he was standing there with his head bowed and eyes lowered, and I knew if I told him that was his life now, then he would do it. I hated having to see him like this. Varistan looked broken, his dauntless will snapped like a twig, the Flame of Faery muzzled and clipped.

And I'd done it to him.

"Stop it," I said.

He lifted his eyes, brows pulled together. "Your grace?"

"Stop it," I said again, my voice growing harsh. "I can't deal with seeing you being a... a... kicked puppy!" I started pacing. "Just... be angry, or... or hate me, I don't know! Not," I gestured at him, "*this*."

"You want me to be... angry?" he asked, sounding perplexed. "Why?"

I kept pacing. I didn't have a good answer.

Varistan watched me for a minute, then asked, "Your grace...?"

"You're making me feel guilty, when you're the one who fucked up," I bit off. "That's not how it's supposed to work, so just... stop it."

After a moment, he sighed. I heard his wings rustling as he shook them out, relaxing away from that posture of diminution. "I hear your grace's spoken will," he said, a non-response if ever I'd heard one. "If you grant me a few minutes, I will strive to select a pleasing outfit for your day."

Varistan ended up putting me into something that looked like it had been made for going out riding, the brocade bodice protective instead of constricting and the pants sturdy. He wasn't good at the task. The length of his claws meant that he couldn't use his fingertips for buttons or ties; he had to pinch them between two fingers and slowly, carefully move them. I'd seen his short temper a hundred times, but even when a button slipped his grasp for the fourth time in a row, all he did was close his eyes, take a careful breath, and try again.

I didn't intervene. I let him take the time he needed to succeed, my heart aching from his care and control, and left without looking back.

People didn't look at me when I stepped out into Nyx Shaeras. I blessed the fae habit of turning one's eyes away when people were embroiled in private affairs, because it didn't feel like being shunned. They would have done the same if I'd been having sex with Varistan or chasing him down the hallway with a sword. Walking through the castle wearing the ducal signet with my back straight and chin lifted, people moved out of my way and didn't stare or comment, giving me the respect of pretending they didn't see my personal affairs.

I met Sintuviel in Varistan's office. I couldn't manage to convince myself that the room was mine. Everything about it was Varistan's, from the view to the organization of his pens, and short of stripping it to the floorboards and building from the ground up, there was no way to erase him from it. I didn't even bother trying, ignoring his desk by the window and dragging out one of the side tables to sit at.

Sintuviel put his hand over his heart and gave me a small bow. "Your grace, if I may..." He lifted his eyes, meeting mine with a quiet expression. "The partnership of a ruler and her steward relies upon trust between the twain. As such, I would like you to know that until the events of yesterday, I was unaware of your profound link to His Grace—ah, to Varistan," he corrected, his ears dropping for a moment into a pose of self-consciousness. "Had I known, I would have counseled him to cease his duplicity, though I would not have taken it upon myself to supercede his decisions, and make you aware. But I'm ashamed to state that I attributed his great affection for you to mere possessiveness, and I greatly regret that negligence."

That was by far the most emotion I'd ever seen Sintuviel express. I offered him a smile that probably looked terrible, and gestured at the chair across from me. "Be seated, if you will. I appreciate your honesty. To answer it with some of my own..." I sighed, rubbing at my face. "I have no idea what I'm doing. I don't even begin to have the training to run a place like Nyx Shaeras, and I'm not petty enough to spend the next few months ruining the lives of everyone here to get back at Varistan. The last thing I want is for my legacy to be destruction." I gave him another weak smile. "I could use your counsel."

He took the seat, lacing his hands together in his lap. "It seems to me that your best resource is the one you will least desire to work with."

"Varistan," I said, my lip lifting.

Sintuviel flicked one ear. "Part of the duty of a duchess is to set aside one's personal troubles for the sake of those entrusted to your care," he said carefully. "Whether that care is granted by the will of Faery or by that of one's Monarch seems as if it should matter little. If your desire is to rise to the task that has been thrust upon you, then my counsel would be to take grasp of every tool provided, and turn that desire to active pursuit. And..." He pursed his lips. "If you are willing to trust the assessment of one who has recently failed in his perception of the man in question, I believe that... Varistan... is deeply motivated to provide you with the stark truth, and that he will not attempt to manipulate you in your decisions regarding Nyx Shaeras should you choose to accept his counsel."

"It's hard for you to call him by his name, isn't it?" I asked, one corner of my mouth flipping up into wry amusement.

His ear flicked again. "I was his chief of staff when he was merely Lord Yllaxira," Sintuviel said in a dignified manner. "I cannot recall a time when I have had occasion to speak of him with such... informality."

I regarded him for a moment, then breathed a laugh, relaxing back against the chair. "You don't have to," I said, with a truer smile. "Whatever happens between me and him, we're... soulmates," I said, a spark of pain flaring in my chest as I said the word. "No matter who wears the ring or makes the decisions, he's still the Duke of Nyx Shaeras. If it's more comfortable to refer to him by that title, you're welcome to do so."

He wouldn't forget where things stood. There was no reason to make his life more unpleasant than necessary, and I appreciated his professionalism a great deal.

"I appreciate that generosity," Sintuviel said, a fraction of tension leaving his stance. "The habits of millennia are difficult to shed, and I move most comfortably in the world of high formality."

"Then you picked a strange master to serve," I said with another exhalation of laughter. "'High formality' isn't how I'd generally describe him, even with as much as he likes to stand on protocol."

With the words came a thousand memories of Varistan, how much comfort he got from knowing exactly what would come next. His ease in formal negotiations, and the way he never made me follow the rules. *Not once*, I thought, a twist of pain tightening my throat. He'd never once demanded that I do as I was told. He liked my defiance. Followed me when I cut new paths, trusted me not to hurt him—

His scream of pain as I tore a blade through his wing. The sickening feel of my spear breaking through his ribcage.

Nausea twisted in my gut, and I shoved it all away. Grieving what I'd lost and what I'd done didn't help anything.

A tiny smile touched Sintuviel's mouth. I wasn't sure if it was meant for me or for his memories of Varistan. "Perhaps he knew he needed someone with such skills to balance his intemperate nature, your grace."

That was a lot of credit to give Varistan—but, then, a single look around his office ought to remind me that, for all his passion and spark, Varistan loved with single-minded focus. This room was a monument to that care, every detail of Nyx Shaeras bound in gilded leather and written in his hand. He knew who he was, and he'd proven his willingness to rely on the strength of others to balance his weaknesses over and over.

Hadn't he done the same thing with me? Listened when I'd argued with him, surrendered his words to my hands, stepped back and trusted me to care for Nyx Shaeras with the same love he bore for it?

I didn't like thinking about it, but it was hard not to. I'd once fantasized about revenge, leaving Varistan's wings and will broken, but the actuality of it was agony. If anything good was going to come out of this, it couldn't be from the scorched earth of that dueling ring. It would happen here, in the heart of Nyx Shaeras, and it would be hard work.

"Alright," I said, setting myself for the days ahead. I could do this. I had to do this. "We've got a lot to do to corner the market on coldwater pearls, especially since Xilvaris has a casket of them and hates our guts. So I suppose we might as well get His Disgraced in here and get started."

Sintuviel looked at me askance, one brow raised.

"I'll keep the sniping to a minimum," I promised with a sigh. "Surely you have to admit it's a *little* humorous, though."

"I grant allowance for your distress," Sintuviel said without reproof, getting to his feet. "Given your soulmate's enjoyment of similar wordplay, I suppose I'll resign myself to ensuring a double dose, your grace."

My lips twitched. I liked him. "Sounds about right, I'm afraid," I said, a bit cheered up by our conversation. "Think you'll survive it?"

"I'm resilient," he said drily. "I'll surely adapt."

I smiled at him, resting my chin on my knuckles. "Good." I wasn't going anywhere. It was time to get to work.

CHAPTER FIFTY-THREE

TURNABOUT'S FAIR PLAY

A s Sintuviel had predicted, Varistan was both an incredible resource and completely dedicated to giving me the information I wanted without trying to sway me. He gave his opinions when requested and wrote the words I dictated in his bold handwriting. From the grimness of his focus that first meeting, I knew he'd been prepared to sign his duchy's death warrant if I demanded it of him. But day by day, as I conducted the business of Nyx Shaeras with him at my right hand, that grim determination eroded, until I could feel the warmth of his regard with every task I completed.

He was proud of me—*impressed* with me. Despite everything, and even as I tried to ignore how that made me feel, I couldn't deny the satisfaction of it. Having the infamous Duke of Nyx Shaeras offer me his opinions in that demure voice, and seeing the admiration in his smile when my choices succeeded, was a heady drug indeed.

The people of the castle clearly didn't know how to treat us, or what to do about the fact that the duke's cocky bondservant was now the one calling the shots while he stood in her shadow. Despite the awkwardness, I made time to go down to the training grounds once each feast week. That first fortnight, only humans were willing to get into the ring with me, but the third time I joined them, Stellaris challenged me to a bout. When she didn't end up brutalized – when, in fact, she claimed a victory – the other fae stopped pussyfooting around and started easing back into treating me like a companion-in-arms again.

She flashed me a wink after that match, a tiny smirk on her full mouth. But she didn't suggest to anyone that I'd thrown the fight, and I certainly wasn't going to let on that my history in the pit meant that I knew how to do exactly that while in front of a crowd.

Some secrets are better kept secret.

Varistan never came to watch me duel. He never had, and I wouldn't ask it of him now. I wasn't sure I could bear the memories, or see the pain on his face. I couldn't bear it even in my nightmares.

I tried reaching out to Darius, but there were a lot of eyes on me, and I didn't want to bring too much scrutiny onto him or Alpha. Varistan and I weren't declaring our connection to the world yet – it was barely the beginning of spring, and the earliest part of the social season wouldn't start for another six weeks or so – but there was no sidestepping the truth anymore. Too many people had seen that duel, and rumor always flickered across the landscape faster than ravens flew. We'd have to deal with it sooner or later, and when the sword inevitably fell, I didn't want it to fall on my fellow mortals.

When my days were full, I could almost forget the pain of betrayal or the aching loneliness of my position, so I filled every waking hour I could. It got easier to have Varistan at my right hand—to see him, day after day. I started looking forward to the mornings again, and to the hours spent working with Varistan in our office.

The aurora pearls took the Court by storm, and correspondence started pouring in from the wealthy of Raven, Pinesap, and Minnow Court, nobility and merchants alike. I could see the pain of those letters in the set of Varistan's spine, the same people who'd treated him like shit fawning for his attention now that his star was in ascendancy again.

We wrote back to all of them, with Varistan doing most of the work. I trusted him to do it. He knew how to charm, and all the connections between all those fancy people that he could lean on, and he was committed to acting as my steward... as my partner. Nyx Shaeras would be a hive of activity once the weather warmed; the first revel of the social season was certainly going to make a splash. A mortal woman wearing the signet of Nyx Shaeras? We'd have our work cut out for us to make sure people believed we had no intentions of joining forces with Stag or Windswept Court.

Even his ex-paramour Yesika wrote, all curling words and conciliation. When I read the letter aloud, my voice tight with rage, Varis looked like he'd been gutted.

Perhaps I was as intemperate as the Flame of Faery. My response was very simple, and I pressed the signet into the blood-red wax seal with vicious satisfaction.

To the Lady Yesika Laeshant,

He's <u>mine</u>.
Fuck off.

Her Grace Isabela Keris, the Duchess of Nyx Shaeras, soulmate of His Grace Varistan Yllaxira, the Duke of Nyx Shaeras, the Flame of Faery, and scion of the Raven King.

The contrast of that peak of emotion to the reality of my life came crashing in when night fell and Varistan closed the door between our rooms. Alone in that huge bed with my stuffed rabbit clutched up against my chest, that single door between us felt like a prison barricade. We worked together every day. He dressed me. He brushed my hair with the quiet dedication of a lover. Sometimes we even laughed together, forgetting the distance for one bright moment.

And then, every night, I got into bed alone and forced myself to pretend I wanted it that way.

Tears pricked at my eyes with stinging heat. He'd hurt me so badly, but I couldn't rouse enough anger to cover over how much I simply *missed* him. Lying in bed, I could almost see the way he always smiled when he was curled up in bed with me, his expression full of warmth. I loved that look almost as much as the wicked sparkle in his eyes when he teased me, and at that moment I couldn't think of anything I wanted more.

I couldn't get the image out of my mind, tossing and turning as I tried to find a position comfortable enough to fall asleep in. Gods, I hated sleeping alone. He was *right there*, a distance I'd crossed a hundred times, and I'd never slept better than I did in his arms.

He was probably sleeping. Waking him up because I couldn't was childish. (*"Who cares if it is?"* asked past Isabela.) And I hated losing. Why should he be the one to win? (*"He already lost. Remember?"* asked reasonable Isabela.) It wasn't like I hadn't slept alone for weeks now. (*"You're as stubborn as he is."* I wasn't sure which Isabela that one was from.)

With a growl of frustration, I got out of bed and stalked over to the door between us. Before I could second-guess myself, I grabbed the handle and turned it.

He hadn't locked it. The door creaked open before I had a chance to regret the action.

Varis wasn't asleep, either, and he rolled over as the wan moonlight fell across him, looking up at me with his hair mussed and expression searching. I wrapped my arms around my chest, not able to meet his eyes.

"Your grace?" he asked, pushing himself up with one arm.

"It's cold," I said, by way of explanation.

It wasn't.

He didn't say anything for a long moment, then sat all the way up, the sheets pooling around his hips. "Would you like me to warm your bed for you?" he asked in a rough voice. He cleared his throat; one corner of his mouth lifted into a sorrow-tinged smile. "I've been told bondservants sometimes provide such a service."

I nodded, not trusting myself to speak without a moment to swallow back the threatening tears. "Yeah," I said, my voice cracking. "You're always so warm."

"I am," Varis said gently. "If you'll allow me a moment to put something on, your grace, I'll come join you."

"Okay." My eyes stung again, and I swiped at them with the heel of my hand, feeling pathetic. "Don't tarry."

"I won't," he promised.

He didn't move, waiting for me, so I closed the door again, turning and leaning against it as I tried to get my breathing under control. I wouldn't cry. It didn't matter how much I missed him. He deserved to have to live through this.

Do you, though, Bells? some traitor part of my mind asked. *Aren't you supposed to be getting what you want out of this bargain?*

Shut up, I told myself, swiping at my eyes again. I started pacing, not able to make myself get back into that enormous, empty bed on my own. This was justice. That's what I wanted. Wasn't it?

The door opened. "Your grace?" Varistan asked.

I turned and looked back at him, feeling haunted.

He closed the distance between us, stopping in front of me and brushing my hair back as he cupped my face in his hands. "Come to bed, your grace," he murmured. "You should get some sleep."

"So should you." I didn't want to move, not when he was looking at me like that. Not with that quiet smile curving his perfect mouth, that soft expression in his eyes, the unsullied affection I was so hungry for—

"I'll do that a great deal better lying next to you," he said quietly. When I didn't respond, just looking up at him with yearning, Varis stepped closer and scooped me into his arms. "Allow me to assist, your grace," he murmured, his heartbeat picking up as I leaned against him.

I could feel his pulse where my body rested along his, closing my eyes and letting myself melt into his warmth. He carried me over to the bed and tucked me back under the blankets, his touch careful, then turned to walk to the other side of the mattress. Before I could second-guess the impulse, I caught him by the wrist, looking up into his eyes. Varis froze, his gaze on his mine and a look of such desperate want startled onto his face that I started losing the battle against tears.

When I tugged on his arm, he followed me down to the bed, moving with care. Varis slipped under the sheets next to me, his legs brushing against mine and tail curling around me. It felt so good to have him next to me again—so *right.* He'd been made to be mine, and I'd been made to be his. Where had it gone so wrong?

I buried my face against his bare chest, hot tears tracking down my face. "I'm so tired of being alone," I got out in a hoarse whisper, the words thickened by the tension in my throat. Everything hurt, my muscles taut and throat so tight I could barely swallow. One sob escaped, my fingers digging into his skin as I clung to him. "I just want to know *why.*"

Varistan wrapped his arms around me, holding me, his breathing growing ragged. "There's no answer that will make it better," he said, sounding like he might join me in tears. "I could give you a hundred, and it wouldn't matter. Darling," he said, sounding desperate as I started sobbing in earnest against his chest. "Isabela, darling, I was selfish and stubborn, and terrified of the aftermath. If I tore up the foundation we'd built everything on, I knew it would all crash down, and you're the best thing I've ever possessed. Every day, there was more to lose."

His body shook, the blunt metal capping his claws digging against my sides. "I was still going to tell you," he said, sounding hopeless. "That's what I was going to tell you. Gods." He shuddered. "I was going to tell you."

"I know," I choked out, my whole body shivering from trying to fight my tears. "I'm so sorry."

He inhaled sharply, his body tensing from hearing me apologize. "Wh... what?"

I sobbed out a laugh, digging my fingers against him as I tried to curl up. "In the duel. I was— I was horrible. All the things I said. What I did to you." I shook, guilt and grief tearing at me like vultures on a carcass. "I *humiliated* you. I made it *hurt.* I— I—"

"Oh, Bells," Varis said, sounding heartbroken for me. "You don't have to feel guilty for that. It's alright. I—" He swallowed, hard. "I don't hold it against you. I let go of it even as you did it. I don't know how to make it better, but I understand, and I understood even then."

I clenched my teeth so hard my jaw hurt. The tumult was too much. I didn't know how to handle this—how to live through this. With a snarl of frustration, I balled my hand up into a fist and hit him on the shoulder like a child having a tantrum. "You're so *stupid,*" I said, squeezing my eyes tight. "Why can't you just hate me?"

His lips turned up against my hair. His warm tail settled up along my back, and he started stroking my hair. "Because I love you," Varis said, sure as the sunrise.

I went still, my pulse pounding in my ears.

"Besides," he added, nuzzling my scalp. "You granted me an enormous measure of grace when you agreed to bargain with me after I broke your heart in front of our entire duchy. It would be beyond churlish to answer that grace with bitterness." Varis sighed, tucking his wing around me to brush away my tears with his thumb. "It's not as if you're doing something to me that I didn't do to you, nor that I didn't earn. If you intended it as punishment, though, I'm afraid you've already remedied the worst of it."

I sniffed, reaching up and swiping at my nose. "I have?"

"Have you any idea what a delight it was to be your figurehead while you won Maestrizen for us? Watching you step into your power is unlikely to ever lose its allure, and now is no different." He gave me a gentle squeeze. "I'm pleased to be at your right hand, your grace, no matter what that means. It's being held apart from you that hurts."

"Don't let it go to your head," I muttered, my cheeks heating. "You're just here to keep me warm."

"Tell yourself whatever you like," he said with that smug confidence I'd so missed. "If laying my summer against your chilled skin is your favored excuse for taking me to bed again—"

I smacked him on the shoulder.

Varistan caught my hand with a laugh, pecking a kiss onto my palm in a quick gesture of affection. "Spitfire mortal," he said fondly. "I think I'm in little danger of the stillness so common to my kind with you by my side."

"Assuming this means we'll find affectionate balance?" I asked, my chest going tight, the pain coming back to the fore.

"Willing to do whatever it takes to find it." Varis tucked my hand between us, wrapping his warm hand around mine. "And feeling rather more hopeful than I was when we parted this evening."

I made a disgruntled noise, cuddling a little closer. "You're trying to charm me," I said, without any malice in the words.

"Is it working?" he asked. "I've been told I can be very charming when I put my mind to it, and the potential rewards are certainly worth the effort."

I just grunted again, the familiar scent of his skin soothing me. Musk and copper, with faint traces of cedarwood from the last shower he'd taken. I would know his scent among a thousand. He was as familiar to me as my own body. Sighing softly, I let myself relax into his warmth, the depth of the night feeling like a time outside of time. I ran my nose up along his strong chest, resting my face against his throat with his quickening pulse against my lips.

I loved his scent. His *heat*. The way his body responded to my touch, and how perfectly he fit against me. I'd put pen to paper to declare that he was mine – my *soulmate* – so I couldn't really pretend otherwise now. I didn't even really want to. Why should I have to be the one to give him up when he was so clearly mine to claim?

Without thinking about it, I opened my mouth so I could scent him better. The ghost of his taste made me salivate, hunger flaring to life in the wake of unhappiness, as if opening the door between our rooms had opened the floodgates of my heart. He was mine, and I wanted him. With Varis this close, it was hard to even remember why I'd ever wanted any distance between us. When I shifted closer, he made a tiny sound of want in the back of his throat, and with an answering hum of appreciation I nipped him on the neck.

The embrace of his wing tightened on me. "Please don't do that," Varis whispered, the sound of his voice vibrating through me. "Please. I can survive the distance, but that will surely break me."

"Even if it's an invitation?" I asked, my mouth still touching his skin.

He stopped breathing, his heartbeat thudding against my chest. I started smiling, the cat in the songbird's cage.

Varistan took a juddering breath, the hand of his wing closing down around my shoulder. "Is it?" he asked, sounding strangled. "Not five minutes ago you were wetting my skin with tears."

"I'm a changeable mortal," I said, my blood heating as I considered throwing away any pretense of distance. But then, I'd had him buried scales-deep in me while I'd still been his bondservant... surely turnabout was fair play. "All full of emotions and animal hunger. Maybe I want something to burn off the sorrow."

"No games," Varis said, the words coming too fast. "Mean it or don't ask. I can't— I can't— I can't—" He caught himself, panting and tense, claws digging into my sides. "Please," he said in a whisper. "You can have me if you desire me, but I need you to truly desire me, not simply the escape of ecstasy. *Me.*"

I pulled back so I could look him in the eyes, at that look of raw want as his hot breath fanned against my face. "I want you, Varis," I told him, meaning every word. There was no denying it, not when I'd all but spat in his ex's face for coming slinking back around. "Not just sex. *You.* I want my fingers buried in your curls and your summer against my skin, and I want to come with your name on my tongue. I can give myself an orgasm, but you're the only one who can give me that." I leaned forward, hunger lighting my eyes. "Are you amenable?"

"Yes," he said in a low moan, his fingers tightening in my hair and thigh slipping between mine. "Gods, *yes*—" A heartbeat later his mouth was on mine, and I surrendered to that desperate passion with total relief.

Chapter Fifty-Four

PIECE BY PIECE

Varistan kissed me like he wanted to forget the taste of air, moaning into my mouth as our tongues twined together. The shock of his heat shot straight to my groin, my core throbbing with desire. Oh, gods, I'd forgotten how good this was, the fucking Flame of Faery with his hands on my skin and his thigh forcing my legs open and his forked tongue in my mouth—

He shoved me onto my back, following with his whole body. I buried my fingers in those thick curls and ground myself up against the powerful muscle of his thigh, pleasure singing through me. It was so easy to forget everything else in the face of how perfect it felt to be tangled up with Varis, my hunger for him roaring through my veins. My fucking *soulmate*.

His tongue licked along mine, touch searing, and then he had his mouth on my throat. "Fuck," he groaned, grinding his hips against my thigh. "You undo me, Bells."

I grabbed him by the ass, hauling him down against me with demand. The twin lengths of his cock pressed against my thigh, the proof of his lust sending a spike of want through me. My whole body felt hypersensitive. Even the touch of my clothing was too rough. All I wanted was his skin against mine, smooth heat and the friction of desire. Unwilling to wait for it, I hooked my fingers over the band of his boxer-briefs and shoved them down.

They got caught on his cocks. *Ugh, of course.* Growling my frustration, I started hauling his tail through the hole, wiggling up against him.

He laughed breathlessly, face against my neck, and helped me disentangle tail and shafts. "You could simply *ask*," he crooned, dropping his hips back down against my bare thigh. Heat shocked through me from the feel of his studded lengths sliding along my sensitive skin. "I'm disinclined to deny you anything—" Varis punctuated the words with a thrust, moaning in the back of his throat. "—let alone my body," he finished, hot breath panting against my neck.

"Prove it," I panted out. I hooked my thumbs over my panties and shoved *them* down. Varistan assisted, his tail wrapping around them and dragging them off my legs.

"As her grace insists." He lifted my back off the bed and tugged my shirt off, then raked his gaze down my body. "What's your pleasure?"

"Stop being so damn cocky," I said with a growl. "Keep it up and I'm going to find something else to do with that tongue of yours."

Varis ran his tongue along his sharp canine, voicing his draconic snarl with wings mantled over me and tail snapping behind him. His cocks flexed, pre-come dripping down to wet my belly. "Is that supposed to be a threat?" he asked in a throaty voice, practically purring the words. "If so, I fully intend to lean into my arrogance—"

I bared my teeth, grabbed his curls, and *yanked*.

Varistan cried out with raw pleasure, his back arching and tail lifting into a fuck-me pose worthy of a cat in heat. I didn't release him, forcing his body down closer to mine. With my other hand, I grabbed his cocks and started stroking. Fucker. I would take him to *pieces*.

"Let's get one thing clear," I said, panting. "You're *mine*. I get to do what I want with you. Got it?"

"Yes," he gasped out.

"Yes, what?" I snapped, predatory hunger sharpening my focus. I squeezed his cocks, making him cry out. "Yes, *what*, Varis?" I tugged on his hair again, hooking one leg over his thigh and dragging him down against me.

"Yes, your grace," he got out through his whimper of pleasure. "Yes, I'm yours, I'm yours, do as you like with me—"

Pleasure thudded into me at that admission, my pulse throbbing between my legs. I let go of him to slide my fingers between my legs, my clit singing with silver pleasure as I ran my slick fingers along myself. "Bite me," I said, rubbing circles against myself with his cocks pressing into the vee between my thigh and groin.

"What?" he said, sounding like he was on the verge of falling apart.

"Fucking *bite me*, Varis, I'm not going to beg for it—"

He groaned and sank his teeth into my shoulder.

I cried out from the contact, arching up against him with the spike of pleasure shooting down my spine. "Fuck," I moaned, grabbing him by the cock and guiding him to my pussy. "Oh, fuck, do it again."

Varis licked me with hunger, breathing hard. "Yes, your grace," he said in a moan of his own. He paired the force of his bite with a thrust of his hips, one cock sliding into me and the other running between my legs and across my ass.

I bucked up into that contact, driving him deeper into me, and Varis didn't make me ask for it. With his mouth against my throat, my soulmate started rocking his hips, slow strokes that stoked the fire inside me. The studs of his cock left my pussy aching with pleasure and my ass tingling in answering need, and when I clenched down on him Varis nipped me on the neck.

"Both?" he asked, breathy and full of hunger.

"Uh-huh," I gasped out in return, clinging to him. Gods, I was the one undone by him. I couldn't think beyond the thrust and drag of his cock inside me, except to crave *more*. I needed it—needed him—couldn't believe I'd gone weeks without this. "Fuck, Varis, now, please—"

Something hit the floor as Varistan fumbled with the bedside table. He snarled a curse, then simply yanked the drawer fully out of the table and snatched the bottle of oil out of the ensuing chaos. He stroked oil down along the spade of his tail, shuddering from it. With a low growl, he shifted and bit the other side of my neck, his hips snapping against mine. "Gods, Bells, I love feeling your cunt grab me when I sink these dragon's fangs into your pretty neck—"

I matched his pace, thrusting up against him with animal need making my pussy throb. With a moan, I squeezed him with my core again, earning a hiss of pleasure. "What happened to 'your grace'?" I asked, barely able to sound coherent.

"You did," Varis said, planting an open-mouthed kiss against my throat. "Your touch. Your fire. How could I ever be the same?" His hot tail slid beneath his cock, the slick tip pressing into my ass. "I want to forget what it's like to have my cock anywhere else but buried inside you."

My hole spasmed around him, followed by my pussy—and the answering shock of pleasure triggered the tension building in my core. Ecstasy rocked through me, every clench of my body down around his cock and the slender tip of his tail robbing me of my breath. I couldn't think, could barely see, my fingernails skidding against his slick scales and my entire soul consumed with the perfection of his body inside of mine.

Varistan took the opportunity, fucking his tail deeper into me with a moan of satisfaction. He kissed his way up to my jaw, then claimed my mouth and focus, tongue hot and slick against mine. All I could do was surrender to the onslaught of sensation, whimpering up into his kiss. My Varis, *fuck*, my gods-damned soulmate—

He pulled his tail out of me, wrapped it around his own cock to line himself up with my body, and rocked into me. I arched up into that contact with a groan of pleasure, the pressure of being doubly filled making my core spasm down against him.

"Ohh, gods," Varis groaned, deepening his strokes as he took me. One of his canines dug against my throat, his panting breath leaving my skin stinging from the heat. "Oh, fuck, darling, I, I, I, I—" He made a sharp sound of frustration, then hooked his arms under my thighs and hauled my hips up. "Fuck," he said, a growl behind the words. "I hate that." He snapped his hips forward, driving his cocks in me to the hilt, flame lighting the air above me.

I rocked myself up against him as he started fucking me in earnest. "So talk less," I advised, moaning when he replied by slamming his cocks home. Then his oiled tail found my clit, and I didn't have any sass left. I could only sprawl there and take it as Varis rutted into me, starting to tremble from the coiling tension growing inside me.

He wrapped his tail around the base of his cocks, rocking the studs of it against my clit with unerring aim. Every thrust slammed him into my depths with a flare of pleasure, the need turning into inevitability.

"Varis— Varis—" I gasped his name out between panting breaths, clawing at the sheets for purchase.

He snarled his pleasure to me and redoubled his effort, hauling my hips against his with every demanding stroke. The world fell away, piece by piece, my wide eyes going unseeing as the pleasure soared—and then crashed into me with all-consuming ecstasy. My pussy and ass slammed down on his cocks with a tidal wave of force, gripping him until he cried out his own release. His wings beat at the air, forcing his cocks deeper, and the heat of his come flooded me, radiating through my core alongside the rolling bliss.

All thought vanished. There was only the incredible surge of brilliant pleasure, my body and soul wrapped around Varistan's, his fire the immovable center of the world. I whimpered, head thrown back, every clench of my orgasm washing bliss through me.

Varis lowered my hips down to the bed while I was still coming down from the aftershocks, everything warm and swimmy. He let go of my thighs and braced himself over me, sweat sheening his skin and wetting his loose curls.

I reached up and ran my fingers down along one curl, moaning when his cocks flexed inside me. Gods, he was beautiful. Beautiful and *mine.*

"Bells," he said softly, his bliss-hazed expression nervous. "Was that... was that good?"

I breathed a laugh, cupping his face with one hand. "Really good, sweetheart. You don't have to worry about that."

"Truly?" he asked, lowering himself down to sprawl across me without pulling out. "No regrets?"

"None," I said, tracing the contour of his sharp-tipped ear. "That was wonderful. I really..." I swallowed, feeling a little self-conscious. "I really missed you."

He relaxed against me, burrowing his face against my neck and inhaling deeply. "I missed you, too," he whispered, all in one rush. Varistan shuddered, his tail wrapping around my foot. "You're the best thing in my life."

"You're the best thing in mine," I answered in a quiet voice, saying it before I could talk myself out of it. "That's why it's so awful."

I felt him hesitate, but a moment later Varistan tilted his face and pressed a gentle kiss to the base of my jaw. "I know." He paused again, then added in a small voice. "May I stay?"

"Don't you dare leave," I said sleepily, running my fingers along the edge of his wing. "What if I get cold?"

Varistan shivered under my touch. "As your grace desires," he said in a low murmur. He shifted, pulling out of me and replacing his hips with cloth. "Shall I carry you to the lavatory? Lest you draw Lianka's ire."

I reached up and traced one finger down the bridge of his nose, appreciating having his body under my hands again. "If you insist," I said with a lazy smile. "I like getting taken care of."

"That's good," he said, clambering off the bed and picking me up, "since your devoted servant is longing to do precisely that."

"Is that what you are?" I rested my head against his heartbeat, the sound soothing me more than anything else ever had.

"The list of things I am is quite long by now, but being your servant is certainly among them," Varis said, padding over to the bathroom. "Scion, survivor, servant, sinner..." He set me down on my feet, tilting my chin up to meet my eyes, the softest smile warming his expression. "Soulmate."

For the first time, it didn't hurt to hear.

CHAPTER FIFTY-FIVE

ULTIMATUM

I woke up totally content, sprawled on my back in the center of my huge bed with Varis curled up around me like an enormous cat. The sheets had ended up tangled around my calves, but with one wing tucked over my chest and a heavy thigh slung across my legs, I was far from cold. Varistan's tail curved in an arc around my whole body, going over the pillow and wrapping around my wrist in a gentle grasp. His gorgeous blood-red curls spread in a tangled sweep over my shoulder, one tickling my nose.

I blew it out of my face with a smile, appreciating having him alongside me again. Things weren't all the way better, but they were definitely improved, and I was a lot more hopeful about the future than I'd been the evening before. I could feel our connection like a path I'd always known, a sensation akin to striding through the Tangle in the darkness of night. The possibilities were falling away as we found our footing with each other again. One day – maybe one day soon – there would only be one left, and we'd have the choice to take it, or to separate forever.

I already knew what he would choose. No one would endure humiliation, sacrifice everything they'd ever worked for, accept penance with open relief, and then walk away. It made it so much easier to stay. There wasn't any risk for me any longer. He'd already made his decision. Now all that was left was for me to make mine.

A cheerful trill drew my attention to the mirrors by the wardrobes and made Varistan's ear twitch. On top of the central mirror, a tawny bird about the size of a crow perched, sporting a crest of cerulean feathers and wearing a harness. It chirped again, ducking its head to scratch vigorously, then gave itself a shake and fluffed out all its feathers, looking content.

That was... that was a flicker-bird. There was a flicker-bird in my bedroom. People didn't send flicker-birds directly to individuals unless the missive was both private and serious, and most of the time it wasn't even possible. You had to have both a talented bird and a strong connection to the person in question so that you could send it to the right location. Varistan knew a lot of nobles, but for someone to send a bird directly to his *bedroom*...

Something glinted on the harness, round and black with inlaid golden lines that matched the brand on Varistan's ankle.

"Varistan..." I said, my fear coming out in my voice.

He made an incoherent sound; his tail tugged on my arm.

"Varis, sweetheart, you really should wake up." I patted him on the thigh. "C'mon. Please wake up before I freak out."

He groaned, pushing himself up a little bit so he could look blearily down at me. "Bells, what..."

I pointed at the flicker-bird.

Varistan followed my hand, paling when he saw the royal crest on the flicker-bird's harness. "That's surely not good."

"Yes," I said, feeling light-headed despite lying down. "Really, really, really not good."

With a heavy exhale, Varis pushed himself up and shook out his wings. "Alright. Give me... give me a moment." He stayed there for a minute, elbows locked as he pulled himself together, then rolled off the bed and stalked over to the adjoining bedroom.

Not particularly wanting to be naked for whatever the flicker-bird had brought, I hauled myself out of bed and dug around for something to wear. I put on one of the outfits I'd brought from Lylvenore, feeling oddly displaced from the familiar clothing. It had been a long time since I'd dressed like a common woman... and I wasn't one any longer, not with Varistan by my side.

He came out of his room wearing a pair of pants, apparently having had the same idea as me. I raked my hair back and tied it up, watching him as he held his arm up like a falconer and whistled. The bird perked up, trilling at him before hopping off of the mirror. It glided over and lit on his wrist.

"Good bird," he said. It nibbled on his fingers in reply. Moving like he'd done it a thousand times (and maybe he had), Varistan undid the snaps on the bird's harness, pulling out a sheet of creamy paper and breaking the seal with a swipe of one claw. His eyes narrowed as he scanned it.

Varis looked up at me, expression hard, and licked his lips.

"'My Varistan,'" he read, returning his fiery gaze to the sheet. "'The leeway I grant you as my scion does not extend to consorting with monsters and mortals. Provide me the assurance that you are not the disloyal wildling you appear. A mortal's life is so fragile, and wild beasts ought to be subjugated, not treated with. To consort with such creatures as if they are your equals sullies your royal blood. Lift your hand and strike down that which seduces you. Are you my true child, or are you as much a Fury as the monsters my traitor son created?'"

My heart thundered, blood roaring in my ears. I fumbled for a chair and dropped heavily into it, my palms prickling with sweat. After the weeks of trade discussions in Maestrizen, I was familiar enough with formal fae speech to know that the King was telling Varistan to kill me and conquer Maestrizen—and that this was a command, not a request.

"'I eagerly await proof of your fidelity, yet as long as you keep your soulmate affectionately by your side, I will not provide you with the protection of my aegis,'" Varistan continued, his voice flat and eyes as cold as rubies. "'Your signet will be forfeit by right of conquest, and I assure you that there are many who hunger for it. Seal your next letter in her blood. Bear not my enmity. Prove out the blood you claim from me, or be blotted from my annals.'" His tail snapped behind him, the spade flared with anger. "'With a father's love, Tathalin Xirangyl.'"

He crumpled the paper and set it aflame with a sharp exhale of dragonfire. The flicker-bird danced nervously; he jerked his wrist upwards, tossing the bird into the air. It vanished, flickering home without any message to bear—and that silence would be message enough.

With the letter still burning in the palm of his hand, Varistan lifted his eyes back to mine. "Do you know what that means?" he asked, his controlled fury clipping the words.

"He can't openly attack you because you're his nephew and the Court will intervene, but he's given his tacit consent for anyone in Raven Court to wage war on us." I sounded distant to my own ears, the fallout of our relationship so much worse than I'd hoped for. "Do you think it was Yesika who told him?"

Varis snorted, closing his fingers around the smoldering paper to crush out the flame. "Yesika is surely still reeling from that message you sent. Even if she's managed to recover, I doubt she would think to involve my uncle." He sighed and walked over to the fireplace, dumping his handful of ash. "No, I suspect we have another enemy who would gladly twist the knife of exposing my deceit to the world."

I winced. "Xilvaris."

"Yes." He wiped his hand off on his pants, leaving a sooty smudge. "I doubt that message was sent in secret. We're likely to be entertaining armies within a day."

"What do you mean?" It wasn't like armies could be roused within a couple hours, and the closest access points were by sea or via the same winding mountain road Varistan and I had traveled from Lylvenore.

"That letter was surely not written on a moment's thought. It's been weeks since our... duel," Varistan said, his tail flaring for a moment and shame darkening his expression. "Tathalin is ancient, and while he may be consumed by bitterness and cracked from the sudden loss of his sons and his land, in the past decades he has still seemed to act with forethought." He raked his claws through his curls, starting to pace. "He has known me nearly since birth. Surely he was aware when he penned that missive that I would not comply, and acted accordingly. The less time an enemy has to prepare, the better, no?"

I rubbed my sweaty palms against my pants, feeling nauseous. "So, what? He's lost three sons already; what's one more?" I watched him pacing, tracking his movement with my eyes. "I know you're only his nephew, but that doesn't seem right."

"The Annihilation War broke him, Bells. How badly, I cannot say for certain, but in the span of a week his two oldest sons were killed and he lost hundreds of miles of territory, and he has lain a great deal of the blame at the feet of his youngest son and that son's human soulmate." Varis stopped pacing, turning towards me with a rueful smile. "He surely didn't name me a Fury by accident. My connection to Ayre is inescapable. He may simply already believe me to be his enemy, and be treating me as such."

"You're not, though," I said, searching his expression.

"No, I'm not. But we surely cannot convince him of such and remain in alliance, and there is nothing in this world that could convince me to spill your life's-blood for the sake of my uncle's favor." He took a deep breath, settling his shoulders back into a confident stance and folding his wings behind him. "So. If there's one thing you could do before you were deposed, your grace, what would it be?"

He wasn't afraid. I realized it with dawning surprise, looking at his calm aplomb. We stood to lose everything but each other – our land, our reputation, even his family name – and he wasn't afraid of it. A smile slowly spread across my face with the recognition. He knew what he wanted—and so did I.

"Free them all," I said, my skin tingling with anticipation. "Every bondservant. He can't undo that."

Varistan started smiling, too, a predatory expression coming into his eyes. "Why stop there?" he asked. "Laws are bound to their land, and unless the Raven King supercedes a lord's declaration, they will stand. While the rest of the nobility may dislike your rulings, they will surely rage if their privileges are revoked, and Tathalin's power over them has been unsteady since the Annihilation War. You could require all bondservants taken into Nyx Shaeras be freed. You could even forbid discrimination within your lands based on the effects of wild magic, which would protect mortals and wildlings alike."

I looked at him for a long moment, at the fire in his crimson eyes and the eager set of his wings, then stood and pulled the signet ring off my thumb. Smiling as those eyes went wide, I held it out to him. "You do it."

"Wh-wh-wh-what?" he stammered out, staring at the ring. "I— You—"

Wearing the expression of a hungry jackal, I sauntered towards him. "You might want to sit down."

"What?" he asked again, eyes darting up to mine before dropping back to my hand. "Why—"

I backed him up to a chair, set my arms on his shoulders, and lowered him into it.

"What are you..." Varis stopped talking when I picked up his left hand. He stared at me in shock when I spread his fingers and held his ring finger out.

I put one knee on the seat next to his thigh, leaning close enough that my lips brushed against his ear. "I forgive you," I crooned, sliding the signet onto his finger. "And I release you from our bargain."

Varistan arched up off the chair, voicing a shuddering cry from the pleasure flooding him. He grabbed me with one wing and hand, clinging to me as his whole body went stiff. "*Fuck*," he gasped out, his whole body shaking. In desperation, he grabbed my hand and shoved it against his groin, bucking up once, twice—and came with a sharp sound of release, his half-hard cocks throbbing against my palm in redirected ecstasy.

"Look at you, your grace," I purred into his ear, stroking him through his pants as he fell into bliss, desire throbbing between my legs. "You really are a kinky little slut, aren't you?"

He whined in protest, wilting back down into the chair. "That's not playing fair," he said in a breathy moan, looking up at me with the echoes of pleasure on his yearning face. "And it's *embarrassing.*"

"Poor baby," I said with mock sympathy, grinning down at him. "Shall I hold you to every promise and bargain from here on out, then?"

"Gods, no," Varis said, without any hesitation. His mouth slanted up to one side. "Have you met me? The only time I seem to have full control over my tongue is when it's put to the task of pleasure instead of speech."

I stuck my own tongue out at him, still grinning.

Varistan tugged me down to him, kissing me on the mouth with a low sound of satisfaction. "Your grace," he murmured against my lips, his warm hand gentle against the back of my neck. "Are you prepared to defy our King alongside me?"

"Your grace," I replied, smiling as he sighed out his pleasure, "let's commit a little treason."

CHAPTER FIFTY-SIX

REVOLUTION

O nce the decision was made, it was surprisingly easy to enact. We got dressed for real, in a pair of coordinating black-and-smoke outfits and matching sword and dagger that made us look like a pair of Generals heading into a formal meeting.

Sintuviel met us in the Sea Room. At my invitation, so did Alpha.

Varistan gave her a sidelong glance when we walked in. "Friend of yours, Bells?"

I grinned like a shark. "Varistan, meet the alpha of Nyx Shaeras' vermin control."

His brows lifted. "'Vermin control'?"

"The removal of those who turn society into their personal feeding grounds, or who ruin the work and lives of others for their own pleasure," Alpha replied with an air of amusement, strolling over to the war table. "Us mortals are rather more organized than your kind like to think, though most of us in this region are actually in the business of search-and-rescue. Isabela's the one who does vermin control."

He opened his mouth. Closed it. Opened it again. Turned to me. "You're part of a murder society?" he asked in a strangled voice. "There's a whole secret murder society for mortals? And you're *in it*?"

"Aw, don't say it like that," I said, with a playful pout, enjoying how appalled he was. "It's not *all* murder."

"Besides, we like you," Alpha said, a tiny smirk hovering on her lips. "You're on the no-kill list. We've even thwarted a few assassination attempts."

He gave me a pained expression. "So why the spears in the night?"

"We were planning on stabbing Lord Sairal, not you," I said cheerfully.

At the man's name, Varistan growled, his ears pinning back. "He certainly deserves such."

"And you gave it to him, if you'll recall," I said, wrapping an arm around his waist. "Sintuviel, how long do we have until our neighbors descend upon us like locusts?"

"Perhaps ask your duke," he said, apparently unperturbed by Alpha's presence. "He's the one bearing the signet."

Varis made a low sound and closed his eyes, a small line appearing between his brows. I could feel him leaning into the land-sense of Nyx Shaeras, my own connection to it weaker now that I wasn't wearing the ring. I couldn't follow him—but that had more to do with practice than anything, I suspected. Varistan loved this land, and knew it intimately. He would know if anything was out-of-place.

"Nightfall," he said, sounding distant. "At least for land forces. There's troops en route from Lylvenore, and they're moving in War Army formation. How unfortunate." He opened his eyes, blinking several times to re-focus on the room. "I can't tell at sea, of course, so we may be entertaining warships before then. I suppose they truly were ready to march at a moment's notice."

I made a face. "Ugh. No time like the present, I guess. Alpha, we're planning on freeing all of the bondservants that look to Nyx Shaeras, and requiring that all bondservants on our land be freed. Any opposition?"

Her lips turned up into a sharp smile. "None. You may want to add in a clause limiting re-bonding to cases of unforced life-debt, since you might find yourself short one signet ring by morning."

"Nyx Shaeras can surely withstand a siege for more than a single night," Varis said, sounding amused. "But, yes. Limiting the circumstances of life-bonding seems wise." He glanced over at Sintuviel, who was taking notes. "Any thoughts, my friend?"

"Plenty, your grace," our steward said, with a faint smile. "This is hardly what I expected to be doing this morning."

"You need not be part of it if it discomfits you," Varistan said, his voice kind. "We've stood by each other for millennia, and I would greatly miss you, but if you desire freedom from this, I won't hold you to it."

Sintuviel's ears shifted, canting forward before settling into a neutral position. "I can't say I ever expected to be part of a rebellion against the Raven King, but I've been at your side for too long to balk now. I trust you, your grace." He offered my soulmate a determined smile. "I'm with you."

The warmth in Varistan's eyes made my heart rate pick up. He wasn't used to people standing by him. Seeing him have that – seeing the loyalty he'd won with his love – was like watching the sun rise.

"Do you have any advice for me?" Varis asked in a serious tone. "I trust your judgment."

"I've been following the events in Stag Court as they've freed their bond-servants, and have some ideas as to how to avoid several of the troubles they encountered. If you grant me leave, I'm pleased to put them to paper." The two men nodded to each other; permission granted and accepted. Sintuviel paused, his ears shifting again as he looked towards Alpha. "Young woman," he said, with an air of mild interest, "what reach do you have among the mortals of Nyx Shaeras? Would you be able to ensure that all knew their debts had been forgiven?"

Her brows drew together, and she pursed her lips. "Maybe not within a fort-night, but surely within a season, and likely sooner." Alpha tilted her head to the side, birdlike. "You fear masters simply not telling their former bondservants."

Sintuviel lifted one shoulder in a slight shrug. "The cost of labor is far greater than the cost of feeding a laborer, is it not? And those of us who are bound to our word tend to twist it to our benefit." He turned a sheet of vellum and slid it across the table to Varistan. "To forgive the debts, your grace," he said, looking up into Varistan's eyes with determination. "By your leave, I will set in writing the legal declarations for life-bonding and for non-discrimination, with what protections I can discern. I should have them before nightfall."

Varistan eyed the paper warily. "You know," he said in a conversational tone that belied the flared tail wrapping its way up my leg, "I think you ought to seal this one, Isabela."

My lips twitched. "Too much forgiveness for your grace?"

He took off the signet, picked up my hand, and plopped it into my palm. "There are upwards of eighty thousand souls across the span of Nyx Shaeras," Varis said, starting to sound strained. "While I have frowned upon the use of human bondservants for my full tenure as its duke, and thus the number of bondservants tied to Nyx Shaeras is more limited than elsewhere in Raven Court, that's still significantly more than ten thousand life-debts to forgive. Need I remind you of how forgiveness affects a fae such as myself?"

An expression of discomfort crawled across Sintuviel's face. A similar ex-pression crossed Varistan's, for very different reasons.

I dropped a kiss on his shoulder. As fascinating as it would have been to see what ten thousand life-debts would do to him, the release of one high-intensity bargain had been enough to make him dry-orgasm. Probably amping that up by ten thousand would trespass far beyond pleasure into raw agony. I was fine taking a pass on that.

Sintuviel passed me the sealing wax. I held it over the paper, looking up at Varistan with a smile. He kissed me on the temple, then leaned down and exhaled a thin stream of flame, melting the red wax.

"Well," I said. "Here goes nothing."

Nothing obvious happened when I pressed the signet into the wax, save that Varistan shivered. He let out the breath that he was holding, burying his face against my neck. "That wasn't so terrible. Merely a faint echo."

He didn't ask for the ring back, but I slid it back onto his finger, anyway. I knew it made him feel better to have his land-sense, and until we were balanced it would be difficult for him to access through me.

"Thank you," he murmured against my skin, almost too quietly to hear. Then he took a deep breath and stood again, putting his shoulders back and loosening his tail's grasp on my leg. "Sintuviel, will you have any time aside from drafting the declarations?"

Our steward dropped his gaze. "I fear not, your grace."

"Then I ask you for no more than that." Varistan looked over at me. "Though it ended poorly, I have experience defending against a siege," he said, flicking his wings with a wry smile. "I was never in command of any assault forces, though, let alone a naval force. I doubt I could successfully set up two within the span of a day, let alone all three."

"If you're asking if I have any experience in warfare, the answer is definitely 'no'," I said with a laugh. I leaned my hip against the table. "I've spent a solid chunk of time with both the First Army and War Army garrisons, though, so I know who to talk to."

"Both armies look to the Raven King, not to me—to us," Varis said, correcting himself. "As he's removed his protection from Nyx Shaeras, they need not protect us."

"Which is why it's good that Stellaris and Tjarrek are my friends," I said cheerfully.

He opened his mouth, closed it, and gave me a puzzled look. "You're on first-name basis with Commander Ruexhan and Commander Ylhain?" he asked, clearly taken aback. "I don't think they've ever once offered such to me, and I've known them a great deal longer."

"That's because your spine goes ramrod straight in outrage any time anyone below the rank of duke dares address you by your name, and I'm soldier enough to get garrison informality," I said, smirking at him. "The fact that you liked me using your name probably should have been a clue that I was a duchess, but hindsight's a great deal better than foresight."

Varistan grunted, but he didn't challenge me on it, merely resettling his wings. "Very well. Then I shall seek the defense of the castle, and I ask you to seek defense of land and sea. Is there aught else?"

"Well," Alpha said, practically purring the word. "How would you feel about a little sabotage?"

His brows raised. "Sabotage?"

She smiled cuttingly. "Armies are made up of people, and people do like their creature comforts. Wouldn't it be a shame if their access to food, water, and safe housing was compromised?"

He opened his mouth, paused, and then laughed. "I don't think I'm even going to ask. Do as you like, Alpha. Consider my resources at your disposal for the purposes of providing defense to this duchy."

Alpha put her hand over her heart and bowed, fae-style. "As you desire, your grace."

The first thing we did once we'd concluded our meeting was to make the formal announcement to the castle. There was a lot to say – ranging from the King allowing us to be invaded to the freeing of the bondservants – but apparently the dealings with Maestrizen and the experience of having a human in charge of the castle for more than a month had prepared our people for strange happenings, because there was a lot less upheaval than I expected. Some of that was surely due to the fact that Varistan had never allowed the mistreatment of bondservants, too, though I supposed there was no way to tease it apart.

That wasn't to say there wasn't upheaval. The bondservant system kept humans in an underclass, and even when it was better to be a slave in Nyx Shaeras than elsewhere, that still didn't make it a favored status. Mostly it was kept to shouted questions and a general sense of uneasiness from the fae who no longer possessed greater rights than their mortal compatriots. A few people – fae and mortal alike – simply turned around and walked out. One burly human pushed his way through the crowd and punched a fae man directly in the nose.

In true fae fashion, the resulting fisticuffs were ignored by all present.

(The mortal won.)

We didn't have any soothing things to say to the fae who expressed fear that their positions might be changed, because they surely would. But the shouts and anxiety subsided over the course of the two hours we spent in the grand hall. I was pretty sure that was mainly due to Varistan's utter certainty that this was the right thing to do—the best thing for his duchy. Everyone who lived in Nyx Shaeras, and especially those in the castle itself, knew how much Varis loved Nyx Shaeras. So if he believed in this... they would trust him.

We told them about the laws we were sealing that evening, too. They might as well know it all before we went into battle.

I went to the First Army garrison after lunch. Stellaris was already preparing for castle defense, so I gave her a salute and left her to it. It took a little longer to find Tjarrek – he was down at the harbor – but when I did, he smiled at me with the type of warm admiration that can stop hearts.

"Your grace," he said, looking at me like I'd done something amazing. "Come to ensure I'm preparing our sea defense?"

"Came to ask you if you would." I wasn't sure what I'd done to deserve a look like that—then caught sight of his tail as it curled behind him.

I'd known he was wildling almost from the start; you can't really hide a tail in public showers. But Tjarrek never showed it otherwise, keeping it bound tightly to his leg and wearing loose-fitting clothing so it wouldn't be noticeable. He was showing it now, though. He must have modified a piece of clothing in the past hour. Perhaps someone had glamored it for him.

"I'm ready to defend Nyx Shaeras with my life, if necessary," he said. He flicked his tail again, glancing down at it with a smirk. "Though I'd like to enjoy the freedom for a bit longer than a single day."

"I'll leave you to it, then, Commander," I said, a helpless smile starting to spread across my face. "Guess I'll see to the War Army, since you and Stellaris have the First Army well in hand."

He gave me a salute, barking a quick command at a sailor before turning back to me. "Best of luck, your grace."

"You, too," I said, and headed back up the slope with unexpected pride warming my heart.

Varistan joined me on the outer wall as the sun set, dropping down from the sky and landing with clean precision close enough that the wind made the soldier next to me take a step back. "Your grace," he said in a placid voice, in opposition to his nervously shifting ears. "Might I have a moment of your time?" He glanced over at the soldiers. "Alone?"

"Of course." I passed my spear to my companion and walked over, putting my arms around Varistan's neck. "Wherever you like, your grace."

He swallowed and picked me up, launching us into the sky as soon as I was in his arms. He didn't land, either, catching one of the dying thermals off the basalt and soaring higher. I leaned my head against his chest and didn't rush him. Facing an invasion couldn't be easy for him.

"I realized something," he said at last, resting his face against my head as he slowly wheeled through the sky. "One of us is surely going to need to face the Raven King tonight, and I believe it needs to be me."

"Oh?" I asked, when he didn't continue.

Varis exhaled, beating his wings once to switch thermals, his arms tightening on me. "This is ultimately his land." Varistan's voice was steady, but I felt the quaver in his grip. "We may be able to repel our attackers on our own, but if the King seizes control of Nyx Shaeras and steps in, he can shatter our walls and let our enemies in. I suspect..." His voice hitched, but he caught himself. "I suspect he will attempt to do exactly that, Bells."

"Kings can do that?" I asked in shock, craning my neck to look at him.

He nodded with a bitter laugh, sorrow tensing his face. "It's easier the younger a Court is, and the closer to the palace heart of the Court, but yes, a King may call upon the wild magic of his land to work his will." He took a deep breath, beating his wings again to take us over the castle, the warm air off the black stone buoying us up. "Raven Court is one of the oldest Courts on the continent, we're far from the Winged Palace, and because of our blood-tie, Tathalin can't directly attempt to cause me physical harm. I believe I can resist him, and keep hold of Nyx Shaeras."

The other option was abandoning Nyx Shaeras—leaving that golden ring on the throne in the grand hall to whoever had come for us and fleeing, turning our backs on all of this. But Varis loved Nyx Shaeras more than anything else in the world. He would never surrender it if he could defend it.

"What do I need to do?" I asked, resigned to the inevitable. It always came down to blood and pain. Why would this be any different?

Another fine tremor ran through him. "If he wins," he said, the words catching in his throat. "Bells. If he wins, he'll be... in me. In my body. If you—" Varis shuddered, hands spasming on me. "If you kill me, he'll fall. You'll— You'll still be duchess. Pelleas will surely be King, and he's... young. He's not eaten with hatred. It— It— It—" He let out a sob, shaking his head sharply. "Promise me," Varis said, while I was still in the grip of horror. "Promise me you'll do it if I... fall."

"Varis," I said, staring up at him, my skin cold and clammy. "Don't ask that of me."

"Please," he whispered, not meeting my eyes. "He can't harm me, but he can use my body to slaughter you while I'm forced to experience it, and he surely will if he has the chance. Don't make me live through that. Please."

I closed my eyes, feeling as if my heart was being crushed into a small knot of pain. "Okay. I promise," I said, not knowing how I'd ever manage to follow through. "But don't lose."

His claws dug into my skin. I imagined I could feel his devastation burrowing into me through the tips of them, graveworms coiling under my skin.

"I'll strive not to," he said, his voice level and his heart locked away.

When he set my feet on solid ground again and kissed me farewell, I couldn't even watch him leave. There wasn't any time to mourn. It was time for war.

CHAPTER FIFTY-SEVEN

BESIEGED

"What are they waiting for?" I muttered, squinting out at the small fires dotting the hills. It was after midnight, and though the soldiers from Lylvenore had arrived not long after dark, they'd made no move to attack, even when their ships engaged our navy in the seas outside Nyx Shaeras.

At least, we were assuming they were the same force. Neither ships nor army were flying any flags, probably because they were technically Court forces. But without that declaration, they might as well have been pirates and marauders. That plausible deniability would let Raven Court go to war with itself.

"I thought it was for setting up siege equipment, but as far as we can tell, they neither brought siege engines with them, nor are they felling trees to build them," Stellaris said, leaning against the crenellation next to me. "We haven't even faced any attempts to pierce the defenses via glamor. It's as if they're waiting for something."

My gut twisted. If they hadn't brought anything for the siege, that meant they didn't expect there to *be* a siege.

"The King," I whispered. "They expect him to take down the walls." Varistan had been sure he could fight back, but if they were that confident—

Her grip on the stone tightened. "Shit. They must have another signet with them, something for him to focus on." Stellaris exhaled through her teeth. "His Grace can shield his own signet, but if there's a nearby signet worn by a willing soul, it will be much, much easier for the King to pierce that defense and engage with Nyx Shaeras."

"That's something the King can do?" I asked, feeling unsteady. "The Vicere-ine of Lylvenore—is that something she would do?"

"I don't know." She shook her head, a sharp motion. "It doesn't have to be her. Any of the landed nobles would do, as long as they were willing to be ridden by our King's power. There's always a chance it will kill you, or leave you a burned-out husk, so I didn't think anyone would dare..." Stellaris trailed off, then turned and met my eyes, hers wide in her too-pale face. "They're too confident. Go," she said. "Warn him. Go, *now*."

I turned and ran.

People stepped out of my way as I bolted down the wall. Luckily, I didn't meet anyone on the stairs; I took them three at a time and narrowly evaded impaling the soldier at the bottom. Spears, while excellent on the battlefield, aren't exactly easy to maneuver around corners.

I took off at a dead run, not bothering to follow the road. Even in the dark, as long as I focused on the ground ahead of me, the weak access I had to the duchy's land-sense meant I wouldn't trip or turn my ankle.

I needed that edge. The outer wall was more than a mile from the castle. The army had been ready for *hours*, waiting as the gibbous moon rose—waiting for the moment when their King would enter the fray.

Varistan needed to know, and he needed to know hours ago.

My breath tore at my throat before I reached the inner wall, heart pounding and sides aching from leaping into action with unwarmed muscles. Ahead of me, I heard a single shout. The sound cut off with the clash of steel—and then was drowned out by the shrieking sound of stone as it sheared, one of the massive gates cracking free and falling, slowly, ponderously, to smash on the ground beneath.

Shit.

I *saw* the force of the Raven King's will as he attacked Varistan, the ripple of the ground billowing towards me as if a giant was shaking out a tablecloth. With timing born solely from my connection to Nyx Shaeras, I threw myself into the air as the ground rose up to heave me off, stumbling as my feet hit the dirt long before they should have. I fell. My knee screamed with pain as the friction tore my skin beneath armor and cloth. In a moment I was up again, dashing across the shivering earth as my soulmate grappled for control against the King who'd been born with Raven Court.

Pebbles danced across the ground. Grass swayed. Behind me, I could hear the roar of battle, and I didn't dare look back.

I jumped up onto the broken gate and bolted for the dark tunnel through the wall. It shifted under me, but I was sure-footed and I still had my land-sense. It flared and fogged, the duel between Varistan and the Raven King turning it into a roil all around me, but it didn't break. Varis was still holding his own.

I ducked a falling fragment of stone and took another on my shoulder. A full block from the archway fell behind me, smashing the cobblestones and spitting shards against the back of my legs.

Then I was free of the dark tunnel, and the moonlight almost dazzled me.

A man stood in a ring of dead soldiers, breathing hard. He swiped his arm across his face, the moonlight making the blood that ran from his nose look black. The King had used his body, but the power of a Court only belongs to its Monarch and its patron deity. To have that sort of power sizzling through your veins... the power to slaughter soldiers and tumble walls... he was lucky to be alive. To be *sane*.

The soldiers hadn't stood a chance. I only would because the King had abandoned his willing host to attack my Varis.

The man turned, his eyes finding mine in the moonlit night.

"Xilvaris," I breathed, shocked into it. He wasn't a landed noble—had no bloodline that would offer him such an opportunity. I knew he hated us, but he shouldn't have been able to do this.

"That's the Marquess of Norvaldt to you, your grace," he said in a mocking tone. He wiped the underside of his wrist across his mouth again, smearing the blood. The light glinted off a silver signet on his right hand. "I almost feel as if I owe you a debt of thanks for how blindingly our King hates you. Wearing the signet of a marquess is astonishing enough, but to claim a duchy by right of conquest? *This* duchy, which you so appallingly snatched from my grasp?" He licked the blood off his lips, looking like a wolf lifting his muzzle from the kill. "Delightful."

"I won't let you have it," I said, shifting my stance as I caught my breath. "You'll never be the Duke of Nyx Shaeras."

"A pity you're not fae," he said, with an air of amusement. "I would so love to see your soul torn asunder by your failure to keep true to those bold words." Xilvaris stepped out of the ring of corpses, sauntering towards me. "Our King may be too busy dueling to kill you for me, but I'm pleased to pick up the slack."

The ground shivered beneath our feet. More stones fell out of the archway behind me, the crash of impact vibrating against my soles.

"You can try." I started moving, keeping my eyes on him as I tried to find a good place for a battle. He would be faster—but in the darkness, I would know the ground better than him. The rougher, the better.

"I'm not your soulmate, little girl. Your words mean naught to me, and my body isn't yours to know." He twisted his wrist, the bloody length of his sword catching the moonlight, and drew a long dagger with his offhand. "Surrender, and perhaps I'll allow you and your precious Vee to escape with your lives. Fight, and I'll seek to claim both."

I didn't bother answering. I knew he'd never let either of us go free.

Xilvaris made a sound of disgust. "Don't say I didn't warn you."

He struck with the slick speed of a weasel, darting forward across the broken ground as if it was the flat sands of the dueling ring. I met him with a sharp jerk of my spear, his dagger sparking against my spear-tip and sword biting a chip out of the haft. *Tak-tak!*, and then he was springing out of the way of my answering jab.

His tongue flickered out, licking at the blood that still ran from his nostrils. The moonlight reflected off his eyes, cold and clear.

Cleaner even than Stellaris, I thought, circling backwards. *He's a practiced killer.*

Blades flashed, his movements precise and quick. I let him drive me backwards, all but staggering, acting the broken-winged bird for him. A tremor rocked the ground, harder than before, and I dropped to one knee as if it had felled me.

He barked a derisive laugh as I barely batted off his attack, scrambling up to my feet.

My knee throbbed, reminding me of my injury. I could feel a trickle of blood running down my leg, the scab cracking back open. Minor annoyances. Neither would hurt my ability to fight.

Xilvaris stalked towards me like a monster in a nightmare, his sharp-tipped ears lifted in high focus and his blood-streaked teeth bared.

I stumbled backwards, opening my mouth and lifting my shoulders as I breathed, as if I was gasping for breath. That look of supercilious pride on his face hardened into mockery, Xilvaris believing every action that fit his version of the world: the pathetic human struggling to hold her own, and the superior fae certain of his victory.

I'm not your soulmate, either, I thought with vicious satisfaction. *You have no idea who you're dealing with.*

He feinted, snapping his blades at me. I flinched like I was supposed to, stepping backwards and to the side, choking up on my spear like a frightened novice. The darkness of the collapsing gateway loomed to my left, stones pattering to the ground with each new tremor.

Xilvaris struck for me again, using his twin blades to catch my spear, his teeth bared with feral hunger. He was so close I could hear the rasp of his breath over the sound of stones rattling across the shivering earth.

I gave him a polite smile, and whipped my spear up and around.

The spiked base of my spear tore a gouge into his inner thigh, the force of the blow making my hands ache. Suddenly freed from my spear, his blades shot forward, but I was already dropping, following my swing with a sideswipe that used my thigh as a fulcrum.

My blade crashed into his elbow with enough force to crush the joint of his armor. Xilvaris staggered backwards into the darkness of the archway with a hoarse shout, blood soaking down his leg and seeping through his armor at his elbow.

I followed him like an avenging angel. The darkness of the tunnel embraced me. Every footstep met solid ground as I drove forward, dancing over fallen blocks of stone and moving with the shudders of the tortured earth.

Xilvaris darted for the light. I blocked him with a vicious swing, sparks flying as my spear sliced across his armor. He tried again, and again. I kept him cornered, not needing to see to hold my ground. I could feel every clumsy footstep as he fought for footing on the shifting earth. The shadow of his body against the dark shifted; I met his attack with confident ease, the movements of my spear precise—and far less tiring than the swing of a sword.

The ground bucked. Pebbles fell, and more than pebbles. Xilvaris cried out as a rock struck him; I sidestepped without thinking why. A massive stone smashed down next to me, a fist-sized piece flying off and slamming into my hip with bruising force.

"Surrender," I said, all but snarling the words, "and perhaps I'll allow you to escape with your life."

With a scream of rage, Xilvaris threw himself at me, committing himself. He was *fast*, and even with the advantage of the dark I couldn't keep him at bay. He took my spear across the side and kept coming, sacrificing his dagger to trap my weapon between his arm and body.

Stones thundered as the wall's archway started falling in earnest. I flung my spear between us and threw myself backwards, a massive rock smashing where I'd stood a heartbeat before, giving me a moment's reprieve. I dropped to the ground, evading Xilvaris as he leapt over the stone, forcing us back into moonlight.

My fingers closed around a long piece of the broken gate as I scrambled away from the falling stone, heart pounding in my throat.

Snarling like an animal, Xilvaris leapt for me.

I waited until the very last second before throwing myself to my knees. His sword clipped the armor of my shoulder, the wind ruffling my hair—and I drove the foot-long shard of saltwood into the gouge I'd left on his inner thigh.

Arterial blood sprayed me as I took Xilvaris' knee to the head. I struck the ground, my ears ringing, and scrabbled for purchase. Had to get up, couldn't be on the ground, wouldn't die—

I got to my feet in time to stagger out of the way of his final attack, a weak swing of his sword that missed my side by inches.

"Bitch," he gasped out, his sword clattering out of his lax fingers.

"That's the Duchess of Nyx Shaeras to you, my lord," I said, panting for air.

He didn't answer. His lip lifted for a moment in a sneer... and then his body slumped, the light leaving his eyes and his final breath stirring the air. I stood there for a moment, breathing hard. I didn't feel any satisfaction from the bloodshed. It had been necessary... but it was still a life taken, and an eternity cut short.

I shook my head, regretting the senselessness of it all, and my eyes fell on the silver of his signet ring. Xilvaris had already served his purpose to the King, but there was no reason to leave that thing sitting there. With businesslike calm, I got down on one knee – grunting as my bruised hip complained – and tugged the ring free. It didn't seem wise to put it on, in case the Raven King was paying attention; I didn't want to give him the chance to kill me.

I tucked it into my pocket instead and shoved myself back up, swaying a little. Damn. I must have gotten hit harder on the head than I'd hoped.

Another crash: the other half of the gate falling, the archway crumbling. I jumped back as rubble fell, my eyes flying to the castle.

It was getting worse. Varis was losing.

I relieved a corpse of his spear and started up the slope, my eyes hard. The Raven King might have had Xilvaris, but Varis had *me*, and there was nothing I wouldn't do for him. *I'm coming for you*, I thought, praying he could feel me as I ran towards him. *Hold on, Varis. I'm coming.*

Chapter Fifty-Eight

REMATCH

Two quakes hit before I reached the castle, the second one throwing me to the ground so hard my teeth snapped together and I could feel my knee grinding when I got up. I limped the last hundred feet to the castle door, and flung it open.

Varistan whirled, panting flame, his wings spread and tail lashing. Blood dripped from one nostril and from his fisted hands, his talons impaled in his palms.

"Varis," I said, walking slowly towards him, holding one hand out. "Varis, it's alright. It's me."

He started laughing, the sound harsh. It didn't sound like him. "Isabela Keris," he said, taking one step towards me. He didn't move like he should; too careful, too measured. "You came." His mouth moved, but that wasn't the cadence of his voice. That wasn't him at all.

A horrible sense of wrongness twisted my gut. That was the Raven King in my soulmate's skin, an ancient fae puppetting my Varis like a hand in a sock.

I gripped my spear automatically, feeling sick to my stomach. "Let him go." I swallowed, my vision swimming as I tried not to cry. "Varis. Varis, you have to fight. Please, sweetheart." A tear tracked down my cheek as he laughed again, uncurling his hands, moving more easily. "Please fight," I whispered, my voice shaking.

"Aren't you pleased?" he asked in a mocking voice, spreading his hands as he walked towards me. "As long as my focus is here with you, my nephew can keep me from tearing down the walls of this castle."

I started circling without thinking, stepping to my good side. My injured knee throbbed. My bruised hip ached. It would slow me down; make me slower. And I'd fought Xilvaris across rough ground, and run all the way here. I didn't think I could take Varis in a fight—

Except it's not Varis, I thought, watching the purposefulness of each step. This wasn't Tathalin's body. Varistan's body wasn't even fully *fae*. The Raven King didn't know how to use it.

Blood dripped off his fingertips, spattering on the pale marble floor.

"Of course," he crooned, "I don't think this state of things will last for long." Tathalin drew Varistan's sword, fingers closing around it with care. "You're injured. You're tired." He bared his teeth. "You're *human*."

I rolled the shoulder Xilvaris had struck, gauging the injury, the cold necessity wrapping around my heart and my tears drying. It wasn't terrible, but I'd be weaker on that side, and it would hurt to use. I leaned into the power of Nyx Shaeras, trusting Varistan to keep me safe as I asked that power to heal my wounds. The longer I could keep the Raven King talking, the more able to fight I'd be.

"Let him go, Tathalin," I said quietly, watching his chest for movement. "I don't want to kill you, but I will."

He made a sound of disgust. "You mortals," he said, sneering the words. "I was born when an ochre handprint pressed to the wall of a cave was the height of creativity. You are *nothing*. How many of those great artists are remembered now? Faugh!" Tathalin circled with me, tail dragging on the floor like a dead limb and wings shifting as he tried to keep his balance in the unfamiliar body. "Do you think time will remember you? That you'll leave your mark upon Faery?"

"You talk too much," I advised him. "Has anyone ever told you that?"

The power of Nyx Shaeras tingled along my skin, soothing my pain. I kept circling, waiting for him to make the first move.

He bared Varistan's teeth, blood dripping off his upper lip. The bleeding from his hands had already stopped. Only the brutality of the power coursing through him was preventing the delicate membranes of his nose from regenerating, too.

"Such hubris." He rolled Varistan's shoulders, settling himself slowly into a fighting stance. He was getting better at moving, I realized. Time was not my friend in this battle. "Have you the least idea of who I am? Of the force of power you're choosing to challenge? Raven Court is *mine*. It, and everything in it. Your Varistan is mine. *You* are—"

I moved, closing the distance between us with sudden speed. He stepped out of the way, avoiding my strikes with infuriating ease, leaning out of the way of each stab just enough that the tip wouldn't strike, stepping back and back and back, Varistan's tail still dragging on the floor.

"Pathetic girl," he said, starting to laugh. "Do you truly think you can defeat *me*? I have faced spears since before your kind could *write*—"

With a snarl, I lifted my foot, and drove the heel of my boot into the spade of Varistan's tail.

Pain hit Tathalin like a battering ram, so much that he couldn't even *scream*, his sword falling out of nerveless fingers and eyes going glassy. He staggered backwards, gasping for breath.

"Bells," he choked out—*Varistan* choked out. "*Now*. Please—"

I flung myself at Varistan, seeing his agony as he struggled to keep control, my focus narrowing down onto his expression like a stooping falcon. Tathalin tried to flee, my Varis fighting to hold the Raven King in his body. I drove my spear for his unprotected throat, my predatory focus on the terror of a King—and in the moment before I struck, I saw him tear free.

Yes!

At the last second, I jerked my spear inches to the side, my blade whistling past Varistan's throat. I didn't check my speed, slamming into him and driving him against the wall, my spear clattering to the floor.

"Bells," he sobbed. "Bells, you— you promised—"

"I lied," I said, starting to cry again as I stroked his curls back from his face. "I'm mortal. I can do that. Varis, sweetheart. Varis—"

"Bells, he's— he's—" His eyes went unfocused for a moment, but he dragged himself back to me. "Bells, please."

"It's okay, darling. Let the walls fall. Just stay with me." My throat felt like I'd swallowed broken glass, my heart pounding and hands shaking. "*Please*, Varis. The rest of it doesn't matter. We did everything we could. Let's run away. We can go to Maestrizen. You like it there, right? Remember? Just take off the ring, let it go—"

He snarled, body shaking and posture shifting as Tathalin seized control. The Raven King grabbed my wrists and slammed me up against the wall, teeth bared and flame glowing in his throat. "*Pitiful girl—*"

Heedless of the danger, I kissed him full on the mouth, sliding my tongue between those deadly fangs. He went stiff—and then Varistan moaned into my mouth, his grip easing enough that I could tear my hands free.

Varis cried out in pain, his back bowing and mouth breaking from mine. His talons screeched along the wall, his left hand shoved so hard against the stone that his arm shook and fingers went bloodless. "He— he won't let me, Bells—"

"Okay, okay, it's okay," I said, crying in earnest. "It's okay, sweetheart. Just let him have everything else. Stay with me, *mi cielo*, please—"

"He doesn't want anything else." Varistan sobbed out a laugh, his breathing rasping and blood starting to trace down his face from his eyes. "Bells, you should have killed me when you had the chance, you would have had Nyx Shaeras—" He cried out again, agony wracking him as Tathalin tried to claw back control.

"No, Varis, no." I stroked his face, my body shaking from the effort of not simply sobbing in his arms. "Don't you understand? It's never been about Nyx Shaeras. It's *you*. You're the one I love." My fingers curled around his jaw.

"You're everything to me. Please, darling." My throat closed, tears blinding me. "Varis, *please*, you have to know how much I love you. You have to know. I need you to stay. Please, I can't do this without you—"

He choked out another sob of laughter, pressing his forehead to mine with such force that it hurt. His broken tail wrapped around my legs with deliberate care. "Bells. He's never going to let me go. There's only one way out."

"*No*, sweetheart, please—"

"You don't understand," he said, shuddering as he warred with the Raven King. His tail gripped my legs so tightly it hurt. "Bells. I choose *you*."

And with a tortured cry, my soulmate yanked my feet out from under me.

Chapter Fifty-Nine

REBIRTH

Everything happened at once.

I struck the ground at the same moment a wash of brutal heat slammed into me, the air so dry my nose started bleeding. I could barely feel the pain, gasping for air as our soulmate bond fell into eternal balance. My awareness of Nyx Shaeras flared back into the strength it had had when I'd been wearing its signet as everything between me and Varis snapped into focus.

He was *mine*—body, heart, and soul. People called him the Flame of Faery, but they didn't understand the truth of those words. Varis was my flame in the night, his soul like a Midwinter bonfire, driving off the darkness with the boldness of his spirit. Everything constricted to that beautiful flare of light, my soul singing out with the bronze voice of a temple bell as the universe fell into alignment, the land we loved shifting to embrace us as we chose each other above all else.

I reached up for my soulmate, and the world exploded.

My senses shattered into the night, the world recoiling in all directions from our epicenter. It might have taken my mind with it, torn me to shreds like a cobweb in a hurricane, except for the burning anchor in the heart of my soul. Varis, gods, Varis, was he alright

My eyes focused on him. Caught sight of his dazed expression of love and loss. Recognized the soot and char of his hottest flame.

Molten gold dripped down his arm.

He'd destroyed the signet of Nyx Shaeras. He'd sacrificed the duchy he loved to free himself—to stay with me. To *choose* me.

Imminence held us in its grip, a sense not of falling, but of being *about* to fall, my heart pounding and breath sharpening as it wound tighter and tighter. I could still feel the dying flickers of my land-sense, sparkling at the edge of my mind. My vision tunneled, my ears roaring with the rush of my blood beneath my skin.

Varistan started shaking, hyperventilating from the loss of the land-sense he'd had for sixteen centuries.

"Varis, sweetheart—" I scrambled to my feet, needing to take care of him—

His crimson eyes met mine, wide and shocked. "Bells— Oh, *fuck*—" he gasped out, sounding like he was about to orgasm.

With the force of a tsunami, Nyx Shaeras crashed back into us.

My vision completely blacked out as the full strength of land-sense flooded into me without the diminution of a signet ring to dull its power. The strength of it wasn't even directed at me, and I barely kept my footing as everything around me came to the fore: the living stones spreading out under our feet, the clash of soldiers against the fractured walls, the scream of tortured wood as the ram of a ship broke through the hull of another. Ancient trees stretched skyward, their salt-soaked power spreading into the bedrock through their taproots. Energy hummed in the wind and the calls of the sea-birds, a force so alien as to be nearly unimaginable.

Wild magic.

All if it twined through and around Varistan, my soulmate clinging to me as the land he'd loved so well for so long answered that affection with total devotion. He'd set Nyx Shaeras free—and instead of returning to the Raven King's grasp, it chose *him*.

He started laughing, helplessly, the thunder of the land's love growing no less yet answering to his practiced hand. Varistan pushed himself upright, looking down into my face with wildness on his. The red of his eyes glowed with the power coursing through him, illuminating his bloodied face. He bared his teeth in a feral grin, as much war-dragon in that moment as fae.

"Watch this," he snarled, and covered my eyes with his hand.

Through the connection to our duchy – to our *Court* – I felt the brilliance of the starry sky turn to darkness. A storm boiled into being from the wrath of a King, blotting out the stars and moon with angry black clouds.

The sky opened. Hundreds of bolts of lightning broke the night, the *CRACK* of their combined thunder leaving my ears ringing as Varistan set enemy ships ablaze and struck down enemy soldiers. The deluge flattened those outside the walls, wind whipping the sea into froth and snatching arrows from the sky.

He lashed out with lightning again, his draconic territoriality leaving him growling like an animal as he drove terrified soldiers back from his castle. I could feel him losing control, the all-consuming pleasure of obeying the hungry land starting to drive him instead of fueling him. Thunder boomed through the halls of Nyx Shaeras again, my soulmate's wings mantled and fangs bared.

"Stop," I said, grabbing either side of his face without bothering to take his hand off my eyes. I didn't need to see to know where he was in space, not anymore. I would always be able to find the other half of my soul. "Stop it, Varis. No more."

Lightning cracked through the sky alongside his snarl of rage, but I'd spent enough time with Nyx Shaeras worn on my hand that I could lean into the same power he controlled, shoving the killing force of those bolts so that they struck the sea and trees instead of ships and men.

"I said *stop*," I snapped, my eyes focusing on his face when he tried to shove me away. "What sort of mate are you? Are you seriously ignoring me so you can go show off for someone else?"

Varis growled, trying to shake my hands off.

I smacked him on the cheek, just enough that it would sting. "Hey!" I did it again, which at least got him to look at me. "Pay attention to *me*."

The eldritch light in his eyes slowly faded as he focused on me, breathing hard. "Bells," he said, panting shallowly. "Bells, they're *still there—*"

"I know," I said, stroking his hair back as he wrapped his warm hands around my wrists and his tail around one of my ankles. "We won, sweetheart. It's okay. Let them limp home."

"They... they..." He closed his eyes and rested his forehead against mine. "Fuck, Bells," he groaned, starting to shiver. "I want them *dead.* Should, I should, please, they hurt me, I want to kill, kill, ki—kill them—"

"Not you, sweetheart." I leaned up and pressed a kiss to his mouth. "Nyx Shaeras. Come back to me again, Varis. Breathe with me."

He nodded, his tail tightening around my ankle as he matched the pace of his breathing to mine. "Y-yes," he said, his breath hitching. "Gods. It's so much. I never expected—"

"Shh." I stroked my thumbs across his cheeks. "It's alright. Let it go."

Our hearts slowed in tandem, the tension easing as the pouring rain outside shifted from the fury of a King to a natural storm. He stopped shaking, and then he stopped having to fight for control, his focus easing as the newborn Court begrudgingly settled into its ancient patterns.

It was done.

We were safe.

It was going to be alright.

At last, Varistan took a deep breath, his warm breath sighing across my face as he exhaled, the last of his stress falling out of his shoulders.

"Well," he murmured. "I guess we don't need to move to Maestrizen."

Laughter bubbled out of me with total surprise, a smile spreading across my face. I leaned back, letting him lower my hands. Varistan started laughing, too, joy lighting his expression.

"Gods," he said with a grin, tugging my hips up against his and wrapping his arms around me. "Did you feel that we claimed Norvaldt March, the one between us and Pinesap Court? *That's* surely going to be an interesting conversation."

My cheeks went hot. "Oh. Um." I fished in my pocket for the signet ring I'd taken from Xilvaris. "That's 'cause Tathalin gave it to Xilvaris so he could besiege us."

Varistan's eyebrows crawled up. "I take it you murdered him and looted his corpse, then."

I sniffed at him, unable to keep the smile off my face for long enough to appear serious. "You make it sound so pedestrian. I'll have you know that when duchesses murder people and loot their corpses, it's called 'emerging from a political discussion with capital gains.'"

"Oh?" he asked archly. "Do educate me. What's it called when a Queen does it?"

"Same thing, but said in a snootier tone," I said, snickering at his look of delight. "Wanna go pull together a formal thingamie to introduce Lightning Court?"

"'Thingamie'?" Varis asked, sounding pained. "Do you mean 'proclamation'? I like the name, though."

"Seems apropos, since Nyx Shaeras is our palace," I said, resting my arms on his shoulders and leaning back into his hold to look up at him. "I'm sure Stellaris and Tjarrek can mop up what you left behind, emphasis on 'mop'," I added, glancing towards the open doorway at the heavy rain. "So can we maybe go hide before anyone finds us and makes us do stuff out in the cold rain?"

"*Isabela!*" Lianka yelled, her voice cutting through the air.

"Too late," I muttered, letting go of Varis and turning towards the entrance to Nyx Shaeras with a sigh. "Can't this wait?" I called back, giving her a pleading expression.

She scowled at me. "You fuckers called this nightmare storm, and if you don't sally out and suffer with us, my fantasies of wreaking vengeance on you for it may need to become reality." She stabbed her finger at a bedraggled soldier holding the reins of a horse. "Get your royal fucking ass out here, your majesty. And, ah, you, too, your majesty," Lianka added, directing her polite bow solely at Varistan.

Well, that pretty much sealed my fate. The vengeance of a healer wasn't one I wanted to toy with, even when she was my friend.

Grousing, I stalked towards the door, with Varistan sauntering behind me. "I already killed a marquess and dueled the Raven King—" I started.

"And now you ought to get on a horse and go claim surrender from your foes," she said mercilessly, water sheeting down her body.

I looked up at the sky with a frown—and got shoved out into the downpour by Varistan. I yelped as rain started soaking into me, Varis keeping his hand on my back to prevent me from leaping backwards.

"Your intervention is appreciated," Varistan said with calm aplomb, stepping out into the rain with me, apparently unbothered. But, then, he liked to go flying in storms, and unlike me he didn't get cold. "If you'll be so kind as to ensure Isabela joins us, my desire is to take to the sky."

"Of course, your majesty," she said, not batting an eye.

Varistan launched himself skyward from the courtyard in a thunder of wing-beats, leaving me to Lianka's mercy. I didn't subject myself to the indignity of getting thrown onto a horse by her. I swiped my wet hair out of my face, put my foot in the stirrup, and hauled myself onto the back of the sodden animal with a grunt.

"Alright," I said, resigned to the task now that I was already wet. "Let's go sally."

CHAPTER SIXTY

SERVICES RENDERED

T here wasn't much mopping up to do, in the end. Varistan's display of pique had made it very clear that the fight between the Duke of Nyx Shaeras and the Raven King hadn't gone the way of the ravens, and fae could feel wild magic, to boot. Every fae in Lightning Court, and for some distance around us, had felt the birth of the Court. With an eldritch storm overhead and a new Court underfoot, none of the enemy combatants were interested in fighting. It was simply a matter of collecting surrenders and figuring out what to do with a bunch of half-burned ships and wet soldiers.

By dawn, I was thoroughly chilled and beyond exhausted, but the enemy combatants had been corralled and the rain had stopped, so after tidying up my injuries Lianka released me from her captivity. I started slogging my way up the slope towards the castle, only to be met by an aggravatingly chipper Varistan.

He dropped out of the sky, clad only in a loose pair of pants; he must have gotten changed once the rain stopped. "Your majesty!" he said, landing in a crouch in front of me. "Why the sourpuss expression?"

I made a rude gesture at him with a growl and trudged past.

Varistan hooked an arm around my waist and flipped me into his arms. I yelped and wiggled, but he threw us into the sky before I could manage to escape his grasp.

"Now, now," he crooned into my ear, breath warm and powerful wings carrying us towards the castle. "Is that any way to treat your devotee?"

I stuck my tongue out at him and clonked my head against his shoulder. "Is that what you are?"

"Why not?" he asked, climbing for altitude. Varis dropped a kiss onto my temple. "I doubt any two soulmate balances are exactly the same, so the names are mostly for the sake of categorization, but given my possessive focus, it seems apropos."

"Mm." I shivered, the cold wind sweeping across my sodden clothing chilling me despite Varistan's warmth. "I suppose I *was* ready to die rather than face a world without you in it."

His arms tightened on me, talons digging into my skin. That memory was going to take a long time to grow distant.

As he dropped to the roof, I leaned up and kissed him at the join of his jaw. "Alright. Devotees it is. I like it."

Varis hit the stone, running a few steps to bleed momentum instead of backwinging. He strode for the door, which was standing open, and grabbed the doorstop with his tail as we passed. "I could settle for calling us 'trueloves'." He took the stairs at a trot, heading for our bedroom with purpose. "As long as you're mine, and I'm yours."

I laughed as he opened the door with his hip, rubbing my cheek against his shoulder. "Can't you feel it?" I asked, looking up at him. "It's like having a bonfire in my soul."

"I can," he said, smiling back at me with unfettered joy. "Like the first ray of sunlight breaking through stormclouds, and the light of a temple on a hill through the winter night. Now," Varis said, setting my feet on the ground. "I know I've been released from our bargain, but there's one service you rendered me that I feel I ought to get the chance to repay."

"Oh?" I asked, humor in my voice as he started stripping me of my wet clothing and armor. He didn't even set it anywhere reasonable, letting the sodden cloth splat on the floor and chucking the armor onto the couch.

"That's right." He dropped to his knees, grinning up at me as he tugged down my wet pants and underthings. "Can you guess?"

"You gonna shove me up against a wall and bossily eat my pussy?" I asked, laughing.

Varis growled playfully and gave my clit a quick lick, making me squeak. "I can do that later, if you like," he said, hopping back up. He swept me into his arms again and strode for the bathroom. "But you're wet, cold, and quite frankly, you're filthy." Varistan stopped in front of the tub, which was filled with steaming water, the scent of cedar and keskyr filling the air. "I'd like to bathe you."

"Don't you hate hot water?" I swung my legs girlishly, basking in his happiness.

Moving with liquid strength, Varistan sank to his knees and lowered me into the bath, smiling at me like he couldn't stop. "Does that matter?"

I settled into the hot water with a moan of pleasure. The contrast between the heat of the bath and my cold blood made me shudder, my spine tingling. Varis traced his fingers through the water, resting his face against his other hand.

"Well, your majesty?" he asked. "May I be at your service for one more night?"

"It's not night," I said, sinking down in the hot water until only my face and knees poked up above the surface. "But I suppose I can be persuaded."

"Good." Varistan stood and tugged down his pants, kicking them to the side. He wasn't wearing anything underneath. "Sit up, please."

I peered up at him through one eye. "I don't recall getting into that cold bath with you."

"Perhaps I'm greedy."

That made me laugh. With a dramatic sigh, I shoved myself upright, glancing at him sidelong. "Well, be quick about it—"

Varis didn't need to be told twice. He stepped into the bath behind me and lowered himself in with a soft sound of discomfort, then sprawled down. "Come here, darling."

Obediently, I scooted back into the vee of his legs, leaning back against his strong chest with a sigh of pleasure. I loved feeling his heartbeat. I loved the press of his skin against mine, and the way our bodies fit together. Gods. How had I ever imagined I would be happy without him? How had I managed to ignore being so ludicrously in love with the Duke of Nyx Shaeras?

The King of Lightning Court, I thought with a smile, my eyes closing. *That'll take some getting used to.*

"Think we can get my father's debts forgiven as part of ransoming our captives of war?" I asked, melting into Varistan's heat. "I'd like to see him again."

His answering chuckle rumbled through me. "Still thinking about work, Bells?" I felt him shifting, then heard the lathering of soap. "Some of those soldiers are Lylvenoran. I feel certain the vicereine will agree to such a trade, and I'm inclined to be generous."

"Are you." I pressed up into his touch as he ran soap-slick hands down my chest.

"Indeed." Varis cupped my breasts, his thumbs brushing across my nipples as he dragged his palms along my front. "I'm in a very good mood. But let's save business for later, hmm?"

The contact sharpened my nipples and made my core tingle, my pulse quickening. Varis' hands ran across my belly and down my thighs. A tingling wake followed his touch, making me exhale in pleasure. He slid them back up, the dull points of his brass-capped talons dragging along the sensitive skin of my legs before he traced them up my midline. His long fingers splayed across my ribs—and then Varis took them away.

I made a tiny sound of protest, pouting.

Varis only laughed again, and a moment later cupped my breasts with freshly-soaped hands. He circled his thumbs on my stiff nipples, the roughness of his sword-calluses sending jolts of pleasure into me with every movement.

I bit my lip, arching my back and dropping my head against his shoulder. "You know, I don't remember this part of bathing you, either," I said in a breathy moan, tilting my hips up.

His warm hands slid down my taut abs and down between my legs, strong fingers digging into my inner thighs. He teased my folds on the way back up, the sides of his fingers brushing along my cleft. One talon ran along my entrance, lifting before it touched my clit. "It could have been like this," he crooned to me, running his slippery hands back down my inner thighs. His tail caressed my calf. "I wanted it."

"And you didn't." I writhed up against him, trying to get him to put his hands where I wanted them. "You said you didn't."

Varistan slid one hand down my arm and wrapped his warm fingers around my wrist. "Because of this," he said, dragging my palm up along his thigh before putting it behind my back, setting my hand on his swelling groin. "If you'd touched me like I'm touching you, I would never have been able to hide my desire. I barely could as it was." He rocked his hips up against my hand, groaning as I pressed my fingertips into the heat of his slit. "I was so certain it would disgust you. It certainly disgusted me. But if I'd known then how well you'd enjoy my cock, perhaps my feelings towards being ridden by a mortal would have been more favorable."

"*Fuck*, Varis," I moaned, arching into his touch. "I wanted you then, too. I always have."

His shafts slid into my hand, hot and slick. His fingers slid between my legs, palm cupping my mound. "I love you," he said, lips brushing my ear. Varis licked up along the curve, the forks of his tongue framing it and heat shocking down my spine from the contact. "I crave you. I suspect it will be many years before I no longer mourn the body I lost, but your hunger for the body I possess seems to match the hunger I have for you, and while I cannot yet say that I love my form, I love what it does to you and for you."

I moaned, wrapping my fingers around his cocks. "I love everything about you," I said, panting out the words. "Your body is absolutely included."

"I'm glad, for it belongs to you, and will for as long as we live." Breathing hard, Varistan gripped me by the inner thighs, his forearms pressing against my hips to hold me down as he ground up against me. "Are you warm enough?" he asked in a breathy rush.

"...What?" I asked, surprised at the topic change.

He bucked up into my grip again with a growl. "You were chilled. Are you warmed? I have a very pressing desire to remove you from this bath and do something else entirely."

I laughed at him, more than a little breathlessly. "I'm warm, but I'm still dirty, and now I'm soapy, to boot."

"I don't care." Varis shoved himself up, grabbing me roughly, and stood. Water sheeted off of us, sloshing out of the tub. He stepped out without any regard for the wet, crossing the room in three strides.

"You're making a mess," I said, sliding my fingers between my legs to ease my aching clit.

"Again, I don't care. If I have to go much longer without having you, I may go mad." He swept his tail across the counter, dumping everything into the sink, and set me down on the stone.

I yelped from the cold, starting to laugh when Varis yanked me almost off the edge, dropping his hips between my legs.

"Don't laugh, darling," he growled, though he was grinning at me. He hooked his arms under my knees and jerked me closer, grinding his studded cock against my pussy. "Being tied to a ravenous newborn Court is amplifying *my* hunger." Varis laced his fingers through my hair, bending down to lick a stripe up my neck, his searing breath making my skin sting and sending sparks of pleasure down my spine. "You may be spending the next few centuries dealing with an aggressive, demanding, *libidinous* King—"

"Oh, no, whatever will I do?" I asked, trying to sound horrified. The effect was somewhat dampened by the way I kept rocking my hips against his cocks, and entirely ruined by a moan as Varistan sank his teeth into my shoulder. "Oh, *fuck*, Varis, if you're going to eat me, start at my pussy, will you?"

He burst out laughing, dropping his forehead against my shoulder. "Such greed," he said, nipping me on the neck. "*Fine.*" Without further warning, Varistan dropped to his knees and planted his hot mouth on my pussy, shoving his tongue into me.

I grabbed him by the horns with a shocked sound of pleasure, mouth open and channel spasming. Varis groaned his satisfaction against me, the vibration divine. He opened his mouth wider and pushed his tongue deeper—then bit down.

The sudden sensation made me cry out, bucking my hips against his face, his teeth digging into me only enough to hit the edge of pain. I whimpered when he released me, and with a growl that sent vibrating pleasure shooting up my clit, Varistan shifted his head and bit me again, one long canine digging into the shaft of my clit with a blinding spike of pleasure.

He kept growling as he started licking me, the rumbling vibration translating through his mouth into tingling pleasure. His long canines pressed against my skin in hard ivory bars, a sharp counterpoint to the slick demand of his tongue. I gave myself to him with a moan, my hands wrapped around his horns and legs splayed over his shoulders. Varis responded to that surrender with a pleased snarl, his wings mantling and tail lashing, the flat of his tongue rubbing against my clit with every stroke.

Even with as tired as I was from the sleepless night, it only took minutes for him to take me from enjoyment to taut need, my abs clenching and thighs closing against his face. With a feral sound of delight, Varistan wrapped his hands around my legs and forced them apart so he could seat his mouth more firmly against my pussy. His capped claws dug into my inner thighs, making me whimper from the counterpoint to the hot demand of his tongue.

Oh, fuck, it felt so good, tension building in my core with shivering need. My whole body throbbed with it, my focus narrowing to the heat of Varistan's mouth against my needy clit. I bucked up against him, thighs shaking, hands closing on his horns in helpless spasms, chasing it—

Varistan rumbled a dangerous laugh—and every sensation in my body spiked to apocalyptic heights.

I came with a scream of pleasure, my nerves on fire with ecstasy. Distantly, I felt come squirting out of me, everything releasing as my core slammed down on itself, my whole body falling into orgasm with the force of an earthquake. I just shook with it, sobbing for air with my vision sparkling, wracked with pleasure, Varistan's mouth pressed hard against me as he stroked and stroked and *stroked* my clit with his tongue, gripping me with the forks of it.

"*Va-aris,*" I whimpered out, overwhelmed and overstimulated, my whole body shaking as aftershocks sang through me.

He growled, but the pleasure ebbed like the tide going out, leaving me sprawled against the wall. Bliss came in its wake, seeping into me, my muscles going lax and fingers falling off his horns.

With a pleased sound, Varis stood, wiping off his wet face with the back of his arm. "Well," he said in a low purr, "that was satisfying."

"What'd you..." I moaned out, slurring my words.

He licked his lips. "A little trick I learned in battle last night." My soulmate ran his hands up my inner thighs and spread my folds with his thumbs, his garnet eyes focused on my pussy. "Using the power of a Court to amplify the physical sensations of one connected to it."

I moaned again as he set the head of his lower shaft against my entrance. "Cruel."

"Perhaps," Varis said in a croon, his lashes lowered. He pressed his hips forward, sliding into me with ease, his studded cock spreading me open and the smooth underside of his upper shaft running along my clit. A smirk turned up his reddened mouth, wickedness lighting his eyes. "Whatever are you going to do with me?"

His cock felt amazing, the heat melting me from within. My pussy closed down against him with an echo of ecstasy, his expression dropping into lash-fluttering bliss from the pleasure.

"Love you," I said, dropping my head back. "Fuck you." I rocked my hips, taking him to the hilt, and wrapped one hand around his other shaft. "Spend eternity with you."

Varis started thrusting, slow deep strokes that sent pleasure curling into me. "I don't know that a man could ask for a better fate." He leaned forward, wings shadowing me. "You're my bliss, Isabela. Paradise in truth."

I answered him with a clench of my core that made him gasp in pleasure. He panted, eyes hazed, then snarled and snapped his hips forward. As if that single stroke had broken his control, Varis started fucking me with increasing desperation, his wings fanning the air.

"Fuck," he gasped out, gripping me by the back of the neck and hooking one arm and his tail under my legs to drag me closer to his body. "Bells, may I come? I'll make it up to you—"

I squeezed him again, earning myself a low groan, his precome slicking my fingers. "Making me promises, Varistan?"

"If they start killing me, release me from them," Varistan said, his breath hot against my neck and his voice halfway to a moan. He lowered his head and nipped my throat, then ran his tongue along my skin to ease the sting. "I love the feeling of being bound to you. I want to feel your fingers tangled in my soul. To be *possessed* by you." Varis held me against him as he rutted up into me, his lips pressed against my skin and his hips moving with demand. "Is that so much to ask?"

I buried my fingers in his hair and tightened my grip. "It's not." I put my lips against his ear, breathing hard. "So, darling," I demanded, "*come for me.*"

He made a sharp sound, almost a sob, his body tensing. It only took two hard thrusts to tip him over the edge into ecstasy, his teeth sinking into my shoulder as heat flooded my core. I dragged on his hair, my pussy spasming against his throbbing cock. Fuck, he was perfect, his pleasure even more of a reward than my own.

And he was mine. Mine, forever. Gods, what a gift.

I stroked his upper shaft as he came down, milking another spurt of come and a whimper out of him. "What a good mate you are. So very obedient," I said in a purr, tracing my tongue along his ear. Grinning at his whine of protest, I let go of his hair and cock, leaning back on my hands. "Am I wrong?"

Varistan made a face at me, tracing his eyes down my body and lingering on the white of his come on my belly. "No matter how fiercely I begin, you do seem to take me in hand with terrible ease," he said, one corner of his mouth flipping up. He rocked his hips against me one more time, winning a little sound of pleasure, then pulled out with care. Varis caught his come in one hand as it dripped out of me, looking like he instantly regretted the decision.

Giggling, I passed him a towel.

"Thank you," he said, with careful dignity, and stuck it between my legs with his sullied hand. "I suppose we now both need to bathe."

"I'm thinking shower, not bath," I said, still grinning. "If you try to bathe me like that again, we're just going to end up here again."

His lips twitched. "I would be amenable to shower sex."

"You're gonna be a problem, aren't you?" I asked, sliding down from the counter.

"Almost certainly, yes," Varistan said, draping himself across my shoulders and nuzzling my neck. "If you need to escape, you likely have several centuries where I'll literally be unable to follow you over the border or set foot on a seafaring ship, so—"

"If you think I'm ever setting foot on a ship again, you're out of your damn mind," I said with a laugh, pulling out the plug for the bath and turning on the water for the shower. "You'll carry me, or I won't go. Besides, why would I want to run away? You may be a problem, but you're *my* problem. I'm not going anywhere without you."

He shivered, his tail wrapping around me and body warm against mine. "I'm glad," he said in a hoarse whisper. "I love troubling you."

"And I love trouble," I said, leaning back against him with a sleepy smile. "C'mon, devotee. Can't have morning sex if we don't get clean and go to bed."

Varis made an interested sound, releasing me and stepping warily into the shower. When he discovered it was merely cool, he sighed in pleasure, tipping his head back. "Wouldn't it be afternoon sex?" he asked. "Assuming we're going to bed after showering, and assuming that we sleep a reasonable amount of time before I wake you with my hungry tongue, begging for the honey from your chalice."

"Is that a promise?" I asked with a raised brow, joining him in the shower.

"A hypothetical," he said, a wicked edge to his smile.

I started laughing, shaking my head at him. "We're gonna have to figure out a schedule, because I'm definitely not going to survive you being in rut for centuries."

"I'm not in *rut*," he said with a playful whine, wrapping his tail around my ankle. "For one, I have to eat. For another, I still need a full measure of sleep. Since you typically sleep a great deal less than I do, that's a full two hours of your waking day where you'll surely be able to do as you like—three, if you count my preferred grooming regimen." Varis paused, frowning, his ears shifting. "At least, I think so. I might be able to call on the Court's strength to ease my physical needs for a time."

"Let's not find out," I laughed, grabbing the shampoo. "We've got armies to ransom, a whole march to figure out how to manage, Court establishment to handle..."

He harrumphed. "If you insist."

"As if!" I flicked water at him and got a curl of flame blown at me for my trouble. "*You're* the bookish dork, not me. As soon as you get all the records from Norvaldt, you're going to be impossible to pry out of your office."

"I suppose I could fuck you on the desk, as long as I moved the papers first..." Varis said, sounding thoughtful.

I grinned at him. "That's my Varis. It's a deal."

EPILOGUE

Despite his threats, I woke well before Varis. Solely for the sake of proving I could hold my own, and certainly not because I was as hungry as he, I woke him up the way he'd threatened to wake me. The strokes of my tongue up his slit, and then along his cocks as he slowly roused, left me burning with want that the sharp taste of his come didn't satisfy. The lust-soaked expression on his face when I finally lifted my mouth off of him helped—but, gods, the revenge he dealt with that forked tongue was so much better.

We probably could have stayed in bed all day, and if things had been in a state where a honeymoon was at all reasonable, we surely would have. You can't exactly keep prisoners of war penned up like livestock, though – at least, not without committing a few war crimes – and Varistan and I weren't the only hungry creatures to deal with.

The *Court*, newborn and bursting with power, was busily gnawing away at the edges of Raven Court. There wasn't a lot we could do about that; Courts could be influenced by warfare and subjugation, but Varistan and Tathalin were close blood relatives. Courts didn't tolerate Monarchs offing potential heirs, or vice-versa; if either directly attacked the other physically or via command, the Court would kill the attacker. So, they couldn't directly wage war on each other. The bordering lords could, though, so we spent the next days and weeks in rapid-fire communication with them, in order to set up mock-battles to draw the lines of Lightning Court.

We decided, that first morning, that aggressively expanding our borders by attacking any defensive forces was too risky. There was no easy way to know if the defending armies belonged to the Raven King, or were wielded by their lords independently, and neither of us were particularly interested in having Varistan's life snuffed out by the Court. Tathalin wouldn't even reply to our missives, and aside from a clear answer, it wasn't worth the risk. Thus, we only engaged when we were attacked, and if we were in communication with the lord in question, we were willing to "suffer defeat" and cede the ground.

Fae lords, as it turns out, will sacrifice a great deal to maintain their lands. The concessions we got for assisting them in maintaining theirs in the face of a ravenous newborn Court were the sort of lasting agreements that would see prosperity in Lightning Court for millennia.

It slowed down by late summer. By that time, we'd managed to repatriate all of our prisoners – most of them to *ourselves*, since about sixty percent of the land force and all of the naval one had been Norvaldter – and our borders had expanded by about a third.

Most of that land was wild land, inhabited mainly by nomadic fae and small farming communities and hunting outposts, but not all of it. We'd acquired a number of baronies and knight-manors, the county to the south... and Lylvenore.

In the first forty-eight hours of Lightning Court's existence, it had grown past Nyx Shaeras' traditional border with Lylvenoran territory, right up to the edge of the Tangle. Another fortnight after that, the city was half-surrounded. By the beginning of summer, it was fully enclosed within our Court.

The vicereine had soldiers and city guards. She'd sent many with Xilvaris – the remaining forty percent of the land force was mostly hers – but Varis and I were both well-aware that she had many more soldiers available. Once we'd worked out how to get the Court to fall back, we even offered it as part of the ransom deal for her soldiers.

She didn't respond to any of our messages, and she didn't once send soldiers outside the Tangle to push us back. We spent a lot of late nights trying to figure out what in the wilds she was doing, since she was essentially ceding land to us by refusing to engage. When we finally came in person towards the middle of the summer, wary and hyper-aware of the aggressive force Lightning Court was exerting on the extent of her power, she challenged Varistan to single combat for the possession of the city.

The laws allowing single combat duels in lieu of warfare were ancient and hallowed. They didn't even have to be fought with live weaponry, merely glamor, which made them a great deal safer than warfare—though, of course, a great deal riskier for the superior force. But we didn't want a war, anyway, and the raging demand our Court had for the city and its tens of thousands of souls was making my soulmate jittery and short-tempered. Varis accepted with a great deal of relief.

They stepped into the ring, Varistan expecting to throw the fight to protect Lylvenore as an exclave of Raven Court—and Vicereine Philomenha didn't even block his first strike, surrendering the city to us without any fight at all. I could have been knocked over with a feather. Varis fully fainted from the sudden release of the pressure to conquer Lylvenore, keeling over like a felled tree.

She gave us an explanation over dinner... once Varistan had been revived, of course. Though she was court fae, her only child was an aberration. He'd spent his entire life glamored; a cruel fate for anyone, since the sensation of glamored flesh was nothing like that of true touch. As vicereine, she couldn't openly defect to Lightning Court, but she'd found the loophole that would let her act against the will of the King, and she'd seized it with both hands.

It was an enormous headache for us, but it did make dealing with the rest of our prisoners of war a lot easier, since we could just send them back home. The upheaval of dealing with the ensuing riots in the city was brutal, though; without Philomenha's assistance, I was fairly sure Lylvenore would have burned to the ground.

Yet I couldn't bring myself to be upset about it. Lylvenore had been my home for a long time, and I loved it and many of the people in it. To be able to give them a better world, even one bought through blood and pain, was more amazing than I ever could have anticipated. It wasn't terrible, either, to get to meet little Illianthe and to offer Estarren a barony for his troubles.

The city helped settle the Court, too. It was an enormous sink for wild magic, and it bled off a great deal of the initial surge of power that was driving Lightning Court to gnaw at the borders. There would probably be a birth surge in the next year—but there were far worse fates than a bloom of new life, and children who would grow up in the sort of world few had dared to believe might happen in their lifespans.

Once we'd claimed Lylvenore, I got the chance, at long-last, to reintroduce Varis to my father. It didn't surprise me when the two men regarded each other with a wary sort of tolerance; I doubted they would ever thaw towards each other. Aside from the horror of their first meeting, they were simply too different to be friends. Father was a down-to-earth man whose mistrust of fae nobility was deep-seated and hard-earned. Varis, on the other hand, was a hedonistic peacock, and in situations where he wasn't comfortable he tended to fall back on his arrogance and physicality.

Suffice it to say that they were like oil and water. I loved them both, and I appreciated their willingness to be in a room together for my sake, but it didn't bother me that Father stayed in Lylvenore, and Varis and I in Nyx Shaeras. I didn't need them to love each other to know that they loved me.

It got me started thinking, though—about family, and especially about heirs. I'd lived my whole life anticipating that I would die young, but now I was liable to live thousands – if not tens of thousands – of years, and maybe significantly more than that. Having a family might actually be in my future.

A little hesitantly, I raised the topic of heirs in the late autumn. I wasn't really sure how Varis imagined our future, but even without necessarily talking about having children, we probably did need to figure out what to do with our Court if he was killed.

Varistan sat there, blinking a little, a bemused expression on his face. "I suppose my mother would be the heir," he said at last, dragging out the words. Grimacing, he dropped back against the back of the couch. "Given that my sire is long dead and I've never sired any children, she's my closest blood relative. Her, and then Tathalin or my grandparents, if either yet live."

"'If'?" I asked, perching on the arm of the couch.

He reached up and tugged me down to sprawl on my back across his lap. "Neither Tathalin nor Kaiah have been forthcoming with me on that topic," he said, using his mother's given name. "They may or may not yet live, and if they live, they may or may not remain identifiably fae. They would be ancient, even by our standards, and surely soaked with wild magic."

I made a little sound of acknowledgement. "Do you think we should invite Kaiah here?" I asked, making a rueful face. "I know you haven't talked to her in ages, and she doesn't seem..."

"...particularly thoughtful towards humanity?" Varis finished wryly. At my answering expression, he laughed, then kissed two of his fingers and pressed them against my lips. "No, I don't think we should bring her here. I suspect she would be disruptive at best, and if I die, she'll surely become Queen regardless of us acknowledging her as heir." He sighed, dropping his head back against the chair. "And if we have children, her presence might sway the Court towards her instead of one of them."

"Children, huh?" I asked with a half-smile, looking up at him.

His skin rouged slightly, ears dropping down into a pose of self-consciousness. "I don't know if I... can," he said, the words hesitant. "Physically, I mean. Sire children." Varis looked away, throat working. "I don't know what was... left."

"Hey." I pushed myself up, changing positions so I was sitting in his lap with my arms over his shoulders. "It's alright if you can't, sweetheart. It doesn't matter to me."

A sad smile flickered onto his face and died. "It matters to me." He rested his forehead against mine, eyes closing. "I've wanted an unbroken family for most of my life. Not knowing if I can ever have that is..." Varistan trailed off, a shudder running through his body. "It's difficult for me."

I tipped his chin up and kissed him softly, an affectionate touch that melted some of the stress out of his shoulders and spine. "There's one person who might know."

"I don't want to talk about him right now." Varis wrapped his arms around me and buried his face against my neck. "I'm not certain I could handle being told by Ayre that if I want children, I'll have to fuck a dragon."

The words were muffled, but bitter, and I flicked Varis on the ear, making him growl. "You're not fucking any dragons," I informed him. "Be anything but loyal, and the likelihood of you getting a chance to sire anything on anyone will soon thereafter become zero."

He shivered again, but for a very different reason. I could practically feel the eagerness radiating off of him. "What happened to encouraging me to find women to slake my lust with?" he said in a low croon, running his mouth along my pulse. "Did you change your mind about my favors?"

"You're mine, and your favors are mine," I said, lips twitching with humor and heat pooling in my belly. "Don't act like you haven't been angling for my possessiveness all along."

"Well, that's very close to true," Varis said with a laugh and a nip to my throat. "You need not worry about my affections straying. You're mine, and I'm something of a loyal mate."

I raised one brow. "Only something of?"

His skin darkened with a blush, ears dropping down a little in self-consciousness. "Incredibly loyal, I'm afraid," he said, sounding embarrassed, and not quite meeting my eyes. "I know that, over the millennia, many long-lasting fae pairings enjoy a pattern of separation and reunification, or, as my parents did, take lovers on the side, but... I..." Varis trailed off, ears shifting in an anxious-animal way. "I hated it when Yesika did it," he said in a rush. "I hated when she had lovers, and I hated when she brought people to our bed, and I hated when—"

I put a finger across his lips. "I'm yours, and my favors are yours," I said, this time with gentleness. "We're balanced soulmates, sweetheart. This isn't merely long-lasting. We belong to each other *forever*."

Varistan's eyes searched my face, brows lifted in the center in an expression of yearning and not-quite-belief. I took my finger away and kissed him instead, relishing the way he melted into my touch. His physicality was such a gift to me. I wasn't always good with words, but I would always be able to reassure him – to show him my love – with my touch.

"I love you. All the parts of you," I said when I broke the kiss, rubbing my nose along his. "That includes your possessiveness and loyalty." I gave him another quick kiss, flashing him a wicked smile. "I suppose it even includes your anxiety, in the sense that I'm looking forward to watching you learn to expect being cherished instead of dismissed as needy."

He huffed a soft laugh, relaxing back against the couch. "I'm glad you don't mind reassuring me, though you may have to wait a while for me to no longer desire such."

"Well, we have time," I said with a grin. "Way more time than I ever anticipated having."

"Looking forward to the millennia ahead of you, after all?" he asked, sounding hopeful.

"Mhm. How could I not, when I get to spend them with you?" I draped myself across his chest, resting my elbows on the back of the couch to prop myself up. "Plus, we have so much to do together. After all, there's one other way I can think of to figure out if we can have natural-born children."

"Oh?" he asked, cocking his ears forward with a little smirk. "And what's that, darling?"

"There's this healer in Lylvenore who's great with human fertility," I replied, licking my lips when his chin came up. "If we time it right, I could get her to turn my cycle back on so I'm in heat in a couple weeks so it syncs with your rut—"

Varis growled, his pupils dilating. His tail wrapped around my ankle, flared and hot. "If I'm in rut, land-tied to a newborn Court, *and* scent-driven to breed you..." He shivered, tilting his hips even while he tried to control his breathing. "Bells, you might not get any *sleep.*"

I straddled him with an evil laugh. To say I liked the idea would be quite the understatement. "Don't worry. Your regeneration rubbed off on Nyx Shaeras, and there's still plenty of wild magic in Lightning Court. I'll be just fine."

He blinked in rapid succession. "My... my what?"

"Regeneration," I said smugly, wiggling to settle myself more firmly against his groin. "Didn't you know?"

"I surely did not, and I'm certain you knew that," Varis said, wrapping his arms around my wait. "If you think to distract me from my focus on what having you fertile might do to me, though, rest assured that I'm far too keenly interested to be waylaid."

I smirked. "Bit of a breeding kink?"

"I didn't have one before, but now..." Varistan gripped me by my hips and bucked up against me, sending heat coiling through my core. "Perhaps we ought to practice. Just in case you're wrong about the regeneration."

"Gonna keep me up all night?" I asked, breathing harder from the feel of his hardening cocks pressing up between my legs.

He growled again, low and sultry. "I think I'd like to try." Varis rocked himself against me, leaning up to put his mouth next to my ear, hot breath stirring my face. "Let's see how many times you can come before dawn."

I laced my fingers through his hair, and let my soulmate devour me whole.

ALSO BY

Check out the other standalone romance in the Monsters of Faery world!
"Captured by the Fae Beast" – Meet the Beast of Phazikai, the brutal prince
of Stag Court who ended the Annihilation War. Two years before Varistan and
Isabela meet, a chance encounter in the wilderness leaves a rock climber bound
to the deadly Stag Prince. He's an aggressive, frightening soulmate—but Leah
is determined to discover the man behind the monster.
*Tropes: enemies to lovers, fated mates, grumpy/sunshine, touch her and die, fae
bargains*

"In the Claws of the Raven Prince" – Step back in time to the Annihilation
War—and meet Varistan's cousin Ayre Xirangyl, Raven Court's answer to Stag
Court's monster. The half-fae, half-manticore Raven Prince is a possessive,
animalistic man determined to win the heart of his soulmate, even knowing
that she's Stag Court's spy.
*Tropes: enemies to lovers, fated mates, touch her and die, target/spy, dual
consciousness*

ABOUT THE AUTHOR

Mallory is a monster aficionado who spends her time reading, writing, and dreaming about beastly lovers. When she doesn't have monsters on the mind, she can be found hiking with her two borzoi or watching survival shows with avid glee. She makes her home on the East Coast alongside a small menagerie of animals, all of whom are pretty sure they're the actual boss of the household..

If you enjoyed the book, she'd love to hear from you! Leave a review, join the newsletter at mallorydunlin.com to see pet pics, or reach out at mallory.dunlin@gmail.com!

Made in the USA
Las Vegas, NV
28 November 2023

81725637R00225